Dear Reader,

In this duo of classic love stories from *New York Times* bestselling author Nora Roberts, we meet two couples who are unexpectedly thrown together, much to their initial chagrin. But as they grudgingly get to know each other they discover a magic that neither expected.

In *A Will and a Way* rivals Pandora McVie and Michael Donohue are none too happy to discover that in order to claim their inheritance, they'll have to live under the same roof for half a year. Though things get off to a rocky start, a winter stranded together in a cozy Catskill getaway may be exactly what these two headstrong people need to melt their hearts…and find their way to each other.

In *Loving Jack*, confirmed bachelor Nathan Powell has his life mapped out before him—until he discovers author Jackie "Jack" MacNamara in *his* hot tub wearing nothing but her birthday suit! These mismatched, *temporary* housemates may be like oil and water, but romance writer Jackie knows the makings of a good love story when she sees it…she'll just have to convince commitment-shy Nathan that he would make a perfect leading man!

We hope these stories inspire you to go after your own happy ending!

The Editors,

Silhouette Books

# NORA ROBERTS

## Happy Endings

Silhouette Books

Published by Silhouette Books

**America's Publisher of Contemporary Romance**

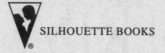

SILHOUETTE BOOKS

HAPPY ENDINGS

ISBN-13: 978-0-373-28169-5

Recycling programs for this product may not exist in your area.

Copyright © 2013 by Harlequin Books S.A.

The publisher acknowledges the copyright holder of the individual works as follows:

A WILL AND A WAY
Copyright © 1986 by Nora Roberts

LOVING JACK
Copyright © 1989 by Nora Roberts

# CONTENTS

# A WILL AND A WAY

For my family members, who, fortunately, aren't as odd as the relatives in this book.

# *Chapter One*

One hundred fifty million dollars was nothing to sneeze at. No one in the vast, echoing library of Jolley's Folley would have dared. Except Pandora. She did so with more enthusiasm than delicacy into a tattered tissue. After blowing her nose, she sat back, wishing the antihistamine she had taken would live up to its promise of fast relief. She wished she'd never caught the wretched cold in the first place. More, she wished she were anywhere else in the world.

Surrounding her were dozens of books she'd read and hundreds more she'd never given a thought to, though she'd spent hours and hours in the library. The scent of the leather-bound volumes mixed with the lighter, homier scent of dust. Pandora preferred either to the strangling fragrance of lilies that filled three stocky vases.

In one corner of the room was a marble-and-ivory

chess set, where she'd lost a great many highly disputed matches. Uncle Jolley, bless his round, innocent face and pudgy fingers, had been a compulsive and skilled cheat. Pandora had never taken a loss in stride. Maybe that's why he'd so loved to beat her, by fair means or foul.

Through the three arching windows the light shone dull and a little gloomy. It suited her mood and, she thought, the proceedings. Uncle Jolley had loved to set scenes.

When she loved—and she felt this emotion for a select few who'd touched her life—she put everything she had into it. She'd been born with boundless energy. She'd developed iron-jawed stubbornness. She'd loved Uncle Jolley in her uninhibited, expansive fashion, acknowledging then accepting all of his oddities. He might have been ninety-three, but he'd never been dull or fussy.

A month before his death, they'd gone fishing—poaching actually—in the lake that was owned and stocked by his neighbor. When they'd caught more than they could eat, they'd sent a half-dozen trout back to the owner, cleaned and chilled.

She was going to miss Uncle Jolley with his round cherub's face, high, melodious voice and wicked humors. From his ten-foot, extravagantly framed portrait, he looked down at her with the same little smirk he'd worn whether he'd been making a million-dollar merger or handing an unsuspecting vice-president a drink in a dribble glass. She missed him already. No one else in her far-flung, contrasting family understood and accepted her with the same ease. It had been one more reason she'd adored him.

Miserable with grief, aggravated by a head cold, Pandora listened to Edmund Fitzhugh drone on, and on, with the preliminary technicalities of Uncle Jolley's will. Maximillian Jolley McVie had never been one for brevity. He'd always said if you were going to do something, do it until the steam ran out. His last will and testament bore his style.

Not bothering to hide her disinterest in the proceedings, Pandora took a comprehensive survey of the other occupants of the library.

To have called them mourners would have been just the sort of bad joke Jolley would have appreciated.

There was Jolley's only surviving son, Uncle Carlson, and his wife. What was her name? Lona—Mona? Did it matter? Pandora saw them sitting stiff backed and alert in matching shades of black. They made her think of crows on a telephone wire just waiting for something to fall at their feet.

Cousin Ginger—sweet and pretty and harmless, if rather vacuous. Her hair was Jean Harlow blond this month. Good old Cousin Biff was there in his black Brooks Brothers suit. He sat back, one leg crossed over the other as if he were watching a polo match. Pandora was certain he wasn't missing a word. His wife—was it Laurie?—had a prim, respectful look on her face. From experience, Pandora knew she wouldn't utter a word unless it were to echo Biff. Uncle Jolley had called her a silly, boring fool. Hating to be cynical, Pandora had to agree.

There was Uncle Monroe looking plump and successful and smoking a big cigar despite the fact that his sister, Patience, waved a little white handkerchief in front of her nose. Probably because of it, Pandora corrected. Uncle Monroe liked nothing better than to make his ineffectual sister uncomfortable.

Cousin Hank looked macho and muscular, but hardly more than his tough athletic wife, Meg. They'd hiked the Appalachian Trail on their honeymoon. Uncle Jolley had wondered if they stretched and limbered up before lovemaking.

The thought caused Pandora to giggle. She stifled it halfheartedly with the tissue just before her gaze wandered over to cousin Michael. Or was it second cousin Michael? She'd never been able to get the technical business straight. It seemed a bit foolish when you weren't talking blood relation anyway. His mother had been Uncle Jolley's niece by Jolley's son's second marriage. It was a complicated state of affairs, Pandora thought. But then Michael Donahue was a complicated man.

They'd never gotten along, though she knew Uncle Jolley had favored him. As far as Pandora was concerned, anyone who made his living writing a silly television series that kept people glued to a box rather than doing something worthwhile was a materialistic parasite. She had a momentary flash of pleasure as she remembered telling him just that.

Then, of course, there were the women. When a man dated centerfolds and showgirls it was obvious he wasn't interested in intellectual stimulation. Pandora smiled as she recalled stating her view quite clearly the last time Michael had visited Jolley's Folley. Uncle Jolley had nearly fallen off his chair laughing.

Then her smile faded. Uncle Jolley was gone. And if she was honest, which she was often, she'd admit that of all the people in the room at that moment, Michael

Donahue had cared for and enjoyed the old man more than anyone but herself.

You'd hardly know that to look at him now, she mused. He looked disinterested and slightly arrogant. She noticed the set, grim line around his lips. Pandora had always considered Donahue's mouth his best feature, though he rarely smiled at her unless it was to bare his teeth and snarl.

Uncle Jolley had liked his looks, and had told Pandora so in his early stages of matchmaking. A hobby she'd made sure he'd given up quickly. Well, he hadn't given it up precisely, but she'd ignored it all the same.

Being rather short and round himself, perhaps Jolley had appreciated Donahue's long lean frame, and the narrow intense face. Pandora might have liked it herself, except that Michael's eyes were often distant and detached.

At the moment he looked like one of the heroes in the action series he wrote—leaning negligently against the wall and looking just a bit out of place in the tidy suit and tie. His dark hair was casual and not altogether neat, as though he hadn't thought to comb it into place after riding with the top down. He looked bored and ready for action. Any action.

It was too bad, Pandora thought, that they didn't get along better. She'd have liked to have reminisced with someone about Uncle Jolley, someone who appreciated his whimsies as she had.

There was no use thinking along those lines. If they'd elected to sit together, they'd have been picking little pieces out of each other by now. Uncle Jolley, smirking down from his portrait, knew it very well.

With a half sigh she blew her nose again and tried

to listen to Fitzhugh. There was something about a bequest to whales. Or maybe it was whalers.

Another hour of this, Michael thought, and he'd be ready to chew raw meat. If he heard one more *whereas*... On a long breath, Michael drew himself in. He was here for the duration because he'd loved the crazy old man. If the last thing he could do for Jolley was to stand in a room with a group of human vultures and listen to long rambling legalese, then he'd do it. Once it was over, he'd pour himself a long shot of brandy and toast the old man in private. Jolley had had a fondness for brandy.

When Michael had been young and full of imagination and his parents hadn't understood, Uncle Jolley had listened to him ramble, encouraged him to dream. Invariably on a visit to the Folley, his uncle had demanded a story then had settled himself back, bright-eyed and eager, while Michael wove on. Michael hadn't forgotten.

When he'd received his first Emmy for *Logan's Run*, Michael had flown from L.A. to the Catskills and had given the statuette to his uncle. The Emmy was still in the old man's bedroom, even if the old man wasn't.

Michael listened to the dry impersonal attorney's voice and wished for a cigarette. He'd only given them up two days before. Two days, four hours and thirty-five minutes. He'd have welcomed the raw meat.

He felt stifled in the room with all these people. Every one of them had thought old Jolley was half-mad and a bit of a nuisance. The one hundred fifty-million-dollar estate was different. Stocks and bonds were extremely sane. Michael had seen several assessing glances roaming over the library furniture. Big, ornate Georgian might not suit some of the streamlined life-styles, but it would liquidate into very tidy cash. The old man, Michael knew, had loved every clunky chair and oversize table in the house.

He doubted if any of them had been to the big echoing house in the past ten years. Except for Pandora, he admitted grudgingly. She might be an annoyance, but she'd adored Jolley.

At the moment she looked miserable. Michael didn't believe he'd ever seen her look unhappy before—furious, disdainful, infuriated, but never unhappy. If he hadn't known better, he'd have gone to sit beside her, offer some comfort, hold her hand. She'd probably chomp it off at the wrist.

Still, her shockingly blue eyes were red and puffy. Almost as red as her hair, he mused, as his gaze skimmed over the wild curly mane that tumbled, with little attention to discipline or style, around her shoulders. She was so pale that the sprinkling of freckles over her nose stood out. Normally her ivory-toned skin had a hint of rose in it—health or temperament, he'd never been sure.

Sitting among her solemn, black-clad family, she stood out like a parrot among crows. She'd worn a vivid blue dress. Michael approved of it, though he'd never say so to Pandora. She didn't need black and crepe and lilies to mourn. That he understood, if he didn't understand her.

She annoyed him, periodically, with her views on his life-style and career. When they clashed, it didn't take long for him to hurl criticism back at her. After all, she was a bright, talented woman who was content to play around making outrageous jewelry for boutiques rather than taking advantage of her Master's degree in education.

She called him materialistic, he called her idealistic. She labeled him a chauvinist, he labeled her a pseudo-intellectual. Jolley had sat with his hands folded and chuckled every time they argued. Now that he was gone, Michael mused, there wouldn't be an opportunity for any more battles. Oddly enough, he found it another reason to miss his uncle.

The truth was, he'd never felt any strong family ties to anyone but Jolley. Michael didn't think of his parents very often. His father was somewhere in Europe with his fourth wife, and his mother had settled placidly into Palm Springs society with husband number three. They'd never understood their son who'd opted to work for a living in something as bourgeois as television.

But Jolley had understood and appreciated. More, much more important to Michael, he'd enjoyed Michael's work.

A grin spread over his face when he heard Fitzhugh drone out the bequest for whales. It was so typically Jolley. Several impatient relations hissed through their teeth. A hundred fifty thousand dollars had just spun out of their reach. Michael glanced up at the larger-than-life-size portrait of his uncle. You always said you'd have the last word, you old fool. The only trouble is you're not here to laugh about it.

"To my son, Carlson…" All the quiet muttering and whispers died as Fitzhugh cleared his throat. Without much interest Pandora watched her relatives come to attention. The charities and servants had their bequests. Now it was time for the big guns. Fitzhugh glanced up briefly before he continued. "Whose—aaah—mediocrity was always a mystery to me, I leave my entire collection of magic tricks in hopes he can develop a sense of the ridiculous."

Pandora choked into her tissue and watched her uncle turn beet red. First point Uncle Jolley, she thought and prepared to enjoy herself. Maybe he'd left the whole business to the A.S.P.C.A.

"To my grandson, Bradley, and my granddaughter by marriage, Lorraine, I leave my very best wishes. They need nothing more."

Pandora swallowed and blinked back tears at the reference to her parents. She'd call them in Zanzibar that evening. They would appreciate the sentiment even as she did.

"To my nephew Monroe who has the first dollar he ever made, I leave the last dollar I made, frame included. To my niece, Patience, I leave my cottage in Key West without much hope she'll have the gumption to use it."

Monroe chomped on his cigar while Patience looked horrified.

"To my grand-nephew, Biff, I leave my collection of matches, with the hopes that he will, at last, set the world on fire. To my pretty grand-niece, Ginger, who likes equally pretty things, I leave the sterling silver mirror purported to have been owned by Marie Antoinette. To my grand-nephew, Hank, I leave the sum of 3528. Enough, I believe, for a lifetime supply of wheat germ."

The grumbles that had begun with the first bequest continued and grew. Anger hovered on the edge of outrage. Jolley would have liked nothing better. Pandora made the mistake of glancing over at Michael. He didn't seem so distant and detached now, but full of admiration. When their gazes met, the giggle she'd been holding back spilled out. It earned her several glares.

Carlson rose, giving new meaning to the phrase controlled outrage. "Mr. Fitzhugh, my father's will is nothing more than a mockery. It's quite obvious that he wasn't in his right mind when he made it, nor do I have any doubt that a court will overturn it."

"Mr. McVie." Again Fitzhugh cleared his throat. The sun began to push its way through the clouds but no one seemed to notice. "I understand perfectly your sentiments in this matter. However, my client was perfectly well and lucid when this will was drawn. He may have worded it against my advice, but it is legal and binding. You are, of course, free to consult with your own counsel. Meanwhile, there's more to be read."

"Hogwash." Monroe puffed on his cigar and glared at everyone. "Hogwash," he repeated while Patience patted his arm and chirped ineffectually.

"Uncle Jolley liked hogwash," Pandora said as she balled her tissue. She was ready to face them down, almost hoped she'd have to. It would take her mind off her grief. "If he wanted to leave his money to the Society for the Prevention of Stupidity, it was his right."

"Easily said, my dear." Biff polished his nails on his lapel. The gold band of his watch caught a bit of the sun and gleamed. "Perhaps the old lunatic left you a ball of twine so you can string more beads."

"You haven't got the matches yet, old boy." Michael spoke lazily from his corner, but every eye turned his way. "Careful what you light."

"Let him read, why don't you?" Ginger piped up,

quite pleased with her bequest. Marie Antoinette, she mused. Just imagine.

"The last two bequests are joint," Fitzhugh began before there could be another interruption. "And, a bit unorthodox."

"The entire document's unorthodox," Carlson tossed out, then harrumphed. Several heads nodded in agreement.

Pandora remembered why she always avoided family gatherings. They bored her to death. Quite deliberately, she waved a hand in front of her mouth and yawned. "Could we have the rest, Mr. Fitzhugh, before my family embarrasses themselves any further?"

She thought, but couldn't be sure, that she saw a quick light of approval in the fusty attorney's eyes. "Mr. McVie wrote this portion in his own words." He paused a moment, either for effect or courage. "To Pandora McVie and Michael Donahue," Fitzhugh read. "The two members of my family who have given me the most pleasure with their outlook on life, their enjoyment of an old man and old jokes, I leave the rest of my estate, in entirety, all accounts, all business interests, all stocks, bonds and trusts, all real and personal property, with all affection. Share and share alike."

Pandora didn't hear the half-dozen objections that sprang out. She rose, stunned and infuriated. "I can't take his money." Towering over the family who sat around her, she strode straight up to Fitzhugh. The lawyer, who'd anticipated attacks from other areas, braced for the unexpected. "I wouldn't know what to do with it. It'd just clutter up my life." She waved a hand at the papers on the desk as if they were a minor annoyance. "He should've asked me first."

"Miss McVie..."

Before the lawyer could speak again, she whirled on Michael. "You can have it all. You'd know what to do with it, after all. Buy a hotel in New York, a condo in L.A., a club in Chicago and a plane to fly you back and forth, I don't care."

Deadly calm, Michael slipped his hands in his pockets. "I appreciate the offer, cousin. Before you pull the trigger, why don't we wait until Mr. Fitzhugh finishes before you embarrass yourself any further?"

She stared at him a moment, nearly nose to nose with him in heels. Then, because she'd been taught to do so at an early age, she took a deep breath and waited for her temper to ebb. "I don't want his money."

"You've made your point." He lifted a brow in the cynical, half-amused way that always infuriated her. "You're fascinating the relatives by the little show you're putting on."

Nothing could have made her find control quicker. She angled her chin at him, hissed once, then subsided. "All right then." She turned and stood her ground. "I apologize for the interruption. Please finish reading, Mr. Fitzhugh."

The lawyer gave himself a moment by taking off his glasses and polishing them on a big white handkerchief. He'd known when Jolley had made the will the day would come when he'd be forced to face an enraged family. He'd argued with his client about it, cajoled, reasoned, pointed out the absurdities. Then he'd drawn up the will and closed the loopholes.

"I leave all of this," he continued, "the money, which is a small thing, the stocks and bonds, which are necessary but boring, the business interests, which are interesting weights around the neck. And my home and all in it, which is everything important to me, the memories made there, to Pandora and Michael because they understood and cared. I leave this to them, though it may annoy them, because there is no one else in my family I can leave what is important to me. What was mine is Pandora and Michael's now, because I know they'll keep me alive. I ask only one thing of each of them in return."

Michael's grip relaxed, and he nearly smiled again. "Here comes the kicker," he murmured.

"Beginning no more than a week after the reading of this document, Pandora and Michael will move into my home in the Catskills, known as Jolley's Folley. They will live there together for a period of six months, neither one spending more than two nights in succession under another roof. After this six-month period, the estate reverts to them, entirely and without encumbrance, share and share alike.

"If one does not agree with this provision, or breaks the terms of this provision within the six-month period, the estate, in its entirety will be given over to all my surviving heirs and the Institute for the Study of Carnivorous Plants in joint shares.

"You have my blessing, children. Don't let an old, dead man down."

For a full thirty seconds there was silence. Taking advantage of it, Fitzhugh began straightening his papers.

"The old bastard," Michael murmured. Pandora would've taken offense if she hadn't agreed so completely. Because he judged the temperature in the room to be on the rise, Michael pulled Pandora out, down the hall and into one of the funny little parlors that could be found throughout the house. Just before he closed the door, the first explosion in the library erupted.

Pandora drew out a fresh tissue, sneezed into it, then plopped down on the arm of a chair. She was too flabbergasted and worn-out to be amused. "Well, what now?"

Michael reached for a cigarette before he remembered he'd quit. "Now we have to make a couple of decisions."

Pandora gave him one of the long lingering stares she'd learned made most men stutter. Michael merely sat across from her and stared back. "I meant what I said. I don't want his money. By the time it's divided up and the taxes dealt with, it's close to fifty million apiece. Fifty million," she repeated, rolling her eyes. "It's ridiculous."

"Jolley always thought so," Michael said, and watched the grief come and go in her eyes.

"He only had it to play with. The trouble was, every time he played, he made more." Unable to sit, Pandora paced to the window. "Michael, I'd suffocate with that much money."

"Cash isn't as heavy as you think."

With something close to a sneer, she turned and sat on the window ledge. "You don't object to fifty million or so after taxes I take it."

He'd have loved to have wiped that look off her face. "I haven't your fine disregard for money, Pandora, probably because I was raised with the illusion of it rather than the reality."

She shrugged, knowing his parents existed, and always had, mainly on credit and connections. "So, take it all then."

Michael picked up a little blue glass egg and tossed it from palm to palm. It was cool and smooth and worth several thousand. "That's not what Jolley wanted."

With a sniff, she snatched the egg from his hand. "He wanted us to get married and live happily ever after. I'd like to humor him…." She tossed the egg back again. "But I'm not that much of a martyr. Besides, aren't you engaged to some little blond dancer?"

He set the egg down before he could heave it at her. "For someone who turns their pampered nose up at television, you don't have the same intellectual snobbery about gossip rags."

"I *adore* gossip," Pandora said with such magnificent exaggeration Michael laughed.

"All right, Pandora, let's put down the swords a minute." He tucked his thumbs in his pockets and rocked back on his heels. Maybe they could, if they concentrated, talk civilly with each other for a few minutes. "I'm not engaged to anyone, but marriage wasn't a term of the will in any case. All we have to do is live together for six months under the same roof."

As she studied him a sense of disappointment ran through her. Perhaps they'd never gotten along, but she'd respected him if for nothing more than what she'd seen as his pure affection for Uncle Jolley. "So, you really want the money?"

He took two furious steps forward before he caught himself. Pandora never flinched. "Think whatever you like." He said it softly, as though it didn't matter. Oddly enough, it made her shudder. "You don't want the money, fine. Put that aside a moment. Are you going to stand by and watch this house go to the clan out there or a bunch of scientists studying Venus's-flytraps? Jolley loved this place and everything in it. I always thought you did, too."

"I do." The others would sell it, she admitted. There wasn't one person in the library who wouldn't put the house on the market and run with the cash. It would be lost to her. All the foolish, ostentatious rooms, the ridiculous archways. Jolley might be gone, but he'd left the house like a dangling carrot. And he still held the stick.

"He's trying to run our lives still."

Michael lifted a brow. "Surprised?"

With a half laugh, Pandora glanced over. "No."

Slowly she walked around the room while the sun shot through the diamond panes of glass and lit her hair. Michael watched her with a sense of detached admiration. She'd look magnificent on the screen. He'd always thought so. Her coloring, her posture. Her arrogance. The five or ten pounds the camera would add couldn't hurt that too angular, bean-pole body, either. And the fire-engine-red hair would make a statement on the screen while it was simply outrageous in reality. He'd often wondered why she didn't do something to tone it down.

At the moment he wasn't interested in any of that—just in what was in her brain. He didn't give a damn about the money, but he wasn't going to sit idly by and watch everything Jolley had had and built go to the vultures. If he had to play rough with Pandora, he would. He might even enjoy it.

Millions. Pandora cringed at the outrageousness of it. That much money could be nothing but a headache, she was certain. Stocks, bonds, accountants, trusts, tax shelters. She preferred a simpler kind of living. Though no one would call her apartment in Manhattan primitive.

She'd never had to worry about money and that was just the way she liked it. Above or below a certain income level, there were nothing but worries. But if you found a nice, comfortable plateau, you could just cruise. She'd nearly found it.

It was true enough that a share of this would help her tremendously professionally. With a buffer sturdy enough, she could have the artistic freedom she wanted and continue the life-style that now caused a bit of a strain on her bank account. Her work was artistic and critically acclaimed but reviews didn't pay the rent. Outside of Manhattan, her work was usually considered too unconventional. The fact that she often had to create more mainstream designs to keep her head above water grated constantly. With fifty or sixty thousand to back her, she could…

Furious with herself, she blocked it off. She was thinking like Michael, she decided. She'd rather die. He'd sold out, turned whatever talent he had to the main chance, just as he was ready to turn these circumstances to his own financial advantage. She would think of other areas. She would think first of Jolley.

As she saw it, the entire scheme was a maze of problems. How like her uncle. Now, like a chess match, she'd have to consider her moves.

She'd never lived with a man. Purposely. Pandora liked running by her own clock. It wasn't so much that she minded sharing *things*, she minded sharing space. If she agreed, that would be the first concession.

Then there was the fact that Michael was attractive,

attractive enough to be unsettling if he hadn't been so annoying. Annoying and easily annoyed, she recalled with a flash of amusement. She knew what buttons to push. Hadn't she always prided herself on the fact that she could handle him? It wasn't always easy; he was too sharp. But that made their altercations interesting. Still, they'd never been together for more than a week at a time.

But there was one clear, inarguable fact. She'd loved her uncle. How could she live with herself if she denied him a last wish? Or a last joke.

Six months. Stopping, she studied Michael as he studied her. Six months could be a very long time, especially when you weren't pleased with what you were doing. There was only one way to speed things up. She'd enjoy herself.

"Tell me, cousin, how can we live under the same roof for six months without coming to blows?"

"We can't."

He'd answered without a second's hesitation, so she laughed again. "I suppose I'd be bored if we did. I can tidy up loose ends and move in in three days. Four at the most."

"That's fine." When his shoulders relaxed, he realized he'd been tensed for her refusal. At the moment he didn't want to question why it mattered so much. Instead he held out a hand. "Deal."

Pandora inclined her head just before her palm met his. "Deal," she agreed, surprised that his hand was hard and a bit callused. She'd expected it to be rather soft and limp. After all, all he did was type. Perhaps the next six months would have some surprises.

"Shall we go tell the others?"

"They'll want to murder us."

Her smile came slowly, subtly shifting the angles of her face. It was, Michael thought, at once wicked and alluring. "I know. Try not to gloat."

When they stepped out, several griping relatives had spilled out into the hallway. They did what they did best together. They argued.

"You'd blow your share on barbells and carrot juice," Biff said spitefully to Hank. "At least I know what to do with money."

"Lose it on horses," Monroe said, and blew out a stream of choking cigar smoke. "Invest. Tax deferred."

"You could use yours to take a course in how to speak in complete sentences." Carlson stepped out of the smoke and straightened his tie. "I'm the old man's only living son. It's up to me to prove he was incompetent."

"Uncle Jolley had more competence than the lot of you put together." Feeling equal parts frustration and disgust, Pandora stepped forward. "He gave you each exactly what he wanted you to have."

Biff drew out a flat gold cigarette case as he glanced over at his cousin. "It appears our Pandora's changed her mind about the money. Well, you worked for it, didn't you, darling?"

Michael put his hand on Pandora's shoulder and squeezed lightly before she could spring. "You'd like to keep your profile, wouldn't you, cousin?"

"It appears writing for television's given you a taste for violence." Biff lit his cigarette and smiled. If he'd thought he could get in a blow below the belt… "I think I'll decline a brawl," he decided.

"Well, I think it's fair." Hank's wife came forward, stretching out her hand. She gave both Pandora and

Michael a hearty shake. "You should put a gym in this place. Build yourself up a little. Come on, Hank."

Silent, and his shoulders straining the material of his suit, Hank followed her out.

"Nothing but muscles between the head," Carlson mumbled. "Come, Mona." He strode ahead of his wife, pausing long enough to level a glare at Pandora and Michael. The inevitable line ran though Michael's mind before Carlson opened his mouth and echoed it. "You haven't heard the last of this."

Pandora gave him her sweetest smile. "Have a nice trip home, Uncle Carlson."

"Probate," Monroe said with a grunt, and waddled his way out behind them.

Patience fluttered her hands. "Key West, for heaven's sake. I've never been south of Palm Beach. My, oh my."

"Oh, Michael." Fluttering her lashes, Ginger placed a hand on his arm. "When do you think I might have my mirror?"

He glanced down into her perfectly lovely, heart-shaped face. Her eyes were as pure a blue as tropical waters. He thanked God Jolley hadn't asked that he spend six months with Cousin Ginger. "I'm sure Mr. Fitzhugh will have it shipped to you as soon as possible."

"Come along, Ginger, we'll give you a ride to the airport." Biff pulled Ginger's hand through his arm, patted it and smiled down at Pandora. "I'd be worried if I didn't know you better. You won't last six days with Michael much less six months. Beastly temper," he said confidentially to Michael. "The two of you'll murder each other before a week's out."

"Don't spend the old man's money yet," Michael warned. "We'll make the six months if for no other reason than to spite you." He smiled when he said it, a chummy, well-meaning smile that took the arrogance from Biff's face.

"We'll see who wins the game." Straight backed, Biff turned toward the door. His wife walked out behind him without having said a word since she'd walked in.

"Biff," Ginger began as they walked out. "What are you going to do with all those matches?"

"Burn his bridges, I hope," Pandora muttered. "Well, Michael, though I can't say there was a lot of love before, there's nearly none lost now."

"Are you worried about alienating them?"

With a shrug of her shoulders, she walked toward a bowl of roses, then gave him a considering look. "Well, I've never had any trouble alienating you. Why is that, do you suppose?"

"Jolley always said we were too much alike."

"Really?" Haughty, she lifted a brow. "I find myself disagreeing with him again. You and I, Michael Donahue, have almost nothing in common."

"If that's so we have six months to prove it." On impulse he moved closer and put a finger under her chin. "You know, darling, you might've been stuck with Biff."

"I'd've given the place to the plants first."

He grinned. "I'm flattered."

"Don't be." But she didn't move away from him. Not yet. It was an interesting feeling to be this close without snarling. "The only difference is you don't bore me."

"That's enough," he said with a hint of a smile. "I'm easily flattered." Intrigued, he flicked a finger down her cheek. It was still pale, but her eyes were direct and steady. "No, we won't bore each other, Pandora. In six months we might experience a lot of things, but boredom won't be one of them."

It might be an interesting feeling, she discovered, but it wasn't quite a safe one. It was best to remember that he didn't find her appealing as a woman but would, for the sake of his own ego, string her along if she permitted it. "I don't flatter easily. I haven't decided exactly what your reasons are for going through with this farce, but I'm doing it only for Uncle Jolley. I can set up my equipment here quite easily."

"And I can write here quite easily."

Pandora plucked a rose from the bowl. "If you can call those implausible scripts writing."

"The same way you call the bangles you string together art."

Color came back to her cheeks and that pleased him. "You wouldn't know art if it reached up and bit you on the nose. My jewelry expresses emotion."

His smile showed pleasant interest. "How much is lust going for these days?"

"I would have guessed you'd be very familiar with the cost." Pandora fumbled for a tissue, sneezed into it, then shut her bag with a click. "Most of the women you date have price tags."

It amused him, and it showed. "I thought we were talking about work."

"My profession is a time-honored one, while yours—yours stops for commercial breaks. And furthermore—"

"I beg your pardon."

Fitzhugh paused at the doorway of the library. He wanted nothing more than to be shed of the McVie clan and have a quiet, soothing drink. "Am I to assume that you've both decided to accept the terms of the will?"

Six months, she thought. It was going to be a long, long winter.

Six months, he thought. He was going to have the first daffodil he found in April bronzed.

"You can start counting the days at the end of the week," he told Fitzhugh. "Agreed, cousin?"

Pandora set her chin. "Agreed."

## Chapter Two

It was a pleasant trip from Manhattan along the Hudson River toward the Catskills. Pandora had always enjoyed it. The drive gave her time to clear her mind and relax. But then, she'd always taken it at her own whim, her own pace, her own convenience. Pandora made it a habit to do everything just that way. This time, however, there was more involved than her own wants and wishes. Uncle Jolley had boxed her in.

He'd known she'd have to go along with the terms of the will. Not for the money. He'd been too smart to think she could be lured into such a ridiculous scheme with money. But the house, her ties to it, her need for the continuity of family. That's what he'd hooked her with.

Now she had to leave Manhattan behind for six months. Oh, she'd run into the city for a few hours here and there, but it was hardly the same as living in the center of things. She'd always liked that—being in the center, surrounded by movement, being able to watch and become involved whenever she liked. Just as she'd always liked long weekends in the solitude of Jolley's Folley.

She'd been raised that way, to enjoy and make the most of whatever environment she was in. Her parents were gypsies. Wealth had meant they'd traveled first class instead of in covered wagons. If there'd been campfires, there had also been a servant to gather kindling, but the spirit was the same.

Before she'd been fifteen, Pandora had been to more than thirty countries. She'd eaten sushi in Tokyo, roamed the moors in Cornwall, bargained in Turkish markets. A succession of tutors had traveled with them so that by her calculations, she'd spent just under two years in a classroom environment before college.

The exotic, vagabond childhood had given her a taste for variety—in people, in foods, in styles. And oddly enough the exposure to widely diverse cultures and mores had formed in her an unshakable desire for a home and a sense of belonging.

Though her parents liked to meander through countries, recording everything with pen and film, Pandora had missed a central point. Where was home? This year in Mexico, next year in Athens. Her parents made a name for themselves with their books and articles on the unusual, but Pandora wanted roots. She'd discovered she'd have to find them for herself.

She'd chosen New York, and in her way, Uncle Jolley.

Now, because her uncle and his home had become her central point, she was agreeing to spend six months living with a man she could hardly tolerate so that she could inherit a fortune she didn't want or need. Life, she'd discovered long ago, never moved in straight lines.

Jolley McVie's ultimate joke, she thought as she turned up the long drive toward his Folley. Well, he could throw them together, but he couldn't make them stick.

Still, she'd have felt better if she'd been sure of Michael. Was it the lure of the millions of dollars, or an affection for an old man that would bring him to the Catskills? She knew his *Logan's Run* was in its very successful fourth year, and that he'd had other lucrative ventures in television. But money was a seduction itself. After all, her Uncle Carlson had more than he could ever spend, yet he was already taking the steps for a probate of the will.

That didn't worry her. Uncle Jolley had believed in hiring the best. If Fitzhugh had drawn up the will, it was air-tight. What worried her was Michael Donahue.

Because of the trap she'd fallen into, she'd found herself thinking of him a great deal too much over the past couple of days. Ally or enemy, she wasn't sure. Either way, she was going to have to live with him. Or around him. She hoped the house was big enough.

By the time she arrived, she was worn-out from the drive and the lingering head cold. Though her equipment and supplies had been shipped the day before, she still had three cases in the car. Deciding to take one at a time, Pandora popped the trunk, then simply looked at Jolley's Folley.

He'd built it when he'd been forty, so the house was already over a half century old. It went in all directions at once, as if he'd never been able to decide where he wanted to start and where he wanted to finish. The truth about Jolley, she admitted, was that he'd never wanted to finish. The project, the game, the puzzle, was always more interesting to him before the last pieces were in place.

Without the wings, it might have been a rather somber and sedate late-nineteenth-century mansion. With them, it was a mass of walls and corners, heights and widths. There was no symmetry, yet to Pandora it had always seemed as sturdy as the rock it had been built on.

Some of the windows were long, some were wide, some of them were leaded and some sheer. Jolley had made up his mind then changed it again as he'd gone along.

The stone had come from one of his quarries, the wood from one of his lumberyards. When he'd decided to build a house, he'd started his own construction firm. McVie Construction, Incorporated was one of the five biggest companies in the country.

It struck her suddenly that she owned half of Jolley's share in the company and her mind spun at how many others. She had interests in baby oil, steel mills, rocket engines and cake mix. Pandora lifted the case and set her teeth. What on earth had she let herself in for?

From the upstairs window, Michael watched her. The jacket she wore was big and baggy with three vivid colors, blue, yellow and pink patched in. The wind caught at her slacks and rippled them from thigh to ankle. She wasn't looking teary-eyed and pale this time, but grim and resigned. So much the better. He'd been tempted to comfort her during their uncle's funeral. Only the knowledge that too much sympathy for a woman like Pandora was fatal had prevented him.

He'd known her since childhood and had consid-

ered her a spoiled brat from the word go. Though she'd
often been off for months at a time on one of her parents' journalistic safaris, they'd seen enough of each
other to feed a mutual dislike. Only the fact that she
had cared for Jolley had given Michael some tolerance
for her. And the fact, he was forced to admit, that she
had more honesty and humanity in her than any of their
other relations.

There had been a time, he recalled, a brief time, during late adolescence that he'd felt a certain…stirring
for her. A purely shallow and physical teenage hunger,
Michael assured himself. She'd always had an intriguing face; it could be unrelentingly plain one moment
and striking the next, and when she'd hit her teens…
well, that had been a natural enough reaction. And it
had passed without incident. He now preferred a woman
with more subtlety, more gloss and femininity—and
shorter fangs.

Whatever he preferred, Michael left the arranging
of his own office to wander downstairs.

"Charles, did my shipment come?" Pandora pulled
off her leather driving gloves and dropped them on a
little round table in the hall. Since Charles was there,
the ancient butler who had served her uncle since before she was born, she felt a certain pleasure in coming.

"Everything arrived this morning, miss." The old
man would have taken her suitcase if she hadn't waved
him away.

"No, don't fuss with that. Where did you have them
put everything?"

"In the garden shed in the east yard, as you instructed."

She gave him a smile and a peck on the cheek, both

of which pleased him. His square bulldog's face grew slightly pink. "I knew I could count on you. I didn't tell you before how happy I was that you and Sweeney are staying. The place wouldn't be the same without you serving tea and Sweeney baking cakes."

Charles managed to pull his back a bit straighter. "We wouldn't think about going anywhere else, miss. The master would have wanted us to stay."

But made it possible for them to go, Pandora mused. Leaving each of them three thousand dollars for every year of service. Charles had been with Jolley since the house was built, and Sweeney had come some ten years later. The bequest would have been more than enough for each to retire on. Pandora smiled. Some weren't made for retirement.

"Charles, I'd love some tea," she began, knowing if she didn't distract him, he'd insist on carrying her bags up the long staircase.

"In the drawing room, miss?"

"Perfect. And if Sweeney has any of those little cakes…"

"She's been baking all morning." With only the slightest of creaks, he made his way toward the kitchen.

Pandora thought of rich icing loaded with sugar. "I wonder how much weight a person can gain in six months."

"A steady diet of Sweeney's cakes wouldn't hurt you," Michael said from above her head. "Men are generally more attracted to flesh than bone."

Pandora spun around, then found herself in the awkward position of having to arch her neck back to see Michael at the top of the stairs. "I don't center my life around attracting men."

"I'd be the last one to argue with that."

He looked quite comfortable, she thought, feeling the first stirrings of resentment. And negligently, arrogantly attractive. From several feet above her head, he leaned against a post and looked down on her as though he was the master. She'd soon put an end to that. Uncle Jolley's will had been very clear. Share and share alike.

"Since you're already here and settled in, you can come help me with the rest of my bags."

He didn't budge. "I always thought the one point we were in perfect agreement on was feminism."

Pandora paused at the door to toss a look over her shoulder. "Social and political views aside, if you don't help me up with them before Charles comes back, he'll insist on doing it himself. He's too old to do it and too proud to be told he can't." She walked back out and wasn't surprised when she heard his footsteps on the gravel behind her.

She took a deep breath of crisp autumn air. All in all, it was a lovely day. "Drive up early?"

"Actually, I drove up late last night."

Pandora turned at the open trunk of her car. "So eager to start the game, Michael?"

If he hadn't been determined to start off peacefully, he'd have found fault with the tone of her voice, with the look in her eyes. Instead he let it pass. "I wanted to get my office set up today. I was just finishing it when you drove in."

"Work, work, work," she said with a long sigh. "You must put in slavish hours to come up with an hour of chase scenes and steam a week."

Peace wasn't all that important. As she reached for a suitcase, he closed a hand over her wrist. Later he'd think about how slim it was, how soft. Now he could only think how much he wished she were a man. Then he could've belted her. "The amount of work I do and what I produce is of absolutely no concern to you."

It occurred to Pandora, oddly, she thought, just how much she enjoyed seeing him on the edge of temper. All of her other relatives were so bland, so outwardly civilized. Michael had always been a contrast, and therefore of more interest. Smiling, she allowed her wrist to stay limp.

"Did I indicate that it was? Nothing, I promise you, could be further from the truth. Shall we get these in and have that tea? It's a bit chilly."

He'd always admired, grudgingly, how smoothly she could slip into the lady-of-the-manor routine. As a writer who wrote for actors and for viewers, he appreciated natural talent. He also knew how to set a scene to his best advantage. "Tea's a perfect idea." He hauled one case out and left the second for her. "We'll establish some guidelines."

"Will we?" Pandora pulled out the case, then let the trunk shut quietly. Without another word, she started back toward the house, holding the front door open for him, then breezing by the suitcase she'd left in the main hall. Because she knew Michael was fond of Charles, she hadn't a doubt he'd pick it up and follow.

The room she always took was on the second floor in the east wing. Jolley had let her decorate it herself, and she'd chosen white on white with a few startling splashes of color. Chartreuse and blazing blue in throw pillows, a long horizontal oil painting, jarring in its colors of sunset, a crimson waist-high urn stuffed with ostrich plumes.

Pandora set her case by the bed, noted with satisfaction that a fire had been laid in the small marble fireplace, then tossed her jacket over a chair.

"I always feel like I'm walking into *Better Homes*," he commented as he let her cases drop.

Pandora glanced down at them briefly, then at him. "I'm sure you're more at home in your own room. It's more—*Field and Stream*. I expect tea's ready."

He gave her a long, steady survey. Her jacket had concealed the trim cashmere sweater tucked into the narrow waist of her slacks. It reminded Michael quite forcibly just what had begun to attract him all those teenage years ago. For the second time he found himself wishing she were a man.

Though they walked abreast down the stairs, they didn't speak. In the drawing room, amid the Mideast opulence Jolley had chosen there, Charles was setting up the tea service.

"Oh, you lit the fire. How lovely." Pandora walked over and began warming her hands. She wanted a moment, just a moment, because for an instant in her room she thought she'd seen something in Michael's eyes. And she thought she'd felt the same something in response. "I'll pour, Charles. I'm sure Michael and I won't need another thing until dinner."

Casually she glanced around the room, at the flowing drapes, the curvy brocade sofas, the plump pillows and brass urns. "You know, this has always been one of my favorite rooms." Going to the tea set, she began to fill cups. "I was only twelve when we visited Turkey, but this room always makes me remember it vividly. Right down to the smells in the markets. Sugar?"

"No." He took the cup from her, plopped a generous slice of cake on a dish, then chose a seat. He preferred the little parlor next door with its tidy English country air. This was the beginning, he thought, with the old butler and plump cook as witnesses. Six months from today, they'd all sign a document swearing that the terms of the will had been adhered to and that would be that. It was the time in between that concerned him.

"Rule number one," Michael began without preamble. "We're both in the east wing because it makes it easier for Charles and Sweeney. But—" he paused, hoping to emphasize his point "—both of us will, at all times, respect the other's area."

"By all means." Pandora crossed her legs and sipped her tea.

"Again, because of the staff, it seems fair that we eat at the same time. Therefore, in the interest of survival, we'll keep the conversations away from professional matters."

Pandora smiled at him and nibbled on cake. "Oh yes, let's do keep things personal."

"You're a nasty little package—"

"See, we're off to a perfect start. Rule number two. Neither of us, no matter how bored or restless, will disturb the other during his or her set working hours. I generally work between ten and one, then again between three and six."

"Rule number three. If one of us is entertaining, the other will make him or herself scarce."

Pandora's eyes narrowed, only for a moment. "Oh, and I so wanted to meet your dancer. Rule number four. The first floor is neutral ground and to be shared equally unless specific prior arrangements are made and agreed upon." She tapped her finger against the arm of the chair. "If we both play fair, we should manage."

"I don't have any trouble playing fair. As I recall, you're the one who cheats."

Her voice became very cool, her tone very rounded. "I don't know what you're talking about."

"Canasta, poker, gin."

"That's absurd and you have absolutely no proof." Rising, she helped herself to another cup of tea. "Besides, cards are entirely different." Warmed by the fire, soothed by the tea, she smiled at him. As Michael recalled, that particular smile was lethal. And stunning. "Are you still holding a grudge over that five hundred I won from you?"

"I wouldn't if you'd won it fairly."

"I won it," she countered. "That's what counts. If I cheated and you didn't catch me, then it follows that I cheated well enough for it to be legal."

"You always had a crooked sense of logic." He rose as well and came close. She had to admire the way he moved. It wasn't quite a swagger because he didn't put the effort into it. But it was very close. "If we play again, whatever we play, you won't cheat me."

Confident, she smiled at him. "Michael, we've known each other too long for you to intimidate me." She reached a hand up to pat his cheek and found her wrist captured a second time. And a second time she saw and felt that same dangerous something she'd experienced upstairs.

There was no Uncle Jolley as a buffer between them now. Perhaps they'd both just begun to realize it. Whatever was between them that made them snarl and snap would have a long, cold winter to surface.

Perhaps neither one of them wanted to face it, but both were too stubborn to back down.

"Perhaps we're just beginning to know each other," Michael murmured.

She believed it. And didn't like it. He wasn't a posturing fool like Biff nor a harmless hulk like Hank. He might be a cousin by marriage only, but the blood between them had always run hot. There was violence in him. It showed sometimes in a look in his eyes, in the way he held himself. As though he wouldn't ward off a blow but counter it. Pandora recognized it because there was violence in her, as well. Perhaps that was why she always felt compelled to shoot darts at him, just to see how many he could boomerang back at her.

They stood as they were a moment, gauging each other, reassessing. The wise thing to do was for each to acknowledge a hit and step aside. Pandora threw up her chin. Michael set for the volley. "We'll go to the mat another time, Michael. At the moment, I'm a bit tired from the drive. If you'll excuse me?"

"Rule number five," he said without releasing her. "If one of us takes potshots at the other, they'll damn well pay the consequences." When he freed her arm, he went back for his cup. "See you at dinner, cousin."

Pandora awoke just past dawn fully awake, rested and bursting with energy. Whether it had been the air in the mountains or the six hours of deep sleep, she was ready and eager to work. Breakfast could wait, she decided as she showered and dressed. She was going out to the garden shed, organizing her equipment and diving in.

The house was perfectly quiet and still dim as she

made her way downstairs. The servants would sleep another hour or two, she thought as she stuck her head in the pantry and chose a muffin. As she recalled, Michael might sleep until noon.

They had made it through dinner without incident. Perhaps they'd been polite to each other because of Charles and Sweeney or perhaps because both of them had been too tired to snipe. Pandora wasn't sure herself.

They'd dined under the cheerful lights of the big chandelier and had talked, when they'd talked, about the weather and the food.

By nine they'd gone their separate ways. Pandora to read until her eyes closed and Michael to work. Or so he'd said.

Outside the air was chill enough to cause Pandora's skin to prickle. She hunched up the collar of her jacket and started across the lawn. It crunched underfoot with the early thin frost. She liked it—the absolute solitude, the lightness of the air, the incredible smell of mountain and river.

In Tibet she'd once come close to frostbite because she hadn't been able to resist the snow and the swoop of rock. She didn't find this slice of the Catskills any less fascinating. The winter was best, she'd always thought, when the snow skimmed the top of your boots and your voice came out in puffs of smoke.

Winter in the mountains was a time for the basics. Heat, food, work. There were times Pandora wanted only the basics. There were times in New York she'd argue for hours over unions, politics, civil rights because the fact was, she loved an argument. She wanted the stimulation of an opposing view over broad issues or niggling ones. She wanted the challenge, the heat and the exercise for her brain. But...

There were times she wanted nothing more than a quiet sunrise over frost-crisped ground and the promise of a warm drink by a hot fire. And there were times, though she'd rarely admit it even to herself, that she wanted a shoulder to lay her head against and a hand to hold. She'd been raised to see independence as a duty, not a choice. Her parents had the most balanced of relationships, equal to equal. Pandora saw them as something rare in a world where the scales tipped this way or that too often. At age eighteen, Pandora had decided she'd never settle for less than a full partnership. At age twenty, she decided marriage wasn't for her. Instead she put all her passion, her energy and imagination into her work.

Straight-line dedication had paid off. She was successful, even prominent, and creatively she was fulfilled. It was more than many people ever achieved.

Now she pulled open the door of the utility shed. It was a big square building, as wide as the average barn, with hardwood floors and paneled walls. Uncle Jolley hadn't believed in the primitive. Hitting the switch, she flooded the building with light.

As per her instructions, the crates and boxes she'd shipped had been stacked along one wall. The shelves where Uncle Jolley had kept his gardening tools during his brief, torrid gardening stage had been packed away. The plumbing was good, with a full-size stainless-steel sink and a small but more than adequate bath with shower enclosed in the rear. She counted five workbenches. The light and ventilation were excellent.

It wouldn't take her long, Pandora figured, to turn the shed into an organized, productive workroom.

It took three hours.

Along one shelf were boxes of beads in various sizes—jet, amethyst, gold, polished wood, coral, ivory. She had trays of stones, precious and semiprecious, square cut, brilliants, teardrops and chips. In New York, they were kept in a safe. Here, she never considered it. She had gold, silver, bronze, copper. There were solid and hollow drills, hammers, tongs, pliers, nippers, files and clamps. One might have thought she did carpentry. Then there were scribes and drawplates, bottles of chemicals, and miles of string and fiber cord.

The money she'd invested in these materials had cost her every penny of an inheritance from her grandmother, and a good chunk of savings she'd earned as an apprentice. It had been worth it. Pandora picked up a file and tapped it against her palm. Well worth it.

She could forge gold and silver, cast alloys and string impossibly complex designs with the use of a few beads or shells. Metals could be worked into thin, threadlike strands or built into big bold chunks. Pandora could do as she chose, with tools that had hardly changed from those used by artists two centuries earlier.

It was and always had been, both the sense of continuity and the endless variety that appealed to her. She never made two identical pieces. That, to her, would have been manufacturing rather than creating. At times, her pieces were elegantly simple, classic in design. Those pieces sold well and allowed her a bit of artistic freedom. At other times, they were bold and brash and exaggerated. Mood guided Pandora, not trends. Rarely, very rarely, she would agree to create a piece along specified lines. If the lines, or the client, interested her.

She turned down a president because she'd found his ideas too pedestrian but had made a ring at a new father's request because his idea had been unique. Pandora had been told that the new mother had never taken the braided gold links off. Three links, one for each of the triplets she'd given birth to.

At the moment, Pandora had just completed drafting the design for a three-tiered necklace commissioned to her by the husband of a popular singer. Emerald. That was her name and the only requirement given to Pandora. The man wanted lots of them. And he'd pay, Pandora mused, for the dozen she'd chosen just before leaving New York. They were square, three karats apiece and of the sharp, sharp green that emeralds are valued for.

This was, she knew, her big chance, professionally and, most importantly, artistically. If the necklace was a success, there'd not only be reviews for her scrapbook, but acceptance. She'd be freer to do more of what she wanted without compromise.

The trick would be to fashion the chain so that it held like steel and looked like a cobweb. The stones would hang from each tier as if they'd dripped there.

For the next two hours, she worked in gold.

Between the two heaters at each end of the shed and the flame from her tools, the air became sultry. Sweat rolled down under her sweater, but she didn't mind. In fact, she barely noticed as the gold became pliable. Again and again, she drew the wire through the drawplate, smoothing out the kinks and subtly, slowly, changing the shape and size. When the wire looked like angel hair she began working it with her fingers, twisting and braiding until she matched the design in her head and on her drawing paper.

It would be simple—elegantly, richly simple. The emeralds would bring their own flash when she attached them.

Time passed. After careful, meticulous use of draw-plate, flame and her own hands, the first thin, gold tier formed.

She'd just begun to stretch out the muscles in her back when the door of the shed opened and cool air poured in. Her face glowing with sweat and concentration, she glared at Michael.

"Just what the hell do you think you're doing?"

"Following orders." He had his hands stuffed in his jacket pockets for warmth, but hadn't buttoned the front. Nor, she noticed, had he bothered to shave. "This place smells like an oven."

"I'm working." She lifted the hem of the big apron she wore and wiped at her brow. It was being interrupted that annoyed her, Pandora told herself. Not the fact that he'd walked in on her when she looked like a steelworker. "Remember rule number three?"

"Tell that to Sweeney." Leaving the door ajar, he wandered in. "She said it was bad enough that you skipped breakfast, but you're not getting away with missing lunch." Curious, he poked his finger into a tray that held brilliant colored stones. "I have orders to bring you back."

"I'm not ready."

He picked up a tiny sapphire and held it to the light. "I had to stop her from tramping out here herself. If I go back alone, she's going to come for you. Her arthritis is acting up again."

Pandora swore under her breath. "Put that down," she ordered, then yanked the apron off.

"Some of this stuff looks real," he commented. Though he put the sapphire back, he picked up a round, winking diamond.

"Some of this stuff is real." Pandora crouched to turn the first heater down.

The diamond was in his hand as he scowled down at her head. "Why in hell do you have it sitting out like candy? It should be locked up."

Pandora adjusted the second heater. "Why?"

"Don't be any more foolish than necessary. Someone could steal it."

"Someone?" Straightening, Pandora smiled at him. "There aren't many someones around. I don't think Charles and Sweeney are a problem, but maybe I should worry about you."

He cursed her and dropped the diamond back. "They're your little bag of tricks, cousin, but if I had several thousand dollars sitting around that could slip into a pocket, I'd be more careful."

Though under most circumstances she fully agreed, Pandora merely picked up her jacket. After all, they weren't in Manhattan but miles away from anyone or anything. If she locked everything up, she'd just have to unlock it again every time she wanted to work. "Just one of the differences between you and me, Michael. I suppose it's because you write about so many dirty deeds."

"I also write about human nature." He picked up the sketch of the emerald necklace she had drawn. It had the sense of scale that would have pleased an architect and the flair and flow that would appeal to an artist. "If you're so into making bangles and baubles, why aren't you wearing any?"

"They get in the way when I'm working. If you write about human nature, how come the bad guy gets caught every week?"

"Because I'm writing for people, and people need heroes."

Pandora opened her mouth to argue, then found she agreed with the essence of the statement. "Hmm," was all she said as she turned out the lights and went out ahead of him.

"At least lock the door," Michael told her.

"I haven't a key."

"Then we'll get one."

"*We* don't need one."

He shut the door with a snap. "*You* do."

Pandora only shrugged as she started across the lawn. "Michael, have I mentioned that you've been more crabby than usual?"

He pulled a piece of hard candy out of his pocket and popped it into his mouth. "Quit smoking."

The candy was lemon. She caught just a whiff. "So I noticed. How long?"

He scowled at some leaves that skimmed across the lawn. They were brown and dry and seemed to have a life of their own. "Couple weeks. I'm going crazy."

She laughed sympathetically before she tucked her arm into his. "You'll live, darling. The first month's the toughest."

Now he scowled at her. "How would you know? You never smoked."

"The first month of anything's the toughest. You

just have to keep your mind occupied. Exercise. We'll jog after lunch."

"We?"

"And we can play canasta after dinner."

He gave a quick snort but brushed the hair back from her cheek. "You'll cheat."

"See, your mind's already occupied." With a laugh, she turned her face up to his. He looked a bit surly, but on him, oddly, it was attractive. Placid, good-natured good looks had always bored her. "It won't hurt you to give up one of your vices, Michael. You have so many."

"I like my vices," he grumbled, then turned his head to look down at her. She was giving him her easy, friendly smile, one she sent his way rarely. It always made him forget just how much trouble she caused him. It made him forget he wasn't attracted to dramatically bohemian women with wild red hair and sharp bones. "A woman who looks like you should have several of her own."

Her mouth was solemn, her eyes wicked. "I'm much too busy. Vices take up a great deal of time."

"When Pandora opened the box, vices popped out."

She stopped at the back stoop. "Among other miseries. I suppose that's why I'm careful about opening boxes."

Michael ran a finger down her cheek. It was the sort of gesture he realized could easily become a habit. She was right, his mind was occupied. "You have to lift off the lid sooner or later."

She didn't move back, though she'd felt the little tingle of tension, of attraction, of need. Pandora didn't believe in moving back, but in plowing through. "Some things are better off locked up."

He nodded. He didn't want to release what was in their private box any more than she did. "Some locks aren't as strong as they need to be."

They were standing close, the wind whistling lightly between them. Pandora felt the sun on her back and the chill on her face. If she took a step nearer, there'd be heat. That she'd never doubted and had always avoided. He'd use whatever was available to him, she reminded herself. At the moment, it just happened to be her. She let her breath come calmly and easily before she reached for the doorknob.

"We'd better not keep Sweeney waiting."

# *Chapter Three*

The streets are almost deserted. A car turns a corner and disappears. It's drizzling. Neon flashes off puddles. It's garish rather than festive. There's a gray, miserable feel to this part of the city. Alleyways, cheap clubs, dented cars. The small, neatly dressed blonde walks quickly. She's nervous, out of her element, but not lost. Close-up on the envelope in her hands. It's damp from the rain. Her fingers open and close on it. Tires squeal offscreen and she jolts. The blue lights of the club blink off and on in her face as she stands outside. Hesitates. Shifts the envelope from hand to hand. She goes in. Slow pan of the street. Three shots and freeze.

Three knocks sounded at the door of Michael's office. Before he could answer, Pandora swirled in. "Happy anniversary, darling."

Michael looked up from his typewriter. He'd been

up most of the night working the story line out in his mind. It was nine in the morning, and he'd only had one cup of coffee to prime him for the day. Coffee and cigarettes together were too precious a memory. The scene that had just jelled in his mind dissolved.

"What the hell are you talking about?" He reached his hand into a bowl of peanuts and discovered he'd already eaten all but two.

"Two full weeks without any broken bones." Pandora swooped over to him, clucked her tongue at the disorder, then chose the arm of a chair. It was virtually the only free space. She brushed at the dust on the edge of the table beside her and left a smear. "And they said it wouldn't last."

She looked fresh with her wild mane of red pulled back from her face, comfortable in sweater and slacks that were too big for her. Michael felt like he'd just crawled out of a cave. His sweatshirt had ripped at the shoulder seam two years before, but he still favored it. A few weeks before, he'd helped paint a friend's apartment. The paint smears on his jeans showed her preference for baby pink. His eyes felt as though he'd slept facedown in the sand.

Pandora smiled at him like some bright, enthusiastic kindergarten teacher. She had a fresh, clean, almost woodsy scent. "We have a rule about respecting the other's work space," he reminded her.

"Oh, don't be cranky." It was said with the same positive smile. "Besides, you never gave me any schedule. From what I've noticed in the past couple of weeks, this is early for you."

"I'm just starting the treatment for a new episode."

"Really?" Pandora walked over and leaned over his

shoulder. "Hmm," she said, though she wondered who had shot whom. "Well, I don't suppose that'll take long."

"Why don't you go play with your beads?"

"Now you're being rude when I came up here to invite you to go with me into town." After brushing off the sleeve of her sweater, she sat on the edge of the desk. She didn't know exactly why she was so determined to be friendly. Maybe it was because the emerald necklace was nearly finished and was exceeding even her standards. Maybe it was because in the past two weeks she'd found a certain enjoyment in Michael's company. Mild enjoyment, Pandora reminded herself. Nothing to shout about.

Suspicious, Michael narrowed his eyes. "What for?"

"I'm going in for some supplies Sweeney needs." She found the turtle shell that was his lampshade intriguing, and ran her fingers over it. "I thought you might like to get out for a while."

He would. It had been two weeks since he'd seen anything but the house and grounds. He glanced back at the page in his typewriter. "How long will you be?"

"Oh, two, three hours I suppose." She moved her shoulders. "It's an hour's round trip to begin with."

He was tempted. Free time and a change of scene. But the half-blank sheet remained in his typewriter. "Can't. I have to get this fleshed out."

"All right." Pandora rose from the desk a bit surprised by the degree of disappointment she felt. Silly, she thought. She loved to drive alone with the radio blaring. "Don't strain your fingers."

He started to growl something at her back, then because his bowl of nuts was empty, thought better of it.

"Pandora, how about picking me up a couple pounds of pistachios?"

As she stopped at the door, she lifted a brow. "Pistachios?"

"Real ones. No red dye." He ran a hand over the bristle on his chin and wished for a pack of cigarettes. One cigarette. One long deep drag.

She glanced at the empty bowl and nearly smiled. The way he was nibbling, he'd lose that lean, rangy look quickly. "I suppose I could."

"And a copy of the *New York Times*."

Her brow rose. "Would you like to make me a list?"

"Be a sport, will you? Next time Sweeney needs supplies, I'll go in."

She thought about it a moment. "Very well then, nuts and news."

"And some pencils," he called out.

She slammed the door smartly.

Nearly two hours passed before Michael decided he deserved another cup of coffee. The story line was bumping along just as he'd planned, full of twists and turns. The fans of *Logan's Run* expected the gritty with occasional bursts of color and magic. That's just the way it was panning out.

Critics of the medium aside, Michael enjoyed writing for the small screen. He liked knowing his stories would reach literally millions of people every week and that for an hour, they could involve themselves with the character he had created.

The truth was, Michael liked Logan—the reluctant but steady heroism, the humor and the flaws. He'd made Logan human and fallible and reluctant because

Michael had always imagined the best heroes were just that.

The ratings and the mail proved he was on target. His writing for Logan had won him critical acclaim and awards, just as the one-act play he'd written had won him critical acclaim and awards. But the play had reached a few thousand at best, the bulk of whom had been New Yorkers. *Logan's Run* reached the family of four in Des Moines, the steelworkers in Chicago and the college crowd in Boston. Every week.

He didn't see television as the vast wasteland but as the magic box. Michael figured everyone was entitled to a bit of magic.

Michael switched off the typewriter so that the humming died. For a moment he sat in silence. He'd known he could work at the Folley. He'd done so before, but never long-term. What he hadn't known was that he'd work so well, so quickly or be so content. The truth was, he'd never expected to get along half so well with Pandora. Not that it was any picnic, Michael mused, absently running the stub of a pencil between his fingers.

They fought, certainly, but at least they weren't taking chunks out of each other. Or not very big ones. All in all he enjoyed the evenings when they played cards if for no other reason than the challenge of trying to catch her cheating. So far he hadn't.

Also true was the odd attraction he felt for her. That hadn't been in the script. So far he'd been able to ignore, control or smother it. But there were times… There were times, Michael thought as he rose and stretched, when he'd like to close her smart-tongued mouth in a more satisfactory way. Just to see what it'd be like, he told himself. Curiosity about people was part of his makeup. He'd be interested to see how Pandora would react if he hauled her against him and kissed her until she went limp.

He let out a quick laugh as he wandered to the window. Limp? Pandora? Women like her never went soft. He might satisfy his curiosity, but he'd get a fist in the gut for his trouble. Even that might be worth it....

She wasn't unmoved. He'd been sure of that since the first day they'd walked back together from her workshop. He'd seen it in her face, heard it, however briefly in her voice. They'd both been circling around it for two weeks. Or twenty years, Michael speculated.

He'd never felt about another woman exactly the way he felt about Pandora McVie. Uncomfortable, challenged, infuriated. The truth was that he was almost always at ease around women. He liked them—their femininity, their peculiar strengths and weaknesses, their style. Perhaps that was the reason for his success in relationships, though he'd carefully kept them short-term.

If he romanced a woman, it was because he was interested in her, not simply in the end result. True enough he was interested in Pandora, but he'd never considered romancing her. It surprised him that he'd caught himself once or twice considering seducing her.

Seducing, of course, was an entirely different matter than romancing. But all in all, he didn't know if attempting a casual seduction of Pandora would be worth the risk.

If he offered her a candlelight dinner or a walk in the moonlight—or a mad night of passion—she'd come back with a sarcastic remark. Which would, inevitably, trigger some caustic rebuttal from him. The merry-go-round would begin again.

In any case, it wasn't romance he wanted with Pandora. It was simply curiosity. In certain instances, it was best to remember what had happened to the intrepid cat. But as he thought of her, his gaze was drawn toward her workshop.

They weren't so very different really, Michael mused. Pandora could insist from dawn to dusk that they had nothing in common, but Jolley had been closer to the mark. They were both quick-tempered, opinionated and passionately protective of their professions. He closed himself up for hours at a time with a typewriter. She closed herself up with tools and torches. The end result of both of their work was entertainment. And after all, that was...

His thoughts broke off as he saw the shed door open. Odd, he hadn't thought she was back yet. His rooms were on the opposite end of the house from the garage, so he wouldn't have heard her car, but he thought she'd drop off what she'd picked up for him.

He started to shrug and turn away when he saw the figure emerge from the shed. It was bundled deep in a coat and hat, but he knew immediately it wasn't Pandora. She moved fluidly, unselfconsciously. This person walked with speed and wariness. Wariness, he thought again, that was evident in the way the head swiveled back and forth before the door was closed again. Without stopping to think, Michael dashed out of the room and down the stairs.

He nearly rammed into Charles at the bottom. "Pandora back?" he demanded.

"No, sir." Relieved that he hadn't been plowed down,

Charles rested a hand on the rail. "She said she might stay in town and do some shopping. We shouldn't worry if—"

But Michael was already halfway down the hall.

With a sigh for the agility he hadn't had in thirty years, Charles creaked his way into the drawing room to lay a fire.

The wind hit Michael the moment he stepped outside, reminding him he hadn't stopped for a coat. As he began to race toward the shed, his face chilled and his muscles warmed. There was no one in sight on the grounds. Not surprising, he mused as he slowed his pace just a bit. The woods were close at the edge, and there were a half a dozen easy paths through them.

Some kid poking around? he wondered. Pandora would be lucky if he hadn't pocketed half her pretty stones. It would serve her right.

But he changed his mind the minute he stood in the doorway of her workshop.

Boxes were turned over so that gems and stones and beads were scattered everywhere. Balls of string and twine had been unraveled and twisted and knotted from wall to wall. He had to push some out of his way to step inside. What was usually almost pristine in its order was utter chaos. Gold and silver wire had been bent and snapped, tools lay where they'd been carelessly tossed to the floor.

Michael bent down and picked up an emerald. It glinted sharp and green in his palm. If it had been a thief, he decided, it had been a clumsy and shortsighted one.

"Oh, God!" Pandora dropped her purse with a thud and stared.

When Michael turned, he saw her standing in the doorway, ice pale and rigid. He swore, wishing he'd had a moment to prepare her. "Take it easy," he began as he reached for her arm.

She shoved him aside forcibly and fought her way into the shed. Beads rolled and bounced at her feet. For a moment there was pure shock, disbelief. Then came a white wall of fury. "How could you?" When she turned back to him she was no longer pale. Her color was vivid, her eyes as sharp as the emerald he still held.

Because he was off guard, she nearly landed the first blow. The air whistled by his face as her fist passed. He caught her arms before she tried again. "Just a minute," he began, but she threw herself bodily into him and knocked them both against the wall. Whatever had been left on the shelves shuddered or fell off. It took several moments, and a few bruises on both ends, before he managed to pin her arms back and hold her still.

"Stop it." He pressed her back until she glared up at him, dry-eyed and furious. "You've a right to be upset, but putting a hole in me won't accomplish anything."

"I knew you could be low," she said between her teeth. "But I'd never have believed you could do something so filthy."

"Believe whatever the hell you want," he began, but he felt her body shudder as she fought for control. "Pandora," and his voice softened. "I didn't do this. Look at me," he demanded with a little shake. "Why would I?"

Because she wanted to cry, her voice, her eyes were hard. "You tell me."

Patience wasn't one of his strong points, but he tried again. "Pandora, listen to me. Try for common sense a minute and just listen. I got here a few minutes before you. I saw someone coming out of the shed from my window and came down. When I got here, this is what I found."

She was going to disgrace herself. She felt the tears backing up and hated them. It was better to hate him. "Let go of me."

Perhaps he could handle her anger better than her despair. Cautiously Michael released her arms and stepped back. "It hasn't been more than ten minutes since I saw someone coming out of here. I figured they cut through the woods."

She tried to think, tried to clear the fury out of her head. "You can go," she said with deadly calm. "I have to clean up and take inventory."

Something hot backed up in his throat at the casual dismissal. Remembering his own reaction when he'd opened the shed door, he swallowed it. "I'll call the police if you like, but I don't know if anything was stolen." He opened his palm and showed her the emerald. "I can't imagine any thief leaving stones like this behind."

Pandora snatched it out of his hand. When her fingers closed over it, she felt the slight prick of the hoop she'd fastened onto it only the day before. The emerald seemed to grow out of the braided wire.

Her heart was thudding against her ribs as she walked to her worktable. There was what was left of the necklace she'd been fashioning for two weeks. The deceptively delicate tiers were in pieces, the emeralds that had hung gracefully from them, scattered. Her own nippers had been used to destroy it. She gathered up the pieces in her hands and fought back the urge to scream.

"It was this, wasn't it?" Michael picked up the sketch from the floor. It was stunning on paper—at once fanciful and bold. He supposed what she had drawn had some claim to art. He imagined how he'd feel if someone took scissors to one of his scripts. "You'd nearly finished."

Pandora dropped the pieces back on the table. "Leave me alone." She crouched and began to gather up stones and beads.

"Pandora." When she ignored him, Michael grabbed her by the shoulders and shook. "Dammit, Pandora, I want to help."

She sent him a long, cold look. "You've done enough, Michael. Now leave me alone."

"All right, fine." He released her and stormed out. Anger and frustration carried him halfway across the lawn. Michael stopped, swore and wished bitterly for a cigarette. She had no right to accuse him. Worse, she had no right to make him feel responsible. The guilt he was experiencing was nearly as strong as it would have been if he'd actually vandalized her shop. Hands in his pockets, he stood staring back at the shed and cursing her.

She really thought he'd done that to her. That he was capable of such meaningless, bitter destruction. He'd tried to talk to her, soothe her. Every offer of help had been thrown back at him. Just like her, he thought with his teeth gritted. She deserved to be left alone.

He nearly started back to the house again when he remembered just how shocked and ill she'd looked in the doorway of the shed. Calling himself a fool, he went back.

When he opened the door of the shed again, the chaos was just as it had been. Sitting in the middle of it on the floor by her workbench was Pandora. She was weeping quietly.

He felt the initial male panic at being confronted with feminine tears and surprise that they came from Pandora who never shed them. Yet he felt sympathy for someone who'd been dealt a bull's-eye blow. Without saying a word, he went to her and slipped his arms around her.

She stiffened, but he'd expected it. "I told you to go away."

"Yeah. Why should I listen to you?" He stroked her hair.

She wanted to crawl into his lap and weep for hours. "I don't want you here."

"I know. Just pretend I'm someone else." He drew her against his chest.

"I'm only crying because I'm angry." With a sniff, she turned her face into his shirt.

"Sure." He kissed the top of her head. "Go ahead and be angry for a while. I'm used to it."

She told herself it was because she was weakened by shock and grief, but she relaxed against him. The tears came in floods. When she cried, she cried wholeheartedly. When she was finished, she was done.

Tears dry, she sat cushioned against him. Secure. She wouldn't question it now. Along with the anger came a sense of shame she was unaccustomed to. She'd been filthy to him. But he'd come back and held her. Who'd have expected him to be patient, or caring? Or strong enough to make her accept both. Pandora let out a long breath and kept her eyes shut for just a moment. He smelled of soap and nothing else.

"I'm sorry, Michael."

She was soft. Hadn't he just told himself she wouldn't be? He let his cheek brush against her hair. "Okay."

"No, I mean it." When she turned her head her lips skimmed across his cheek. It surprised them both. That kind of contact was for friends—or lovers. "I couldn't think after I walked in here. I—" She broke off a moment, fascinated by his eyes. Wasn't it strange how small the world could become if you looked into someone's eyes? Why hadn't she ever noticed that before? "I need to sort all this out."

"Yeah." He ran a fingertip down her cheek. She was soft. Softer than he'd let himself believe. "We both do."

It was so easy to settle herself in the crook of his arm. "I can't think."

"No?" Her lips were only an inch from his—too close to ignore, too far to taste. "Let's both not think for a minute."

When he touched his mouth to hers, she didn't draw away but accepted, experimented with the same sense of curiosity that moved through him. It wasn't an explosion or a shock, but a test for both of them. One they'd both known would come sooner or later.

She tasted warm, and her sweetness had a bite. He'd known her so long, shouldn't he have known that? Her body felt primed to move, to act, to race. Soft, yes, she was soft, but not pliant. Perhaps he'd have found pliancy too easy. When he slipped his tongue into her mouth hers met it teasingly, playfully. His stomach knotted. She made him want more, much more of that unapologetically earthy scent, the taut body. His fingers tangled in her hair and tightened.

He was as mysterious and bold as she'd always thought he would be. His hands were firm, his mouth giving. Sometimes she'd wondered what it would be like to meet him on these terms. But she'd always closed her mind before any of the answers could slip through. Michael Donahue was dangerous simply because he was Michael Donahue. By turns he'd attracted and alienated her since they'd been children. It was more than any other man had been able to do for more than a week.

Now, as her mouth explored his, she began to understand why. He was different, for her. She didn't feel altogether safe in his arms, and not completely in control. Pandora had always made certain she was both those things when it came to a man. The scrape of his unshaved cheek didn't annoy her as she'd thought it would. It aroused. The discomfort of the hard floor seemed suitable, as was the quick rush of cold air through the still-open door.

She felt quietly and completely at home. Then the quick nip of his teeth against her lip made her feel as though she'd just stepped on uncharted land. New territory was what she'd been raised on, and yet, in all her experience, she'd never explored anything so unique, so exotic or so comfortable.

She wanted to go on and knew she had to stop.

Together they drew away.

"Well." She scrambled for composure as she folded her hands in her lap. Be casual, she ordered herself while her pulse thudded at her wrists. Be careless. She couldn't afford to say anything that might make him laugh at her. "That's been coming for a while, I suppose."

He felt as though he'd just slid down a roller coaster without a cart. "I suppose." He studied her a moment, curious and a bit unnerved. When he saw her fingers twist together he felt a small sense of satisfaction. "It wasn't altogether what I'd expected."

"Things rarely are." Too many surprises for one day, Pandora decided, and rose unsteadily to her feet. She made the mistake of looking around and nearly sunk to the floor again.

"Pandora—"

"No, don't worry." She shook her head as he rose. "I'm not going to fall apart again." Concentrating on breathing evenly, she took one long look at her workshop. "It looks like you were right about the locks. I suppose I should be grateful you haven't said I told you so."

"Maybe I would if it applied." Michael picked up the emeralds scattered on her table. "I'm no expert, cousin, but I'd say these are worth a few thousand."

"So?" She frowned as her train of thought began to march with his. "No thief would've left them behind." Reaching down, she picked up a handful of stones. Among them were two top-grade diamonds. "Or these."

As was his habit, he began to put the steps together in a sort of mental scenario. Action and reaction, motive and result. "I'd wager once you've inventoried, you won't be missing anything. Whoever did this didn't want to risk more than breaking and entering and vandalism."

With a huff, she sat down on her table. "You think it was one of the family."

"'They said it wouldn't last,'" he quoted, and stuck his hands in his pockets. "You may've had something there, Pandora. Something neither of us considered when we were setting out the guidelines. None of them believed we'd be able to get through six months together. The fact is, we've gotten through the first two weeks without a hitch. It could make one of them nervous enough to want to throw in a complication. What was your first reaction when you saw all this?"

She dragged her hand through her hair. "That you'd done it for spite. Exactly what our kith and kin would expect me to think. Dammit, I hate to be predictable."

"You outsmarted them once your mind cleared."

She sent him a quick look, not certain if she should thank him or apologize again. It was best to do neither. "Biff," Pandora decided with relish. "This sort of low-minded trick would be just up his alley."

"I'd only vote for Biff if you find a few rocks missing." Michael rocked back on his heels. "He'd never be able to resist picking up a few glitters that could be liquidated into nice clean cash."

"True enough." Uncle Carlson—no, it seemed a bit crude for his style. Ginger would've been too fascinated with the sparkles to have done any more than fondle. Pulling a hand through her hair, she tried to picture one of her bland, civilized relations wielding a pair of nippers. "Well, I don't suppose it matters a great deal which one of them did it. They've put me two weeks behind on my commission." Again she picked up pieces of thin gold. "It'll never be quite the same," she murmured. "Nothing is when it's done over."

"Sometimes it's better."

With a shake of her head, she walked over to a heater. If he gave her any more sympathy now, she wouldn't be able to trust herself. "One way or the other I've got to get started. Tell Sweeney I won't make it in for lunch."

"I'll help you clean this up."

"No." She turned back when he started to frown.

"No, really, Michael, I appreciate it. I need to be busy. And alone."

He didn't like it, but understood. "All right. I'll see you at dinner."

"Michael…" He paused at the doorway and looked back. Amid the confusion she looked strong and vivid. He nearly closed the door and went back to her. "Maybe Uncle Jolley was right."

"About what?"

"You may have one or two redeeming qualities."

He smiled at her then, quick and dashing. "Uncle Jolley was always right, cousin. That's why he's still pulling the strings."

Pandora waited until the door shut again. Pulling the strings he was, she mused. "But you're not playing matchmaker with my life," she mumbled. "I'm staying free, single and unattached. Just get that through your head."

She wasn't superstitious, but Pandora almost thought she heard her uncle's high, cackling laugh. She rolled up her sleeves and got to work.

# *Chapter Four*

Because after a long, tedious inventory Pandora discovered nothing missing, she vetoed Michael's notion of calling in the police. If something had been stolen, she'd have seen the call as a logical step. As it was, she decided the police would poke and prod around and lecture on the lack of locks. If the vandal had been one of the family—and she had to agree with Michael's conclusion there—a noisy, official investigation would give the break-in too much importance and undoubtedly too much publicity.

Yes, the press would have a field day. Pandora had already imagined the headlines. "Family vs. family in the battle of eccentric's will." There was, under her independent and straightforward nature, a prim part of her that felt family business was private business.

If one or more of the members of the family were

keeping an eye on Jolley's Folley and the goings-on there, Pandora wanted them to think that she'd brushed off the vandalism as petty and foolish. As a matter of pride, she didn't want anyone to believe she'd been dealt a stunning blow. As a matter of practicality, she didn't want anyone to know that she had her eyes open. She was determined to find out who had broken into her shop and how they'd managed to pick such a perfect time for it.

Michael hadn't insisted on calling the police because his thoughts had run along the same lines as Pandora's. He'd managed, through a lot of maneuvering and silence, to keep his career totally separate from his family. In his business, he was known as Michael Donahue, award-winning writer, not Michael Donahue, relative of Jolley McVie, multimillionaire. He wanted to keep it that way.

Stubbornly, each had refused to tell the other of their reasons or their plans for some personal detective work. It wasn't so much a matter of trust, but more the fact that neither of them felt the other could do the job competently. So instead, they kept the conversation light through one of Sweeney's four-star meals and let the vandalism rest. More important, they carefully avoided any reference that might trigger some remark about what had happened on a more personal level in Pandora's workshop.

After two glasses of wine and a generous portion of chicken fricassee, Pandora felt more optimistic. It would have been much worse if any of her stock or tools had been taken. That would have meant a trip into Manhattan and days, perhaps weeks of delay. As it was, the worst crime that she could see was the fact that she'd been spied on. Surely that was the only explanation for the break-in coinciding so perfectly with her trip to town. And that would be her first order of business.

"I wonder," Pandora began, probing lightly, "if the Saundersons are in residence for the winter."

"The neighbors with the pond." Michael had thought of the Saunderson place himself. There were certain points on that property where, with a good set of binoculars, someone could watch the Folley easily. "They spend a lot of time in Europe, don't they?"

"Hmm." Pandora toyed with her chicken. "He's in hotels, you know. They tend to pop off here or there for weeks at a time."

"Do they ever rent the place out?"

"Oh, not that I know of. I'm under the impression that they leave a skeleton staff there even when they fly off. Now that I think of it, they were home a few months ago." The memory made her smile. "Uncle Jolley and I went fishing and Saunderson nearly caught us. If we hadn't scrambled back to the cabin—" She broke off as the thought formed.

"Cabin." Michael picked up where she'd left off. "That old two-room wreck Jolley was going to use as a hunting lodge during his eat-off-the-land stage? I'd forgotten all about it."

Pandora shrugged as though it meant nothing while her mind raced ahead. "He ended up eating more beans than game. In any case, we caught a bundle of trout, ate like pigs and sent the rest along to Saunderson. He never sent a thank-you note."

"Poor manners."

"Well, I've heard his grandmother was a barmaid in Chelsea. More wine?"

"No, thanks." He thought it best to keep a clear head if he was going to carry out the plans that were just beginning to form. "Help yourself."

Pandora set the bottle down and sent him a sweet smile. "No, I'm fine. Just a bit tired really."

"You're entitled." It would clear his path beautifully if he could ship her off to bed early. "What you need is a good night's sleep."

"I'm sure you're right." Both of them were too involved with their own moves to notice how excruciatingly polite the conversation had become. "I'll just skip coffee tonight and go have a bath." She feigned a little yawn. "What about you? Planning to work late?"

"No—no, I think I'll get a fresh start in the morning."

"Well then." Pandora rose, still smiling. She'd give it an hour, she calculated, then she'd be out and gone. "I'm going up. Good night, Michael."

"Good night." Once the light in her room was off, he decided, he'd be on his way.

Pandora sat in her darkened room for exactly fifteen minutes and just listened. All she had to do was get outside without being spotted. The rest would be easy. Opening her door a crack, she held her breath, waited and listened a little longer. Not a sound. It was now or never, she decided and bundled into her coat. Into the deep pockets, she shoved a flashlight, two books of matches and a small can of hair spray. As good as mace, Pandora figured, if you ran into something unfriendly. She crept out into the hall and started slowly down the stairs, her back to the wall.

An adventure, she thought, feeling the familiar pulse

of excitement and anxiety. She hadn't had one since Uncle Jolley died. As she let herself out one of the side doors, she thought how much he'd have enjoyed this one. The moon was only a sliver, but the sky was full of stars. The few clouds that spread over them were hardly more than transparent wisps. And the air—she took a deep breath—was cool and crisp as an apple. With a quick glance over her shoulder at Michael's window, she started toward the woods.

The starlight couldn't help her there. Though the trees were bare, the branches were thick enough to block out big chunks of sky. She dug out her flashlight and, turning it side to side, found the edges of the path. She didn't hurry. If she rushed, the adventure would be over too soon. She walked slowly, listened and imagined.

There were sounds—the breeze blew through pine needles and scattered the dry leaves. Now and again there was a skuttle in the woods to the right or left. A fox, a raccoon, a bear not quite settled down to hibernate? Pandora liked not being quite certain. If you walked through the woods alone, in the dark, and didn't have some sense of wonder, it was hardly worth the trip.

She liked the smells—pine, earth, the hint of frost that would settle on the ground before morning. She liked the sense of being alone, and more, of having something up ahead that warranted her attention.

The path forked, and she swung to the left. The cabin wasn't much farther. She stopped once, certain she'd heard something move up ahead that was too big to be considered a fox. For a moment she had a few uncomfortable thoughts about bears and bobcats. It was one thing to speculate and another to have to deal with them. Then there was nothing. Shaking her head, Pandora went on.

What would she do if she got to the cabin, and it wasn't dusty and deserted? What would she do if she actually found one of her dear, devoted relatives had set up housekeeping? Uncle Carlson reading the *Wall Street Journal* by the fire? Aunt Patience fussing around the rocky wooden table with a dust cloth? The thought was almost laughable. Almost, until Pandora remembered her workshop.

Drawing her brows together, she walked forward. If someone was there, they were going to answer to her. In moments, the shadow of the cabin loomed up before her. It looked as it was supposed to look, desolate, deserted, eerie. She kept her flashlight low as she crept toward the porch, then nearly let out a scream when her own weight caused the narrow wooden stair to creak. She held a hand to her heart until it no longer felt as though it would break her ribs. Then slowly, quietly, stealthily, she reached for the doorknob and twisted it.

The door moaned itself open. Wincing at the sound, Pandora counted off ten seconds before she took the next step. With a quick sweep of her light, she stepped in.

When the arm came around her neck, she dropped the flashlight with a clatter. It rolled over the floor, sending an erratic beam over the log walls and brick fireplace. Even as she drew the breath to scream, she reached in her pocket for the hair spray. After she was whirled around, she found herself face-to-face with Michael. His fist was poised inches from her face, her can inches from his. Both of them stood just as they were.

"Dammit!" Michael dropped his arm. "What are you doing here?"

"What are you doing here?" she tossed back. "And what do you mean by grabbing me that way? You may've broken my flashlight."

"I almost broke your nose."

Pandora shook back her hair and walked over to retrieve her light. She didn't want him to see her hands tremble. "Well, I certainly think you should find out who someone is before you throw a headlock on them."

"You followed me."

She sent him a cool, amused look. It helped to be able to do so when her stomach was still quaking. "Don't flatter yourself. I simply wanted to see if something was going on out here, and I didn't want you to interfere."

"Interfere." He shone his own light directly in her face so that she had to throw up a hand in defense. "And what the hell were you going to do if something was going on? Overpower them?"

She thought of how easily he'd taken her by surprise. It only made her lift her chin higher. "I can take care of myself."

"Sure." He glanced down at the can she still held. "What have you got there?"

Having forgotten it, Pandora looked down herself, then had to stifle a chuckle. Oh, how Uncle Jolley would've appreciated the absurdity. "Hair spray," she said very precisely. "Right between the eyes."

He swore, then laughed. He couldn't have written a scene so implausible. "I guess I should be glad you didn't get a shot off at me."

"I look before I pounce." Pandora dropped the can

back into her pocket. "Well, since we're here, we might as well look around."

"I was doing just that when I heard your catlike approach." She wrinkled her nose at him, but he ignored her. "It looks like someone's been making themselves at home." To prove his point, Michael shone his light at the fireplace. Half-burnt logs still smoldered.

"Well, well." With her own light, Pandora began to walk around the cabin. The last time she'd been there, the chair with the broken rung had been by the window. Jolley had sat there himself, keeping a lookout for Saunderson while she'd opened a tin of sardines to ward off starvation. Now the chair was pulled up near the fire. "A vagrant, perhaps."

Watching her, Michael nodded. "Perhaps."

"But not likely. Suppose they'll be back?"

"Hard to say." The casual glance showed nothing out of place. The cabin was neat and tidy. Too tidy. The floor and table surfaces should have had a film of dust. Everything had been wiped clean. "It could be they've done all the damage they intend to do."

Disgruntled, Pandora plopped down on the bunk and dropped her chin in her hands. "I'd hoped to catch them."

"And what? Zap them with environmentally safe hair spray?"

She glared up at him. "I suppose you had a better plan."

"I think I might've made them a bit more uncomfortable."

"Black eyes and broken noses." She made an impatient sound. "Really, Michael, you should try to get your mind out of your fists."

"I suppose you just wanted to talk reasonably with whichever member of our cozy family played search and destroy with your workshop."

She started to snap, caught herself, then smiled. It was the slow, wicked smile Michael could never help admiring. "No," she admitted. "Reason wasn't high on my list. Still, it appears we've both missed our chance for brute force. Well, you write the detective stories— so to speak—shouldn't we look for clues?"

His lips curved in something close to a sneer. "I didn't think to bring my magnifying glass."

"You can almost be amusing when you put your mind to it." Rising, Pandora began to shine her light here and there. "They might've dropped something."

"A name tag?"

"Something," she muttered, and dropped to her knees to look under the bunk. "Aha!" Hunkering down, she grabbed at something.

"What is it?" Michael was beside her before she'd straightened up.

"A shoe." Feeling foolish and sentimental, she held it in both hands. "It's nothing. It was Uncle Jolley's."

Because she looked lost, and more vulnerable than he'd expected, Michael offered the only comfort he knew. "I miss him, too."

She sat a moment, the worn sneaker in her lap. "You know, sometimes it's as though I can almost feel him. As though he's around the next corner, in the next room, waiting to pop up and laugh at the incredible joke he's played."

With a quick laugh, Michael rubbed a hand over her back. "I know what you mean."

Pandora looked at him, steady, measuring. "Maybe

you do," she murmured. Briskly she set the sneaker on the bunk and rose. "I'll have a look in the cupboards."

"Let me know if you find any cookies." He met the look she tossed over her shoulder with a shrug. "In the early stages of nonsmoking, you need a lot of oral satisfaction."

"You ought to try chewing gum." Pandora opened a cupboard and shone her light over jars and cans. There was peanut butter, chunky, and caviar, Russian. Two of Jolley's favorite snacks. She passed over taco sauce and jumbo fruit cocktail, remembering that her ninety-three-year-old uncle had had the appetite of a teenager. Then reaching in, she plucked out a can and held it up.

"Aha!"

"Again?"

"Tuna fish," Pandora announced waving the can at Michael. "It's a can of tuna."

"Right you are. Any mayo to go with it?"

"Don't be dense, Michael. Uncle Jolley hated tuna."

Michael started to say something sarcastic, then stopped. "He did, didn't he?" he said slowly. "And he never kept anything around he didn't like."

"Exactly."

"Congratulations, Sherlock. Now which of the suspects has an affection for canned fish?"

"You're just jealous because I found a clue and you didn't."

"It's only a clue," Michael pointed out, a little annoyed at being outdone by an amateur, "if you can do something with it."

He'd never give her credit, she thought, for anything, not her craft, her intelligence and never her womanhood. There was an edge to her voice when she spoke again. "If you're so pessimistic, why did you come out here?"

"I was hoping to find someone." Restless, Michael moved his light from wall to wall. "As it is all we've done is prove someone was here and gone."

Pandora dropped the can of tuna in disgust. "A waste of time."

"You shouldn't've followed me out."

"I didn't follow you out." She shone her light back at him. He looked too male, too dangerous in the shadows. She wished, only briefly, that she had the spectacular build and stunning style that would bring him whimpering to his knees. Their breath came in clouds and merged together. "For all I know, you followed me."

"Oh, I see. That's why I was here first."

"Beside the point. If you'd planned to come out here tonight, why didn't you tell me?"

He came closer. But if he came too close to her, he discovered, he began to feel something, something like an itch along the skin. Try to scratch it, he reminded himself, and she'd rub you raw in seconds. "For the same reason you didn't tell me. I don't trust you, cousin. You don't trust me."

"At least we can agree on something." She started to brush by him and found her arm captured. In one icy movement, she tilted her head down to look at his hand, then up to look at his face. "That's a habit you should try to break, Michael."

"They say when you break one habit, you pick up another."

The ice in Pandora's voice never changed, but her blood was warming. "Do they?"

"You're easier to touch than I'd once thought, Pandora."

"Don't be too sure, Michael." She took a step back, not in retreat, she told herself. It was a purely offensive move. Still, he moved with her.

"Some women have trouble dealing with physical attraction."

The temper that flared in her eyes appealed to him as much as the passion he'd seen there briefly that afternoon. "Your ego's showing again. This dominant routine might work very well with your centerfolds, but—"

"You've always had an odd fascination with my sex life." Michael grinned at her, pleased to see frustration flit over her face.

"The same kind of educated fascination one has with the sex lives of lower mammals." It infuriated her that her heart was racing. And not from anger. She was too honest to pretend it was anger. She'd come looking for an adventure, and she'd found one. "It's getting late," she said, using the tone of a parochial schoolteacher to a disruptive student. "You'll have to excuse me."

"I've never asked about your sex life." When she took another step away, he boxed her neatly into a corner. Pandora's hand slipped into her pocket and rested on the can of hair spray. "Let me guess. You prefer a man with a string of initials after his name who philosophizes about sex more than he acts on it."

"Why you pompous, arrogant—"

Michael shut her mouth the way he'd once fantasized. With his own.

The kiss was no test this time, but torrid, hot, edging toward desperate. Whatever she might feel, she'd dissect later. Now she'd accept the experience. His mouth was warm, firm, and he used it with the same cocky male confidence that would have infuriated her at any other time. Now she met it with her own.

He was strong, insistent. For the first time Pandora felt herself body to body with a man who wouldn't treat her delicately. He demanded, expected and gave a completely uninhibited physicality. Pandora didn't have to think her way through the kiss. She didn't have to think at all.

He'd expected her to rear back and take a swing at him. Her instant and full response left him reeling. Later Michael would recall that nothing as basic and simple as a kiss had made his head spin for years.

She packed a punch, but she did it with soft lips. If she knew just how quickly she'd knocked him out, would she gloat? He wouldn't think of it now. He wouldn't think of anything now. Without a moment's hesitation, he buried his consciousness in her and let the senses rule.

The cabin was cold and dark without even a single stream of moonlight for romance. It smelled of dying smoke and settling dust. The wind had kicked up enough to moan grumpily at the windows. Neither of them noticed. Even when they broke apart, neither of them noticed.

He wasn't steady. That was something else he'd think about later. At least he had the satisfaction of seeing she wasn't steady, either. She looked as he felt, stunned, off balance and unable to set for the next blow. Needing some equilibrium, he grinned at her.

"You were saying?"

She wanted to slug him. She wanted to kiss him

again until he didn't have the strength to grin. He'd expect her to fall at his feet as other women probably did. He'd expect her to sigh and smile and surrender so he'd have one more victory. Instead she snapped, "Idiot."

"I love it when you're succinct."

"Rule number six," Pandora stated, aiming a killing look. "No physical contact."

"No physical contact," Michael agreed as she stomped toward the doorway, "unless both parties enjoy it."

She slammed the door and left him grinning.

When two people are totally involved in their own projects, they can live under the same roof for days at a time and rarely see each other. Especially if the roof is enormous and the people very stubborn. Pandora and Michael brushed together at meals and otherwise left each other alone. This wasn't out of any sense of politeness or consideration. It was simply because each of them was too busy to heckle the other.

Separately, however, each felt a smug satisfaction when the first month passed. One down, five to go.

When they were into their second month, Michael drove into New York for a day to handle a problem with a script that had to be dealt with personally. He left, cross as a bear and muttering about imbeciles. Pandora prepared to enjoy herself tremendously in his absence. She wouldn't have to keep up her guard or share the Folley for hours. She could do anything she wanted without worrying about anyone coming to look over her shoulder or make a caustic remark. It would be wonderful.

She ended up picking at her dinner, then watching for his car through the heavy brocade drapes. Not because she missed *him*, she assured herself. It was just that she'd become used to having someone in the house.

Wasn't that one of the reasons she'd never lived with anyone before? She wanted to avoid any sense of dependence. And dependence, she decided, was natural when you shared the same space—even when it was with a two-legged snake.

So she waited, and she watched. Long after Charles and Sweeney had gone to bed, she continued to wait and watch. She wasn't concerned, and certainly not lonely. Only restless. She told herself she didn't go to bed herself because she wasn't tired. Wandering the first floor, she walked into Jolley's den. Game room would have been a more appropriate name. The decor was a cross between video arcade and disco lounge with its state-of-the-art components and low, curved-back sofas.

She turned on the huge, fifty-four-inch television, then left it on the first show that appeared. She wasn't going to *watch* it. She just wanted the company.

There were two pinball tables where she passed nearly an hour trying to beat the high scores Jolley had left behind. Another legacy. Then there was an arcade-size video game that simulated an attack on the planet Zarbo. Under her haphazard defense system, the planet blew up three times before she moved on. There was computerized chess, but she thought her mind too sluggish to take it on. In the end she stretched out on the six-foot sofa in front of the television. Just to rest, not to watch.

Within moments, she was hooked on the late-night syndication of a cop show. Squealing tires and blasting bullets. Head pillowed on her arms, one leg thrown over the top of the sofa, she relaxed and let herself be entertained.

When Michael came to the doorway, she didn't notice him. He'd had a grueling day and had hit some nasty traffic on the drive back. The fact was he'd considered staying in the city overnight—the sensible thing to do. He'd found himself making a dozen weak excuses why he had to go back instead of accepting the invitation of the assistant producer—a tidily built brunette with big brown eyes.

He'd intended to crawl upstairs, fall into his bed and sleep until noon, but he'd seen the lights and heard the racket. Now, here was Pandora, self-proclaimed critic of the small screen, sprawled on a sofa watching reruns at one in the morning. She looked suspiciously as though she were enjoying herself.

Not a bad show, Michael mused, recognizing the series. In fact, he'd written a couple of scripts for it in his early days. The central character had a sly sort of wit and a fumbling manner that caused the perpetrator to spill out enough information for an arrest by the end of the show.

Michael watched Pandora as she shifted comfortably on the couch. He waited until the commercial break. "Well, how the mighty have fallen."

She nearly did, rolling quickly to look back toward the doorway. She sat up, scowled and searched her mind for a plausible excuse. "I couldn't sleep," she told him, which was true enough. She wouldn't add it was because he hadn't been home. "I suppose television is made for the insomniac. Valium for the mind."

He was tired, bone tired, but he realized how glad

he was she'd had a comeback. He came over, plopped down beside her and propped his feet on a coffee table made out of a fat log. "Who done it?" he asked, and sighed. It was good to be home.

"The greedy business partner." She was too pleased to have him back to be embarrassed. "There's really very little challenge in figuring out the answers."

"This show wasn't based on the premise of figuring out who did the crime, but in how the hero maneuvers them into betraying themselves."

She pretended she wasn't interested, but shifted so that she could still see the screen. "So, how did things go in New York?"

"They went." Michael pried off one shoe with the toe of the other. "After several hours of hair tearing and blame casting, the script's intact."

He looked tired. Really tired, she realized, and unbent enough to take off his other shoe. He merely let out a quick grunt of appreciation. "I don't understand why people would get all worked up about one silly hour a week."

He opened one eye to stare at her. "It's the American way."

"What's there to get so excited about? You have a crime, the good guys chase the bad guys and catch them before the final credits. Seems simple enough."

"I can't thank you enough for clearing that up. I'll point it out at the next production meeting."

"Really, Michael, it seems to me things should run fairly smoothly, especially since you've been on the air with this thing for years."

"Know anything about ego and paranoia?"

She smiled a little. "I've heard of them."

"Well, multiply that with artistic temperament, the ratings race and an escalating budget. Don't forget to drop in a good dose of network executives. Things haven't run smoothly for four years. If *Logan* goes another four, it still won't run smoothly. That's show biz."

Pandora moved her shoulders. "It seems a foolish way to make a living."

"Ain't it just," Michael agreed, and fell sound asleep.

She let him doze for the next twenty minutes while she watched the sly, fumbling cop tighten the ropes on the greedy business partner. Satisfied that justice had been done, Pandora rose to switch off the set and dim the lights.

She could leave him here, she considered as she watched Michael sleep. He looked comfortable enough at the moment. She thought about it as she walked over to brush his hair from his forehead. But he'd probably wake up with a stiff neck and a nasty disposition. Better get him upstairs into bed, she decided, and shook his shoulder.

"Michael."

"Mmm?"

"Let's go to bed."

"Thought you'd never ask," he mumbled, and reached halfheartedly for her.

Amused, she shook him harder. "Never let your reach exceed your grasp. Come on, cousin, I'll help you upstairs."

"The director's a posturing idiot," he grumbled as she dragged him to his feet.

"I'm sure he is. Now, see if you can put one foot in front of the other. That's the way. Here we go." With an arm around his waist, she began to lead him from the room.

"He kept screwing around with my script."

"Of all the nerve. Here come the steps."

"Said he wanted more emotional impact in the second act. Bleaches his hair," Michael muttered as she half pulled him up the steps. "Lot he knows about emotional impact."

"Obviously a mental midget." Breathlessly she steered him toward his room. He was heavier than he looked. "Here we are now, home again." With a little strategy and a final burst of will, she shoved him onto the bed. "There now, isn't that cozy?" Leaving him fully dressed, she spread an afghan over him.

"Aren't you going to take my pants off?"

She patted his head. "Not a chance."

"Spoilsport."

"If I helped you undress this late at night, I'd probably have nightmares."

"You know you're crazy about me." The bed felt like heaven. He could've burrowed in it for a week.

"You're getting delirious, Michael. I'll have Charles bring you some warm tea and honey in the morning."

"Not if you want to live." He roused himself to open his eyes and smile at her. "Why don't you crawl in beside me? With a little encouragement, I could show you the time of your life."

Pandora leaned closer, closer, until her mouth was inches from his. Their breath mixed quickly, intimately. She hovered there a moment while her hair fell forward and brushed his cheek. "In a pig's eye," she whispered.

Michael shrugged, yawned and rolled over. "'Kay."

In the dark, Pandora stood for a moment with her

hands on her hips. At least he could've acted insulted. Chin up, she walked out—making sure she slammed the door at her back.

# Chapter Five

Tier by painstaking tier, Pandora had completed the emerald necklace. When it was finished, she was pleased to judge it perfect. This judgment pleased her particularly because she was her own toughest critic. Pandora didn't feel emotionally attached or creatively satisfied by every piece she made. With the necklace, she felt both. She examined it under a magnifying glass, held it up in harsh light, went over the filigree inch by inch and found no flaws. Out of her own imagination she'd conceived it, then with her own skill created it. With a kind of regret, she boxed the necklace in a bed of cotton. It wasn't hers any longer.

With the necklace done, she looked around her workshop without inspiration. She'd put so much into that one piece, all her concentration, her emotion, her skill. She hadn't made a single plan for the next project. Restless, wanting to work, she picked up her pad and began to sketch.

Earrings perhaps, she mused. Something bold and chunky and ornate. She wanted a change after the fine, elegant work she'd devoted so much time to. Circles and triangles, she thought. Something geometric and blatantly modern. Nothing romantic like the necklace.

Romantic, she mused, and sketched strong, definite lines. She'd been working with a romantic piece; perhaps that's why she'd nearly made a fool of herself with Michael. Her emotions were involved with her work, and her work had been light and feminine and romantic. It made sense, she decided, satisfied. Now, she'd work with something strong and brash and arrogant. That should solve the problem.

There shouldn't be a problem in the first place. Teeth gritted, she flipped a page and started over. Her feelings for Michael had always been very definite. Intolerance. If you were intolerant of someone, it went against the grain to be attracted to him.

It wasn't real attraction in any case. It was more some sort of twisted…curiosity. Yes, curiosity. The word satisfied her completely. She'd been curious, naturally enough, to touch on the sexuality of a man she'd known since childhood. Curious, again naturally, to find out what it was about Michael Donahue that attracted all those poster girls. She'd found out.

So he had a way of making a woman feel utterly a woman, utterly involved, utterly willing. It wasn't something that had happened to her before nor something she'd looked for. As Pandora saw it, it was a kind of skill. She decided he'd certainly honed it as meticulously as any craftsman. Though she found it difficult to fault him for that, *she* wasn't about to fall in with the horde. If he knew, if he even suspected, that she'd had the same reaction to him that she imagined dozens of other women had, he'd gloat for a month. If he guessed that from time to time she'd wished—just for a moment—that he'd think of her the way he thought of those dozens of other women, he'd gloat for twice as long. She wouldn't give him the pleasure.

Individuality was part of her makeup. She didn't want to be one of his women, even if she could. Now that her curiosity had been satisfied, they'd get through the next five months without any more…complications.

Just because she'd found him marginally acceptable as a human being, almost tolerable as a companion wouldn't get in the way. It would, if anything, make the winter pass a bit easier.

And when she caught herself putting the finishing touches on a sketch of Michael's face, she was appalled. The lines were true enough, though rough. She'd had no trouble capturing the arrogance around the eyes or the sensitivity around the mouth. Odd, she realized; she'd sketched him to look intelligent. She ripped the sheet from her pad, crumpled it up in a ball and tossed it into the trash. Her mind had wandered, that was all. Pandora picked up her pencil again, put it down, then dug the sketch out again. Art was art, after all, she told herself as she smoothed out Michael's face.

He wasn't having a great deal of success with his own work. Michael sat at his desk and typed like a maniac for five minutes. Then he stared into space for fifteen. It wasn't like him. When he worked, he worked steadily, competently, smoothly until the scene was set.

Leaning back in his chair, he picked up a pencil and ran his fingers from end to end. Whatever the statistics said, he should never have given up smoking. That's what had him so edgy. Restless, he pushed away from the desk and wandered over to the window. He stared down at Pandora's workshop. It looked cheerful under a light layer of snow that was hardly more than a dusting. The windows were blank.

That's what had him so edgy.

She wasn't what he'd expected. She was softer, sweeter. Warmer. She was fun to talk to, whether she was arguing and snipping and keeping you on the edge of temper, or whether she was being easy and companionable. There wasn't an overflow of small talk with Pandora. There weren't any trite conversations. She kept your mind working, even if it was in defense of her next barb.

It wasn't easy to admit that he actually enjoyed her company. But the weeks they'd been together at the Folley had gone quickly. No, it wasn't easy to admit he liked being with her, but he'd turned down an interesting invitation from his assistant producer because... Because, Michael admitted on a long breath, he hadn't wanted to spend the night with one woman when he'd known his thoughts would have been on another.

Just how was he going to handle this unwanted and unexpected attraction to a woman who'd rather put on the gloves and go a few rounds than walk in the moonlight?

Romantic women had always appealed to him because he was, unashamedly, a romantic himself. He enjoyed candlelight, quiet music, long, lonely walks. Michael courted women in old-fashioned ways because he felt comfortable with old-fashioned ways. It didn't interfere with the fact that he was, and had been since college, a staunch feminist. Romance and sociopolitical views were worlds apart. He had no trouble balancing equal pay for equal work against offering a woman a carriage ride through the park.

And he knew if he sent Pandora a dozen white roses, she'd complain about the thorns.

He wanted her. Michael was too much a creature of the senses to pretend otherwise. When he wanted something, he worked toward it in one of two ways. First, he planned out the best approach, then took the steps one at a time, maneuvering subtly. If that didn't work, he tossed out subtlety and went after it with both hands. He'd had just as much success the first way as the second.

As he saw it, Pandora wouldn't respond to patience and posies. She wouldn't go for being swept off her feet, either. With Pandora, he might just have to toss his two usual approaches and come up with a whole new third.

An interesting challenge, Michael decided with a slow smile. He liked nothing better than arranging and rearranging plot lines and shifting angles. And hadn't he always thought Pandora would make a fascinating character? So, he'd work it like a screenplay.

Hero and heroine living as housemates, he began. Attracted to each other but reluctant. Hero is intelligent, charming. Has tremendous willpower. Hadn't he given up smoking—five weeks, three days and fourteen hours ago? Heroine is stubborn and opinionated, often mistakes arrogance for independence. Hero gradually cracks through her brittle shield to their mutual satisfaction.

Michael leaned back in his chair and grinned. He might just make it a play. A great deal of the action would be ad-lib, of course, but he had the general theme. Satisfied, and looking forward to the opening scene, Michael went back to work with a vengeance.

Two hours breezed by with Michael working steadily. He answered the knock at his door with a grunt.

"I beg your pardon, Mr. Donahue." Charles, slightly out of breath from the climb up the stairs, stood in the doorway.

Michael gave another grunt and finished typing the paragraph. "Yes, Charles?"

"Telegram for you, sir."

"Telegram?" Scowling, he swiveled around in the chair. If there was a problem in New York—as there was at least once a week—the phone was the quickest way to solve it. "Thanks." He took the telegram, but only flapped it against his palm. "Pandora still out in her shop?"

"Yes, sir." Grateful for the chance to rest, Charles expanded a bit. "Sweeney is a bit upset that Miss McVie missed lunch. She intends to serve dinner in an hour. I hope that suits your schedule."

Michael knew better than to make waves where Sweeney was concerned. "I'll be down."

"Thank you, sir, and if I may say, I enjoy your television show tremendously. This week's episode was particularly exciting."

"I appreciate that, Charles."

"It was Mr. McVie's habit to watch it every week in my company. He never missed an episode."

"There probably wouldn't have been a *Logan's Run* without Jolley," Michael mused. "I miss him."

"We all do. The house seems so quiet. But I—" Charles reddened a bit at the thought of overstepping his bounds.

"Go ahead, Charles."

"I'd like you to know that both Sweeney and I are pleased to remain in your service, yours and Miss McVie's. We were glad when Mr. McVie left you the house. The others…" He straightened his back and plunged on. "They wouldn't have been suitable, sir. Sweeney and I had both discussed resigning if Mr. McVie had chosen to leave the Folley to one of his other heirs." Charles folded his bony hands. "Will there be anything else before dinner, sir?"

"No, Charles. Thank you."

Telegram in hand, Michael leaned back as Charles went out. The old butler had known him since childhood. Michael could remember distinctly when Charles had stopped calling him Master Donahue. He'd been sixteen and visiting the Folley during the summer months. Charles had called him Mr. Donahue and Michael had felt as though he'd just stepped from childhood, over adolescence and into adulthood.

Strange how much of his life had been involved with the Folley and the people who were a part of it. Charles had served him his first whisky with dignity if not approval on his eighteenth birthday. Years before that, Sweeney had given him his first ear boxing. His parents had never bothered to swat him and his tutors wouldn't have dared. Michael still remembered that after the sting had eased, he'd felt like part of a family.

Pandora had been both bane and fantasy during his adolescence. Apparently that hadn't changed as much as Michael had thought. And Jolley. Jolley had been father, grandfather, friend, son and brother.

Jolley had been Jolley, and Michael had spoken no less than the truth when he'd told Charles he missed the old man. In some part of himself, he always would. Thinking of other things, Michael tore open the telegram.

Your mother gravely ill. Doctors not hopeful. Make arrangements to fly to Palm Springs immediately. L. J. KEYSER.

Michael stared at the telegram for nearly a minute. It wasn't possible; his mother was never ill. She considered it something of a social flaw. He felt a moment's disbelief, a moment's shock. He was reaching for the phone before either had worn off.

When Pandora walked by his room fifteen minutes later, she saw him tossing clothes into a bag. She lifted a brow, leaned against the jamb and cleared her throat. "Going somewhere?"

"Palm Springs." He tossed in his shaving kit.

"Really?" Now she folded her arms. "Looking for a sunnier climate?"

"It's my mother. Her husband sent me a telegram."

Instantly she dropped her cool, sarcastic pose and came into the room. "Is she ill?"

"The telegram didn't say much, but it doesn't sound good."

"Oh, Michael, I'm sorry. Can I do anything? Call the airport?"

"I've already done it. I've got a flight in a couple of

hours. They're routing me through half a dozen cities, but it was the best I could do."

Feeling helpless, she watched him zip up his bag. "I'll drive you to the airport if you like."

"No, thanks anyway." He dragged a hand through his hair as he turned to face her. The concern was there, though he realized she'd only met his mother once, ten, perhaps fifteen years before. The concern was for him and unexpectedly solid. "Pandora, it's going to take me half the night to get to the coast. And then I don't know—" He broke off, not able to imagine his mother seriously ill. "I might not be able to make it back in time—not in forty-eight hours."

She shook her head. "I don't want you to think about it. I'll call Fitzhugh and explain. Maybe he'll be able to do something. After all, it's an emergency. If he can't, he can't."

He was taking a step that could pull millions of dollars out from under her. Millions of dollars and the home she loved. Torn, Michael went to her and rested his hands on her shoulders. She was so slender. He'd forgotten just how fragile a strong woman could be. "I'm sorry, Pandora. If there was any other way…"

"Michael, I told you I didn't want the money. I meant it."

He studied her a moment. Yes, the strength was there, the stubbornness and the basic goodness he often overlooked. "I believe you did," he murmured.

"As for the rest, well, we'll see. Now go ahead before you miss your plane." She waited until he'd grabbed his bag then walked with him to the hall. "Call me if you get the chance and let me know how your mother is."

He nodded, started for the stairs, then stopped. Setting his bag down, he came back and pulled her against him. The kiss was hard and long, with hints of a fire barely banked. He drew her away just as abruptly. "See you."

"Yeah." Pandora swallowed. "See you."

She stood where she was until she heard the front door slam.

She had a long time to think about the kiss, through a solitary dinner, during the hours when she tried to read by the cheery fire in the parlor. It seemed to Pandora that there'd been more passion concentrated in that brief contact than she'd experienced in any of her carefully structured relationships. Was it because she'd always been able to restrict passion to her temper, or her work?

It might have been because she'd been sympathetic, and Michael had been distraught. Emotions had a way of feeding emotions. But for the second time she found herself alone in the house, and to her astonishment, lonely. It was foolish because the fire was bright, the book entertaining and the brandy she sipped warming.

But lonely she was. After little more than a month, she'd come to depend on Michael's company. Even to look forward to it, as strange as that may have been. She liked sitting across from him at meals, arguing with him. She especially liked watching the way he fought, exploding when she poked pins in his work. Perverse? she wondered with a sigh. Perhaps she was, but life was so boring without a bit of friction. No one seemed to provide it more satisfactorily than Michael Donahue.

She wondered when she'd see him again. And she wondered if now they'd have to forgo spending the winter together. If the terms of the will were broken, there would be no reason for them to stay on together. In fact, they'd have no right to stay at the Folley at all. They'd both go back to New York where, due to separate life-styles, they never saw one another. Not until now, when it was a possibility, did Pandora fully realize how much she didn't want it to happen.

She didn't want to lose the Folley. There were so many memories, so many important ones. Wouldn't they begin to fade if she couldn't walk into a room and bring them back? She didn't want to lose Michael. His companionship, she amended quickly. It was more satisfying than she'd imagined to have someone near who could meet you head to head. If she lost that daily challenge, life would be terribly flat. Since it was Michael who was adding that certain spark to the days, it was only natural to want him around. Wasn't it?

With a sigh, Pandora shut the book and decided an early night would be more productive than idle speculation. Just as she reached over to shut out the lamp, it went out on its own. She was left with the glow of the fire.

Odd, she thought and reached for the switch. After turning it back and forth, she rose, blaming a defective bulb. But when she walked into the hall she found it in darkness. The light she'd left burning was out, along with the one always left on at the top of the stairs. Again Pandora reached for a switch and again she found it useless.

Power failure, she decided but found herself hesitating in the dark. There was no storm. Electricity at the Folley went out regularly during snow and thunderstorms, but the back-up generator took over within minutes. Pandora waited, but the house remained dark.

It occurred to her as she stood there hoping for the best, that she'd never really considered how dark dark could be. She was already making her way back into the parlor for a candle when the rest occurred to her. The house was heated with electricity, as well. If she didn't see about the power soon, the house was going to be very cold as well as very dark before too long. With two people in their seventies in the house, she couldn't let it go.

Annoyed, she found three candles in a silver holder and lit them. It wasn't any use disturbing Charles's sleep and dragging him down to the basement. It was probably only a faulty fuse or two. Holding the candles ahead of her, Pandora wound her way through the curving halls to the cellar door.

She wasn't bothered about going down into the cellar in the dark. So she told herself as she stood with her hand on the knob. It was, after all, just another room. And one, if memory served, which was full of the remains of several of Uncle Jolley's rejected hobbies. The fuse box was down there. She'd seen it when she'd helped her uncle cart down several boxes of photographic equipment after he'd decided to give up the idea of becoming a portrait photographer. She'd go down, check for faulty fuses and replace them. After the lights and heat were taken care of, she'd have a hot bath and go to bed.

But she drew in a deep breath before she opened the door.

The stairs creaked. It was to be expected. And they were steep and narrow as stairs were in any self-respecting cellar. The light from her candles set the shadows dancing over the crates and boxes her uncle had stored there. She'd have to see if she could talk Michael into helping her sort through them. On some bright afternoon. She was humming nervously to herself before she reached the bottom stair.

Pandora held the candles high and scanned the floor as far as the light circled. She knew mice had an affection for dark, dank cellars and she had no affection for them. When nothing rushed across the floor, she skirted around two six-foot crates and headed for the fuse box. There was the motorized exercise bike that Uncle Jolley had decided took the fun out of staying fit. There was a floor-to-ceiling shelf of old bottles. He'd once been fascinated by a ten-dollar bottle cutter. And there, she saw with a sigh of relief, was the fuse box. Setting the candles on a stack of boxes, she opened the big metal door and stared inside. There wasn't a single fuse in place.

"What the hell's this?" she muttered. Then as she shifted to look closer, her foot sent something rattling over the concrete floor. Jolting, she stifled a scream and the urge to run. Holding her breath, she waited in the silence. When she thought she could manage it, she picked up the candles again and crouched. Scattered at her feet were a dozen fuses. She picked one up and let it lay in her palm. The cellar might have its quota of mice, but they weren't handy enough to empty a fuse box.

She felt a little shudder, which she ignored as she began to gather up the fuses. Tricks, she told herself. Just silly tricks. Annoying, but not as destructive as the one played in her workshop. It wasn't even a very clever trick, she decided, as it was as simple to put fuses back as it had been to take them out.

Working quickly, and trying not to look over her shoulder, Pandora put the fuses back in place. Whoever had managed to get into the basement and play games had wasted her time, nothing more.

Finished, she went over to the stairs, and though she hated herself, ran up them. But her sigh of relief was premature. The door she'd carefully left open was closed tightly. For a few moments she simply refused to believe it. She twisted the knob, pushed, shoved and twisted again. Then she forgot everything but the fear of being closed in a dark place. Pandora beat on the door, shouted, pleaded, then collapsed half sobbing on the top step. No one would hear her. Charles and Sweeney were on the other side of the house.

For five minutes she gave in to fear and self-pity. She was alone, all alone, locked in a dark cellar where no one would hear her until morning. It was already cold and getting colder. By morning…her candles would go out by then, and she'd have no light at all. That was the worst, the very worst, to have no light.

Light, she thought, and called herself an idiot as she wiped away tears. Hadn't she just fixed the lights? Scrambling up, Pandora hit the switch at the top of the stairs. Nothing happened. Holding back a scream, she held the candles up. The socket over the stairs was empty.

So, they'd thought to take out the bulbs. It had been a clever trick after all. She swallowed fresh panic and tried to think. They wanted her to be incoherent, and she refused to give them the satisfaction. When she found out which one of her loving family was playing nasty games…

That was for later, Pandora told herself. Now she was going to find a way out. She was shivering, but she told herself it was anger. There were times it paid to lie to yourself. Holding the candles aloft, she forced herself to go down the steps again when cowering at the top seemed so much easier.

The cellar was twice the size of her apartment in New York, open and barnlike without any of the ornate decorating Uncle Jolley had been prone to. It was just dark and slightly damp with concrete floors and stone walls that echoed. She wouldn't think about spiders or things that scurried into corners right now. Slowly, trying to keep calm, she searched for an exit.

There were no doors, but then she was standing several feet underground. Like a tomb. That particular thought didn't soothe her nerves so she concentrated on other things. She'd only been down in the cellar a handful of times and hadn't given a great deal of thought to the setup. Now she had to think about it—and pretend her palms weren't clammy.

She eased by a pile of boxes as high as her shoulders, then let out a scream when she ran into a maze of cobwebs. More disgusted than frightened, she brushed and dragged at them. It didn't sit well with her to make a fool out of herself, even if no one was around to see it. Someone was going to pay, she told herself as she fought her way clear.

Then she saw the window, four feet above her head and tiny. Though it was hardly the size of a transom, Pandora nearly collapsed in relief. After setting the candles on a shelf, she began dragging boxes over. Her muscles strained and her back protested, but she hauled and stacked against the wall. The first splinter had her swearing. After the third, she stopped counting. Out of breath, streaming with sweat, she leaned against her makeshift ladder. Now all she had to do was climb it.

With the candles in one hand, she used the other to haul herself up. The light shivered and swayed. The boxes groaned and teetered a bit. The thought passed through her mind that if she fell, she could lie there on the frigid concrete with broken bones until morning. She pulled herself high and refused to think at all.

When she reached the window, she found the little latch rusted and stubborn. Swearing, praying, she balanced the candles on the box under her and used both hands. She felt the latch give, then stick again. If she'd only thought to find a tool before she'd climbed up. She considered climbing back down and finding one, then made the mistake of looking behind her. The stack of boxes looked even more rickety from up there.

Turning back to the window, she tugged with all the strength she had. The latch gave with a grind of metal against metal, the boxes swayed from the movement. She saw her candles start to tip and grabbed for them. Out of reach, they slid from the box and clattered to the concrete, their tiny flames extinguished as they hit the ground. She almost followed them, but managed to fight for balance. Pandora found herself perched nine feet off the floor in pitch-darkness.

She wouldn't fall, she promised herself as she gripped the little window ledge with both hands. Using her touch to guide her, she pulled the window out and open, then began to ease herself through. The first blast of cold air made her almost giddy. After she'd pushed her shoulders through she gave herself a moment to breathe and adjust to the lesser dark of starlight. From somewhere to the west, she heard a hardy night bird call twice and fall silent. She'd never heard anything more beautiful.

Grabbing the base of a rhododendron, she pulled

herself through to the waist. When she heard the crash of boxes behind her, she laid her cheek against the cold grass. Inch by inch, she wiggled her way out, ignoring the occasional rip and scratch. At last, she was flat on her back, looking up at the stars. Cold, bruised and exhausted, she lay there, just breathing. When she was able, Pandora dragged herself up and walked around to the east terrace doors.

She wanted revenge, but first, she wanted a bath.

After three layovers and two plane changes, Michael arrived in Palm Springs. Nothing, as far as he could see, had changed. He never came to the exclusive little community but that he came reluctantly. Now, thinking of his mother lying ill, he was swamped with guilt.

He rarely saw her. True, she was no more interested in seeing him than he was her. Yet, she was still his mother. They had been on a different wavelength since the day he'd been born, but she'd taken care of him. At least, she'd hired people to take care of him. Affection, Michael realized, didn't have to enter into a child's feelings for his parent. The bond was there whether or not understanding followed it.

With no more than a flight bag, he bypassed the crowd at baggage claim and hailed a cab. After giving his mother's address, he sat back and checked his watch, subtracting time zones. Even with the hours he'd gained, it was probably past visiting hours. He'd get around that, but first he had to know what hospital his mother was in. If he'd been thinking straight, he would have called ahead and checked.

If his mother's husband wasn't in, one of the servants could tell him. It might not be as bad as the telegram made it sound. After all his mother was still young. Then it struck Michael that he didn't have the vaguest idea how old his mother was. He doubted his father knew, and certainly not her current husband. At another time, it might have struck him as funny.

Impatient, he watched as the cab glided by the gates and pillars of the elite. His career had caused him to stay in California for extended lengths of time, but he preferred L.A. to Palm Springs. There, at least, was some action, some movement, some edge. But he liked New York best of all; the pace matched his own and the streets were tougher.

He thought of Pandora. Both of them lived in New York, but they never saw each other unless it was miles north of the city at the Folley. The city could swallow you. Or hide you. It was another aspect Michael appreciated.

Didn't he often use it to hide—from his stifling upbringing, from his recurring lack of faith in the human race? It was at the Folley that he felt the easiest, but it was in New York that he felt the safest. He could be anonymous there if he chose to be. There were times he wanted nothing more. He wrote about heroes and justice, sometimes rough but always human. He wrote, in his own fashion, about basic values and simple rights.

He'd been raised with the illusions and hypocrisy of wealth and with values that were just as unstable. He'd broken away from that, started on his own. New York had helped make it possible because in the city backgrounds were easily erased. So easily erased, Michael mused, that he rarely thought of his.

The cab cruised up the long semicircle of macadam, under the swaying palms, toward the towering white house where his mother had chosen to live. Michael remembered there was a lily pond in the back with goldfish the size of groupers. His mother refused to call them carp.

"Wait," he told the driver, then dashed up two levels of stairs to the door. The butler who answered was new. It was his mother's habit to change the staff regularly, before, as she put it, they got too familiar. "I'm Michael Donahue, Mrs. Keyser's son."

The butler glanced over his shoulder at the waiting cab, then back at Michael's disheveled sweater and unshaven face. "Good evening, sir. Are you expected?"

"Where's my mother? I want to go to the hospital directly."

"Your mother isn't in this evening, Mr. Donahue. If you'll wait, I'll see if Mr. Keyser's available."

Intolerant, as always, of cardboard manners, he stepped inside. "I know she's not in. I want to go see her tonight. What's the name of the hospital?"

The butler gave a polite nod. "What hospital, Mr. Donahue?"

"Jackson, where did that cab come from?" Wrapped in a deep-rose smoking jacket, Lawrence Keyser strolled downstairs. He had a thick cigar between the fingers of one hand and a snifter of brandy in the other.

"Well, Lawrence," Michael began over a wave of fury. "You look comfortable. Where's my mother?"

"Well, well, it's—ah, it's Matthew."

"It's Michael."

"Michael, of course. Jackson, pay off Mr. ah, Mr. Donavan's cab."

"No, thanks, Jackson." Michael held up a hand. Another time, he'd have been amused at his stepfather's groping for his name. "I'll use it to get to the hospital. Wouldn't want to put you out."

"No trouble at all, not at all." Big, round and only partially balding, Keyser gave Michael a friendly grin. "Veronica will be pleased to see you, though we didn't know you were coming. How long are you in town?"

"As long as I'm needed. I left the minute I got the telegram. You didn't mention the name of the hospital. Since you're home and relaxing," he said with only the slightest trace of venom, "should I assume that my mother's condition's improved?"

"Condition?" Keyser gave a jovial laugh. "Well now, I don't know how she'd take to that term, but you can ask her yourself."

"I intend to. Where is she?"

"Playing bridge at the Bradleys'. She'll be coming along in about an hour. How about a brandy?"

"Playing bridge!" Michael stepped forward and grabbed his surprised stepfather by the lapels. "What the hell do you mean she's playing bridge?"

"Can't stomach the game myself," Keyser began warily. "But Veronica's fond of it."

It came to Michael, clear as a bell. "You didn't send me a telegram about Mother?"

"A telegram?" Keyser patted Michael's arm, and hoped Jackson stayed close. "No need to send you a telegram about a bridge game, boy."

"Mother's not ill?"

"Strong as a horse, though I wouldn't let her hear me say so just that way."

Michael swore and whirled around. "Someone's going to pay," he muttered.

"Where are you going?"

"Back to New York," Michael tossed over his shoulder as he ran down the steps.

Relieved, Keyser opted against the usual protests about his departure. "Is there a message for your mother?"

"Yeah." Michael stopped with a hand on the door of the cab. "Yeah, tell her I'm glad she's well. And I hope she wins—in spades." Michael slammed the door shut behind him.

Keyser waited until the cab shot out of sight. "Odd boy," Keyser grumbled to his butler. "Writes for television."

# Chapter Six

Pandora, sleeping soundly, was awakened at seven in the morning when Michael dropped on her bed. The mattress bounced. He snuggled his head into the pillow beside her and shut his eyes.

"Sonofabitch," he grumbled.

Pandora sat up, remembered she was naked and grabbed for the sheets. "Michael! You're supposed to be in California. What are you doing in my bed?"

"Getting horizontal for the first time in twenty-four hours."

"Well, do that in your own bed," she ordered, then saw the lines of strain and fatigue. "Your mother." Pandora grabbed for his hand. "Oh, Michael, is your mother—"

"Playing bridge." He rubbed his free hand over his face. Even to him it felt rough and seedy. "I bounced across country, once in a tuna can with propellers, to find out she was sipping sherry and trumping her partner's ace."

"She's better then?"

"She was always better. The telegram was a hoax." He yawned, stretched and settled. "God, what a night."

"You mean…" Pandora tugged on the sheets and glowered. "Well, the rats."

"Yeah. I plotted out several forms of revenge when I was laid over in Cleveland. Maybe our friend who stomped through your workshop figured it was my turn. Now we each owe them one."

"I owe 'em two." Pandora leaned back against the headboard with the sheets tucked under her arms. Her hair fell luxuriously over her naked shoulders. "Last night while you were off on your wild-goose chase, I was locked in the cellar."

Michael's attention shot away from the thin sheet that barely covered her. "Locked in? How?"

Crossing one ankle over the other, Pandora told him what happened from the time the lights went out.

"Climbed up on boxes? To that little window? It's nearly ten feet."

"Yes, I believe I noticed that at the time."

Michael scowled at her. The anger he'd felt at being treated to a sleepless night doubled. He could picture her groping her way around in the dank cellar all too well. Worse, he could see her very clearly climbing on shaky boxes and crates. "You could've broken your neck."

"I didn't. What I did do was rip my favorite pair of slacks, scratch both knees and bruise my shoulder."

Michael managed to hold back his fury. He'd let it go, he promised himself, when the time was right. "It could've been worse," he said lightly, and thought of what he'd do to whoever had locked her in.

"It was worse," Pandora tossed back, insulted. "While you were sipping Scotch at thirty thousand feet, I was locked in a cold, damp cellar with mice and spiders."

"We might reconsider calling the police."

"And do what with them? We can't prove anything. We don't even know whom we can't prove anything against."

"New rule," Michael decided. "We stick together. Neither of us leaves the house overnight without the other. At least until we find out which of our devoted relations is playing games."

Pandora started to protest, then remembered how frightened she'd been, and before the cellar, before the fear, how lonely. "Agreed. Now…" With one hand hanging onto the sheet, she shifted toward him. "I vote for Uncle Carlson on this one. After all, he knows the house better than any of the others. He lived here."

"It's as good a guess as any. But it's only a guess." Michael stared up at the ceiling. "I want to know. Biff stayed here for six weeks one summer when we were kids."

"That's right." Pandora frowned at the ceiling herself. The mirror across the room reflected them lying companionably, hip to hip. "I'd forgotten about that. He hated it."

"He's never had a sense of humor."

"True enough. As I recall he certainly didn't like you."

"Probably because I gave him a black eye."

Pandora's brow lifted. "You would." Then, because

the image of Biff with a shiner wasn't so unappealing, she added: "Why did you? You never said."

"Remember the frogs in your dresser?"

Pandora sniffed and smoothed at the sheets. "I certainly do. It was quite immature of you."

"Not me. Biff."

"Biff?" Astonished, she turned toward him again. "You mean that little creep put the frogs in my underwear?" The next thought came, surprisingly pleasing. "And you punched him for it?"

"It wasn't hard."

"Why didn't you deny it when I accused you?"

"It was more satisfying to punch Biff. In any case, he knows the house well enough. And I imagine if we checked up, we'd find most of our happy clan has stayed here, at least for a few days at a time. Finding a fuse box in the cellar doesn't take a lot of cunning. Think it through, Pandora. There are six of them, seven with the charity added on. Split a hundred fifty million seven ways and you end up with plenty of motive. Every one of them has a reason for wanting us to break the terms of the will. None of them, as far as I'm concerned, is above adding a little pressure to help us along."

"Another reason the money never appealed to me," she mused. "They haven't done anything but vandalize and annoy, but, dammit, Michael, I want to pay them back."

"The ultimate payback comes in just under five months." Without thinking about it, Michael put his arm around her shoulders. Without thinking about it, Pandora settled against him. A light fragrance clung to her skin. "Can't you see Carlson's face when the will holds up and he gets nothing but a magic wand and a trick hat?"

His shoulder felt more solid than she'd imagined. "And Biff with three cartons of matchbooks." Comfortable, she chuckled. "Uncle Jolley's still having the last laugh."

"We'll have it with him in a few months."

"It's a date. And you've got your shoes on my sheets."

"Sorry." With two economical movements, he pried them off.

"That's not exactly what I meant. Don't you want to wander off to your own room now?"

"Not particularly. Your bed's nicer than mine. Do you always sleep naked?"

"No."

"My luck must be turning then." He shifted to press his lips to a bruise on her shoulder. "Hurt?"

She shrugged and prayed it came off as negligent. "A little."

"Poor little Pandora. And to think I always thought you were tough-skinned."

"I am—"

"Soft," he interrupted, and skimmed his fingers down her arm. "Very soft. Any more bruises?" He brushed his lips over the curve of her neck. They both felt her quick, involuntary shudder.

"Not so you'd notice."

"I'm very observant." He rolled, smoothly, so that his body pressed more intimately into hers as he looked down on her. He was tired. Yes, he was tired and more than a little punchy with jet lag, but he hadn't forgotten he wanted her. Even if he had, the way her body yielded, the way her face looked rosy and soft with sleep, would've jogged his memory. "Why don't I look for myself?" He ran his fingers down to where the sheet lay, neat, prim and arousing, at her breast.

She sucked in her breath, incredibly moved by his lightest touch. She couldn't let it show...could she? She couldn't reach out for something that was only an illusion. He wasn't stable. He wasn't real. He was with her now because she was here and no one else was. Why was it becoming so hard to remember that?

His face was close, filling her vision. She saw the little things she'd tried not to notice over the years. The way a thin ring of gray outlined his irises, the straight, almost aristocratic line of his nose that had remained miraculously unbroken through countless fistfights. The soft, sculpted, somehow poetic shape of his mouth. A mouth, she remembered, that was hot and strong and inventive when pressed against hers.

"Michael..." The fact that she hesitated, then fumbled before she reached down to take his hand both pleased and unnerved him. She wasn't as cool and self-contained as she'd always appeared. And because she wasn't, he could slip his way under her skin. But he might not slip out again so easily.

Be practical, she told herself. Be realistic. "Michael, we have almost five months more to get through."

"Good point." He needed the warmth. He needed the woman. Maybe it was time to risk the consequences. He lowered his head and nibbled at her mouth. "Why waste it?"

She let herself enjoy him. For just a moment, she promised herself. For only a moment. He was warm and his hands were easy. The night had been long and cold and frightening. No matter how much she hated to admit it, she'd needed him. Now, with the sun pouring through the tiny square panes in the windows, falling bright and hard on the bed, she had him. Close, secure, comforting.

Her lips opened against his.

He'd had no plan when he'd come into her room. He'd simply been drawn to her; he'd wanted to lie beside her and talk to her. Passion hadn't guided him. Desire hadn't pushed him. There'd only been the basic need to be home, to be home with her. When she'd snuggled against him, hair tousled, eyes heavy, it had been so natural that the longing had snuck up on him. He wanted nothing more than to stay where he was, wrapped around her, slowly heating.

And for her, passion didn't bubble wildly, but easily, like a brew that had been left to simmer through the day while spices were added. One sample, then another, and the taste changed, enriched, deepened. With Michael, there the flavors were only hinted at, an aroma to draw in and savor. She could have gone on, and on, hour after hour, until what they made between them was perfected. She wanted to give in to the need, the beginnings of greed. If she did, everything would change. It was a change she couldn't predict, couldn't see clearly, could only anticipate. So she resisted him and herself and what could happen between them.

"Michael…" But she let her fingers linger in his hair for just a minute more. "This isn't smart."

He kissed her eyes closed. It was something no one had done before. "It's the smartest thing either of us has done in years."

She wanted to agree, felt herself on the edge of agreeing. "Michael, things are complicated enough. If we were lovers and things went wrong, how could we manage to go on here together? We've made a commitment to Uncle Jolley."

"The will doesn't have a damn thing to do with you and me in this bed."

How could she have forgotten just how intense he could look when he was bent on something? How was it she'd never noticed how attractive it made him? She'd have to make a stand now or go under. "The will has everything to do with you and me in this house. If we go to bed together and our relationship changes, then we'll have to deal with all the problems and complications that go with it."

"Name some."

"Don't be amusing, Michael."

"Giving you a laugh wasn't my intention." He liked the way she looked against the pillow—hair spread out like wildfire, cheeks a bit flushed, her mouth on the edge of forming a pout. Strange he'd never pictured her this way before. It didn't take any thought to know he'd picture her like this again and again. "I want you, Pandora. There's nothing amusing about it."

No, that wasn't something she could laugh or shrug off, not when the words brushed over her skin and made her muscles limp. He didn't mean it. He couldn't mean it. But she wanted to believe it. If she couldn't laugh it off, she had to throw up a guard and block it. "Becoming lovers is something that takes a lot of thought. If we're going to discuss it—"

"I don't want to discuss it." He pressed his lips against hers until he felt her body soften. "We're not making a corporate merger, Pandora, we're making love."

"That's just it." She fought back an avalanche of longing. Be practical. It was her cardinal rule. "We're business partners. Worse, we're family business partners, at least for the next few months. If we change that now it could—"

"If," he interrupted. "It could. Do you always need guarantees?"

Her brows drew together as annoyance competed with desire. "It's a matter of common sense to look at all the angles."

"I suppose you have any prospective lover fill out an application form."

Her voice chilled. It was, in a distorted way, close to the truth. "Don't be crude, Michael."

Pushed to the limit, he glared down at her. "I'd rather be crude than have your brand of common sense."

"You've never had any brand of common sense," she tossed back. "Why else would every busty little blonde you've winked at be public knowledge? You don't even have the decency to be discreet."

"So that's it." Shifting, Michael drew her into a sitting position. There was no soft yielding now. She faced him with fire in her eyes. "Don't forget the brunettes and the redheads."

She hadn't. She promised herself she wouldn't. "I don't want to discuss it."

"You brought it up, and we'll finish it. I've gone to bed with women. So put me in irons. I've even enjoyed it."

She tossed her hair behind her shoulder. "I'm sure you have."

"And I haven't had a debate with every one of them

beforehand. Some women prefer romance and mutual enjoyment."

"Romance?" Her brows shot up under her tousled hair. "I've always had another word for it."

"You wouldn't recognize romance if it dropped on your head. Do you consider it discreet to take lovers and pretend you don't? To pledge undying fidelity to one person while you're looking for another? What you want to call discretion, I call hypocrisy. I'm not ashamed of any of the women I've known, in bed or out."

"I'm not interested in what you are or aren't ashamed of. I'm not going to be your next mutual enjoyment. Keep your passion for your dancers and starlets and chorus girls."

"You're as big a snob as the rest of them."

That hit home and had her shoulders stiffening. "That's not true. I've simply no intention of joining a crowd."

"You flatter me, cousin."

"There's another word for that, too."

"Think about this." He gave her a shake, harder than he'd intended. "I've never made love with a woman I didn't care for and respect." Before he cut loose and did more than shake her, he got up and walked to the door while she sat in the middle of the bed clutching sheets and looking furious.

"It appears you give respect easily."

He turned back to study her. "No," he said slowly. "But I don't make people jump through hoops for it."

A cold war might not be as stimulating as an active battle, but with the right participants, it could be equally destructive. For days Pandora and Michael circled around each other. If one made a sarcastic comment, the other reached into the stockpile and used equal sarcasm. Neither drew out the red flag for full-scale attack, instead they picked and prodded at each other while the servants rolled their eyes and waited for bloodshed.

"Foolishness," Sweeney declared as she rolled out the crust for two apple pies. "Plain foolishness." She was a sturdy, red-faced woman, as round as Charles was thin. In her pragmatic, no-nonsense way, she'd married and buried two husbands, then made her way in the world by cooking for others. Her kitchen was always neat and tidy, all the while smelling of the sinfully rich food she prepared. "Spoiled children," she told Charles. "That's what they are. Spoiled children need the back of the hand."

"They've over four months to go." Charles sat gloomily at the kitchen table, hunched over a cup of tea. "They'll never make it."

"Hah!" Sweeney slammed the rolling pin onto a fresh ball of dough. "They'll make it. Too stubborn not to. But it's not enough."

"The master wanted them to have the house. As long as they do, we won't lose it."

"What'll we be doing in this big empty house when both of them go back to the city? How often will either of them be visiting with the master gone?" Sweeney turned the crust into a pan and trimmed it expertly. "The master wanted them to have the house, true enough. And he wanted them to have each other. The house needs a family. It's up to us to see it gets one."

"You didn't hear them over breakfast." Charles

sipped his tea and watched Sweeney pour a moist apple mixture into the crust.

"That has nothing to do with it. *I've* seen the way they look at each other when they think the other one's not noticing. All they need's a push."

With quick, economic movements, she filled the second crust. "We're going to give 'em one."

Charles stretched out his legs. "We're too old to push young people."

Sweeney gave a quick grunt as she turned. Her hands were thick, and she set them on her hips. "Being old's the whole trick. You've been feeling poorly lately."

"No, to tell you the truth, I've been feeling much better this week."

"You've been feeling poorly," Sweeney repeated, scowling at him. "Now here's our Pandora coming in for lunch. Just follow my lead. Look a little peaked."

Snow had come during the night, big fat flakes that piled on the ground and hung in the pines. As she walked, Pandora kicked it up, pleased with herself. Her work couldn't have been going better. The earrings she'd finally fashioned had been unique, so unique, she'd designed a necklace to complement them. It was chunky and oversize with geometric shapes of copper and gold. Not every woman could wear it, but the one who could wouldn't go unnoticed.

It was, to Pandora, a statement of the strong, disciplined woman. She was just as pleased with the shoulder-brushing earrings she was making with jet and silver beads. They had been painstakingly strung together and when finished would be elegantly flirtatious. Another aspect of woman. If her pace kept steady, she'd have a solid inventory to ship off to the boutique she supplied. In time for the Christmas rush, she reminded herself smugly.

When she opened the kitchen door, she was ravenously hungry and in the best of moods.

"…if you're feeling better in a day or two," Sweeney said briskly, then turned as if surprised to see Pandora inside. "Oh, time must've got away from me. Lunch already and I'm just finishing up the pies."

"Apple pies?" Grinning, Pandora moved closer. But Sweeney saw with satisfaction that Pandora was already studying Charles. "Any filling left?" she began, and started to dip her fingers into the bowl. Sweeney smacked them smartly.

"You've been working with those hands. Wash them up in the sink, and you'll have your lunch as soon as I can manage it."

Obediently, Pandora turned on a rush of water. Under the noise, she murmured to Sweeney. "Is Charles not feeling well?"

"Bursitis is acting up. Cold weather's a problem. Just being old's a problem in itself." She pushed a hand at the small of her back as though she had a pain. "Guess we're both slowing down a bit. Aches and pains," Sweeney sighed and cast a sidelong look at Pandora. "Just part of being old."

"Nonsense." Concerned, Pandora scrubbed her hands harder. She told herself she should have been keeping a closer eye on Charles. "You just try to do too much."

"With the holidays coming…" Sweeney trailed off and made a business out of arranging a top crust. "Well, decorating the house is a lot of work, but it's its own reward. Charles and I'll deal with the boxes in the attic this afternoon."

"Don't be silly." Pandora shut off the water and reached for a towel. "I'll bring the decorations down."

"No, now, missy, there're too many boxes and most of them are too heavy for a little girl like you. That's for us to see to. Isn't that right, Charles?"

Thinking of climbing the attic stairs a half-dozen times, Charles started to sigh. A look from Sweeney stopped him. "Don't worry, Miss McVie, Sweeney and I will see to it."

"You certainly will not." Pandora hung the towel back on the hook. "Michael and I will bring everything down this afternoon, and that's that. Now I'll go tell him to come to lunch."

Sweeney waited until the door swung shut behind Pandora before she grinned.

Upstairs, Pandora knocked twice on Michael's office door, then walked in. He kept on typing. Putting her pride on hold, Pandora walked over to his desk and folded her arms. "I need to talk to you."

"Come back later. I'm busy."

Abuse rose up in her throat. Remembering Sweeney's tired voice, she swallowed it. "It's important." She ground her teeth on the word, but said it. "Please."

Surprised, Michael stopped typing in midword. "What? Has one of the family been playing games again?"

"No, it's not that. Michael, we have to decorate the house for Christmas."

He stared at her a moment, swore and turned back to his machine. "I've got a twelve-year-old boy kidnapped and being held for a million-dollar ransom. That's important."

"Michael, will you put away fantasyland for a moment? This is real."

"So's this. Just ask my producer."

"Michael!" Before he could stop her, Pandora pulled the sheet from the typewriter. He was halfway out of his chair to retaliate. "It's Sweeney and Charles."

It stopped him, though he snatched the paper back from her. "What about them?"

"Charles's bursitis is acting up again, and I'm sure Sweeney's not feeling well. She sounded, well, old."

"She is old." But Michael tossed the paper on the desk. "Think we should call in a doctor?"

"No, they'd be furious." She swung around his desk, trying to pretend she wasn't reading part of his script. "I'd rather just keep an eye on them for a few days and make sure they don't overdo. That's where the Christmas decorations come in."

"I figured you'd get to them. Look, if you want to deck the halls, go ahead. I haven't got time to fool with it today."

"Neither do I." She folded her arms in a manner that amused him. "Sweeney and Charles have it in their heads that it has to be done. Unless we want them dragging up and down the attic stairs, we have to take care of it."

"Christmas is three weeks away."

"I know the date." Frustrated, she strode to the window then back. "They're old and they're set on it. You know Uncle Jolley would've had them up the day after Thanksgiving. It's traditional."

"All right, all right." Trapped, Michael rose. "Let's get started."

"Right after lunch." Satisfied she'd gotten her way, Pandora swept out.

Forty-five minutes later, she and Michael were pushing open the attic door. The attic was, in Jolley's tradition, big enough to house a family of five. "Oh, I'd forgotten what a marvelous place this is." Forgetting herself, Pandora grabbed Michael's hand and pulled him in. "Look at this table, isn't it horrible?"

It was. Old and ornate with curlicues and cupids, it had been shoved into a corner to hold other paraphernalia Jolley had discarded. "And the bird cage out of Popsicle sticks. Uncle Jolley said it took him six months to finish it, then he didn't have the heart to put a bird inside."

"Lucky for the bird," Michael muttered, but found himself, as always, drawn to the dusty charm of the place. "Spats," he said, and lifted a pair from a box. "Can't you see him in them?"

"And this hat." Pandora found a huge circular straw hat with a garden of flowers along the brim. "Aunt Katie's. I've always wished I'd met her. My father said she was just as much fun as Uncle Jolley."

Michael watched Pandora tip the brim over her eyes. "If that was her hat, I believe it. How about this?" He found a black derby and tilted it rakishly.

"It's you," Pandora told him with her first easy laugh in days. "All you need's a high white collar and a walking stick. Look." She pulled him in front of a tall cheval mirror that needed resilvering. Together, they studied themselves.

"An elegant pair," Michael decided, though his sweater bagged over his hips, and she already had dust on her nose. "All you need is one of those slim little skirts that sweep the floor and a lace blouse with padded shoulders."

"And a cameo on a ribbon," she added as she tried to visualize herself. "No, I probably would've worn bloomers and picketed for women's rights."

"The hat still suits you." He turned to adjust it just a bit. "Especially with your hair long and loose. I've always liked it long, though you looked appealingly lost and big-eyed when you had it all chopped short."

"I was fifteen."

"And you'd just come back from the Canary Islands with the longest, brownest legs I'd ever seen in my life. I nearly ate my saucer when you walked into the parlor."

"You were in college and had some cheerleader hanging on your arm."

Michael grinned. "You had better legs."

Pandora pretended little interest. She remembered the visit perfectly, but was surprised, and pleased, that he did. "I'm surprised you noticed or remembered."

"I told you I was observant."

She acknowledged the thrust with a slight nod. There were times when it was best to pad quietly over dangerous ground. "We'd better start digging out the decorations. Sweeney said the boxes were back along the left and clearly marked." Without waiting for agreement, she turned and began to look. "Oh good grief." She stopped again when she saw the stacks of boxes, twenty, perhaps twenty-five of them. Michael stood at her shoulder and stuck his hands in his pockets.

"Think we can hire some teamsters?"

Pandora blew out a breath. "Roll up your sleeves."

On some trips, they could pile two or three boxes apiece and maneuver downstairs. On others, it took both of them to haul one. Somewhere along the way they'd stopped arguing. It was just too much effort.

Grimy and sweaty, they dropped the last boxes in the parlor. Ignoring the dust on her slacks, Pandora collapsed in the nearest chair. "Won't it be great fun hauling them all up again after New Year's?"

"Couldn't we've settled on a plastic Santa?"

"It'll be worth it." Drumming up the energy, she knelt on the floor and opened the first box. "Let's get started."

Once they did, they went at it with a vengeance. Boxes were opened, garland strewed and bulbs tested. They squabbled good-naturedly about what looked best where and the proper way to drape lights at the windows. When the parlor, the main hall and the staircase were finished, Pandora stood at the front door and took a long look.

The garland was white and silver, twisting and twining down the banister. There were bright red bells, lush green ribbon and tiny lights just waiting for evening.

"It looks good," she decided. "Really good. Of course, Sweeney and Charles will want to decorate the servants' quarters and that entire box goes into the dining room, but it's a wonderful start."

"Start?" Michael sat on the stairs. "We're not entering a contest, cousin."

"These things have to be done right. I wonder if my parents will make it home for Christmas. Well…" She brushed that off. They always considered wherever they were home. "I'd say we're ready for the tree. Let's go find one."

"You want to drive into town now?"

"Of course not." Pandora was already pulling coats

out of the hall closet. "We'll go right out in the woods and dig one up."

"We?"

"Certainly. I hate it when people cut trees down and then toss them aside after the new year. The woods are loaded with nice little pines. We'll dig one up, then replant it after the holidays."

"How handy are you with a shovel?"

"Don't be a spoilsport." Pandora tossed his coat to him, then pulled on her own. "Besides, it'll be nice to spend some time outside after being in that stuffy attic. We can have some hot buttered rum when we're finished."

"Heavy on the rum."

They stopped at the toolshed for a shovel. Michael picked two and handed one to Pandora. She took it without a blink, then together they walked through the ankle-high snow to the woods. The air had a bite and the scent of pine was somehow stronger in the snow.

"I love it when it's like this." Pandora balanced the shovel on her shoulder and plowed through the woods. "It's so quiet, so—separated. You know, sometimes I think I'd rather live here and visit the city than the other way around."

He'd had the same thought, but was surprised to hear it from her. "I always thought you liked the bright lights and confusion."

"I do. But I like this, too. How about this one?" She paused in front of a spruce. "No, the trunk's too crooked." She walked on. "Besides, I wonder if it wouldn't be more exciting to go into the city for a week now and again and know you had someplace like this to come back to. I seem to work better here. Here's one."

"Too tall. We're better off digging up a young one. Wouldn't it put a crimp in your social life?"

"What?" She studied the tree in question and was forced to agree with him. "Oh. My social life isn't a priority, my work is. In any case, I could entertain here."

He had a picture of her spending long, cozy weekends with flamboyant, artsy types who read Keats aloud. "You don't have to come all the way to the Catskills to play house."

Pandora merely lifted a brow. "No, I don't. This one looks good." She stopped again and took a long study of a four-and-a-half-foot spruce. Behind her, Michael worked hard to keep his mouth shut. "It's just the right size for the parlor."

"Fine." Michael stuck his shovel into the ground. "Put your back into it."

As he bent over to dig, Pandora scooped up a shovelful of snow and tossed it into his face. "Oh, sorry." She smiled and batted her eyes. "Looks like my aim's off." Digging with more effort, she began to hum.

He let it go, probably because he appreciated the move and wished he'd thought of it himself. Within fifteen minutes, they had the hole dug.

"There now." Only a little out of breath, Pandora leaned on her shovel. "The satisfaction of a job well done."

"We only have to carry it back to the house, set it up and…damn, we need something to wrap the roots and dirt in. There was burlap in the shed."

They eyed each other blandly.

"All right," he said after a moment. "I'll go get it, then you have to sweep up the needles and dirt we trail on the floor."

"Deal."

Content, Pandora turned away to watch a cardinal when a snowball slapped into the back of her head. "Sorry." Michael gave her a companionable smile. "Aim must be off." He whistled as he walked back to the shed.

Pandora waited until he was out of sight, then smiling smugly, knelt down to ball snow. By the time he got back, she calculated, she could have an arsenal at hand. He wouldn't have a chance. She took her time, forming and smoothing each ball into a sophisticated weapon. Secure in her advantage, she nearly fell on her face when she heard a sound behind her. She had the ball in her hand and was already set to throw as she whirled. No one was there. Narrowing her eyes, she waited. Hadn't she seen a movement back in the trees? It would be just like him to skirt around and try to sneak up on her. She saw the cardinal fly up again as if startled and heard the quiet plop of snow hitting snow as it was shaken from branches.

"All right, Michael, don't be a coward." She picked up a ball in her left hand, prepared to bombard.

"Guarding your flank?" Michael asked so that this time when she whirled back around, she slid onto her bottom. He grinned at her and dropped the burlap sack in her lap.

"But weren't you…" She trailed off and looked behind her again. How could he be here if he was there? "Did you circle around?"

"No, but from the looks of that mound of balls, I should've. Want to play war?"

"It's just a defense system," she began, then looked over her shoulder again. "I thought I heard you. I would've sworn there was someone just beyond the trees there."

"I went straight to the shed and back." He looked beyond her. "You saw something out there?"

"Michael, if you're playing tricks—"

"No." He cut her off and reached down to pull her to her feet. "No tricks. Let's have a look."

She moved her shoulders but didn't remove her hand from his as they walked deeper into the trees. "Maybe I was a bit jumpy."

"Or expecting me to be sneaky?"

"That, too. It was probably just a rabbit."

"A rabbit with big feet," he murmured as he looked down at the tracks. They were clear enough in the snow, tracks leading to and away from the spot ten yards behind where they'd dug up the tree. "Rabbits don't wear boots."

"So, we still have company. I was beginning to think they'd given the whole business up." She kept her voice light, but felt the uneasiness of anyone who'd been watched. "Maybe it's time we talked to Fitzhugh, Michael."

"Maybe, in the meantime—" The sound of an engine cut him off. He was off in a sprint with Pandora at his heels. After a five-minute dash, they came, clammy and out of breath, to what was hardly more than a logging trail. Tire tracks had churned up the snow and blackened it. "A Jeep, I'd guess." Swearing, Michael stuck his hands in his pockets. If he'd started out right away, he might have caught someone or at least have caught a glimpse of someone.

Pandora let out an annoyed breath. Racing after

someone was one thing, being outmaneuvered another. "Whoever it is is only wasting his time."

"I don't like being spied on." He wanted physical contact. Longed for it. Frustrated, he stared at the tracks that led back to the main road. "I'm not playing cat and mouse for the next four months."

"What are we going to do?"

His smile spread as he looked at the tracks. "We'll spread the word through Fitzhugh that we've been bothered by trespassers. Being as there's any number of valuables on the premises, we've decided to haul out one of Jolley's old .30-.30's."

"Michael! They may be a nuisance, but they're still family." Unsure, she studied him. "You wouldn't really shoot at anyone."

"I'd rather shoot at family than strangers," he countered, then shrugged. "They're also fond of their own skin. I can't think of one of them who wouldn't hesitate to play around if they thought they might be picking buckshot out of embarrassing places."

"I don't like it. Guns, even the threat of guns, are trouble."

"Got a better idea?"

"Let's buy a dog. A really big, mean dog."

"Great, then we can let him loose and have him sink his teeth into one of our favorite relatives. They'd like that a lot better than buckshot."

"He doesn't have to be that mean."

"We'll compromise and do both."

"Michael—"

"Let's call Fitzhugh."

"And take his advice?" Pandora demanded.

"Sure…if I like it."

Pandora started to object, then laughed. It was all as silly as a plot of one of his shows. "Sounds reasonable," she decided, then tucked her arm through his. "Let's get the tree inside first."

# Chapter Seven

"I know it's Christmas Eve, Darla." Michael picked up his coffee cup, found it empty and lifted the pot from his hot plate. Dregs. He bit off a sigh. The trouble with the Folley was that you had to hike a half a mile to the kitchen whenever the pot ran dry. "I know it'll be a great party, but I can't get away."

That wasn't precisely true, Michael mused as he listened to Darla's rambles about a celebration in Manhattan. *Everyone*, according to her estimate, was going to be there. That meant a loud, elbow-to-elbow party with plenty of booze. He could have taken a day and driven into the city to raise a glass or two with friends. He was well ahead of schedule. So far ahead, he could have taken off a week and not felt the strain. The precise truth was, he didn't want to get away.

"I appreciate that...you'll just have to tell everyone

Merry Christmas for me. No, I like living in the country, Darla. Weird? Yeah, maybe." He had to laugh. Darla was a top-notch dancer and a barrel of laughs, but she didn't believe life went on outside of the island of Manhattan. "New Year's if I can manage it. Okay, babe. Yeah, yeah, *ciao.*"

More than a little relieved, Michael hung up. Darla was a lot of fun, but he wasn't used to being clung to by a woman, especially one he'd only dated casually. The truth was, she was just as attracted to the influence he had with certain casting agents as she was interested in him. He didn't hold it against her. She had ambition and talent, a combination that could work in the tough-edged business of entertaining if a dash of luck was added. After the holidays he'd make a few calls and see what he could do.

From the doorway, Pandora watched as Michael ran a hand along the back of his neck. Darla, she repeated silently. She imagined the women his taste leaned toward had names like Darla, or Robin and Candy. Sleek, smooth, sophisticated and preferably empty-headed.

"Popularity's such a strain, isn't it, darling?"

Michael turned in his chair to give her a long, narrowed look. "Eavesdropping's so rude, isn't it, darling?"

She shrugged but didn't come in. "If you'd wanted privacy, you should've closed your door."

"Around here you have to nail it shut for privacy."

One brow raised, head slightly inclined, Pandora looked as aloof as royalty. "Your phone conversations have absolutely no interest for me. I only came up as a favor to Charles. You've a package downstairs."

"Thanks." He didn't bother to hide amusement at her tone. If he knew Pandora, and he did, she'd listened to every word. "I thought these were your sacred working hours."

"Some of us schedule our work well enough that we can take some time off during the holidays. No, no, let's not bicker," she decided abruptly before he could retaliate. "It is nearly Christmas after all, and we've had three weeks of peace from our familial practical jokers. Truce," Pandora offered with a smile Michael wasn't sure he should trust. "Or a moratorium if you prefer."

"Why?"

"Let's just say I'm a sucker for holly and ivy. Besides, I'm relieved we didn't have to buy a big drooling dog or a supply of buckshot."

"For now." Not completely satisfied, Michael tipped back in his chair. "Fitzhugh's notion of notifying the local police of trespassers and spreading the rumor of an official investigation might be working temporarily. Or maybe our friends and family are just taking a holiday break themselves. Either way I'm not ready to relax."

"You'd rather break someone's nose than solve things peaceably," Pandora began, then waved a hand. "Never mind. I, for one, am going to enjoy the holidays and not give any of our dear family a thought." She paused a moment, toying with her braided chain of gold and amethyst. "I suppose Darla was disappointed."

Michael watched the way the stones caught the thin winter light and made sparks from it. "She'll pull through."

Pandora twisted the chain one way, twisted it back, then let it go. It was the sort of nervous gesture Michael hadn't expected from her. "Michael, you know you don't have to stay. I really will be fine if you want to run into New York for the holiday."

"Rule number six," he reminded her. "We stick together, and you've turned down a half-dozen invitations for the holidays yourself."

"My choice." She reached for the chain again, then dropped her hands. "I don't want you to feel obligated—"

"My choice," he interrupted. "Or have you suddenly decided I'm chivalrous and unselfish?"

"Certainly not," she tossed back, but smiled. "I prefer thinking you're just too lazy to make the trip."

He shook his head, but his lips curved in response. "I'm sure you would."

She hesitated in the doorway until he lifted a brow in question. "Michael, would you become totally obnoxious if I told you I'm glad you're staying?"

He studied her as she stood, looking slim and neat in the doorway, her hair a riotous contrast to the trim sweater and stovepipe pants. "I might."

"Then I won't tell you." Without another word, she slipped out of the doorway and disappeared.

Contrary woman, Michael thought. He was close to being crazy about her. And crazy was the perfect word. She baited him or, he admitted, he baited her at every possible opportunity. He could imagine no two people less inclined to peaceful coexistence, much less harmony. And yet…and yet he was close to being crazy about her. Knowing better than to try to go back to work, he rose and followed her downstairs.

He found her in the parlor, rearranging packages under the tree. "How many have you shaken?"

"All of them," she said easily. But she didn't turn because he might have seen how pleased she was he'd come downstairs with her. "I don't want to show any preference. Thing is," she added, poking at an elegantly wrapped box, "I seem to have missed my present from you."

Michael gave her a bland smile. "Who says I got you anything?"

"You would have been terribly rude and insensitive otherwise."

"Yep. In any case, you seem to've done well enough." He crouched down to study the stacks of boxes under the tree. "Who's Boris?" Idly he picked up a small silver box with flowing white ribbon.

"A Russian cellist who defected. He admires my... gold links."

"I bet. And Roger?"

"Roger Madison."

His mouth dropped open, but only for a moment. "The Yankee shortstop who batted .304 last year?"

"That's right. You may've noticed the silver band he wears on his right wrist. I made that for him last March. He seems to think it straightened out his bat or something." She lifted the blue-and-gold box and shook it gently. "He tends to be very generous."

"I see." Michael took a comprehensive study of the boxes. "There don't seem to be a great many packages here for you from women."

"Really?" Pandora took a scan herself. "It appears you make up for that with your pile. Chi-Chi?" she asked as she picked up a box with a big pink bow.

"She's a marine biologist," Michael said with his tongue in his cheek.

"Fascinating. And I imagine Magda's a librarian."

"Corporate attorney," he said blandly.

"Hmm. Well, whoever sent this one's obviously shy."

She picked up a magnum of champagne with a glittering red ribbon. The tag read "Happy Holidays, Michael," and nothing more.

Michael scanned the label with approval. "Some people don't want to advertise their generosity."

"How about you?" She tilted her head. "After all, it is a magnum. Are you going to share?"

"With whom?"

"I should've known you'd be greedy." She picked up a box with her name on it. "Just for that I'm eating this entire box of imported chocolates myself."

Michael eyed the box. "How do you know they're chocolates?"

She only smiled. "Henri always gives me chocolate."

"Imported?"

"Swiss."

Michael put out a hand. "Share and share alike."

Pandora accepted it. "I'll chill the wine."


Hours later when there was starlight on the snow and a fire in the hearth, Pandora lit the tree. Like Michael, she didn't miss any of the crowded, frenzied parties in the city. She was where she wanted to be. It had taken Pandora only a matter of weeks to discover she wasn't as attached to the rush of the city as she'd once thought. The Folley was home. Hadn't it always been? No, she no longer thought of going back to Manhattan in the spring. But what would it be like to live in the Folley alone?

Michael wouldn't stay. True, he'd own half of the Folley in a few months, but his life—including his active social life—was in the city. He wouldn't stay, she thought again, and found herself annoyed with her own sense of regret. Why should he stay? she asked herself as she wandered over to poke at the already crackling fire. How could he stay? They couldn't go on living together indefinitely. Sooner or later she'd have to approach him about her decision to remain there. To do so, she'd have to explain herself. It wouldn't be easy.

Still, she was grateful to Jolley for doing something she'd once resented. Boxing her in. She may have been forced into dealing with Michael on a day-to-day level, but in the few months she'd done so, her life had had more energy and interest than in the many months before. It was that, Pandora told herself, that she hated to give up.

She'd dealt with her attraction to him semisuccessfully. The fact was, he was no more her type than she was his. She jammed hard at a log. From all the many reports, Michael preferred a more flamboyant, exotic sort of woman. Actresses, dancers, models. And he preferred them in droves. She, on the other hand, looked for more intellectual men. The men she spent time with could discuss obscure French novelists and appreciate small, esoteric plays. Most of them wouldn't have known if *Logan's Run* was a television show or a restaurant in SoHo.

The fact that she had a sort of primitive desire for Michael was only a tempest in a teapot. Pandora smiled as she replaced the poker. She couldn't deny she enjoyed a tempest now and again.

When a small one erupted behind her, Pandora turned in disbelief. A little white dog with oversize feet scrambled into the room, slid on the Aubusson carpet and rammed smartly into a table. Barking madly, it rolled over twice, righted itself, then dashed at Pandora to leap halfheartedly and loll its tongue. Entertained,

Pandora crouched down and was rewarded when the puppy sprang onto her lap and licked her face.

"Where'd you come from?" Laughing, and defending herself as best she could, Pandora found the card attached to the red bow around the puppy's neck. It read:

My name is Bruno. I'm a mean, ugly dog looking for a lady to defend.

"Bruno, huh?" Laughing again, Pandora stroked his unfortunately long ears. "How mean are you?" she asked as he contented himself with licking her chin.

"He especially likes to attack discontented relatives," Michael announced as he wheeled in a tray carrying an ice bucket and champagne. "He's been trained to go after anyone wearing a Brooks Brothers suit."

"We might add Italian loafers."

"That's next."

Moved, incredibly moved, she concentrated on the puppy. She hadn't the least idea how to thank Michael without making a fool of herself. "He isn't really ugly," she murmured.

"They promised me he would be."

"They?" She buried her face in the puppy's fur a moment. "Where did you get him?"

"Pound." Watching her, Michael ripped the foil from the champagne. "When we went into town for supplies last week and I deserted you in the supermarket."

"And I thought you'd gone off somewhere to buy pornographic magazines."

"My reputation precedes me," he said half to himself. "In any case, I went to the pound and walked through the kennels. Bruno bit another dog on the—on a sensitive area in order to get to the bars first. Then he grinned at me with absolutely no dignity. I knew he was the one."

The cork came out with a bang and champagne sprayed up and dripped onto the floor. Bruno scrambled out of Pandora's lap and greedily licked it up. "Perhaps his manners are lacking a bit," Pandora observed. "But his taste is first class." She rose, but waited until Michael had poured two glasses. "It was a lovely thing to do, dammit."

He grinned and handed her a glass. "You're welcome."

"It's easier for me when you're rude and intolerable."

"I do the best I can." He touched his glass to hers.

"When you're sweet, it's harder for me to stop myself from doing something foolish."

He started to lift his glass, then stopped. "Such as?"

"Such as." Pandora set down her champagne, then took Michael's and set it on the table as well. Watching him, only him, she put her arms around his neck. Very slowly—unwise acts done slowly often take on a wisdom of their own—she touched her mouth to his

It was, as she'd known it would be, warm and waiting. His hands came to her shoulders, holding her without pressure. Perhaps they'd both come to understand that pressure would never hold her. When she softened, when she gave, she gave through her own volition, not through seduction, not through demand. So it was Pandora who moved closer, Pandora who pressed body to body, offering hints of intimacy with no submission.

It wasn't submission he wanted. It wasn't submission he looked for, though it was often given to him. He didn't look for matching strength, but strength that meshed. In Pandora, where he'd never thought to search for it, he found it. Her scent twisted around him, heightening emotions her taste had just begun to stir. Under his hands, her body was firm with the underlying softness women could exploit or be exploited by. He thought she'd do neither, but would simply be. By being alone, she drew him in.

She didn't resist his touch, not when his hands slipped down to her hips or skimmed up again. It seemed he'd done so before, though only in dreams she'd refused to acknowledge. If this was the time for acceptance, she'd accept. If this was the time for pleasure, she'd take it. If she found both with him, she wouldn't refuse. Even questions could come later. Maybe tonight was a night without questions.

She drew back, but only to smile at him. "You know, I don't think of you as a cousin when I'm kissing you."

"Really?" He nipped at her lips. She had an incredibly alluring mouth—full and pouty. "What do you think of me as?"

She cocked a brow. His arms surrounded her, but didn't imprison. Pandora knew she'd have to analyze the difference later. "I haven't figured that out yet."

"Then maybe we should keep working it out." He started to pull her back, but she resisted.

"Since you've broken tradition to give me my Christmas present a few hours early, I'll do the same." Going to the tree, Pandora reached down and found the square, flat box. "Happy Christmas, Michael."

He sat down on the arm of a chair to open it while Pandora picked up her glass of champagne. She sipped, watching a bit nervously for his reaction. It was only a token after all, she told herself, as she played with the stem of her glass. When he ripped off the paper then said nothing, she shrugged. "It's not as inventive as a guard dog."

Michael stared down at the pencil sketch of their uncle without any idea what to say. The frame she'd made herself, he knew. It was silver and busily ornate in a style Jolley would have appreciated. But it was the sketch that held him silent. She'd drawn Jolley as Michael remembered him best, standing, a bit bent forward from the waist as though he were ready to pop off on a new tangent. What thin hair he'd had left was mussed. His cheeks were stretched out in a big, wide-open grin. It had been drawn with love, talent and humor, three qualities Jolley had possessed and admired. When Michael looked up, Pandora was still twisting the stem of the glass in her hands.

Why, she's nervous, he realized. He'd never expected her to be anything but arrogantly confident about her work. About herself. The secrets he was uncovering were just as unnerving to him as they were to her. A man tended to get pulled into a woman who had soft spots in unexpected places. If he was pulled in, how would he work his way out again? But she was waiting, twisting the stem of her glass in her hand.

"Pandora. No one's ever given me anything that's meant more."

The line between her brows smoothed out as her smile bloomed. The ridiculous sense of pleasure was difficult to mask. "Really?"

He held a hand out to her. "Really." He glanced down at the sketch again and smiled. "It looks just like him."

"It looks like I remember him." She let her fingers link with Michael's. Pandora could tell herself it was

Jolley who drew them together, and nothing else. She could nearly believe it. "I thought you might remember him that way, too. The frame's a bit gaudy."

"And suitable." He studied it with more care. The silver shone dully, set off with the deep curls and lines she'd etched. It could, he realized, be put in an antique shop and pass for an heirloom. "I didn't know you did this sort of thing."

"Now and again. The boutique carries a few of them."

"Doesn't fit in the same category as bangles and beads," he mused.

"Doesn't it?" Her chin tilted. "I thought about making you a big gold collar with rhinestones just to annoy you."

"It would have."

"Maybe next year then. Or perhaps I'll make one for Bruno." She glanced around. "Where'd he go?"

"He's probably behind the tree gnawing on presents. During his brief stay in the garage, he ate a pair of golf shoes."

"We'll put a stop to that," Pandora declared, and went to find him.

"You know, Pandora, I'd no idea you could draw like this." Michael settled against the back of the chair to study the sketch again. "Why aren't you painting?"

"Why aren't you writing the Great American Novel?"

"Because I enjoy what I'm doing."

"Exactly." Finding no sign of the puppy around the tree, Pandora began to search under the furniture. "Though certainly a number of painters have toyed with jewelry design successfully enough—Dali for one—I feel...Michael!"

He set his untouched champagne back down and hurried over to where she knelt by a divan. "What is it?" he demanded, then saw for himself. Eyes closed, breathing fast and heavy, the puppy lay half under the divan. Even as Pandora reached for him, Bruno whimpered and struggled to stand.

"Oh, Michael, he's sick. We should get him to a vet."

"It'll be midnight before we get to town. We won't find a vet at midnight on Christmas Eve." Gently Michael laid a hand on Bruno's belly and heard him moan. "Maybe I can get someone on the phone."

"Do you think it's something he ate?"

"Sweeney's been supervising his feeding like a new mother." On cue Bruno struggled and shuddered and relieved himself of what offended his stomach. Exhausted from the effort, he lay back and dozed fitfully. "Something he drank," Michael murmured.

Pampering and soothing, Pandora stroked the dog. "That little bit of champagne shouldn't have made him ill." Because the dog was already resting easier, she relaxed a bit. "Charles isn't going to be pleased Bruno cast up his accounts on the carpet. Maybe I should—" She broke off as Michael grabbed her arm.

"How much champagne did you drink?"

"Only a sip. Why—" She broke off again to stare. "The champagne. You think something's wrong with it?"

"I think I'm an idiot for not suspecting an anonymous present." He grabbed her by the chin. "Only a sip. You're sure? How do you feel?"

Her skin had gone cold, but she answered calmly enough. "I'm fine. Look at my glass, it's still full." She turned her head to look at it herself. "You—you think it was poisoned?"

"We'll find out."

Logic seeped through, making her shake her head. "But, Michael, the wine was corked. How could it have been tampered with?"

"The first season on *Logan* I used a device like this." He thought back, remembering how he'd tested the theory by adding food coloring to a bottle of Dom Perignon. "The killer poisoned champagne by shooting cyanide through the cork with a hypodermic."

"Fiction," Pandora claimed, and fought a shiver. "That's just fiction."

"Until we find out differently, we're going to treat it as fact. The rest of the bottle's going into New York to Sanfield Labs for testing."

Shaky, Pandora swallowed. "For testing," she said on an unsteady breath. "All right, I suppose we'll both be easier when we're sure. Do you know someone who works there?"

"We own Sanfield." He looked down at the sleeping puppy. "Or we will own it in a matter of months. That's just one of the reasons someone might've sent us some doctored champagne."

"Michael, if it was poisoned…" She tried to imagine it and found it nearly impossible. "If it was poisoned," she repeated, "this wouldn't just be a game anymore."

He thought of what might have happened if they hadn't been distracted from the wine. "No, it wouldn't be a game."

"It doesn't make any sense." Uneasy and fighting to calm herself, Pandora rose. "Vandalism I can see, petty annoyances I can understand, but I just can't attribute something like this to one of the family. We're probably overreacting. Bruno's had too much excitement. He could very well have picked up something in the pound."

"I had him sent to the vet for his shots before he was delivered here yesterday." Michael's voice was calm, but his eyes were hot. "He was healthy, Pandora, until he lapped up some spilled champagne."

One look at him told her rationalizing was useless. "All right. The wine should be tested in any case so we can stop speculating. We can't do anything about it until day after tomorrow. In the meantime, I don't want to dwell on it."

"Pulling the blinds down, Pandora?"

"No." She picked up Bruno, who whimpered and burrowed into her breast. "But until it's proven, I don't want to consider that a member of my family tried to kill me. I'll fix him something warm to drink, then I'm going to take him upstairs. I'll keep an eye on him tonight."

"All right." Fighting a combination of frustration and fury, Michael stood by the fire.

Long after midnight when he couldn't sleep, couldn't work, Michael looked in on her. She'd left a light burning low across the room so that the white spreads and covers took on a rosy hue. Outside snow was falling again in big, festive flakes. Michael could see her, curled in the wide bed, the blankets up to her chin. The fire was nearly out. On the rug in front of it, the puppy snored. She'd put a mohair throw over him and had set a shallow bowl filled with what looked like tea nearby. Michael crouched beside the dog.

"Poor fella," he murmured. As he stroked, Bruno stirred, whimpered, then settled again.

"I think he's better."

Glancing over, Michael saw the light reflected in Pandora's eyes. Her hair was tousled, her skin pale and soft. Her shoulders, gently sloped, rose just above the covers pooled around her. She looked beautiful, desirable, arousing. He told himself he was mad. Pandora didn't fit into his carefully detailed notion of beauty. Michael looked back at the dog.

"Just needs to sleep it off. You could use another log on this fire." Needing to keep busy, Michael dug in the woodbox, then added a log to the coals.

"Thanks. Can't sleep?"

"No."

"Me, either." They sat in silence a moment, Pandora in the big bed, Michael on the hearth rug. The fire crackled greedily at the fresh log and flickered light and shadow. At length, she drew her knees up to her chest. "Michael, I'm frightened."

It wasn't an easy admission. He knew it cost her to tell him. He stirred at the fire a moment, then spoke lightly as he replaced the screen. "We can leave. We can drive into New York tomorrow and stay there. Forget this whole business and enjoy the holidays."

She didn't speak for a minute, but she watched him carefully. His face was turned away toward the fire so that she had to judge his feelings by the way he held himself. "Is that what you want to do?"

He thought of Jolley, then he thought of Pandora. Every muscle in his body tightened. "Sure." He tossed it off like a shrug. "I've got to think about myself." He said it as if to remind himself it had once been true.

"For someone who earns his living by making up stories, you're a lousy liar." She waited until he turned to face her. "You don't want to go back. What you want is to gather all our relatives together and beat them up."

"Can you see me pounding Aunt Patience?"

"With a few exceptions," Pandora temporized. "But the last thing you want is to give up."

"All right, that's me." He rose and, hands in pockets, paced back and forth in front of the fire. He could smell the woodsmoke mixed with some light scent from one of the bottles on Pandora's dresser. "What about you? You didn't want to hassle with this whole business from the beginning. I talked you into it. I feel responsible."

For the first time in hours she felt her humor return. "I hate to dent your ego, Michael, but you didn't talk me into anything. No one does. And I'm completely responsible for myself. I don't want to quit," she added before he could speak. "I said I didn't want the money, and that was true. I also said I didn't need it, and that's not precisely true. Over and above that, there's pride. I'm frightened, yes, but I don't want to quit. Oh, stop pacing around and come sit down." The order was cross and impatient, nearly making him smile. He came over and sat on the bed.

"Better?"

She gave him a long, steady look that had the hint of a smile fading. "Yes. Michael, I've been lying here for hours thinking this thing through. I've realized a few things. You called me a snob once, and perhaps you were right in a way. I've never thought much about money. Never allowed myself to. When Uncle Jolley cut everyone out, I thought of it as a cross between a joke and a slap on the wrist. I figured they'd grumble and complain certainly, but that was all." She lifted her hand palm up. "It was only money, and every one of them has their own."

"Ever heard of greed or the lust for power?"

"That's just it, I didn't think. How much do I know about any of those people? They bore or annoy me from time to time, but I've never thought about them as individuals." Now she ran the hand through her hair so that the blankets fell to her waist. "Ginger must be about the same age as I am, and I can't think of two things we have in common. I'd probably pass Biff's wife on the street without recognizing her."

"I have a hard time remembering her name," Michael put in, and earned a sigh from Pandora.

"That's my point. We don't really know them. The family, in a group, is a kind of parlor joke. Separately, who are they and what are they capable of? I've just begun to consider it. It's not a joke, Michael."

"No, it's not."

"I want to fight back, but I don't know how."

"The surest way is by staying. And maybe," he added, and took her hand. It was cool and soft. "Add a little psychological warfare."

"Such as?"

"What if we sent each one of our relatives a nice bottle of champagne?"

Her smile came slowly. "A magnum."

"Naturally. It'd be interesting to see what sort of reaction we get."

"It would be a nasty gesture, wouldn't it?"

"Uh-hmm."

"Maybe I haven't given your creative brain enough

credit." She fell silent as he wound her hair around his finger. "I suppose we should get some sleep."

"I suppose." But his fingers skimmed down her shoulders.

"I'm not very tired."

"We could play canasta."

"We could." But she made no move to stop him when he nudged the thin straps of her chemise from her shoulders. "There's always cribbage."

"That, too."

"Or…" It was her decision, they both understood that. "We might finish playing out the hand we started downstairs earlier."

He lifted her hand and pressed his lips to the palm. "Always best to finish what you start before going on. As I recall, we were…here." He lowered his mouth to hers. Slowly, on a sigh, she wound her arms around his neck.

"That seems about right."

Holding fast, they sunk into the bed together.

Perhaps it was because they knew each other well. Perhaps it was because they'd already waited a lifetime, but each moved slowly. Desire, for the moment, was comfortable, easy to satisfy with a touch, a taste. Passion curled inside him then unwound with a sigh. There was inch after inch of her to explore with his fingertips, with his lips. He'd waited too long, wanted too long, to miss any part of what they could give to each other.

She was more generous than he'd imagined, less inhibited, more open. She didn't ask to be coaxed, she didn't pretend to need persuasion. She ran her hands over him with equal curiosity. Her mouth took from him and gave again. When his lips parted from hers, her eyes were on him, clouded with desire, dark with amusement of a shared joke. They were together, Michael thought as he buried his face in her hair. About to become lovers. The joke was on both of them.

Her hands were steady when she pulled his sweatshirt over his head, steady still as she ran them over his chest. Her pulse wasn't. She'd avoided this, refused this. Now she was accepting it though she knew there would be consequences she couldn't anticipate.

The fire crackled steadily. The soft light glowed. Consequences were for more practical times.

Her skin slid over his with each movement. Each movement enticed. With his heartbeat beginning to hammer in his head, he journeyed lower. With open-mouthed kisses he learned her body in a way he'd only been able to imagine. Her scent was everywhere, subtle at the curve of her waist, stronger at the gentle underside of her breasts. He drew it in and let it swim in his head.

He felt the instant her lazy enjoyment darkened with power. When her breath caught on a moan, he took her deeper. They reached a point where he no longer knew what they did to each other, only that strength met need and need became desperation.

His skin was damp. She tasted the moistness of it and craved more. So this was passion. This was the trembling, churning hunger men and women longed for. She'd never wanted it. That's what she told herself as her body shuddered. Pleasure and pain mixed, needs and fears tangled. Her mind was as swamped with sensations as her flesh—heat and light, ecstasy and terror. The vulnerability overwhelmed her though her body arched taut and her hands clung. No one had ever brushed back her defenses so effortlessly and taken. Taken and taken.

Breathless and desperate, she dragged his mouth back to hers. They rolled over the bed, rough, racing. Neither had had enough. While she tugged and pulled at his jeans, Michael drove her higher. He'd wanted the madness, for himself and for her. Now he felt the wild strength pouring out of her. No thought here, no logic. He rolled on top of her again, reveling in her frantic breathing.

She curled around him, legs and arms. When he plunged into her, they watched the astonishment on each other's faces. Not like this—it had never been like this. They'd come home. But home, each discovered, wasn't always a peaceful place.

There was silence, stunned, awkward silence. They lay tangled in the covers as the log Michael had set to fire broke apart and showered sparks against the screen. They knew each other well, too well to speak of what had happened just yet. So they lay in silence as their skin cooled and their pulses leveled. Michael shifted to pull the spread up over them both.

"Merry Christmas," he murmured.

With a sound that was both sigh and laugh, Pandora settled beside him.

## Chapter Eight

They left the Folley in the hard morning light the day after Christmas. Sun glared off snow, melting it at the edges and forming icicles down branches and eaves. It was a postcard with biting wind.

After a short tussle they'd agreed that Pandora would drive into the city and Michael would drive back. He pushed his seat back to the limit and managed to stretch out his legs. She maneuvered carefully down the slushy mountain road that led from the Folley. They didn't speak until she'd reached clear highway.

"What if they don't let us in?"

"Why shouldn't they?" Preferring driving to sitting, Michael shifted in his seat. For the first time he was impatient with the miles of road between the Folley and New York.

"Isn't that like counting your chickens?" Pandora

turned the heat down a notch and loosened the buttons of her coat. "We don't own the place yet."

"Just a technicality."

"Always cocky."

"You always look at the negative angles."

"Someone has to."

"Look…" He started to toss back something critical, then noticed how tightly she gripped the wheel. All nerves, he mused. Though the scenery was a print by Currier and Ives, it wasn't entirely possible to pretend they were off on a holiday jaunt. He was running on nerves himself, and they didn't all have to do with doctored champagne. How would he have guessed he'd wake up beside her in the cool light of dawn and feel so involved? So responsible. So hungry.

He took a deep breath and watched the scenery for another moment. "Look," he began again in a lighter tone. "We may not own the lab or anything else at the moment, but we're still Jolley's family. Why should a lab technician refuse to do a little analysis?"

"I suppose we'll find out when we get there." She drove another ten miles in silence. "Michael, what difference is an analysis going to make?"

"I have this odd sort of curiosity. I like to know if someone's tried to poison me."

"So we'll know if, and we'll know why. We still won't know who."

"That's the next step." He glanced over. "We can invite them all to the Folley for New Year's and take turns grilling them."

"Now you're making fun of me."

"No, actually, I'd thought of it. I just figure the time's not quite right." He waited a few minutes. In thin leather gloves, her fingers curled and uncurled on the wheel. "Pandora, why don't you tell me what's really bothering you?"

"Nothing is." Everything was. She hadn't been able to think straight for twenty-four hours.

"Nothing?"

"Nothing other than wondering if someone wants to kill me." She tossed it off arrogantly. "Isn't that enough?"

He heard the edge under the sarcasm. "Is that why you hid in your room all day yesterday."

"I wasn't hiding." She had enough pride to sound brittle. "I was tending to Bruno. And I was tired."

"You hardly ate any of that enormous goose Sweeney slaved over."

"I'm not terribly fond of goose."

"I've had Christmas dinner with you before," he corrected. "You eat like a horse."

"How gallant of you to point it out." For no particular reason, she switched lanes, pumped the gas and passed another car. "Let's just say I wasn't in the mood."

"How did you manage to talk yourself into disliking what happened between us so quickly?" It hurt. He felt the hurt, but it didn't mean he had to let it show. His voice, as hers had been, was cool and hard.

"I haven't. That's absurd." Dislike? She hadn't been able to think of anything else, feel anything else. It scared her to death. "We slept together." She managed to toss it off with a shrug. "I suppose we both knew we would sooner or later."

He'd told himself precisely the same thing. He'd lost count of the number of times. He'd yet to figure out when he'd stopped believing. For himself. "And that's it?"

The question was deadly calm, but she was too preoccupied with her own nerves to notice. "What else?" She had to stop dwelling on a moment of impulse. Didn't she? She couldn't go on letting her common sense be overrun by an attraction that would lead nowhere. Could she? "Michael, there's no use blowing what happened out of proportion."

"Just what is that proportion?"

The car felt stuffy and close. Pandora switched off the heat and concentrated on the road. "We're two adults," she began, but had to swallow twice.

"And?"

"Dammit, Michael, I don't have to spell it out."

"Yes, you do."

"We're two adults," she said again, but with temper replacing nerves. "We have normal adult needs. We slept together and satisfied them."

"How practical."

"I am practical." Abruptly, and very badly, she wanted to weep. "Much too practical to weave fantasies about a man who likes his women in six packs. Too practical," she went on, voice rising, "to picture myself emotionally involved with a man I spent one night with. And too practical to romanticize what was no more than an exchange of normal and basic lust."

"Pull over."

"I will not."

"Pull over to the shoulder, Pandora, or I'll do it for you."

She gritted her teeth and debated calling his bluff. There was just enough traffic on the road to force her hand. With only a slight squeal of tires, Pandora pulled off to the side of the road. Michael turned off the key then grabbed her by the lapels and pulled her half into his seat. Before she could struggle away, he closed his mouth over hers.

Heat, anger, passion. They seemed to twist together into one emotion. He held her there as cars whizzed by, shaking the windows. She infuriated him, she aroused him, she hurt him. In Michael's opinion, it was too much for one man to take from one woman. As abruptly as he'd grabbed her, he released her.

"Make something practical out of that," he challenged.

Breathless, Pandora struggled back into her own seat. In a furious gesture, she turned the key, gunning the motor. "Idiot."

"Yeah." He sat back as she pulled back onto the highway. "We finally agree on something."

It was a long ride into the city. Longer still when you sat in a car in tense silence. Once they entered Manhattan, Pandora was forced to follow Michael's directions to the lab.

"How do you know where it is?" she demanded after they left the car in a parking garage. The sidewalk was mobbed with people hurrying to exchange what had been brightly boxed and wrapped the day before. As they walked, Pandora held her coat closed against the wind.

"I looked the address up in Jolley's files yesterday." Michael walked the half block hatless, his coat flapping open, clutching the box with the champagne under one arm. He wasn't immune to the cold but found it a relief after the hot tension of the drive. With a brisk gesture to Pandora, he pushed through revolving doors and entered the lobby of a steel-and-glass building. "He owned the whole place."

Pandora looked across the marble floor. It sloped upward and widened into a crowded, bustling area with men and women carrying briefcases. "This whole place?"

"All seventy-two floors."

It hit her again just how complicated the estate was. How many companies operated in the building? How many people worked there? How could she possibly crowd her life with this kind of responsibility? If she could get her hands on Uncle Jolley—Pandora broke off, almost amused. How he must be enjoying this, she thought.

"What am I supposed to do with seventy-two floors in midtown?"

"There are plenty of people to do it for you." Michael gave their names to the guard at the elevators. With no delay, they were riding to the fortieth floor.

"So there are people to do it for us. Who keeps track of them?"

"Accountants, lawyers, managers. It's a matter of hiring people to look after people you hire."

"That certainly clears that up."

"If you're worried, think about Jolley. Having a fortune didn't seem to keep him from enjoying himself. For the most part, he looked at the whole business as a kind of hobby."

Pandora watched the numbers above the door. "A hobby."

"Everyone should have a hobby."

"Tennis is a hobby," she muttered.

"The trick is to keep the ball moving. Jolley tossed it in our court, Pandora."

She folded her arms. "I'm not ready to be grateful for that."

"Look at it this way then." He put a hand on her shoulder and squeezed lightly. "You don't have to know how to build a car to own one. You just have to drive steady and follow the signs. If Jolley didn't think we could follow the signs, he wouldn't have given us the keys."

It helped to look at it that way. Still it was odd to consider she was riding on an elevator she would own when the six months were up. "Do we know whom to go to?" Pandora glanced at the box Michael held, which contained the bottle of champagne.

"A man named Silas Lockworth seems to be in charge."

"You did your homework."

"Let's hope it pays off."

When the elevator stopped, they walked into the reception area for Sanfield Laboratories. The carpet was pale rose, the walls lacquered in cream. Two huge split-leaf philodendrons flanked the wide glass doors that slid open at their approach. A woman behind a gleaming desk folded her hands and smiled.

"Good morning. May I help you?"

Michael glanced at the computer terminal resting on an extension of her desk. Top of the line. "We'd like to see Mr. Lockworth."

"Mr. Lockworth's in a meeting. If I could have your names, perhaps his assistant can help you."

"I'm Michael Donahue. This is Pandora McVie."

"McVie?"

Pandora saw the receptionist's eyebrows raise. "Yes, Maximillian McVie was our uncle."

Already polite and efficient, the receptionist became gracious. "I'm sure Mr. Lockworth would have greeted you himself if we'd known you were coming. Please have a seat. I'll ring through."

It took under five minutes.

The man who strode out into reception didn't look like Pandora's conception of a technician or scientist. He was six-three, lean as a gymnast with blond hair brushed back from a tanned, lantern-jawed face. He looked, Pandora thought, more like a man who'd be at home on the range than in a lab with test tubes.

"Ms. McVie." He walked with an easy rolling gait, hand outstretched. "Mr. Donahue. I'm Silas Lockworth. Your uncle was a good friend."

"Thank you." Michael accepted the handshake. "I apologize for dropping in unannounced."

"No need for that." Lockworth's smile seemed to mean it. "We never knew when Jolley was going to drop in on us. Let's go back to my office."

He led them down the corridor. Lockworth's office was the next surprise. It was plush enough, with curvy chairs and clever lithographs, to make you think of a corporate executive. The desk was piled high with enough files and papers to make you think of a harried clerk. It carried the scent from the dozens of leather-bound books on a floor-to-ceiling shelf. Built into one wall was a round aquarium teeming with exotic fish.

"Would you like coffee? I can guarantee it's hot and strong."

"No." Pandora was already twisting her gloves in her hands. "Thank you. We don't want to take too much of your time."

"It's my pleasure," Lockworth assured her. "Jolley certainly spoke often of both of you," Lockworth went on as he gestured to chairs. "There was never a doubt you were his favorites."

"And he was ours," Pandora returned.

"Still you didn't come to pass the time." Lockworth leaned back on his desk. "What can I do for you?"

"We have something we'd like analyzed," Michael began. "Quickly and quietly."

"I see." Silas stopped there, brow raised. Lockworth was a man who picked up impressions of people right away. In Pandora he saw nerves under a sheen of politeness. In Michael he saw violence, not so much buried as thinly coated. He thought he detected a bond between them though they hadn't so much as looked at each other since entering the room.

Lockworth could have refused. His staff was slimmed down during the holidays, and work was backlogged. He was under no obligation to either of them yet. But he never forgot his obligation to Jolley McVie. "We'll try to accommodate you."

In silence, Michael opened the box and drew out the bottle of champagne. "We need a report on the contents of this bottle. A confidential report. Today."

Lockworth took it and examined the label. His lips curved slightly. "Seventy-two. A good year. Were you thinking of starting a vineyard?"

"We need to know what's in there other than champagne."

Rather than showing surprise, Lockworth leaned back on the desk again. "You've reason to think there is?"

Michael met the look. "We wouldn't be here otherwise."

Lockworth only inclined his head. "All right. I'll run it through the lab myself."

With a quick scowl for Michael's manners, Pandora rose and offered her hand. "We appreciate the trouble, Mr. Lockworth. I'm sure you have a great many other things to do, but the results are important to Michael and me."

"No problem." He decided he'd find out why it was important after he'd analyzed the wine. "There's a coffee shop for the staff. I'll show you where it is. You can wait for me there."

"There was absolutely no reason to be rude." Pandora settled herself at a table and looked at a surprisingly varied menu.

"I wasn't rude."

"Of course you were. Mr. Lockworth was going out of his way to be friendly, and you had a chip on your shoulder. I think I'm going to have the shrimp salad."

"I don't have a chip on my shoulder. I was being cautious. Or maybe you think we should spill everything to a total stranger."

Pandora folded her hands and smiled at the waitress. "I'd like the shrimp salad and coffee."

"Two coffees," Michael muttered. "And the turkey platter."

"I've no intention of spilling, as you put it, everything to a total stranger." Pandora picked up her napkin. "However, if we weren't going to trust Lockworth, we'd have been better off to buy a chemistry set and try to handle it ourselves."

"Drink your coffee," Michael muttered, and picked up his own the moment the waitress served it.

Pandora frowned as she added cream. "How long do you think it'll take?"

"I don't know. I'm not a scientist."

"He didn't look like one, either, did he?"

"Bronc rider." Michael sipped his black coffee and found it as strong as Lockworth had promised.

"What?"

"Looks like a bronc rider. I wonder if Carlson or any of the others have any interest in this building."

Pandora set her coffee down before she tasted it. "I hadn't thought of that."

"As I remember, Jolley turned over Tristar Corporation to Monroe about twenty-five years ago. I remember my parents talking about it."

"Tristar. Which one is that?"

"Plastics. I know he gave little pieces of the pie out here and there. He told me once he wanted to give all his relatives a chance before he crossed them off the list."

After a moment's thought, she shrugged and picked up her coffee again. "Well, if he did give a few shares of Sanfield to one of them, what difference does it make?"

"I don't know how much we should trust Lockworth."

"You'd have felt better if he'd been bald and short with Coke-bottle glasses and a faint German accent."

"Maybe."

"See?" Pandora smiled. "You're just jealous because

he has great shoulders." She fluttered her lashes. "Here's your turkey."

They ate slowly, drank more coffee, then passed more time with pie. After an hour and a half, both of them were restless and edgy. When Lockworth came in, Pandora forgot to be nervous about the results.

"Thank God, here he comes."

After maneuvering around chairs and employees on lunch break, Lockworth set a computer printout on the table and handed the box back to Michael. "I thought you'd want a copy." He took a seat and signaled for coffee. "Though it's technical."

Pandora frowned down at the long, chemical terms printed out on the paper. It meant little more than nothing to her, but she doubted trichloroethanol or any of the other multisyllabic words belonged in French champagne. "What does it mean?"

"I wondered that myself." Lockworth reached in his pocket and drew out a pack of cigarettes. Michael looked at it for a moment with longing. "I wondered why anyone would put rose dust in vintage champagne."

"Rose dust?" Michael repeated. "Pesticide. So it was poisoned."

"Technically, yes. Though there wasn't enough in the wine to do any more than make you miserably ill for a day or two. I take it neither one of you had any?"

"No." Pandora looked up from the report. "My puppy did," she explained. "When we opened the bottle, some spilled and he lapped it up. Before we'd gotten around to drinking it, he was ill."

"Luckily for you, though I find it curious that you'd jumped to the conclusion that the champagne had been poisoned because a puppy was sick."

"Luckily for us, we did." Michael folded the report and slipped it into his pocket.

"You'll have to pardon my cousin," Pandora said. "He has no manners. We appreciate you taking time out to do this for us, Mr. Lockworth. I'm afraid it isn't possible to fully explain ourselves at this point, but I can tell you that we had good reason to suspect the wine."

Lockworth nodded. As a scientist he knew how to theorize. "If you find you need a more comprehensive report, let me know. Jolley was an important person in my life. We'll call it a favor to him."

As he rose, Michael stood with him. "I'll apologize for myself this time." He held out a hand.

"I'd be a bit edgy myself if someone gave me pesticide disguised as Moët et Chandon. Let me know if I can do anything else."

"Well," Pandora began when they were alone. "What next?"

"A little trip to the liquor store. We've some presents to buy."

They sent, first-class, a bottle of the same to each of Jolley's erstwhile heirs. Michael signed the cards simply, "One good turn deserves another." After it was done and they walked outside in the frigid wind, Pandora huffed and pulled on her gloves.

"An expensive gesture."

"Look at it as an investment," Michael suggested.

It wasn't the money, she thought, but the sudden futility she felt. "What good will it do really?"

"Several bottles'll be wondered over, then appreciated. But one," Michael said with relish. "One makes a statement, even a threat."

"An empty threat," Pandora returned. "It's not as if

we'll be there when everyone gets one to gauge reactions."

"You're thinking like an amateur."

Michael was halfway across the street when Pandora grabbed his arm. "Just what does that mean?"

"When an amateur plays a practical joke, he thinks he has to be in on the kill."

Ignoring the people who brushed by them, Pandora held her ground. "Since when is pesticide poisoning a practical joke?"

"Revenge follows the same principle."

"Oh, I see. And you're an expert."

The light changed. Cars started for them, horns blaring. Gritting his teeth, Michael grabbed her arm and pulled her to the curb. "Maybe I am. It's enough for me to know someone's going to look at the bottle and be very nervous. Someone's going to look at it and know we intend to give as good as we get. Your trouble is you don't like to let your emotions loose long enough to appreciate revenge."

"Leave my emotions alone."

"That's the plan," he said evenly, and started walking again.

In three strides she'd caught up with him. Her face was pink from the wind, the anger in her voice came out in thin wisps. "You're not annoyed with Lockworth or about the champagne or over differing views on revenge. You're mad because I defined our relationship in practical terms."

He stared at her as her phrasing worked on both his temper and his humor. "Okay," he declared, turning to walk on. Patience straining, he turned back when

Pandora grabbed his arm. "You want to hash this out right here?"

"I won't let you make me feel inadequate just because I broke things off before you had a chance to."

"Before I had a chance to?" He took her by the coat. With the added height from the heels on her boots, she looked straight into his eyes. Another time, another place, he might have considered her magnificent. "I barely had the chance to recover from what happened before you were shoving me out. I wanted you. Dammit, I still want you. God knows why."

"Well, I want you, too, and I don't like it, either."

"Looks like that puts us in the same fix, doesn't it?"

"So what're we going to do about it?"

He looked at her and saw the anger. But he looked closely enough to see confusion, as well. One of them had to make the first move. He decided it was going to be him. Taking her hand, he dragged her across the street.

"Where are we going?"

"The Plaza."

"The Plaza Hotel? Why?"

"We're going to get a room, put the chain on the door and make love for the next twenty-four hours. After that, we'll decide how we want to handle it."

There were times, Pandora decided, when it was best to go along for the ride. "We don't have any luggage."

"Yeah. My reputation's about to be shattered."

She made a sound that might have been a laugh. When they walked into the elegant lobby, the heat warmed her skin and stirred up her nerves. It was all impulse, she told herself. She knew better than to make any important decision on impulse. He could change everything. That was something she hadn't wanted to admit but had known for years. When she started to draw away, his hand locked on her arm.

"Coward," he murmured. He couldn't have said anything more perfectly designed to make her march forward.

"Good afternoon." Michael smiled at the desk clerk. Pandora wondered briefly if the smile would have been so charming if the clerk had been a man. "Checking in."

"You have a reservation?"

"Donahue. Michael Donahue."

The clerk punched some buttons and stared at her computer screen. "I'm afraid I don't show anything under Donahue for the twenty-sixth."

"Katie," Michael said on a breath of impatience. He sent Pandora a long suffering look. "I should never have trusted her to handle this."

Catching the drift, Pandora patted his hand. "You're going to have to let her go, Michael. I know she's worked for your family for forty years, but when a person gets into their seventies…" She trailed off and let Michael take the ball.

"We'll decide when we get home." He turned back to the desk clerk. "Apparently there's been a mix-up between my secretary and the hotel. We'll only be in town overnight. Is anything available?"

The clerk went back to her buttons. Most people in her experience raised the roof when there was a mix-up in reservations. Michael's quiet request touched her sympathies. "You understand there's a problem because of the holiday." She punched more buttons, wanting to help. "We do have a suite available."

"Fine." Michael took the registration form and filled

it out. With the key in his hand, he sent the clerk another smile. "I appreciate the trouble." Noting the bellhop hovering at his elbow, he handed him a bill. "We'll handle it, thanks."

The clerk looked at the twenty in his palm and the lack of luggage. "Yes, sir!"

"He thinks we're having an illicit affair," Pandora murmured as they stepped onto the elevator.

"We are." Before the doors had closed again, Michael grabbed her to him and locked her in a kiss that lasted twelve floors. "We don't know each other," he told her as they stepped into the hallway. "We've just met. We don't have mutual childhood memories or share the same family." He put the key in the lock. "We don't give a damn what the other does for a living nor do we have any long-standing opinions about each other."

"Is that supposed to simplify things?"

Michael drew her inside. "Let's find out."

He didn't give her a chance to wonder, a chance to debate. The moment the door was shut behind them, he had her in his arms. He took questions away. He took choice away. For once, she wanted him to. In a fury of passions, of hungers, of cravings, they came together. Each fought to draw more, still more out of the other, to touch faster, to possess more quickly. They forgot what they knew, what they thought and reveled in what they felt.

Coats, still chill from the wind, were pushed to the floor. Sweaters and shirts followed. Hardly more than a foot inside the door, they slid to the carpet.

"Damn winter," Michael muttered as he fought with her boots.

Laughing, Pandora struggled with his, then moaned when he pressed his lips to her breast.

It was a race, part warring, part loving. Neither gave the other respite. When their clothes were shed, they sprinted ahead, hands reaching, lips arousing. There was none of the dreamy déjà vu they'd experienced the first time. This was new. The fingers tracing her skin had never been felt before. The lips, hot and searing, had never been tasted. Fresh, erotically fresh, their mouths met and clung.

Her heart had never beat so fast. She was sure of it. Her body had never ached and pulsed so desperately. She'd never wanted it to. Now she wanted more, everything. Him. She rolled so that she could press quick, hungry kisses over his face, his neck, his chest. Everywhere.

His mind was teeming with her, with every part of her that he could touch or taste or smell. She was wild in a way he'd never imagined. She was demanding in a way any man would desire. His body seemed to fascinate her, every curve, every angle. She exploited it until he was half mad, then he groped for her.

She'd never known a man could give so much. Racked with sensations, she arched under him. Hot and ready, she offered. But he was far from through. The taste of her thighs was subtle, luring him toward the heat. He found her, drove her and kept her helplessly trapped in passion. Helplessly. The sensation shivered over her. She'd never known what it had meant to be truly vulnerable to another. He could have taken anything from her then, asked anything and she couldn't have refused. But he didn't ask, he gave.

She crested wave after wave. Between heights and

depths she pinwheeled, delighting in the spin. On the rug with the afternoon light streaming through the windows, she was locked in blinding darkness without any wish to see. *Make me feel,* her mind seemed to shout. More. Again. Still.

And he was inside her, joined, melded. She found there was more. Impossibly more.

They stayed where they were, sprawled on scattered clothes. Gradually Pandora found her mind swimming back to reality. She could see the pastel walls, the sunlight. She could smell the body heat that was a mix of hers and his. She could feel Michael's hair brushing over her cheek, the beat of his heart, still fast, against her breast.

It happened so fast, she thought. Or had it taken hours? All she was certain of was that she'd never experienced anything like it. Never permitted herself to, she amended. Strange things could happen to a woman who lifted the lid from her passion. Other things could sneak in before the top closed again. Things like affection, understanding. Even love.

She caught herself stroking Michael's hair and let her hand fall to the carpet. She couldn't let love in, not even briefly. Love took as well as gave. That she'd always known. And it didn't always give and take in equal shares. Michael wasn't a man a woman could love practically, and certainly not wisely. That she understood. He wouldn't follow the rules.

She'd be his lover, but she wouldn't love him. Though there would be no pretending they could live with each other for the next three months platonically, she wouldn't risk her heart. For an instant Pandora thought she felt it break, just a little. Foolishness, she told herself. Her heart was strong and unimpaired. What she and Michael had together was a very basic, very uncomplicated arrangement. Arrangement, she thought, sounded so much more practical than romance.

But her sigh was quiet, and a little wistful.

"Figure it all out?" He shifted a little as he spoke, just enough so that he could brush his lips down her throat.

"What do you mean?"

"Have you figured out the guidelines for our relationship?" Lifting his head, he looked down at her. He wasn't smiling, but Pandora thought he was amused.

"I don't know what you're talking about."

"I can almost hear the wheels turning. Pandora, I can see just what's going on in your head."

Annoyed that he probably could, she lifted a brow. "I thought we'd just met."

"I'm psychic. You're thinking...." He trailed off to nibble at her lips. "That there should be a way to keep our...relationship on a practical level. You're wondering how you'll keep an emotional distance when we're sleeping together. You've decided that there'll be absolutely no romantic overtones to any arrangement between us."

"All right." He made her feel foolish. Then he ran a hand over her hip and made her tremble. "Since you're so smart, you'll see that I've only been using common sense."

"I like it better when your skin gets hot, and you haven't any sense at all. But—" he kissed her before she could answer "—we can't stay in bed all the time. I don't believe in practical affairs, Pandora. I don't believe in emotional distance between lovers."

"You've had a great deal of experience there."

"That's right." He sat up, drawing her with him. "And I'll tell you this. You can wall up your emotions all you want. You can call whatever we have here by any practical term you can dream up. You can turn up your nose at candlelight dinners and quiet music. It's not going to make any difference." He gathered her hair in his hand and pulled her head back. "I'm going to get to you, cousin. I'm going to get to you until you can't think of anything, anyone but me. If you wake up in the middle of the night and I'm not there, you'll wish I were. And when I touch you, any time I touch you, you're going to want me."

She had to fight the shudder. She knew, as well as she'd ever known anything, that he was right. And she knew, perhaps they both did, that she'd fight it right down to the end. "You're arrogant, egocentric and simpleminded."

"True enough. And you're stubborn, willful and perverse. The only thing we can be sure of at this point is that one of us is going to win."

Sitting on the pile of discarded clothes, they studied each other. "Another game?" Pandora murmured.

"Maybe. Maybe it's the only game." With that, he stood and lifted her into his arms.

"Michael, I don't need to be carried."

"Yes, you do."

He walked across the suite toward the bedroom. Pandora started to struggle, then subsided. Maybe just this once, she decided, and relaxed in his arms.

# Chapter Nine

January was a month of freezing wind, pelting snow and gray skies. Each day was as bitterly cold as the last, with tomorrow waiting frigidly in the wings. It was a month of frozen pipes, burst pipes, overworked furnaces and stalled engines. Pandora loved it. The frost built up on the windows of her shop, and the inside temperature always remained cool even with the heaters turned up. She worked until her fingers were numb and enjoyed every moment.

Throughout the month, the road to the Folley was often inaccessible. Pandora didn't mind not being able to get out. It meant no one could get in. The pantry and freezer were stocked, and there was over a cord of wood stacked beside the kitchen door. The way she looked at it, they had everything they needed. The days were short and productive, the nights long and relaxing. Since the incident of the champagne, it had been a quiet, uneventful winter.

Uneventful, Pandora mused, wasn't precisely the right term. With quick, careful strokes, she filed the edges of a thick copper bracelet. It certainly wasn't as though nothing had happened. There'd been no trouble from outside sources, but... Trouble, as she'd always known, was definitely one of Michael Donahue's greatest talents.

Just what was he trying to pull by leaving a bunch of violets on her pillow? She was certain a magic wand would have been needed to produce the little purple flowers in January. When she'd questioned him about them, he'd simply smiled and told her violets didn't have thorns. What kind of an answer was that? Pandora wondered, and examined the clasp of the bracelet through a magnifying glass. She was satisfied with the way she'd designed it to blend with the design.

Then, there'd been the time she'd come out of the bath to find the bedroom lit with a dozen candles. When she'd asked if there'd been a power failure, Michael had just laughed and pulled her into bed.

He did things like reaching for her hand at dinner and whispering in her ear just before dawn. Once he'd joined her in the shower uninvited and silenced her protests by washing every inch of her body himself. She'd been right. Michael Donahue didn't follow the rules. He'd been right. He was getting to her.

Pandora removed the bracelet from the vise, then absently began to polish it. She'd made a half a dozen others in the last two weeks. Big chunky bracelets, some had gaudy stones, some had ornate engraving. They suited her mood—daring, opinionated and a bit silly.

She'd learned to trust her instincts, and her instincts told her they'd sell faster than she could possibly make them—and be copied just as quickly.

She didn't mind the imitations. After all, there was only one of each type that was truly a Pandora McVie. Copies would be recognized as copies because they lacked that something special, that individuality of the genuine.

Pleased, she turned the bracelet over in her hand. No one would mistake any of her work for an imitation. She might often use glass instead of precious or semi-precious stones because glass expressed her mood at the time. But each piece she created carried her mark, her opinion and her honesty. She never gave a thought to the price of a piece when she crafted it or its market value. She created what she needed to create first, then after it was done, her practical side calculated the profit margin. Her art varied from piece to piece, but it never lied.

Looking down at the bracelet, Pandora sighed. No, her art never lied, but did she? Could she be certain her emotions were as genuine as the jewelry she made? A feeling could be imitated. An emotion could be fraudulent. How many times in the past few weeks had she pretended? Not pretended to feel, Pandora thought, but pretended not to feel. She was a woman who'd always prided herself on her honesty. Truth and independence went hand in hand with Pandora's set of values. But she'd lied—over and over again—to herself, the worst form of deception.

It was time to stop, Pandora told herself. Time to face the truth of her feelings if only in the privacy of her own heart and mind.

How long had she been in love with Michael? She had to stand and move around the shop as the question formed in her mind. Weeks? Months? Years? It wasn't something she could answer because she would never be sure. But she was certain of the emotion. She loved. Pandora understood it because she loved only a few people, and when she did, she loved boundlessly. Perhaps that was the biggest problem. Wasn't it a sort of suicide to love Michael boundlessly?

Better to face it, she told herself. No problem resolved itself without being faced first and examined second. However much a fool it made her, she loved Michael. Pandora rubbed at the steam on the windows and looked out at the snow. Strange, she'd really believed once she accepted it she'd feel better. She didn't.

What options did she have? She could tell him. And have him gloat, Pandora thought with a scowl. He would, too, before he trotted off to his next conquest. *She* certainly wasn't fool enough to think he'd be interested in a long-term relationship. Of course, she wasn't interested in one either, Pandora told herself as she began to noisily pack her tools.

Another option was to cut and run. What the relatives hadn't been able to accomplish with their malice and mischief, her own heart would succeed in doing. She could get in the car, drive to the airport and fly to anywhere. Escape was the honest word. Then, she'd not only be a coward, she'd be a traitor. No, she wouldn't let Uncle Jolley down; she wouldn't run. That left her, as Pandora saw it, with one option.

She'd go on as she was. She'd stay with Michael, sleep with Michael, share with Michael—share with him everything but what was in her heart. She'd take the two months they had left together and prepare herself to walk away with no regrets.

He'd gotten to her, Pandora admitted. Gotten to her in places no other man had touched. She loved him for it. She hated him for it. With her mood as turbulent as her thoughts, she locked the shop and stomped across the lawn.

"Here she comes now." With a new plan ready to spring, Sweeney turned away from the kitchen window and signaled to Charles.

"It's never going to work."

"Of course it is. We're going to push those children together for their own good. Any two people who spat as much as they do should be married."

"We're interfering where it's not our place."

"What malarkey!" Sweeney took her seat at the kitchen table. "Whose place is it to interfere if not ours, I'd like to know? Who'll be knocking around this big empty house if they go back to the city if not us? Now pick up that cloth and fan me. Stoop over a bit and look feeble."

"I am feeble," Charles muttered, but picked up the cloth.

When Pandora walked into the kitchen she saw Sweeney sprawled back in a chair, eyes closed, with Charles standing over her waving a dishcloth at her face.

"God, what's wrong? Charles, did she faint?" Before he could answer, Pandora had dashed across the room. "Call Michael," she ordered. "Call Michael quickly." She brushed Charles away and crouched. "Sweeney, it's Pandora. Are you in pain?"

Barely suppressing a sigh of satisfaction, Sweeney let her eyes flutter open and hoped she looked pale. "Oh, missy, don't you worry now. Just one of my spells is all. Now and then my heart starts to flutter so that I feel it's coming right out of my head."

"I'm going to call the doctor." Pandora had taken only one step when her hand was caught in a surprisingly strong grip.

"No need for that." Sweeney made her voice thin and weary. "Saw him just a few months past and he told me I'd have to expect one of these now and again."

"I don't believe that," Pandora said fiercely. "You're just plain working too hard, and it's going to stop."

A little trickle of guilt worked its way in as Sweeney saw the concern. "Now, now, don't fret."

"What is it?" Michael swung through the kitchen door. "Sweeney?" He knelt down beside her and took her other hand.

"Now look at all this commotion." Mentally she leaped up and kicked her heels. "It's nothing but one of my little spells. The doctor said I'd have to watch for them. Just a nuisance, that's all." She looked hard at Charles when he came in. Eventually she looked hard enough so that he remembered his cue.

"And you know what he said."

"Now, Charles—"

"You're to have two or three days of bed rest."

Pleased that he'd remembered his lines, Sweeney pretended to huff. "Pack of nonsense. I'll be right as rain in a few minutes. I've dinner to cook."

"You won't be cooking anything." In a way Sweeney considered properly masterful, Michael picked her up. "Into bed with you."

"Just who'll take care of things?" Sweeney demanded. "I'll not have Charles spreading his germs around my kitchen."

Michael was nearly out of the room with Sweeney before Charles remembered the next step. He coughed into his hand, looked apologetic and coughed again.

"Listen to that!" Pleased, Sweeney let her head rest against Michael's shoulder. "I won't go to bed and let him infect my kitchen."

"How long have you had that cough?" Pandora demanded. When Charles began to mutter, she stood up. "That's enough. Both of you into bed. Michael and I will take care of everything." Taking Charles's arm, she began to lead him into the servants' wing. "Into bed and no nonsense. I'll make both of you some tea. Michael, see that Charles gets settled, I'll look after Sweeney."

Within a half hour, Sweeney had them both where she wanted them. Together.

"Well, they're all settled in and there's no fever." Satisfied, Pandora poured herself a cup of tea. "I suppose all they need is a few days' rest and some pampering. Tea?"

He made a face at the idea and switched on the coffee. "Since the days of house calls are over, I'd think they'd be better off here in bed than being dragged into town. We can take turns keeping an eye on them."

"Mmm-hmm." Pandora opened the refrigerator and studied. "What about meals? Can you cook?"

"Sure." Michael rattled cups in the cupboard. "Badly, but I can cook. Meat loaf's my specialty." When this was met with no enthusiasm, he turned his head. "Do you?"

"Cook?" Pandora lifted a plastic lid hopefully. "I

can broil a steak and scramble eggs. Anything else is chancy."

"Life's nothing without a risk." Michael joined her in her rummage through the refrigerator. "Here's almost half an apple cobbler."

"That's hardly a meal."

"It'll do for me." He took it out and went for a spoon. Pandora watched as he sat down at the table and dug in. "Want some?"

She started to refuse on principle, then decided not to cut off her nose. Going to the cupboard, she found a bowl. "What about the bedridden?" she asked as she scooped out cobbler.

"Soup," Michael said between bites. "Nothing better than hot soup. Though I'd let them rest awhile first."

With a nod of agreement, she sat across from him. "Michael…" She trailed off as she played with her cobbler. The steam from her tea rose up between them. She'd been thinking about how to broach the subject for days. It seemed the time had come. "I've been thinking. In two months, the will should be final. When Fitzhugh wrote us last week, he said Uncle Carlson's lawyers were advising him to drop the probate."

"So?"

"The house, along with everything else, will be half yours, half mine."

"That's right."

She took a bite of cobbler, then set down her spoon. "What're you smiling at?"

"You're nice to look at. I find it relaxing to sit here alone in the kitchen, in the quiet, and look at you."

It was that sort of thing, just that sort of thing, that left her light-headed and foolish. She stared at him a moment, then dropped her gaze to her bowl. "I wish you wouldn't say things like that."

"No, you don't. So you've been thinking," he prompted.

"Yes." She gave herself a moment, carefully spooning out another bite of cobbler. "We'll have the house between us, but we won't be living here together any longer. Sweeney and Charles will be here alone. I've worried about that for a while. Now, after this, I'm more concerned than ever. They can't stay here alone."

"No, I think you're right. Ideas?"

"I mentioned before that I was considering moving here on a semipermanent basis." She found she had no appetite after all and switched back to her tea. "I think I'm going to make it permanent all around."

He heard a trace of nervousness in her voice. "Because of Charles and Sweeney?"

"Only partly." She drank more tea, set the cup down and toyed with her cobbler again. She wasn't accustomed to discussing her decisions with anyone. Though she found it difficult, Pandora had already resolved that she had an obligation to do so. More, she'd realized she needed to talk to him, to be, as she couldn't be on other levels, honest. "I always felt the Folley was home, but I didn't realize just how much of a home. I need it, for myself. You see, I never had one." She lifted her gaze and met his. "Only here."

To say her words surprised him was to say too little. All his life he'd seen her as the pampered pet, the golden girl with every advantage. "But your parents—"

"Are wonderful," Pandora said quickly. "I adore them. There's nothing about them I'd change. But..." How could she explain? How could she not? "We never had a kitchen like this—a place you could come back

to day after day and know it'd be the same. Even if
you changed the wallpaper and the paint, it would be
the same. It sounds silly." She shifted restlessly. "You
wouldn't understand."

"Maybe I would." He caught her hand before she
could rise. "Maybe I'd like to."

"I want a home," she said simply. "The Folley's been
that to me. I want to stay here after the term's up."

He kept her hand in his, palm to palm. "Why are you
telling me this, Pandora?"

Reasons. Too many reasons. She chose the only one
she could give him safely. "In two months, the house
belongs to you as much as to me. According to the terms
of the will—"

He swore and released her hand. Rising, he stuck his
hands in his back pockets and strode to the window.
He'd thought for a moment, just for a moment, she'd
been ready to give him more. By God, he'd waited long
enough for only a few drops more. There'd been something in her voice, something soft and giving. Perhaps
he'd just imagined it because he'd wanted to hear it.
Terms of the will, he thought. It was so like her to see
nothing else.

"What do you want, my permission?"

Disturbed, Pandora stayed at the table. "I suppose I
wanted you to understand and agree."

"Fine."

"You needn't be so curt about it. After all, you
haven't any plans to use the house on a regular basis."

"I haven't made any plans," he murmured. "Perhaps
it's time I did."

"I didn't mean to annoy you."

He turned slowly, then just as slowly smiled. "No,

I'm sure you didn't. There's never any doubt when you annoy me intentionally."

There was something wrong here, something she couldn't quite pinpoint. So she groped. "Would you mind so much if I were to live here?"

It surprised him when she rose to come to him, offering a hand. She didn't make such gestures often or casually. "No, why should it?"

"It would be half yours."

"We could draw a line down the middle."

"That might be awkward. I could buy you out."

"No."

He said it so fiercely, her brows shot up. "It was only an offer."

"Forget it." He turned to look for soup.

Pandora stood back a moment, watching his back, the tension in the muscles. "Michael…" With a sigh, she wrapped her arms around his waist. She felt him stiffen, but didn't realize it was from surprise. "I seem to be saying all the wrong things. Maybe I have an easier time when we snap at each other than when I try to be considerate."

"Maybe we both do." He turned to frame her face with his hands. For a moment they looked like friends, like lovers. "Pandora…." Could he tell her he found it impossible to think about leaving her or her leaving him? Would she understand if he told her he wanted to go on living with her, being with her? How could she possibly take in the fact that he'd been in love with her for years when he was just becoming able to accept it himself? Instead he kissed her forehead. "Let's make soup."

* * *

They couldn't work together without friction, but they discovered over the next few days that they could work together. They cooked meals, washed up, dusted furniture while the servants stayed in bed or sat, bundled up, on sofas drinking tea. True, there were times when Sweeney itched to get up and be about her business, or when Charles suffered pangs of conscience, but they were convinced they were doing their duty. Both servants felt justified when they heard laughter drift through the house.

Michael wasn't sure there had been another time in his life when he'd been so content. He was, in essence, playing house, something he'd never had the time or inclination for. He would write for hours, closed off in his office, wrapped up in plots and characters and what-ifs. Then he could break away and reality was the scent of cooking or furniture polish. He had a home, a woman, and was determined to keep them.

Late in the afternoon, he always laid a fire in the parlor. After dinner they had coffee there, sometimes quietly, sometimes during a hard-fought game of rummy. It seemed ordinary, Michael admitted. It was ordinary, unless you added Pandora. He was just setting fire to the kindling when Bruno raced into the room and upset a table. Knickknacks went flying.

"We're going to have to send you to charm school," Michael declared as he rose to deal with the rubble. Though it had been just over a month, Bruno had nearly doubled in size already. He was, without a doubt, going to grow into his paws. After righting the table, he saw the dog wiggling its way under a sofa. "What've you got there?"

Besides being large, Bruno had already earned a reputation as a clever thief. Just the day before, they'd lost a slab of pork chops. "All right, you devil, if that's tonight's chicken, you're going into solitary confinement in the garage." Getting down on all fours, Michael looked under the couch. It wasn't chicken the dog was gnawing noisily on, but Michael's shoe.

"Damn!" Michael made a grab but the dog backed out of reach and kept on chewing. "That shoe's worth five times what you are, you overgrown mutt. Give it here." Flattening, Michael scooted halfway under the sofa. Bruno merely dragged the shoe away again, enjoying the game.

"Oh, how sweet." Pandora walked into the parlor and eyed Michael from the waist down. He did, she decided, indeed have some redeeming qualities. "Are you playing with the dog, Michael, or dusting under the sofa?"

"I'm going to make a rug out of him."

"Dear, dear, we sound a little cross this evening. Bruno, here baby." Carrying the shoe like a trophy, Bruno squirmed out from under the couch and pranced over to her. "Is this what you were after?" Pandora held up the shoe while petting Bruno with her other hand. "How clever of you to teach Bruno to fetch."

Michael pulled himself up, then yanked the shoe out of her hand. It was unfortunately wet and covered with teeth marks. "That's the second shoe he's ruined. And he didn't even have the courtesy to take both from one pair."

She looked down at what had been creamy Italian leather. "You never wear anything but tennis shoes or boots anyway."

Michael slapped the shoe against his palm. Bruno, tongue lolling, grinned up at him. "Obedience school."

"Oh, Michael, we can't send our child away." She patted his cheek. "It's just a phase."

"This phase has cost me two pairs of shoes, my dinner and we never did find that sweater he dragged off."

"You shouldn't drop your clothes on the floor," Pandora said easily. "And that sweater was already ratty. I'm sure Bruno thought it was a rag."

"He never chews up anything of yours."

Pandora smiled. "No, he doesn't, does he?"

Michael gave her a long look. "Just what're you so happy about?"

"I had a phone call this afternoon."

Michael saw the excitement in her eyes and decided the issue of the shoe could wait. "And?"

"From Jacob Morison."

"The producer?"

"*The* producer," Pandora repeated. She'd promised herself she wouldn't overreact, but the excitement threatened to burst inside her. "He's going to be filming a new movie. Jessica Wainwright's starring."

Jessica Wainwright, Michael mused. Grande dame of the theater and the screen. Eccentric and brilliant, her career had spanned two generations. "She's retired. Wainwright hasn't made a film in five years."

"She's making this one. Billy Mitchell's directing."

Michael tilted his head in consideration as he studied Pandora's face. It made him think of the cat and the canary. "Sounds like they're pulling out all the stops."

"She plays a half-mad reclusive countess who's dragged back to reality by a visit from her granddaughter. Cass Barkley's on the point of signing for the part of the granddaughter."

"Oscar material. Now, are you going to tell me why Morison called you?"

"Wainwright's an admirer of my work. She wants me to design all her jewelry for the movie. All!" After an attempt to sound businesslike, Pandora laughed and did a quick spin. "Morison said the only way he could talk her out of retirement was to promise her the best. She wants me."

Michael grabbed her close and spun her around. Bruno raced around the room barking and shaking tables. "We'll celebrate," he decided. "Champagne with our fried chicken."

Pandora held on tight. "I feel like an idiot."

"Why?"

"I've always thought I was, well, beyond star adoration. I'm a professional." Bubbling with excitement, she clung to Michael. "While I was talking to Morison I told myself it was a great career opportunity, a wonderful chance to express myself in a large way. Then I hung up and all I could think was Jessica Wainwright! A Morison production! I felt as silly as any bubble-headed fan."

"Proves you're not half the snob you think you are." Michael cut off her retort with a kiss. "I'm proud of you," he murmured.

That threw her off. All of her pleasure in the assignment was dwarfed by that one sentence. No one but Jolley had ever been proud of her. Her parents loved her, patted her head and told her to do what she wanted. Pride was a valued addition to affection. "Really?"

Surprised, Michael drew her back and kissed her again. "Of course I am."

"But you've never thought much of my work."

"No, that's not true. I've never understood why people feel the need to deck themselves out in bangles, or why you seemed content to design on such a small scale. But as far as your work goes I'm not blind, Pandora. Some of it's beautiful, some of it's extraordinary and some of it's incomprehensible. But it's all imaginative and expertly crafted."

"Well." She let out a long breath. "This is a red-letter day. I always thought you felt I was playing with beads because I didn't want to face a real job. You even said so once."

He grinned. "Only because it made you furious. You're spectacular to look at when you're furious."

She thought about it a moment, then let out a sigh. "I suppose this is the best time to tell you."

He tensed, but forced his voice to come calmly. "To tell me what?"

"I watch the Emmy Awards every time you're nominated."

Tension flowed out in a laugh. There'd been guilt in every syllable. "What?"

"Every time," Pandora repeated, amazed that her cheeks were warm. "It made me feel good to watch you win. And…" She paused to clear her throat. "I've watched a few episodes of *Logan's Run*."

Michael wondered if she realized she sounded as though she was confessing a major social flaw. "Why?"

"Uncle Jolley was always going on about it; I'd even hear it discussed at parties. So I thought I'd see for myself. Naturally, it was just a matter of intellectual curiosity."

"Naturally. And?"

She moved her shoulders. "Of its kind—"

He stopped that line of response by twisting her ear. "Some people only tell the truth under duress."

"All right." Half laughing, she reached to free herself. "It's good!" she shouted when he held on. "I liked it."

"Why?"

"Michael, that hurts!"

"We have ways of making you talk."

"I liked it because the characters are genuine, the plots are intelligent. And—" she had to swallow hard on this one "—it has style."

When he let go of her ear to kiss her soundly, she gave him a halfhearted shove. "If you repeat that to anyone, I'll deny it."

"It'll be our little secret." He kissed her again, not so playfully.

Pandora was almost becoming used to the sensation of having her muscles loosen and feeling as if her bones were dissolving. She moved closer, delighting in the feeling of having her body mold against his. When his heart thudded, she felt the pulse inside herself. When his tiny moan escaped, she tasted it on her tongue. When the need leaped forward, she saw it in his eyes.

She pressed her mouth to his again and let her own hunger rule. There would be consequences. Hadn't she already accepted it? There would be pain. She was already braced for it. She couldn't stop what would happen in the weeks ahead, but she could direct what would happen tonight and perhaps tomorrow. It had to be enough. Everything she felt, wanted, feared, went into the kiss.

It left him reeling. She was often passionate, wildly so. She was often demanding, erotically so. But he'd never felt such pure emotion from her. There was a softness under the strength, a request under the urgency. He drew her closer, more gently than was his habit, and let her take what she wanted.

Her head tilted back, inviting, luring. His grip tightened. His fingers wound into her hair and were lost in the richness of it. He felt the need catapult through his body so that he was tense against her sudden, unexpected yielding. She never submitted, and until that moment he hadn't known how stirring it could be to have her do so. Without a thought to time and place, they lowered to the sofa.

Because she was pliant, he was tender. Because he was gentle, she was patient. In a way they'd never experienced, they made love without rush, without fire, without the whirlwind. Thoroughly, they gave to each other. A touch, a taste, a murmured request, a whispered answer. The fire sizzled gently behind them as night fell outside the windows. Fingers brushed, lips skimmed so that they learned the power of quiet arousal. Though they'd been lovers for weeks, they brought love to passion for the first time.

The room was quiet, the light dim. If she'd never looked for romance, it found her there, wrapped easily in Michael's arms. Closer they came, but comfortably. Deeper they dived, but lazily. As they came together, Pandora felt her firm line of independence crack to let him in. But the weakness she'd expected didn't follow. Only contentment.

It was contentment that followed her into that quick and final burst of pleasure.

They were still wrapped together, half dozing, when the phone rang. With a murmur of complaint, Michael reached over his head to the table and lifted the receiver.

"Hello."

"Michael Donahue, please."

"Yeah, this is Michael."

"Michael, it's Penny."

He rubbed a hand over his eyes as he tried to put a face with the name. Penny—the little blonde in the apartment next to his. Wanted to be a model. He remembered vaguely leaving her the number of the Folley in case something important was delivered to his apartment. "Hi." He watched Pandora's eyes flutter open.

"Michael, I hate to do this, but I had to call. I've already phoned the police. They're on their way."

"Police?" He struggled into a half-sitting position. "What's going on?"

"You've been robbed."

"What?" He sat bolt upright, nearly dumping Pandora on the floor. "When?"

"I'm not sure. I got home a few minutes ago and noticed your door wasn't closed all the way. I thought maybe you'd come back so I knocked. Anyway, I pushed the door open a bit. The place was turned upside down. I came right over here and called the cops. They asked me to contact you and told me not to go back over."

"Thanks." Dozens of questions ran through his mind but there was no one to answer them. "Look, I'll try to come in tonight."

"Okay. Hey, Michael, I'm really sorry."

"Yeah. I'll see you."

"Michael?" Pandora grabbed his hand as soon as he hung up the receiver.

"Somebody broke into my apartment."

"Oh no." She'd known the peace couldn't last. "Do you think it was—"

"I don't know." He dragged a hand through his hair. "Maybe. Or maybe it was someone who noticed no one had been home for a while."

She felt the anger in him but knew she couldn't soothe it. "You've got to go."

Nodding, he took her hand. "Come with me."

"Michael, one of us has to be here with Sweeney and Charles."

"I'm not leaving you alone."

"You have to go," she repeated. "If it was one of the family, maybe you can find something to prove it. In any case, you have to see to this. I'll be fine."

"Just like the last time I was away."

Pandora lifted a brow. "I'm not incompetent, Michael."

"But you'll be alone."

"I have Bruno. Don't give me that look," she ordered. "He may not be ferocious, but he certainly knows how to bark. I'll lock every door and window."

He shook his head. "Not good enough."

"All right, we'll call the local police. They have Fitzhugh's report about trespassers. We'll explain that I'm going to be alone for the night and ask them to keep an eye on the place."

"Better." But he rose to pace. "If this is a setup..."

"Then we're prepared for it this time."

Michael hesitated, thought it through, then nodded. "I'll call the police."

## Chapter Ten

The moment Michael left, Pandora turned the heavy bolt on the main door. Though it had taken them the better part of an hour, she was grateful he'd insisted on checking all the doors and windows with her. The house, with Pandora safely in it, was locked up tight.

It was entirely too quiet.

In defense, Pandora went to the kitchen and began rattling pots and pans. She had to be alone, but she didn't have to be idle. She wanted to be with Michael, to stand by him when he faced the break-in of his apartment. Was it as frustrating for him to go on alone, she wondered, as it was for her to stay behind? It couldn't be helped. There were two old people in the house who couldn't be left. And they needed to eat.

The chicken was to have been a joint effort and a respite from the haphazard meals they'd managed to date. Michael had claimed to know at least the basics of deep frying. While he'd volunteered to deal with the chicken, she'd been assigned to try her hand at mashing potatoes. She'd thought competition if nothing else would have improved the end result.

Pandora resigned herself to a solo and decided the effort of cooking would keep her mind off fresh trouble. Needing company, she switched on the tuner on the kitchen wall unit and fiddled with the dial until she found a country-music station. Dolly Parton bubbled out brightly. Satisfied, she pulled one of Sweeney's cookbooks from the shelf and began to search the index. Fried chicken went on picnics, she mused. How much trouble could it be?

She had two counters crowded and splattered, and flour up to her wrists when the phone rang. Using a dishcloth, Pandora plucked the receiver from the kitchen extension. Her foot was tapping to a catchy rendition of "On the Road Again."

"Hello."

"Pandora McVie?"

Her mind on more immediate matters, Pandora stretched the cord to the counter and picked up a drumstick. "Yes."

"Listen carefully."

"Can you speak up?" Tongue caught between her teeth, Pandora dipped the drumstick in her flour mixture. "I can't hear you very well."

"I have to warn you and there's not much time. You're in danger. You're not safe in that house, not alone."

The cookbook slid to the floor and landed on her foot. "What? Who is this?"

"Just listen. You're alone because it was arranged. Someone's going to try to break in tonight."

"Someone?" She shifted the phone and listened hard. It wasn't malice she detected, but nervousness. Whoever was on the other end was as shaky as she was. She was certain—almost certain—it was a man's voice. "If you're trying to frighten me—"

"I'm trying to warn you. When I found out…" Already low and indistinct, the voice became hesitant. "You shouldn't have sent the champagne. I don't like what's going on, but it won't stop. No one was going to be hurt, do you understand? But I'm afraid of what might happen next."

Pandora felt fear curl in her stomach. Outside the kitchen windows it was dark, pitch-dark. She was alone in the house with two old, sick servants. "If you're afraid, tell me who you are. Help me stop what's going on."

"I'm already risking everything by warning you. You don't understand. Get out, just get out of the house."

It was a ploy, she told herself. A ploy to make her leave. Pandora straightened her shoulders, but her gaze shifted from blank window to blank window. "I'm not going anywhere. If you want to help, tell me who I should be afraid of."

"Just get out," the voice repeated before the line went dead.

Pandora stood holding the silent receiver. The oil in the fryer had begun to sizzle, competing with the radio. Watching the windows, listening, she hung up the phone. It was a trick, she told herself. It was only a trick to get her out of the house in hopes she'd be frightened enough to stay out. She wouldn't be shooed away by a quivering voice on the telephone.

Besides, Michael had already called the police. They knew she was alone in the house. At the first sign of trouble, she only had to pick up the phone.

Her hands weren't completely steady, but she went back to cooking with a vengeance. She slipped coated chicken into the fryer, tested the potatoes she had cooking, then decided a little glass of wine while she worked was an excellent idea. She was pouring it when Bruno raced into the room to run around her feet.

"Bruno." Pandora crouched and gathered the dog close. He felt warm, solid. "I'm glad you're here," she murmured. But for a moment, she allowed herself to wish desperately for Michael.

Bruno licked her face, made a couple of clumsy leaps toward the counter, then dashed to the door. Jumping up against it, he began to bark.

"Now?" Pandora demanded. "I don't suppose you could wait until morning."

Bruno raced back to Pandora, circled her then raced back to the door. When he'd gone through the routine three times, she relented. The phone call had been no more than a trick, a clumsy one at that. Besides, she told herself as she turned the lock, it wouldn't hurt to open the door and take a good look outside.

The moment she opened it, Bruno jumped out and tumbled into the snow. He began to sniff busily while Pandora stood shivering in the opening and straining her eyes against the dark. Music and the smells of cooking poured out behind her.

There was nothing. She hugged herself against the cold and decided she hadn't expected to see anything.

The snow was settled, the stars bright and the woods quiet. It was as it should have been; a very ordinary evening in the country. She took a deep breath of winter air and started to call the dog back. They saw the movement at the edge of the woods at the same time.

Just a shadow, it seemed to separate slowly from a tree and take on its own shape. A human shape. Before Pandora could react, Bruno began to bark and plow through the snow.

"No, Bruno! Come back." Without giving herself a chance to think, Pandora grabbed the old pea coat that hung beside the door and threw it on. As an afterthought, she reached for a cast-iron skillet before bolting through the door after her dog. "Bruno!"

He was already at the edge of the woods and hot on the trail. Picking up confidence as she went, Pandora raced in pursuit. Whoever had been watching the house had run at the sight of the clumsy, overgrown puppy. She'd found she was susceptible to fear, but she refused to be frightened by a coward. With as much enthusiasm as Bruno, Pandora sprinted into the woods. Out of breath and feeling indestructible, she paused long enough to look around and listen. For a moment there was nothing, then off to the right, she heard barking and thrashing.

"Get 'em, Bruno!" she shouted, and headed toward the chaos. Excited by the chase, she called encouragement to the dog, changing direction when she heard his answering bark. As she ran, snow dropped from the branches to slide cold and wet down the back of her neck. The barking grew wilder, and in her rush, Pandora fell headlong over a downed tree. Spitting out snow and swearing, she struggled to her knees. Bruno bounded out of the woods and sent her sprawling again.

"Not me." Flat on her back, Pandora shoved at the dog. "Dammit, Bruno, if you don't—" She broke off when the dog stiffened and began to growl. Sprawled on the snow, Pandora looked up and saw the shadow move through the trees. She forgot she was too proud to fear a coward.

Though her hands were numb from cold, she gripped the handle of the skillet and, standing, inched her way along toward the nearest tree. Struggling to keep her breathing quiet, she braced herself for attack and defense. Relative or stranger, she'd hold her own. But her knees were shaking. Bruno tensed and hurled himself forward. The moment he did, Pandora lifted the skillet high and prepared to swing.

"What the hell's going on?"

"Michael!" The skillet landed in the snow with a plop as she followed Bruno's lead and hurled herself forward. Giddy with relief, she plastered kisses over Michael's face. "Oh, Michael, I'm so glad it's you."

"Yeah. You sure looked pleased when you were hefting that skillet. Run out of hair spray?"

"It was handy." Abruptly she drew back and glared at him. "Dammit, Michael, you scared me to death. You're supposed to be halfway to New York, not skulking around the woods."

"And you're supposed to be locked in the house."

"I would've been if you hadn't been skulking in the woods. Why?"

In an offhanded gesture, he brushed snow from her face. "I got ten miles away, and I couldn't get rid of this bad feeling. It was too pat. I decided to stop at a gas station and phone my neighbor."

"But your apartment."

"I talked to the police, gave them a list of my valuables. We'll both run into New York in a day or two." Snow was scattered through her hair and matted to her coat. He thought of what might have happened and resisted the urge to shake her. "I couldn't leave you alone."

"I'm going to start believing you're chivalrous after all." She kissed him. "That explains why you're not in New York, but what were you doing in the woods?"

"Just a hunch." He bent to retrieve the frying pan. A good whack with that, he discovered, and he'd have been down for the count.

"The next time you have a hunch, don't stand at the edge of the woods and stare at the house."

"I wasn't." Michael took her arm and headed back toward the house. He wanted her inside again, behind locked doors.

"I saw you."

"I don't know who you saw." Disgusted, Michael looked back at the dog. "But if you hadn't let the dog out we'd both know. I decided to check around outside before coming in, and I saw footprints. I followed them around, then cut into the woods." He glanced over his shoulder, still tight with tension. "I was just coming up behind whoever made them when Bruno tried his attack. I started chasing." He swore and slapped a palm against the skillet. "I was gaining when this hound ran between my legs and sent me face first into the snow. About that time, you started yelling at the dog. Whoever I was chasing had enough time to disappear."

Pandora swore and kicked at the snow. "If you'd let

me know what was going on, we could've worked together."

"I didn't know what was going on until it was already happening. In any case, the deal was you'd stay inside with the doors locked."

"The dog had to go out," Pandora muttered. "And I had this phone call." She looked back over her shoulder and sighed. "Someone called to warn me."

"Who?"

"I don't know. I thought it was a man's voice, but— I'm just not sure."

Michael's hand tightened on her arm. "Did he threaten you?"

"No, no it wasn't like a threat. Whoever it was certainly seemed to know what's been going on and isn't happy about it. That much was clear. He—she said someone was going to try to break into the Folley, and I should get out."

"And, of course, you handled that by running into the woods with a skillet. Pandora." This time he did shake her. "Why didn't you call the police?"

"Because I thought it was another trick and it made me mad." She sent Michael a stubborn look. "Yes, it frightened me at first, then it just plain made me mad. I don't like intimidation. When I looked out and saw someone near the woods, I only wanted to fight back."

"Admirable," he said but took her shoulders. "Stupid."

"You were doing the same thing."

"It's not the same thing. You've got brains, you've got style. I'll even give you guts. But, cousin, you're not a heavyweight. What if you'd caught up with whoever was out there and they wanted to play rough?"

"I can play rough, too," Pandora muttered.

"Fine." With a quick move, he hooked a foot behind hers and sent her bottom first into the snow. She didn't have the opportunity to complain before he was standing over her, gesturing with the skillet. Bruno decided it was a game and leaped on top of her. "I might've come back tomorrow and found you half-buried in the snow." Before she could speak, he hauled her to her feet again. "I'm not risking that."

"You caught me off balance," she began.

"Shut up." He had her by the shoulders again, and this time his grip wasn't gentle. "You're too important, Pandora, I'm through taking chances. We're going inside and calling the cops. We're going to tell them everything."

"What can they do?"

"We'll find out."

She let out a long breath, then leaned against him. The chase might have been exciting, but her knees had yet to stop shaking. "Okay, maybe you're right. We're no farther along now than when we started."

"Calling the police isn't giving up, it's just changing the odds. I might not have come back here tonight, Pandora. The dog may not have frightened anyone off. You'd have been alone." He took both her hands, pressing them to his lips and warming them. "I'm not going to let anything happen to you."

Confused by the sense of pleasure his words gave her, she tried to draw her hands away. "I can take care of myself, Michael."

He smiled but didn't let go. "Maybe. But you're not going to have the chance to find out. Let's go home. I'm hungry."

"Typical," she began, needing to lighten the mood. "You'd think of your stomach—oh my God, the chicken!" Breaking away, Pandora loped toward the house.

"I'm not that hungry." Michael sprinted after her. The relief came again when he scooped her up into his arms. When he'd heard her shout in the woods, had realized she was outside and vulnerable, his blood had simply stopped flowing. "In fact," he said as he scooped her up, "I can think of more pressing matters than eating."

"Michael." She struggled, but laughed. "If you don't put me down, there won't be a kitchen to eat in."

"We'll eat somewhere else."

"I left the pan on. There's probably nothing left of the chicken but charred bones."

"There's always soup." With that, he pushed open the kitchen door.

Rather than a smoky, splattered mess, they found a platter piled high with crisp, brown chicken. Sweeney had wiped up the spills, and had the pans soaking in the sink.

"Sweeney." From her perch in Michael's arms, Pandora surveyed the room. "What are you doing out of bed?"

"My job," she said briskly, but gave them a quick sidelong look. As far as she was concerned, her plans were working perfectly. She imagined Pandora and Michael had decided to take a little air while dinner was cooking, and, as young people would, had forgotten the time.

"You're supposed to be in bed," Pandora reminded her.

"Posh. I've been in bed long enough." And the days

of little or no activity had nearly bored her to tears. It was worth it, however, to see Pandora snug in Michael's arms. "Feeling fit as a fiddle now, I promise you. Wash up for dinner."

Michael and Pandora each took separate and careful studies. Sweeney's cheeks were pink and round, her eyes bright. She bustled from counter to counter in her old businesslike fashion. "We still want you to take it easy," Michael decided. "No heavy work."

"That's right. Michael and I'll take care of the washing up." She saw him scowl, just a little, and patted his shoulder. "We like to do it."

At Michael and Pandora's insistence, all four ate in the kitchen. Charles, sitting next to Sweeney, was left uncertain how much he should cough and settled on a middle road, clearing his throat every so often. In an unspoken agreement, Pandora and Michael decided to keep the matter of trespassers to themselves. Both of them felt the announcement that someone was watching the house would be too upsetting for the two old people while they were recuperating.

On the surface, dinner was an easy meal, but Pandora kept wondering how soon they could nudge the servants along to bed and contact the police. More than once, Pandora caught Sweeney looking from her to Michael with a smug smile. Sweet old lady, Pandora mused, innocently believing the cook to be pleased to have her kitchen back. It made Pandora only more determined to protect her and Charles from any unpleasantness. She concentrated on cleaning up and packing them off to bed, and it was nearly nine before she was able to meet Michael in the parlor.

"Settled?"

She heard the familiar restlessness in his voice and merely nodded, pouring a brandy. "It's a bit like cajoling children, but I managed to find a Cary Grant movie that interested them." She sipped the brandy, waiting for her muscles to relax with it. "I'd rather be watching it myself."

"Another time." Michael took a sip from her snifter. "I've called the police. They'll be here shortly."

She took the glass back. "It still bothers me to take the business to outsiders. After all, anything beyond simple trespass is speculation."

"We'll let the police speculate."

She managed to smile. "Your Logan always handles things on his own."

"Someone told me once that that was just fiction." He poured himself a brandy and toasted her. "I discovered I don't like having you in the middle of a story line."

The brandy and firelight gave the evening an illusion of normalcy. Pandora took his statement with a shrug. "You seem to have developed a protect-the-woman syndrome, Michael. It's not like you."

"Maybe not." He tossed back a gulp. "It's different when it's my woman."

She turned, brow lifted. It was ridiculous to feel pleasure at such a foolish and possessive term. "Yours?"

"Mine." He cupped the back of her neck with his hand. "Got a problem with that?"

Her heart beat steadily in her throat until she managed to swallow. Maybe he meant it—now. In a few months when he was back moving in his own world, with his own people, she'd be no more than his somewhat annoying cousin. But for now, just for now, maybe he meant it. "I'm not sure."

"Give it some thought," he advised before he lowered his mouth to hers. "We'll come back to it."

He left her flustered and went to answer the door.

When he returned, Pandora was sitting calmly enough in a high-backed chair near the fire. "Lieutenant Randall, Pandora McVie."

"How d'you do?" The lieutenant pulled off a wool muffler and stuck it in his coat pocket. He looked, Pandora thought, like someone's grandfather. Comfy, round and balding. "Miserable night," he announced, and situated himself near the fire.

"Would you like some coffee, Lieutenant?"

Randall gave Pandora a grateful look. "Love it."

"Please, have a seat. I'll be back in a minute."

She took her time heating coffee and arranging cups and saucers on a tray. Not putting off, Pandora insisted, just preparing. She'd never had occasion to talk to a policeman on any subject more complex than a parking ticket. She'd come out on the short end on that one. Now, she was about to discuss her family and her relationship with Michael.

Her relationship with Michael, she thought again as she fussed with the sugar bowl. That's what really had her hiding in the kitchen. She hadn't yet been able to dull the feeling that had raced through her when he'd called her his woman. Adolescent, Pandora told herself. It was absolutely absurd to feel giddy and self-satisfied and unnerved because a man had looked at her with passion in his eyes.

But they'd been Michael's eyes.

She found linen napkins and folded them into triangles. She didn't want to be anyone's woman but her own. It had been the strain and excitement of the evening that had made her react like a sixteen-year-old being offered a school ring. She was an adult; she was self-sustaining. She was in love. Talk yourself out of that one, Pandora challenged herself. Taking a long breath, she hefted the tray and went back to the parlor.

"Gentlemen." Pandora set the tray on a low table and stuck on a smile. "Cream and sugar, Lieutenant?"

"Thanks. A healthy dose of both." He set a dog-eared notepad on his knee when Pandora handed him a cup. "Mr. Donahue's been filling me in. Seems you've had a few annoyances."

She smiled at the term. Like his looks, his voice was comfortable. "A few."

"I'm not going to lecture." But he gave them both a stern look. "Still, you should've notified the police after the first incident. Vandalism's a crime."

"We'd hoped by ignoring it, it would discourage repetition." Pandora lifted her cup. "We were wrong."

"I'll need to take the champagne with me." Again, he sent them a look of disapproval. "Even though you've had it analyzed, we'll want to run it through our own lab."

"I'll get it for you." Michael rose and left them alone.

"Miss McVie, from what your cousin tells me, the terms of Mr. McVie's will were a bit unconventional."

"A bit."

"He also tells me he talked you into agreeing to them."

"That's Michael's fantasy, Lieutenant." She sipped her coffee. "I'm doing exactly what I chose to do."

Randall nodded and noted. "You agree with Mr. Donahue's idea that these incidents are connected and one of your relatives is responsible."

"I can't think of any reason to disagree."

"Do you have any reason to suspect one more than another?"

Pandora thought it through as she'd thought it through before. "No. You see, we're not at all a close family. The truth is I don't know any of them very well."

"Except Mr. Donahue."

"That's right. Michael and I often visited our uncle, and we ran into each other here at the Folley." Whether we wanted to or not, she added to herself in her own private joke. "None of the others came by very often."

"The champagne, Lieutenant." Michael brought in the box. "And the report from Sanfield Laboratories."

Randall skimmed the printout, then tucked the sheet into the box. "Your uncle's attorney..." He referred quickly to his notes. "Fitzhugh reported trespassing several weeks ago. We've had a squad car cruise the area, but at this point you might agree to having a man patrol the grounds once a day."

"I'd prefer it," Michael told him.

"I'll contact Fitzhugh." Seeing his cup was empty, Pandora took it and filled it again. "I'll also need a list of the relatives named in the will."

Pandora frowned over her rim. Between her and Michael, they tried to fill in the lieutenant, as best as they could. When they had finished, Pandora sent Randall an apologetic look. "I told you we aren't close."

"I'll get the lawyer to fill in the details." Randall rose and tried not to think about the cold drive back to town. "We'll keep the inquiries as quiet as possible. If anything else happens, call me. One of my men will be around to look things over."

"Thank you, Lieutenant." Michael helped the pudgy man on with his coat.

Randall took another look around the room. "Ever think of installing a security system?"

"No."

"Think again," he advised, and made his way out.

"We've just been scolded," Pandora murmured.

Michael wondered if *Logan's Run* had room for a cranky, well-padded cop. "Seems that way."

"You know, Michael, I have two schools of thought on bringing in the police."

"Which are?"

"It's either going to calm things down or stir things up."

"You pay your money and take your choice."

She gave him a knowing look. "You're counting on the second."

"I came close tonight." He bypassed the coffee and poured another brandy. "I nearly had my hands on something. Someone." When he looked at her, the faint amusement in his eyes had faded. The recklessness was back. "I like my fights in the open, face-to-face."

"It's better if we look at it as a chess game rather than a boxing match." She came close to wrap her arms around him and press her cheek to his shoulder. It was the kind of gesture he didn't think he'd ever get used to from her. As he rested his head on her hair, he realized that the fact that he wouldn't only added to the sweetness of the feeling. When had he stopped remembering that she didn't fit into his long-established picture of the ideal woman? Her hair was too red, her body too thin, her tongue too sharp. Michael nuzzled against her and found they fit very well.

"I've never had the patience for chess."

"Then we'll just leave it to the police." She held him tighter. The need to protect rose as sharply as the desire to be protected. "I've been thinking about what might have happened out there tonight. I don't want you hurt, Michael."

With two fingers under her chin, he lifted it. "Why not?"

"Because..." She looked into his eyes and felt her heart melt. But she wouldn't be a fool; she wouldn't risk her pride. "Because then I'd have to do the dishes by myself."

He smiled. No, he didn't have a great deal of patience, but he could call on it when circumstances warranted. He brushed a kiss on either side of her mouth. Sooner or later, he'd have more out of her. Then he'd just have to decide what to do with it. "Any other reason?"

Absorbing the sensations, Pandora searched her mind for another easy answer. "If you were hurt, you couldn't work. I'd have to live with your foul temper."

"I thought you were already living with it."

"I've seen it fouler."

He kissed her eyes closed in his slow, sensuous way. "Try one more time."

"I care." She opened her eyes, and her look was tense and defiant. "Got a problem with that?"

"No." His kiss wasn't gentle this time, it wasn't patient. He had her caught close and reeling within moments. If there was tension in her still, he couldn't feel it. "The only problem's been dragging it out of you."

"You're family after all—"

With a laugh, he nipped the lobe of her ear. "Don't try to back out."

Indignant, she stiffened. "I never back out."

"Unless you can rationalize it. Just remember this." He had her molded against him again. "The family connection's distant." Their lips met, urgently, then parted. "This connection isn't."

"I don't know what you want from me," she whispered.

"You're usually so quick."

"Don't joke, Michael."

"It's no joke." He drew her away, holding her by the shoulders. Briefly, firmly, he ran his hands down to her elbows, then back. "No, I'm not going to spell it out for you, Pandora. I'm not going to make it easy on you. You have to be willing to admit we both want the same thing. And you will."

"Arrogant," she warned.

"Confident," he corrected. He had to be, or he'd be on his knees begging. There'd come a time, he'd promised himself, when she'd drop the last of her restrictions. "I want you."

A tremor skipped up her spine. "I know."

"Yeah." He linked his fingers with hers. "I think you do."

# Chapter Eleven

Winter raged its way through February. There came a point when Pandora had to shovel her way from the house to her workshop. She found herself grateful for the physical labor. Winter was a long quiet time that provided too many hours to think.

In using this time, Pandora came to several uncomfortable realizations. Her life, as she'd known it, as she'd guided it, would never be the same. As far as her art was concerned, she felt the months of concentrated effort with dashes of excitement had only improved her crafting. In truth, she often used her jewelry to take her mind off what was happening to and around her. When that didn't work, she used what was happening to and around her in her work.

The sudden blunt understanding that her health, even her life, had been endangered made her take a step away from her usual practical outlook. It caused her to appreciate little things she'd always taken for granted. Waking up in a warm bed, watching snow fall while a fire crackled beside her. She'd learned that every second in life was vital.

Already she was considering taking a day to drive back to New York and pack what was important to her. More than packing, it would be a time of decision making. What she kept, what she didn't, would in some ways reflect the changes she'd accepted in herself.

Both the lease on her apartment and the lease on the shop over the boutique were coming up for renewal. She'd let them lapse. Rather than living alone, she'd have the company and the responsibility of her uncle's old servants. Though she'd once been determined to be responsible only to herself and her art, Pandora made the choice without a qualm. Though she had lived in the city, in the rush, in the crowds, she'd isolated herself. No more.

Through it all wove Michael.

In a few short weeks, what they had now would be over. The long winter they'd shared would be something to think of during other winters. As she prepared for a new and different life, Pandora promised herself she'd have no regrets. But she couldn't stop herself from having wishes. Things were already changing.

The police had come, and with their arrival had been more questions. Everything in her shop had to be locked up tightly after dark, and there were no more solitary walks in the woods after a snowfall. It had become a nightly ritual to go through the Folley and check doors and windows that had once been casually ignored. Often when she walked back to the house from her shop, she'd see Michael watching from the window of his room. It should have given her a warm, comfortable feeling, but she knew he was waiting for something else to happen. She knew, as she knew him, that he wanted it. Inactivity was sitting uneasily on him.

Since they'd driven into New York to deal with the break-in at his apartment, he'd been distant, with a restlessness roiling underneath. Though they both understood the wisdom of having the grounds patrolled, she thought they felt intruded upon.

They had no sense of satisfaction from the police investigation. Each one of their relatives had alibis for one or more of the incidents. So far the investigation seemed to have twin results. Since the police had been called in, nothing else had happened. There'd been no anonymous phone calls, no shadows in the woods, no bogus telegrams. It had, as Pandora had also predicted, stirred things up. She'd dealt with an irate phone call from Carlson who insisted they were using the investigation in an attempt to undermine his case against the will.

On the heels of that had come a disjointed letter from Ginger who'd had the idea that the Folley was haunted. Michael had had a two-minute phone conversation with Morgan who'd muttered about private family business, overreacting and hogwash. Biff, in his usual style, had wired a short message:

Cops and robbers? Looks like you two are playing games with each other.

From Hank they heard nothing.
The police lab had confirmed the private analysis of

the champagne; Randall was plodding through the investigation in his precise, quiet way. Michael and Pandora were exactly where they'd been weeks before: waiting.

He didn't know how she could stand it. As Michael made his way down the narrow path Pandora had shoveled, he wondered how she could remain so calm when he was ready to chew glass. It had only taken him a few days of hanging in limbo to realize it was worse when nothing happened. Waiting for someone else to make the next move was the most racking kind of torture. Until he was sure Pandora was safe, he couldn't relax. Until he had his hands around someone's throat, he wouldn't be satisfied. He was caught in a trap of inactivity that was slowly driving him mad. Pausing just outside her shop, he glanced around.

The house looked big and foolish with icicles hanging and dripping from eaves, gutters and shutters. It belonged in a book, he thought, some moody, misty gothic. A fairy tale—the grim sort. Perhaps one day he'd weave a story around it himself, but for now, it was just home.

With his hands in his pockets he watched smoke puff out of chimneys. Foolish it might be, but he'd always loved it. The longer he lived in it, the surer he was that he was meant to. He was far from certain how Pandora would take his decision to remain after the term was over.

His last script for the season was done. It was the only episode to be filmed before the show wrapped until fall. He could, as he often did, take a few weeks in the early spring and find a hot, noisy beach. He could fish, relax and enjoy watching women in undersize bikinis. Michael knew he wasn't going anywhere.

For the past few days, he'd been toying with a screenplay for a feature film. He'd given it some thought before, but somehow something had always interfered. He could write it here, he knew. He could perfect it here with Pandora wielding her art nearby, criticizing his work so that he was only more determined to make it better. But he was waiting. Waiting for something else to happen, waiting to find who it was who'd used fear and intimidation to try to drive them out. And most of all, he was waiting for Pandora. Until she gave him her complete trust, willingly, until she gave him her heart unrestrictedly, he had to go on waiting.

His hands curled into fists and released. He wanted action.

He tried the door and satisfied himself that she'd kept her word and locked it from the inside. "Pandora?" He knocked with the side of his fist. She opened the door with a drill in her hand. After giving her flushed face and tousled hair a quick look, Michael lifted his hands, palms out. "I'm unarmed."

"And I'm busy." But her lips curved. There was a light of pleasure in her eyes. He found it easy to notice such small things.

"I know, I've invaded scheduled working hours, but I have a valid excuse."

"You're letting in the cold," she complained. Once, she might have shut the door in his face without a second thought. This time she shut it behind him.

"Not a hell of a lot warmer in here."

"It's fine when I'm working. Which I am."

"Blame Sweeney. She's sending me in for supplies, and she insisted I take you." He sent Pandora a bland look. "'That girl holes herself up in that shed too much. Needs some sun.'"

"I get plenty of sun," Pandora countered. Still, the idea of a drive into town appealed. It wouldn't hurt to talk to the jeweler in the little shopping center. She was beginning to think her work should spread out a bit, beyond the big cities. "I suppose we should humor her, but I want to finish up here first."

"I'm in no hurry."

"Good. Half an hour then." She went to exchange the drill for a jeweler's torch. Because she didn't hear the door open or shut, she turned and saw Michael examining her rolling mill. "Michael," she said with more than a trace of exasperation.

"Go ahead, take your time."

"Don't you have anything to do?"

"Not a thing," he said cheerfully.

"Not one car chase to write?"

"No. Besides, I've never seen you work."

"Audiences make me cranky."

"Broaden your horizons, love. Pretend I'm an apprentice."

"I'm not sure they can get that broad."

Undaunted, he pointed to her worktable. "What is that thing?"

"This thing," she began tightly, "is a pendant. A waterfall effect made with brass wire and some scraps of silver I had left over from a bracelet."

"No waste," he murmured. "Practical as ever. So what's the next step?"

With a long breath, she decided it would be simpler to play along than to throw him out. "I've just finished adjusting the curves of the wires. I've used different thicknesses and lengths to give it a free-flowing effect. The silver scraps I've cut and filed into elongated teardrops. Now I solder them onto the ends of the wires."

She applied the flux, shifting a bit so that he could watch. After she'd put a square of solder beside each wire, she used the torch to apply heat until the solder melted. Patient, competent, she repeated the procedure until all twelve teardrops were attached.

"Looks easy enough," he mused.

"A child of five could do it."

He heard the sarcasm and laughed as he took her hands. "You want flattery? A few minutes ago I saw a pile of metal. Now I see an intriguing ornament. Ornate and exotic."

"It's supposed to be exotic," Pandora replied. "Jessica Wainwright will wear it in the film. It's to have been a gift from an old lover. The countess claims he was a Turkish prince."

Michael studied the necklace again. "Very appropriate."

"It'll droop down from brass and silver wires twisted together. The lowest teardrop should hang nearly to her waist." Pleased, but knowing better than to touch the metal before the solder cooled, Pandora held up her sketch. "Ms. Wainwright was very specific. She wants nothing ordinary, nothing even classic. Everything she wears should add to the character's mystique."

She set the sketch down and tidied her tools. She'd solder on the hoop and fashion the neck wire when they returned from town. Then if there was time, she'd begin the next project. The gold-plated peacock pin with its three-inch filigree tail would take her the better part of two weeks.

"This thing has potential as a murder weapon," Michael mused, picking up a burnisher to examine the curved, steel tip.

"I beg your pardon?"

He liked the way she said it, so that even with her back turned she was looking down her nose. "For a story line."

"Leave my tools out of your stories." Pandora took the burnisher from him and packed it away. "Going to buy me lunch in town?" She stripped off her apron then grabbed her coat.

"I was going to ask you the same thing."

"I asked first." She locked the shop and welcomed the cold. "The snow's beginning to melt."

"In a few weeks, the five dozen bulbs Jolley planted during his gardening stage will be starting to bloom."

"Daffodils," she murmured. It didn't seem possible when you felt the air, saw the mounds of snow, but spring was closing in. "The winter hasn't seemed so long."

"No, it hasn't." He slipped an arm around her shoulders. "I never expected six months to go so quickly. I figured one of us would've attempted murder by this time."

With a laugh, Pandora matched her step to his. "We've still got a month to go."

"Now we have to behave ourselves," he reminded her. "Lieutenant Randall has his eye on us."

"I guess we blew our chance." She turned to wind her arms around his neck. "There have been times I've wanted to hit you with a blunt instrument."

"Feeling's mutual," he told her as he lowered his mouth. Her lips were cool and curved.

At the side window, Sweeney drew back the drape. "Look at this!" Cackling, she gestured to Charles. "I told you it would work. In a few more weeks, I'll be putting bells on a wedding cake."

As Charles joined Sweeney at the window, Pandora scooped a hand into the snow and tossed it in Michael's face. "Don't count your chickens," he muttered.

In a desperate move to avoid retaliation, Pandora raced to the garage. She ducked seconds before snow splattered against the door. "Your aim's still off, cousin." Hefting the door, she sprinted inside and jumped into his car. Smug, she settled into the seat. He wouldn't, she was sure, mar his spotless interior with a snowball. Michael opened the door, slid in beside her and dumped snow over her head. She was still squealing when he turned the key.

"I'm better at close range."

Pandora sputtered as she wiped at the snow. Because she'd appreciated the move, it was difficult to sound indignant. "One would have thought that a man who drives an ostentatious car would be more particular with it."

"It's only ostentatious if you buy it for status purposes."

"And, of course, you didn't."

"I bought it because it gets terrific gas mileage." When she snorted, he turned to grin at her. "And because it looks great wrapped around redheads."

"And blondes and brunettes."

"Redheads," he corrected, twining her hair around his finger. "I've developed a preference."

It shouldn't have made her smile, but it did. She was still smiling when they started down the long, curvy road. "We can't complain about the road crews," she said idly. "Except for those two weeks last month, the roads've been fairly clear." She glanced toward the mounds of snow the plows had pushed to the side of the road.

"Too bad they won't do the driveway."

"You know you loved riding that little tractor. Uncle Jolley always said it made him feel tough and macho."

"So much so he'd race it like a madman over the yard."

As they came to a curve, Michael eased on the brake and downshifted. Pandora leaned forward and fiddled with the stereo. "Most people have equipment like this in their den."

"I don't have a den."

"You don't have a stereo to put in one, either," she remembered. "Or a television."

He shrugged, but mentally listed what he'd lost from his apartment. "Insurance'll cover it."

"The police are handling that as though it were a normal break-in." She switched channels. "It might've been."

"Or it might've been a smoke screen. I wish we—" He broke off as they approached another curve. He'd pressed the brake again, but this time, the pedal had gone uselessly to the floor.

"Michael, if you're trying to impress me with your skill as a driver, it's not working." Instinctively Pandora grabbed the door handle as the car careered down the curve.

Whipping the steering wheel with one hand, Michael yanked on the emergency brake. The car continued to barrel down. He gripped the wheel in both hands and fought the next curve. "No brakes." As he told her, Michael glanced down to see the speedometer hover at seventy.

Pandora's knuckles turned white on the handle. "We won't make it to the bottom without them."

He never considered lying. "No." Tires squealed as he rounded the next curve. Gravel spit under the wheels as the car went wide. There was the scrape and scream of metal as the fender kissed the guardrail.

She looked at the winding road spinning in front of her. Her vision blurred then cleared. The sign before the S-turn cautioned for a safe speed of thirty. Michael took it at seventy-five. Pandora shut her eyes. When she opened them and saw the snowbank dead ahead, she screamed. With seconds to spare, Michael yanked the car around. Snow flew skyward as the car skidded along the bank.

Eyes intense, Michael stared at the road ahead and struggled to anticipate each curve. Sweat beaded on his forehead. He knew the road, that's what terrified him. In less than three miles, the already sharp incline steepened. At high speed, the car would ram straight through the guardrail and crash on the cliffs below. The game Jolley had begun would end violently.

Michael tasted his own fear, then swallowed it. "There's only one chance; we've got to turn off on the lane leading into the old inn. It's coming up after that curve." He couldn't take his eyes from the road to look at her. His fingers dug into the wheel. "Hang on."

She was going to die. Her mind was numb from the thought of it. She heard the tires scream as Michael dragged at the wheel. The car tilted, nearly going over. She saw trees rush by as the car slid on the slippery edge of the lane. Almost, for an instant, the rubber seemed to grip the gravel beneath. But the turn was too sharp, the speed too fast. Out of control, the car spiraled toward the trees.

"I love you," she whispered, and grabbed for him before the world went black.

He came to slowly. He hurt, and for a time didn't understand why. There was noise. Eventually he turned his head toward it. When he opened his eyes, Michael saw a boy with wide eyes and black hair gawking through the window.

"Mister, hey, mister. You okay?"

Dazed, Michael pushed open the door. "Get help," he managed, fighting against blacking out again. He took deep gulps of air to clear his head as the boy dashed off through the woods. "Pandora." Fear broke through the fog. In seconds, he was leaning over her.

His fingers shook as he reached for the pulse of her neck, but he found it. Blood from a cut on her forehead ran down her face and onto his hands. With his fingers pressed against the wound, he fumbled in the glove compartment for the first-aid kit. He'd stopped the bleeding and was checking her for broken bones when she moaned. He had to stop himself from dragging her against him and holding on.

"Take it easy," he murmured when she began to stir. "Don't move around." When she opened her eyes, he saw they were glazed and unfocused. "You're all right." Gently he cupped her face in his hands and continued to reassure her. Her eyes focused gradually. As they did, she reached for his hand.

"The brakes...."

"Yeah." He rested his cheek against hers a moment. "It was a hell of a trip, but it looks like we made it."

Confused, she looked around. The car was stopped, leaning drunkenly against a tree. It had been the deep, slushy snow that had slowed them down enough to prevent the crash from being fatal. "We—you're all right?" The tears started when she reached out and took his face in her hands as he had with hers. "You're all right."

"Terrific." His wrist throbbed like a jackhammer and his head ached unbelievably, but he was alive. When she started to move, he held her still. "No, don't move around. I don't know how badly you're hurt. There was a kid. He's gone for help."

"It's just my head." She started to take his hand, and saw the blood. "Oh God, you're bleeding. Where?" Before she could begin her frantic search, he gripped her hands together.

"It's not me. It's you. Your head's cut. You probably have a concussion."

Shaky, she lifted her hand and touched the bandage. The wound beneath it hurt, but she drew on that. If she hurt, she was alive. "I thought I was dead." She closed her eyes but tears slipped through the lashes. "I thought we were both dead."

"We're both fine." They heard the siren wail up the mountain road. He was silent until she opened her eyes again. "You know what happened?"

Her head ached badly, but it was clear. "Attempted murder."

He nodded, not turning when the ambulance pulled into the slushy lane. "I'm through waiting, Pandora. I'm through waiting all around."

* * *

Lieutenant Randall found Michael in the emergency-room lounge. He unwrapped his muffler, unbuttoned his coat and sat down on the hard wooden bench. "Looks like you've had some trouble."

"Big time."

Randall nodded toward the Ace bandage on Michael's wrist. "Bad?"

"Just a sprain. Few cuts and bruises and a hell of a headache. Last time I saw it, my car looked something like an accordion."

"We're taking it in. Anything we should look for?"

"Brake lines. It seemed I didn't have any when I started the trip down the mountain."

"When's the last time you used your car?" Randall had his notepad in hand.

"Ten days, two weeks." Wearily, Michael rubbed a temple. "I drove into New York to talk to police about the robbery in my apartment."

"Where do you keep your car?"

"In the garage."

"Locked?"

"The garage?" Michael kept his eye on the hallway where Pandora had been wheeled away. "No. My uncle had installed one of those remote control devices a few years back. Never worked unless you turned on the television. Anyway, he took it out again and never replaced the lock. Pandora's car's in there," he remembered suddenly. "If—"

"We'll check it out," Randall said easily. "Miss McVie was with you?"

"Yeah, she's with a doctor." For the first time in weeks, Michael found himself craving a cigarette. "Her head was cut." He looked down at his hands and remembered her blood on them. "I'm going to find out who did this, Lieutenant, and then I'm going to—"

"Don't say anything to me I might have to use later," Randall warned. There were some people who threatened as a means to let off steam or relieve tension. Randall didn't think Michael Donahue was one of them. "Let me do my job, Mr. Donahue."

Michael gave him a long, steady look. "Someone's been playing games, deadly ones, with someone very important to me. If you were in my place, would you twiddle your thumbs and wait?"

Randall smiled, just a little. "You know, Donahue, I never miss your show. Great entertainment. Some of this business sounds just like one of your shows."

"Like one of my shows," Michael repeated slowly.

"Problem is, things don't work the same way out here in the world as they do on television. But it sure is a pleasure to watch. Here comes your lady."

Michael sprang up and headed for her.

"I'm fine," she told him before he could ask.

"Not entirely." Behind her a young, white coated doctor stood impatiently. "Miss McVie has a concussion."

"He put a few stitches in my head and wants to hold me prisoner." She gave the doctor a sweet smile and linked arms with Michael. "Let's go home."

"Just a minute." Keeping her beside him, Michael turned to the doctor. "You want her in the hospital?"

"Michael—"

"Shut up."

"Anyone suffering from a concussion should be routinely checked. Miss McVie would be wise to remain overnight with professional care."

"I'm not staying in the hospital because I have a bump on the head. Good afternoon, Lieutenant."

"Miss McVie."

Lifting her chin, she looked back at the doctor. "Now, Doctor…"

"Barnhouse."

"Dr. Barnhouse," she began. "I will take your advice to a point. I'll rest, avoid stress. At the first sign of nausea or dizziness, I'll be on your doorstep. I can assure you, now that you've convinced Michael I'm an invalid, I'll be properly smothered and hovered over. You'll have to be satisfied with that."

Far from satisfied, the doctor directed himself to Michael. "I can't force her to stay, of course."

Michael lifted a brow. "If you think I can, you've got a lot to learn about women."

Resigned, Barnhouse turned back to Pandora. "I want to see you in a week, sooner if any of the symptoms we discussed show up. You're to rest for twenty-four hours. That means horizontally."

"Yes, Doctor." She offered a hand, which he took grudgingly. "You were very gentle. Thank you."

His lips twitched. "A week," he repeated and strode back down the hall.

"If I didn't know better," Michael mused, "I'd say he wanted to keep you here just to look at you."

"Of course. I look stunning with blood running down my face and a hole in my head."

"I thought so." He kissed her cheek, but used the gesture to get a closer look at her wound. The stitches were small and neat, disappearing into her hairline. After counting six of them, his determination iced. "Come on, we'll go home so I can start pampering you."

"I'll take you myself." Randall gestured toward the door. "I might as well look around a bit while I'm there."

Sweeney clucked like a mother hen and had Pandora bundled into bed five minutes after she'd walked in the door. If she'd had the strength, Pandora would have argued for form's sake. Instead she let herself be tucked under a comforter, fed soup and sweet tea, and fussed over. Though the doctor had assured her it was perfectly safe to sleep, she thought of the old wives' tale and struggled to stay awake. Armed with a sketch pad and pencil, she whiled away the time designing. But when she began to tire of that, she began to think.

Murder. It would have been nothing less than murder. Murder for gain, she mused, an impossible thing for her to understand. She'd told herself before that her life was threatened, but somehow it had seemed remote. She had only to touch her own forehead now to prove just how direct it had become.

An uncle, a cousin, an aunt? Which one wanted Jolley's fortune so badly to murder for it? Not for the first time, Pandora wished she knew them better, understood them better. She realized she'd simply followed Jolley's lead and dismissed them as boring.

And that was true enough, Pandora assured herself. She'd been to a party or two with all of them. Monroe would huff, Biff would preen, Ginger would prattle, and so on. But boring or not, one of them had slipped over the line of civilized behavior. And they were willing to step over her to do it. Slowly, from memory, she began to sketch each of her relatives. Perhaps that way, she'd see something that was buried in her subconscious.

When Michael came in, she had sketches lined in rows over her spread. "Quite a rogues' gallery."

He'd come straight from the garage, where he and Randall had found the still-wet brake fluid on the concrete. Not all of it, Michael mused. Whoever had tampered with the brakes had left enough fluid in so that the car would react normally for the first few miles. And then, nothing. Michael had already concluded that the police would find a hole in the lines. Just as they'd find one in the lines of Pandora's, to match the dark puddle beneath her car. It had been every bit as lethal as his.

He wasn't ready to tell Pandora that whoever had tried to kill them had been as close as the garage a day, perhaps two, before. Instead he looked at her sketches.

"What do you see?" she demanded.

"That you have tremendous talent and should give serious thought to painting."

"I mean in their faces." Impatient with herself, she drew her legs up Indian style. "There's just nothing there. No spark, no streak of anything that tells me this one's capable of killing."

"Anyone's capable of killing. Oh yes," Michael added when she opened her mouth to disagree. "Anyone. It's simply that the motive has to fit the personality, the circumstances, the need. When a person's threatened, he kills. For some it's only when their lives or the lives of someone they love are threatened."

"That's entirely different."

"No." He sat on the bed. "It's a matter of different degrees. Some people kill because their home is threatened, their possessions. Some kill because a desire is threatened. Wealth, power, those are very strong desires.

"So a very ordinary, even conventional person might kill to achieve that desire."

He gestured to her sketches. "One of them tried. Aunt Patience with her round little face and myopic eyes."

"You can't seriously believe—"

"She's devoted to Morgan, obsessively so. She's never married. Why? Because she's always taken care of him."

He picked up the next sketch. "Or there's Morgan himself, stout, blunt, hard-nosed. He thought Jolley was mad and a nuisance."

"They all did."

"Exactly. Carlson, straitlaced, humorless, and Jolley's only surviving son."

"He tried contesting the will."

"Going the conventional route. Still, he knew his father was shrewd, perhaps better than anyone. Who's to say he wouldn't cover his bases in a more direct way? Biff…" He had a laugh as he looked at the sketch. Pandora had drawn him precisely as he was. Self-absorbed.

"I can't see him getting his hands dirty."

"For a slice of a hundred fifty million? I can. Pretty little Ginger. One wonders if she can possibly be as sweet and spacey as she appears. And Hank." Pandora had drawn him with his arm muscle flexed. "Would he settle for a couple of thousand when he could have millions?"

"I don't know—that's just the point." Pandora shuffled the sketches. "Even when I have them all lined up in front of me, I don't know."

"Lined up," Michael murmured. "Maybe that is the answer. I think it's time we had a nice, family party."

"Party? You don't mean actually invite them all here."

"It's perfect."

"They won't come."

"Oh yes, they will." He was already thinking ahead. "You can bank on it. A little hint that things aren't going well around here, and they'll jump at the chance to give us an extra push. You see the doctor in a week. If he gives you a clean bill of health, we're going to start a little game of our own."

"What game?"

"In a week," he repeated, and took her face in his hands. It was narrow, dominated by the mop of hair and sharp eyes. Not beautiful, but special. It had taken him a long time to admit it. "A bit pale."

"I'm always pale with a concussion. Are you going to pamper me?"

"At least." But his smile faded as he gathered her close. "Oh God, I thought I'd lost you."

The trace of desperation in his voice urged her to soothe. "We'd both have been lost if you hadn't handled the car so well." She snuggled into his shoulder. It was real and solid, like the one she'd sometimes imagined leaning on. It wouldn't hurt, just this once, to pretend it would always be there. "I never thought we'd walk away from that one."

"But we did." He drew back to look at her. She looked tired and drawn, but he knew her will was as strong as ever. "And now we're going to talk about what you said to me right before we crashed."

"Wasn't I screaming?"

"No."

"If I criticized your driving, I apologize."

He tightened his grip on her chin. "You told me you loved me." He watched her mouth fall open in genuine surprise. Some men might have been insulted. Michael could bless his sense of humor. "It could technically be called a deathbed confession."

Had she? She could only remember reaching for him in those last seconds, knowing they were about to die together. "I was hysterical," she began, and tried to draw back.

"It didn't sound like raving to me."

"Michael, you heard Dr. Barnhouse. I'm not supposed to have any stress. If you want to be helpful, see about some more tea."

"I've something better for relaxing the muscles and soothing the nerves." He laid her back against the pillows, sliding down with her. Sweetly, tenderly, he ran his lips down the lines of her cheekbones. "I want to hear you tell me again, here."

"Michael—"

"No, lie back." And his hands, gentle and calm, stilled her. "I need to touch you, just touch you. There's plenty of time for the rest."

He was so kind, so patient. More than once she'd wondered how such a restive, volatile man could have such comforting hands. Taking off only his shoes, he slipped into bed with her. He held her in the crook of his arm and stroked until he felt her sigh of relief. "I'm going to take care of you," he murmured. "When you're well, we'll take care of each other."

"I'll be fine tomorrow." But her voice was thick and sleepy.

"Sure you will." He'd keep her in bed another twenty-four hours if he had to chain her. "You haven't told me again. Are you in love with me, Pandora?"

She was so tired, so drained. It seemed she'd reached a point where she could fight nothing. "What if I am?" She managed to tilt her head back to stare at him. His fingers rubbed gently at her temple, easing even the dull echo of pain. "People fall in and out of love all the time."

"People." He lowered his head so that he could just skim her lips with his. "Not Pandora. It infuriates you, doesn't it?"

She wanted to glare but closed her eyes instead. "Yes. I'm doing my best to reverse the situation."

He snuggled down beside her, content for now. She loved him. He still had time to make her like the idea. "Let me know how it works out," he said, and lulled her to sleep.

# Chapter Twelve

Michael studied the dark stains on the garage floor with a kind of grim fascination. Draining the brake fluid from an intended victim's car was a hackneyed device, one expected from time to time on any self-respecting action-adventure show. Viewers and readers alike developed a certain fondness for old, reliable angles in the same way they appreciated the new and different. Though it took on a different picture when it became personal, the car careering out of control down a steep mountain road was as old as the Model T.

He'd used it himself, just as he'd used the anonymous gift of champagne. And the bogus-telegram routine, he mused as an idea began to stir. Just last season one of *Logan's* heroines of the week had been locked in a cellar—left in the dark after going to investigate a window slamming in the wind. It too was a classic. Each and every one of the ploys used against himself and Pandora could have been lifted from one of his own plots. Randall had pointed it out, though he'd been joking. It didn't seem very funny.

Michael cursed himself, knowing he should have seen the pattern before. Perhaps he hadn't simply because it had been a pattern, a trite one by Hollywood standards. Whether it was accidental or planned, Michael decided he wasn't about to be outplotted. He'd make his next move taking a page from the classic mystery novels. Going into the house, Michael went to the phone and began to structure his scene.

He was just completing his last call when Pandora came down the hall toward him. "Michael, you've got to do something about Sweeney."

Michael leaned back against the newel post and studied her. She looked wonderful—rested, healthy and annoyed. "Isn't it time for your afternoon nap?"

"That's just what I'm talking about." The annoyance deepened between her brows and pleased him. "I don't need an afternoon nap. It's been over a week since the accident." She pulled a leather thong out of her hair and began to run it through her fingers. "I've seen the doctor, and he said I was fine."

"I thought it was more something along the lines of you having a head like a rock."

She narrowed her eyes. "He was annoyed because I healed perfectly without him. The point is, I am healed, but if Sweeney keeps nagging and hovering, I'll have a relapse." It came out as a declaration as she stood straight in front of him, chin lifted, looking as though she'd never been ill a day in her life.

"What would you like me to do?"

"She'll listen to you. For some reason she has the idea that you're infallible. Mr. Donahue this, Mr. Donahue that." She slapped the leather against her palm. "For the past week all I've heard is how charming, handsome and strong you are. It's a wonder I recovered at all."

His lips twitched, but he understood Sweeney's flattery could undo any progress he'd made. "The woman's perceptive. However…" He stopped Pandora's retort by holding up a hand. "Because I'd never refuse you anything—" when she snorted he ignored it "—and because she's been driving me crazy fussing over my wrist, I'm going to take care of it."

Pandora tilted her head. "How?"

"Sweeney's going to be too busy over the next few days to fuss over us. She'll have the dinner party to fuss over."

"What dinner party?"

"The dinner party we're going to give next week for all our relatives."

She glanced at the phone, remembering he'd been using it when she'd come down the hall. "What have you been up to?"

"Just setting the scene, cousin." He rocked back on his heels, already imagining. "I think we'll have Sweeney dig out the best china, though I doubt we'll have time to use it."

"Michael." She didn't want to seem a coward, but the accident had taught her something about caution and self-preservation. "We won't just be inviting relatives. One of them tried to kill us."

"And failed." He took her chin in his hand. "Don't you think he'll try again, Pandora, and again? The police can't patrol the grounds indefinitely. And," he added with his fingers tightening, "I'm not willing to let bygones be bygones." His gaze skimmed up to where her hair just covered the scar on her forehead. The doctor had said it would fade, but Michael's memory of it never would. "We're going to settle this, my way."

"I don't like it."

"Pandora." He gave her a charming smile and pinched her cheek. "Trust me."

The fact that she did only made her more nervous. With a sigh, she took his hand. "Let's tell Sweeney to kill the fatted calf."


Right down to the moment the first car arrived, Pandora was certain no one would come. She'd sat through a discussion of Michael's plan, argued, disagreed, admired and ultimately she'd given up. Theatrics, she'd decided. But there was enough Jolley in her to look forward to the show, especially when she was one of the leads. And she had, as they said in the business, her part cold.

She'd dressed for the role in a slim, strapless black dress. For flair, she'd added a sterling silver necklace she'd fashioned in an exaggerated star burst. Matching earrings dripped nearly to her chin. If Michael wanted drama, who was she to argue? As the night of the dinner party had grown closer, her nerves had steeled into determination.

When he saw her at the top of the stairs, he was speechless. Had he really convinced himself all these years she had no real beauty? At the moment, poised, defiant and enjoying herself, she made every other woman he'd known look like a shadow. And if he told her so, she wouldn't believe it for a moment. Instead he merely nodded and rocked back on his heels.

"Perfect," he told her as she walked down the main stairs. Standing at the base in a dark suit, Michael looked invincible, and ruthless. "The sophisticated heroine." He took her hand. "Cool and sexy. Hitchcock would've made you a star."

"Don't forget what happened to Janet Leigh."

He laughed and sent one of her earrings spinning. "Nervous?"

"Not as much as I'd thought I'd be. If this doesn't work—"

"Then we're no worse off than we are now. You know what to do."

"We've rehearsed it a half-dozen times. I still have the bruises."

He leaned closer to kiss both bare shoulders. "I always thought you'd be a natural. When this is over, we have a scene of our own to finish. No, don't pull back," he warned as she attempted to. "It's too late to pull back." They stood close, nearly mouth to mouth. "It's been too late all along."

Nerves she'd managed to quell came racing back, but they had nothing to do with plots or plans. "You're being dramatic."

With a nod, he tangled his fingers in her hair. "My sense of drama, your streak of practicality. An interesting combination."

"An uneasy one."

"If life's too easy you sleep through it," Michael decided. "It sounds like the first of our guests are arriving," he murmured as they heard the sound of a car. He kissed her briefly. "Break a leg."

She wrinkled her nose at his back. "That's what I'm afraid of."

Within a half hour, everyone who had been at the reading of the will, except Fitzhugh, was again in the library. No one seemed any more relaxed than they'd been almost six months before. Jolley beamed down on them from the oil painting. From time to time Pandora glanced up at it almost expecting him to wink. To give everyone what they'd come for, Pandora and Michael kept arguing about whatever came to mind. Time for the game to begin, she decided.

Carlson stood with his wife near a bookshelf. He looked cross and impatient and glowered when Pandora approached.

"Uncle Carlson, I'm so glad you could make it. We don't see nearly enough of each other."

"Don't soft-soap me." He swirled his scotch but didn't drink. "If you've got the idea you can talk me out of contesting this absurd will, you're mistaken."

"I wouldn't dream of it. Fitzhugh tells me you don't have a chance." She smiled beautifully. "But I have to agree the will's absurd, especially after being forced to live in the same house with Michael all these months." She ran a finger down one of the long, flattened prongs of her necklace. "I'll tell you, Uncle Carlson, there have been times I've seriously considered throwing in the towel. He's done everything possible to make the six months unbearable. Once he pretended his mother was ill, and he had to go to California. Next thing I knew I was locked in the basement. Childish games," she muttered sending Michael a look of utter dislike. Out of the corner of her eye, she saw Carlson take a quick, nervous drink. "Well, the sentence is nearly up." She turned back with a fresh smile. "I'm so glad we could have this little celebration. Michael's finally going to open a bottle of champagne he's been hoarding since Christmas."

Pandora watched Carlson's wife drop her glass on the Turkish carpet. "Dear me," Pandora said softly. "We'll have to get something to mop that up. Freshen your drink?"

"No, she's fine." Carlson took his wife by the elbow. "Excuse me."

As they moved away, Pandora felt a quick thrill of excitement. So, it had been Carlson.

"I quit smoking about six months ago," Michael told Hank and his wife, earning healthy approval.

"You'll never regret it," Hank stated in his slow, deliberate way. "You're responsible for your own body."

"I've been giving that a lot of thought lately," Michael said dryly. "But living with Pandora the past few months hasn't made it easy. She's made this past winter miserable. She had someone send me a fake telegram so I'd go flying off to California thinking my mother was ill." He glanced over his shoulder and scowled at Pandora's back.

"If you've gotten through six months without smoking…" Meg began, guiding the conversation back to Michael's health.

"It's a miracle I have living with that woman. But it's almost over." He grinned at Hank. "We're having champagne instead of carrot juice for dinner. I've been saving this bottle since Christmas for just the right occasion."

He saw Hank's fingers whiten around his glass of Perrier and Meg's color drain. "We don't—" Hank looked helplessly at Meg. "We don't drink."

"Champagne isn't drinking," Michael said jovially. "It's celebrating. Excuse me." He moved to the bar as if to freshen his drink and waited for Pandora to join him. "It's Hank."

"No." She added a splash of vermouth to her glass. "It's Carlson." Following the script, she glared at him. "You're an insufferable bore, Michael. Putting up with you isn't worth any amount of money."

"Intellectual snob." He toasted her. "I'm counting the days."

With a sweep of her skirts, Pandora walked over to Ginger. "I don't know how I manage to hold my temper with that man."

Ginger checked her face in a pretty silver compact. "I've always thought he was kind of cute."

"You haven't had to live with him. We were hardly together a week when he broke into my workshop and vandalized it. Then he tried to pass the whole thing off as the work of a vagrant."

Ginger frowned and touched a bit of powder to her nose. "It didn't seem like something he'd do to me. I told—" She caught herself and looked back at Pandora with a vague smile. "Those are pretty earrings."

Michael steeled himself to listen to Morgan's terse opinion on the stock market. The moment he found an opening, he broke in. "Once everything's settled, I'll have to come to you for advice. I've been thinking about getting more actively involved with one of Jolley's chemical firms. There's a lot of money in fertilizer—and pesticides." He watched Patience flutter her hands and subside at a glare from Morgan.

"Software," Morgan said briefly.

Michael only smiled. "I'll look into it."

Pandora tried unsuccessfully to pump Ginger. The five-minute conversation left her suspicious, confused and with the beginnings of a headache. She decided to try her luck on Biff.

"You're looking well." She smiled at him and nodded at his wife.

"You're looking a bit pale, cousin."

"The past six months haven't been a picnic." She cast a look at Michael. "Of course, you've always detested him."

"Of course," Biff said amiably.

"I've yet to discover why Uncle Jolley was fond of him. Besides being a bore, Michael has an affection for odd practical jokes. He got a tremendous kick out of locking me in the cellar."

Biff smiled into his glass. "He's never quite been in our class."

Pandora bit her tongue, then agreed. "Do you know, he even called me one night, disguising his voice. He tried to frighten me by saying someone was trying to kill me."

Biff's brows drew together as he stared into Pandora's eyes. "Odd."

"Well, things are almost settled. By the way, did you enjoy the champagne I sent you?"

Biff's fingers froze on his glass. "Champagne?"

"Right after Christmas."

"Oh yes." He lifted his glass again, studying her as he drank. "So it was you."

"I got the idea when someone sent Michael a bottle at Christmastime. He promises to finally open it tonight. Excuse me, I want to check on dinner."

Her eyes met Michael's briefly as she slipped from

the room. They'd set his scene, she thought. Now she had to move the action along. In the kitchen she found Sweeney finishing up the final preparation for the meal.

"If they're hungry," Sweeney began, "they'll just have to wait ten minutes."

"Sweeney, it's time to turn off the main power switch."

"I know, I know. I was just finishing this ham."

Sweeney had been instructed to, at Pandora's signal, go down to the cellar, turn off the power, then wait exactly one minute and turn it on again. She had been skeptical about the whole of Michael and Pandora's plan but had finally agreed to participate in it. Wiping her hands on her apron, the cook went to the cellar door. Pandora took a deep breath and walked back to the library.

Michael had positioned himself near the desk. He gave Pandora the slightest of nods when she entered. "Dinner in ten minutes," she announced brightly as she swept across the room.

"That gives us just enough time." Michael took the stage and couldn't resist starting with a tried and true line. He didn't have to see Pandora to know she was taking her position. "You all must be wondering why we brought you here tonight." He lifted his glass and looked from one face to the next. "One of you is a murderer."

On cue, the lights went out and pandemonium struck. Glasses shattered, women screamed, a table was overturned. When the lights blinked on, everyone froze. Lying half under the desk, facedown, was Pandora. Beside her was a letter opener with a curved, ornate hilt and blood on the blade. In an instant Michael was beside her, lifting her into his arms before anyone had a chance to react. Silently, he carried her from the room. Several minutes passed before he returned, alone. He gazed, hot and hard, at every face in the room.

"A murderer," he repeated. "She's dead."

"What do you mean she's dead?" Carlson pushed his way forward. "What kind of game is this? Let's have a look at her."

"No one's touching her." Michael effectively blocked his way. "No one's touching anything or leaving this room until the police get here."

"Police?" Pale and shaken, Carlson glanced around. "We don't want that. We'll have to handle this ourselves. She's just fainted."

"Her blood's all over this," Michael commented gesturing to the bloodstained letter opener.

"No!" Meg pushed forward until she'd broken through the crowd around the desk. "No one was supposed to be hurt. Only frightened. It wasn't supposed to be like this. Hank." She reached out, then buried her face against his chest.

"We were only going to play some tricks," he murmured.

"First degree murder isn't a trick."

"We never—" He looked at Michael in shock. "Not murder," he managed, holding Meg as tightly as she was holding him.

"You didn't want to drink the champagne, either, did you, Hank?"

"That's when I wanted to stop." Still sobbing, Meg turned in her husband's arms. "I even called and tried to warn her. I thought it was wrong all along, just a mean trick, but we needed money. The gym's drained everything we have. We thought if we could make the two of you angry enough with each other, you'd break the terms of the will. But that's all. Hank and I stayed in the cabin and waited. Then he went into Pandora's shop and turned things upside down. If she thought you did it—"

"I never thought she would," Ginger piped up. Two tears rolled down her cheeks. "Really, it all seemed silly and—exciting."

Michael looked at his pretty, weeping cousin. "So you were part of it."

"Well, I didn't really do anything. But when Aunt Patience explained it to me…"

"Patience?" There were patterns and patterns. A new one emerged.

"Morgan deserved his share." The old woman wrung her hands and looked everywhere but at the blood-stained letter opener. She'd thought she'd done the right thing. It all sounded so simple. "We thought we could make one of you leave, then it would all be the way it should be."

"Telegram," Morgan said, puffing wide-eyed on his cigar. "Not murder." He turned to Carlson. "Your idea."

"It's preposterous." Carlson mopped his brow with a white silk handkerchief. "The lawyers were incompetent. They haven't been able to do a thing. I was merely protecting my rights."

"With murder."

"Don't be ridiculous." He nearly sounded staid and stuffy again. "The plan was to get you out of the house. I did nothing more than lock—her—in the cellar. When I heard about the champagne, I had a doubt or two, but after all, it wasn't fatal."

"Heard about the champagne." It was what Michael had waited for. "From whom?"

"It was Biff," Meg told him. "Biff set it all up, promised nothing would go wrong."

"Just an organizer." Biff gauged the odds, then shrugged. "All's fair, cousin. Everyone in this room had their hand in." He held his up, examining it. "There's no blood on mine. I'd vote for you." He gave Michael a cool smile. "After all, it's no secret you couldn't abide each other."

"You set it up." Michael took a step closer. "There's also a matter of tampering with my car."

Biff moved his shoulders again, but Michael saw the sweat bead above his lips. "Everyone in this room had a part in it. Any of you willing to turn yourselves in?" His breath came faster as he backed away. "One of them panicked and did this. You won't find my fingerprints on that letter opener."

"When someone's attempted murder once," Michael said calmly, "it's easier to prove he tried again."

"You won't prove anything. Any of us might have drained the brake lines in your car. You can't prove I did."

"I don't need to." In a quick move, Michael caught him cleanly on the jaw and sent him reeling. Before he could fall, Michael had him by the collar. "I never said anything about draining the lines."

Feeling the trap close, Biff struck out blindly. Fists swinging, they tumbled to the floor. A Tiffany lamp shattered in a pile of color. They rolled, locked together, into a Belker table that shook from the impact. Shocked and ineffective, the rest stepped back and gave them room.

"Michael, that's quite enough." Pandora entered the

room, her hair mussed and her clothes disheveled. "We have company."

Panting, he dragged Biff to his feet. His wrist sang a bit, but he considered it a pleasure. Charles, looking dignified in his best suit, opened the library doors. "Dinner is served."

Two hours later, Pandora and Michael shared a small feast in the library. "I never thought it would work," Pandora said over a mouthful of ham. "It shouldn't have."

"The more predictable the moves, the more predictable the end."

"Lieutenant Randall didn't seem too pleased."

"He wanted to do it his way." Michael moved his shoulders. "Since he'd already discovered Biff had been visiting other members of the family and making calls to them, he was bound to find out something eventually."

"The easy way." She rubbed the back of her neck. "Do you know how uncomfortable it is to play dead?"

"You were great." He leaned over to kiss her. "A star."

"The letter opener with the stage blood was a nice touch. Still, if they'd all work together..."

"We already knew someone was weakening because of the warning call. Turned out that Meg had had enough."

"I've been thinking about investing in their gym."

"It wouldn't hurt."

"What do you think's going to happen?"

"Oh, Carlson'll get off more or less along with the rest of them, excluding Biff. I don't think we have to worry about going to court over the will. As for our dear cousin—" Michael lifted a glass of champagne "—he's going to be facing tougher charges than malicious mischief or burglary. I may never get my television back, but he isn't going to be wearing any Brooks Brothers suits for a while. Only prison blues."

"You gave him another black eye," Pandora mused.

"Yeah." With a grin, Michael drank the wine. "Now you and I only have to cruise through the next two weeks."

"Then it's over."

"No." He took her hand before she could rise. "Then it begins." He slipped the glass from her other hand and pressed her back against the cushions. "How long?"

Pandora struggled to keep the tension from showing. "How long what?"

"Have you been in love with me?"

She jerked, then was frustrated when he held her back. "I'm not sitting here feeding your ego."

"All right, we'll start with me." He leaned back companionably and boxed her in. "I think I fell in love with you when you came back from the Canary Islands and walked into the parlor. You had legs all the way to your waist and you looked down your nose at me. I've never been the same."

"I've had enough games, Michael," she said stiffly.

"So've I." He traced a finger down her cheek. "You said you loved me, Pandora."

"Under duress."

"Then I'll just have to keep you under duress because I'm not giving you up now. Why don't we get married right here?"

She'd started to give him a hefty shove and stopped with her hands pressed against his chest. "What?"

"Right here in the library." He glanced around, ignoring the overturned tables and broken china. "It'd be a nice touch."

"I don't know what you're talking about."

"It's very simple. Here's the plot. You love me, I love you."

"That's not simple," she managed. "I've just been accessible. Once you get back to your blond dancers and busty starlets, you'll—"

"What blond dancers? I can't stand blond dancers."

"Michael, this isn't anything I can joke about."

"Just wait. You buy a nice white dress, maybe a veil. A veil would suit you. We get a minister, lots of flowers and have a very traditional marriage ceremony. After that, we settle into the Folley, each pursuing our respective careers. In a year, two at the most, we give Charles and Sweeney a baby to fuss over. See?" He kissed her ear.

"People's lives aren't screenplays," she began.

"I'm crazy about you, Pandora. Look at me." He took her chin and held it so that their faces were close. "As an artist, you're supposed to be able to see below the surface. That should be easy since you've always told me I'm shallow."

"I was wrong." She wanted to believe. Her heart already did. "Michael, if you're playing games with me, I'll kill you myself."

"Games are over. I love you, it's that simple."

"Simple," she murmured, surprised she could speak at all. "You want to get married?"

"Living together's too easy."

She was more surprised that she could laugh. "Easy?"

"That's right." He shifted her until she was lying flat on the sofa, his body pressed into hers. When his mouth came down, it wasn't patient, wasn't gentle, and everything he thought, everything he felt, communicated itself through that one contact. As she did rarely, as he asked rarely, she went limp and pliant. Her arms went around him. Perhaps it was easy after all.

"I love you, Michael."

"We're getting married."

"It looks that way."

His eyes were intense when he lifted his head. "I'm going to make life tough on you, Pandora. That's just to pay you back for the fact that you'll be the most exasperating wife on record. Do we understand each other?"

Her smile bloomed slowly. "I suppose we always have."

Michael pressed a kiss to her forehead, to the tip of her nose, then to her lips. "He understood both of us."

She followed his gaze to Jolley's portrait. "Crazy old goat has us right where he wants us. I imagine he's having a good laugh." She rubbed her cheek against Michael's. "I just wish he could be here to see us married."

Michael lifted a brow. "Who says he won't be?" He pulled her up and picked up both glasses. "To Maximillian Jolley McVie."

"To Uncle Jolley." Pandora clinked her glass to Michael's. "To us."

\* \* \* \* \*

# LOVING JACK

To Kasey Michaels,
because Jackie is a heroine she'll understand.

# Chapter One

The minute Jackie saw the house, she was in love. Of course, she acknowledged, she did fall in love easily. It wasn't that she was easily impressed, she was just open, wide-open, to emotions—her own and everyone else's.

The house had a lot of emotion in it, she felt, and not all of it serene. That was good. Total serenity would have been all right for a day or two, but boredom would have closed in. She preferred the contrasts here, the strong angles and arrogant juts of the corners, softened occasionally by curving windows and unexpectedly charming archways.

The white-painted walls glittered in the sunlight, set off by stark ebony trim. Though she didn't believe the world was black-and-white, the house made the statement that the two opposing forces could live together in harmony.

The windows were wide, welcoming the view from both east and west, while skylights let in generous slices of sun. Flowers grew in profusion in the side garden and in terra-cotta pots along the terraces. She enjoyed the bold color they added, the touch of the exotic and lush. They'd have to be tended, of course—and religiously, if the heat continued and the rain didn't come. She didn't mind getting dirty, though, especially if there was a reward at the end.

Through wide glass doors she looked out at the crystalline waters of a kidney-shaped tiled pool. That, too, would require tending, but that, too, offered rewards. She could already picture herself sitting beside it, watching the sun set with the scent of flowers everywhere. Alone. That was a small hitch, but one she was willing to accept.

Beyond the pool and the sloping slice of lawn was the Intracoastal Waterway. Its waters were dark, mysterious, but even as she watched, a motorboat putted by. She discovered she liked the sound of it. It meant there were people close enough to make contact but not so close as to interfere.

The water roads reminded her of Venice and a particularly pleasant month she had spent there during her teens. She'd ridden in gondolas and flirted with dark-eyed men. Florida in the spring wasn't as romantic as Italy, but it suited her just fine.

"I love it." She turned back to the wide, sun-washed room. There were twin sofas the color of oatmeal on a steel-blue carpet. The rest of the furniture was an elegant ebony and leaned toward the masculine. Jackie approved of its strength and style. She rarely wasted her time looking for flaws and was willing to accept them when they jumped out at her. But in this house and everything about it she saw perfection.

She beamed at the man standing casually in front of the white marble fireplace. The hearth had been cleaned and swept and was a home for a potted fern. The man's tropical-looking white pants and shirt might have been chosen for precisely that pose. Knowing Frederick Q. MacNamara as she did, Jackie was sure it had been.

"When can I move in?"

Fred's smile lit up his round, boyish face. No one looking at it would have been reminded of a shark. "That's our Jack, always going on impulse." His body was rounded, too—not quite fat, but not really firm, either. Fred's favorite exercise was hailing—cabs or waiters. He moved toward her with a languid grace that had once been feigned but was now second nature. "You haven't even seen the second floor."

"I'll see it when I unpack."

"Jack, I want you to be sure." He patted her cheek—older, more experienced cousin to young scatterbrain. She didn't take offense. "I'd hate for you to regret this in a day or two. After all, you're proposing to live in this house by yourself for three months."

"I've got to live somewhere." She gestured, palm out, with a hand as slim and delicate as the rest of her. Gold and colored stones glittered on four fingers, a sign of her love of the pretty. "If I'm going to be serious about writing, I should be alone. Since I don't think I'd care for a garret, why shouldn't it be here?"

She paused a moment. It never paid to be too casual with Fred, cousin or not. Not that she didn't like him. Jackie had always had a soft spot for Fred, though she

knew he had a habit of skimming off the top and dealing from the bottom.

"You're sure it's all right for you to sublet it to me?"

"Perfectly." His voice was as smooth as his face.
Whatever wrinkles Fred had were carefully camou-
flaged. "The owner only uses it as a winter home, and
then only sporadically. He prefers having someone in
residence rather than leaving it empty. I told Nathan I'd
take care of things until November, but then this business in San Diego came up, and it can't be put off. You
know how it is, darling."

Jackie knew exactly how it was. With Fred, "sudden business" usually meant he was avoiding either a
jealous husband or the law. Despite his unprepossess-
ing looks, he had constant problems with the former,
and not even a prepossessing family name could always
protect him from the latter.

She should have been warier, but Jackie wasn't always wise, and the house—the look, the feel, of it—had
already blinded her.

"If the owner wants it occupied, I'm happy to accommodate him. Let me sign on the dotted line, Fred. I
want to unpack and spend a couple of hours in the pool."

"If you're sure." He was already drawing a paper
from his pocket. "I don't want a scene later—like the
time you bought my Porsche."

"You failed to tell me the transmission was held together with Krazy Glue."

"Let the buyer beware," Fred said mildly, and handed
her a monogrammed silver pen.

She had a quick flash of trepidation. This was Cousin
Fred, after all. Fred of the easy deal and the can't-miss
investment. Then a bird flew into the garden and began

to sing cheerily, and Jackie took it as an omen. She signed the lease in a bold, flowing hand before drawing out her checkbook.

"A thousand a month for three months?"

"Plus five hundred damage deposit," Fred added.

"Right." She supposed she was lucky dear cousin Fred wasn't charging her a commission. "Are you leaving me a number, an address or something so I can get in touch with the owner if necessary?"

Fred looked blank for a moment, then beamed at her. It was that MacNamara smile, charming and guileless. "I've already told him about the turnover. Don't worry about a thing, sweetie. He'll be in touch with you."

"Fine." She wasn't going to worry about details. It was spring, and she had a new house, a new project. New beginnings were the best thing in the world. "I'll take care of everything." She touched a large Chinese urn. She'd begin by putting fresh flowers in it. "Will you be staying tonight, Fred?"

The check was already stashed in the inside pocket of his jacket. He resisted the urge to add a loving pat. "I'd love to hang around, indulge in some family gossip, but since we've got everything squared away, I should catch a flight to the Coast. You'll need to get to the market pretty soon, Jack. There're some essentials in the kitchen, but not much else." As he spoke, he started across the room toward a pile of baggage. It never occurred to him to offer to take his cousin's bags upstairs for her, or for her to ask him to. "Keys are there on the table. Enjoy yourself."

"I will." When he hefted his cases she walked over to open the door for him. She'd meant her invitation to spend the night sincerely, and she was just as sincerely glad he'd refused. "Thanks, Fred. I really appreciate this."

"My pleasure, darling." He leaned down to exchange a kiss with her. Jackie got a whiff of his expensive cologne. "Give my love to the family when you talk to them."

"I will. Safe trip, Fred." She watched him walk out to a long, lean convertible. It was white, like his suit. After stowing his cases, Fred scooted behind the wheel and sent her a lazy salute. Then she was alone.

Jackie turned back to the room and hugged herself. She was alone, and on her own. She'd been there before, of course. She was twenty-five, after all, and had taken solo trips and vacations, had her own apartment and her own life. But each time she started out with something new it was a fresh adventure.

As of this day...was it March 25, 26? She shook her head. It didn't matter. As of this day, she was beginning a new career. Jacqueline R. MacNamara, novelist.

It had a nice ring, she thought. The first thing she was going to do was unpack her new typewriter and begin chapter one. With a laugh, she grabbed the typewriter case and her heaviest suitcase and started upstairs.

It didn't take long to acclimate herself, to the South, to the house, to her new routine. She rose early, enjoying the morning quiet with juice and a piece of toast—or flat cola and cold pizza, if that was handier. Her typing improved with practice, and by the end of the third day her machine was humming nicely. She would break in the afternoon to have a dip in the pool, lie in the sun and think about the next scene, or plot twist.

She tanned easily and quickly. It was a gift Jackie attributed to the Italian great-grandmother who had breached the MacNamara's obsessively Irish ranks. The color pleased her, and most of the time she remembered the face creams and moisturizers that her mother had always touted. "Good skin and bone structure make a beauty, Jacqueline. Not style or fashion or clever makeup," she'd often declared.

Well, Jackie had the skin and bone structure, though even her mother had to admit she would never be a true beauty. She was pretty enough, in a piquant, healthy sort of way. But her face was triangular rather than oval, her mouth wide rather than bowed. Her eyes were just a shade too big, and they were brown. The Italian again. She hadn't inherited the sea green or sky blue that dominated the rest of her family. Her hair was brown, as well. During her teens she'd experimented with rinses and streaks, often to her mother's embarrassment, but had finally settled for what God had given her. She'd even come to like it, and the fact that it curled on its own meant she didn't have to spend precious time in salons. She kept it short, and its natural fullness and curl made a halo around her face.

She was glad of its length now, because of her afternoon dips. It only took a few shakes and a little finger-combing to make it spring back to its casual style.

She took each morning as it came, diving headfirst into writing after she woke, then into the pool each afternoon. After a quick forage for lunch, she went back to her machine and worked until evening. She might play in the garden then, or sit and watch the boats or read on the terrace. If the day had been particularly productive, she would treat herself to the whirlpool, letting the bubbling water and the sultry heat of the glass enclosure make her pleasantly tired.

She locked the house for the owner's benefit rather than for her own safety. Each night Jackie slipped into bed in the room she'd chosen with perfect peace of mind and the tingling excitement of what the next morning would bring.

Whenever her thoughts turned to Fred, she smiled. Maybe the family was wrong about Fred after all. It was true that more than once he'd taken some gullible relative for a ride down a one-way street and left him—or her—at a dead end. But he'd certainly done her a good turn when he'd suggested the house in Florida. On the evening of the third day, Jackie lowered herself into the churning waters of the spa and thought about sending cousin Fred some flowers.

She owed him one.

He was dead tired, and happy as hell to be home at last. The final leg of the journey had seemed interminable. Being on American soil again after six months hadn't been enough. When Nathan had landed in New York, the first real flood of impatience had struck. He was home, yet not home. For the first time in months he had allowed himself to think of his own house, his own bed. His own private sacrosanct space.

Then there had been an hour's delay that had left him roaming the airport and almost grinding his teeth. Even once he'd been airborne he hadn't been able to stop checking and rechecking his watch to see how much longer he had to hang in the sky.

The airport in Fort Lauderdale still wasn't home. He'd spent a cold, hard winter in Germany and he'd had enough of the charm of snow and icicles. The warm, moist air and the sight of palms only served to annoy him, because he wasn't quite there yet.

He'd arranged to have his car delivered to the airport, and when he'd finally eased himself into the familiar interior he'd felt like himself again. The hours of flying from Frankfurt to New York no longer mattered. The delays and impatience were forgotten. He was behind the wheel, and twenty minutes from pulling into his own driveway. When he went to bed that night it would be between his own sheets. Freshly laundered and turned back by Mrs. Grange, who Fred MacNamara had assured him would have the house ready for his arrival.

Nathan felt a little twist of guilt about Fred. He knew he'd hustled the man along to get him up and out of the house before his arrival, but after six months of intense work in Germany he wasn't in the mood for a houseguest. He'd have to be sure to get in touch with Fred and thank him for keeping an eye on things. It was an arrangement that had solved a multitude of problems with little fuss. As far as Nathan was concerned, the less fuss the better. He definitely owed Frank MacNamara a very large thank-you.

In a few days, Nathan thought as he slipped his key into the lock. After he'd slept for twenty hours and indulged in some good, old-fashioned sloth.

Nathan pushed open the door, hit the lights and just looked. Home. It was so incredibly good to be home, in the house he'd designed and built, among things chosen for his own taste and comfort.

Home. It was exactly as he—no, it wasn't exactly as he'd left it, he realized quickly. Because his eyes were gritty with fatigue, he rubbed them as he studied the room. His room.

Who had moved the Ming over to the window and stuck irises in it? And why was the Meissen bowl on the table instead of the shelf? He frowned. He was a meticulous man, and he could see a dozen small things out of place.

He'd have to speak to Mrs. Grange about it, but he wasn't going to let a few annoyances spoil his pleasure at being home.

It was tempting to go straight to the kitchen and pour himself something long and cold, but he believed in doing first things first. Hefting his cases, he walked upstairs, relishing each moment of quiet and solitude.

He flipped on the lights in his bedroom and stopped short. Very slowly, he lowered the suitcases and walked to the bed. It wasn't turned down, but made up haphazardly. His dresser, the Chippendale he'd picked up at Sotheby's five years before, was crowded with pots and bottles. There was a definite scent here, not only from the baby roses that had been stuck in the Waterford—which belonged in the dining room cabinet—but a scent of woman. Powder, lotion and oil. Neither strong nor rich, but light and intrusive. His eyes narrowed when he saw the swatch of color on the spread. Nathan picked up the thin, almost microscopic bikini panties.

Mrs. Grange? The very idea was laughable. The sturdy Mrs. Grange wouldn't be able to fit one leg inside that little number. If Fred had had a guest... Nathan turned the panties over under the light. He supposed he could tolerate Fred having had a companion, but not in his room. And why in hell weren't her things packed and gone?

He got an image. It might have been the architect in him that enabled him to take a blank page or an empty lot and fill it completely in his mind. He saw a tall, slim woman, sexy, a little loud and bold. Ready to party. A redhead, probably, with lots of teeth and a rowdy turn of mind. That was fine for Fred, but the agreement had been that the house was to be empty and back in order on Nathan's return.

He gave the bottles on his dresser one last glance. He'd have Mrs. Grange dispose of them. Without thinking, he stuffed the thin piece of nylon in his pocket and strode out to see what else wasn't as it should be.

Jackie, her eyes shut and her head resting on the crimson edge of the spa, sang to herself. It had been a particularly good day. The tale was spinning out of her head and onto the page so quickly it was almost scary. She was glad she'd picked the West for her setting, old Arizona, desolate, tough, dusty and full of grit. That was just the right backdrop for her hard-bitten hero and her primly naive heroine.

They were already bumping along the rocky road to romance, though she didn't think even they knew it yet. She loved being able to put herself back in the 1800s, feeling the heat, smelling the sweat. And of course there was danger and adventure at every step. Her convent-raised heroine was having a devil of a time, but she was coping. Strong. Jackie couldn't have written about a weak-minded woman if she'd had to.

And her hero. Just thinking about him made her smile. She could see him perfectly, just as if he'd popped out of her imagination into the tub with her. That dark black hair, thick, glinting red in the sun when he removed his hat. Long enough that a woman could get a handful of it. The body lean and hard from riding, brown from the sun, scarred from the trouble he never walked away from.

You could see that in his face, a lean, bony face that was often shadowed by the beard he didn't bother to shave. He had a mouth that could smile and make a woman's heart pump fast. Or it could tighten and send shivers of fear up a man's spine. And his eyes. Oh, his eyes were a wonder. Slate gray and fringed by long, dark lashes, crinkled at the corners from squinting into the Arizona sun. Flat and hard when he pulled the trigger, hot and passionate when he took a woman.

Every woman in Arizona was in love with Jake Redman. And Jackie was pleased to be a little in love with him herself. Didn't that make him real? she thought as the bubbles swirled around her. If she could see him so clearly, and feel for him this intensely, didn't it mean she was doing the job right? He wasn't a good man, not through and through. It would be up to the heroine to mine the gold from him, and accept the rough stones along with it. And boy, was he going to give Miss Sarah Conway a run for her money. Jackie could hardly wait to sit down with them so that they could show her what happened next. If she concentrated hard enough, she could almost hear him speak to her.

"What in the hell are you doing?"

Still dreaming, Jackie opened her eyes and looked into the face of her imagination. Jake? she thought, wondering if the hot water had soaked into her brain. Jake didn't wear suits and ties, but she recognized the look that meant he was about to draw and fire. Her mouth fell open and she stared.

His hair was shorter, but not by much, and the

shadow of beard was there. She pressed her fingers to her eyes and got chlorine in them, then blinked them open. He was still there, a little closer now. The sound of the spa's motor seemed louder as it filled her head.

"Am I dreaming?"

Nathan's eyes narrowed. She wasn't the rowdy redhead he'd pictured, but a cute, doe-eyed brunette. Either way, she didn't belong in his house. "What you're doing is trespassing. Now who the hell are you?"

The voice. Good grief, even the voice was right. Jackie shook her head and struggled to get a grip on herself. This was the twentieth century, and no matter how real her characters seemed on paper, they didn't come to life in five-hundred-dollar suits. The simple fact was that she was alone with a stranger and in a very vulnerable position.

She wondered how much she remembered from her karate course, then took another look at the man's broad shoulders and decided it just wasn't going to be enough.

"Who are you?" The edge of fear gave her voice haughty, rounded tones her mother would have been proud of.

"You're the one who has questions to answer," he countered. "But I'm Nathan Powell."

"The architect? Oh, I've admired your work. I saw the Ridgeway Center in Chicago, and…" She started to scoot up, no longer afraid, but then she remembered she hadn't bothered to put on a suit and slumped back again. "You have a marvelous flair for combining aesthetics with practicality."

"Thanks. Now—"

"But what are you doing here?"

His eyes narrowed again, and for the second time

Jackie saw something of her gunslinger in them. "That's my question. This is my house."

"Yours?" She rubbed the back of her wrist over her eyes as she tried to think. "You're Nathan? Fred's Nathan?" Relieved, she smiled again. "Well, that explains things."

A dimple appeared at the corner of her mouth when she smiled. Nathan noticed it, then ignored it. He was a fastidious man, and fastidious men didn't come home to find strange women in their tubs. "Not to me. I'm going to repeat myself. Who the hell are you?"

"Oh. Sorry. I'm Jack." When his brow rose, she smiled again and extended a wet hand. "Jackie—Jacqueline MacNamara. Fred's cousin."

He glanced at her hand, and at the glitter of jewels on it, but didn't take it in his. He was afraid that if he did he might just haul her out onto the tiled floor. "And why, Miss MacNamara, are you sitting in my spa, and sleeping in my bed?"

"Is that your room? Sorry, Fred didn't say which I was to take, so I took the one I liked best. He's in San Diego, you know."

"I don't give a damn where he is." He'd always been a patient man. At least that was what he'd always believed. Right now, though, he was finding he had no patience at all. "What I want to know is why you're in my house."

"Oh, I sublet it from Fred. Didn't he get ahold of you?"

"You what?"

"You know, it's hard to talk with this motor running. Wait." She held up a hand before he could hit the off button. "I'm, ah…well, I wasn't expecting anyone, so I'm not exactly dressed for company. Would you mind?"

He glanced down automatically to where the water churned hot and fast at the subtle curve of her breast. Nathan set his teeth. "I'll be in the kitchen. Make it fast."

Jackie let out a long breath when she was alone. "I think Fred did it again," she muttered as she hauled herself out of the tub and dried off.

Nathan made himself a long gin and tonic, using a liberal hand with the gin. As far as homecomings went, this one left a lot to be desired. There might have been men who'd be pleasantly surprised to come home after an exhausting project and find naked women waiting in their sunrooms. Unfortunately, he just wasn't one of them. He took a deep drink as he leaned back against the counter. It was, he supposed, just a question of taking one step at a time—and the first would be disposing of Jacqueline MacNamara.

"Mr. Powell?"

He glanced over to see her step into the kitchen. She was still dripping a bit. Her legs were lightly tanned and long—very long, he noticed—skimmed at the thighs by a terry-cloth robe that was as boldly striped as Joseph's coat of many colors. Her hair curled damply around her face in a soggy halo, with a fringe of bangs that accented dark, wide eyes. She was smiling, and the dimple was back. He wasn't sure he liked that. When she smiled she looked as though she could sell you ten acres of Florida swampland.

"It appears we're going to have to discuss your cousin."

"Fred." Jackie nodded, still smiling, and slipped onto

a rattan stool at the breakfast bar. She'd already decided she'd do best by being totally at ease and in control. If he thought she was nervous and unsure of her position… Well, she wasn't positive, but she had a very good idea she'd find herself standing outside the house, bag in hand. "He's quite a character, isn't he? How did you meet him?"

"Through a mutual friend." He grimaced a little, thinking he was going to have to talk with Justine, as well. "I had a project in Germany that was going to keep me out of the country for a few months. I needed someone to house-sit. He was recommended. As I knew his aunt—"

"Patricia—Patricia MacNamara's my mother."

"Adele Lindstrom."

"Oh, Aunt Adele. She's my mother's sister." It was more than a smile this time. Something wickedly amused flashed in Jackie's eyes. "She's a lovely woman."

There was something droll, a bit too droll, in the comment. Nathan chose to ignore it. "I worked with Adele briefly on a revitalization project in Chicago. Because of the connection, and the recommendation, I decided to have Fred look out for the house while I was away."

Jackie bit her bottom lip. It was her first sign of nerves, and though she didn't realize it, that small gesture cleared a great deal of ground for her. "He wasn't renting it from you?"

"Renting it? Of course not." She was twisting her rings, one at a time, around her fingers. Don't get involved, he warned himself. Tell her to pack up and move out. No explanations, no apologies. You can be in bed in ten minutes. Nathan felt rather than heard his own sigh. Not many people knew that Nathan Powell was a sucker. "Is that what he told you?"

"I suppose I'd better tell you the whole story. Could I have one of those?"

When she indicated his glass, he nearly snapped at her. Manners had been bred carefully into him, and he was irritated at his oversight, even though she was hardly a guest. Without speaking, he poured and mixed another drink, then sat it in front of her. "I'd appreciate it if you could condense the whole story and just give me the highlights."

"Okay." She took a sip, bracing herself. "Fred called me last week. He'd heard through the family grapevine that I was looking for a place to stay for a few months. A nice quiet place where I could work. I'm a writer," she said with the audacious pride of one who believed it. When this brought no response, she drank again and continued. "Anyway, Fred said he had a place that might suit me. He told me he'd been renting this house.... He described it," Jackie explained, "and I just couldn't wait to see it. It's a beautiful place, so thoughtfully designed. Now that I know who you are, I can see why— the strength and charm of the structure, the openness of the space. If I hadn't been so intent on what I was doing, I'd have recognized your style right away. I studied architecture for a couple of semesters at Columbia."

"That's fascinating, I'm sure. . . . LaFont?"

"Yes, he's a wonderful old duck, isn't he? So pompous and sure of his own worth."

Nathan raised a brow. He'd studied with LaFont himself—a lifetime ago, it seemed—and was well aware that the old duck, as Jackie had termed him, only took on the most promising students. He opened his mouth again, then shut it. He wouldn't be drawn out. "Let's get back to your cousin, Miss MacNamara."

"Jackie," she said, flashing that smile again. "Well, if I hadn't been really anxious to get settled, I probably would have said thanks but no thanks. Fred's always got an angle. But I came down. I took one look at the place, and that was that. He said he had to leave for San Diego right away on business and that the owner—you—didn't want the house empty while you were away. I suppose you don't really just use it as a winter home sporadically, do you?"

"No." He drew a cigarette out of his pocket. He'd successfully cut down to ten a day, but these were extenuating circumstances. "I live here year-round, except when a project takes me away. The arrangement was for Fred to live here during my absence. I called two weeks ago to let him know when I'd be arriving. He was to contact Mrs. Grange and leave his forwarding address with her."

"Mrs. Grange?"

"The housekeeper."

"He didn't mention a housekeeper."

"Why doesn't that surprise me?" Nathan murmured, and finished off his drink. "That takes us to the point of your occupation."

Jackie drew a long breath. "I signed a lease. Three months. I wrote Fred a check for the rent, in advance, plus a damage deposit."

"That's unfortunate." He wouldn't feel sorry for her. He'd be damned if he would. "You didn't sign a lease with the owner."

"With your proxy. With whom I thought was your proxy," she amended. "Cousin Fred can be very smooth."

He wasn't smiling, Jackie noted. Not even a glimmer. It was a pity he couldn't see the humor in the situation. "Look, Mr. Powell—Nathan—it's obvious Fred's pulled something on both of us, but there must be a way we can work it out. As far as the thirty-five hundred dollars goes—"

"Thirty-five hundred?" Nathan said. "You paid him thirty-five hundred dollars?"

"It seemed reasonable." She was tempted to pout because of his tone, but she didn't think it would help. "You do have a beautiful home, and there was the pool, and the sunroom. Anyway, with a bit of family pressure, I may be able to get some of it back. Sooner or later." She thought about the money a moment longer, then dismissed it. "But the real problem is how to handle this situation."

"Which is?"

"My being here, and your being here."

"That's easy." Nathan tapped out his cigarette. There was no reason, absolutely no reason, why he should feel guilty that she'd lost money. "I can recommend a couple of excellent hotels."

She smiled again. She was sure he could, but she had no intention of going to one. The dimple was still in place, but if Nathan had looked closely he would have seen that the soft brown eyes had hardened with determination.

"That would solve your part of the problem, but not mine. I do have a lease."

"You have a worthless piece of paper."

"Very possibly." She tapped her ringed fingers on the counter as she considered. "Did you ever study law? When I was at Harvard—"

"Harvard?"

"Very briefly." She brushed away the hallowed halls with the back of her hand. "I didn't really take to it, but I do think it might be difficult and, worse, annoying to toss me out on my ear." She swirled her drink and considered. "Of course, if you wanted to get a warrant and take it to court, dragging Cousin Fred into it, you'd win eventually. I'm sure of that. In the meantime," she continued before he could find the right words, "I'm sure we can come up with a much more suitable solution for everyone. You must be exhausted." She changed her tone so smoothly he could only stare. "Why don't you go on up and get a good night's sleep? Everything's clearer on a good night's sleep, don't you think? We can hash through all this tomorrow."

"It's not a matter of hashing through anything, Miss MacNamara. It's a matter of your packing up your things." He shoved a hand into his pocket, and his fingers brushed the swatch of nylon. Gritting his teeth, he pulled it out. "These are yours?"

"Yes, thanks." Without a blush, Jackie accepted her underwear. "It's a little late to be calling the cops and explaining all of this to them. I imagine you could throw me out bodily, but you'd hate yourself for it."

She had him there. Nathan began to think she had a lot more in common with her cousin than a family name. He glanced at his watch and swore. It was already after midnight, and he didn't—quite—have the heart to dump her in the street. The worst of it was that he was nearly tired enough to see double and couldn't seem to come up with the right, or the most promising, arguments. So he'd let it ride—for the moment.

"I'll give you twenty-four hours, Miss MacNamara. That seems more than reasonable to me."

"I knew you were a reasonable man." She smiled at him again. "Why don't you go get some sleep? I'll lock up."

"You're in my bed."

"I beg your pardon?"

"Your things are in my room."

"Oh." Jackie scratched at her temple. "Well, I suppose if it was really important to you, I could haul everything out tonight."

"Never mind." Maybe it was all a nightmare. A hallucination. He'd wake up in the morning and discover everything was as it should be. "I'll take one of the guest rooms."

"That's a much better idea. You really do look tired. Sleep well."

He stared at her for nearly a full minute. When he was gone, Jackie laid her head down on the counter and began to giggle. Oh, she'd get Fred for this, make no mistake. But now, just now, it was the funniest thing that had happened to her in months.

# Chapter Two

When Nathan woke, it was after ten East Coast time, but the nightmare wasn't over. He realized that as soon as he saw the muted striped paper on the wall of the guest room. He was in his own house, but he'd somehow found himself relegated to the position of guest.

His suitcases, open but still packed, sat on the mahogany chest under the garden window. He'd left his drapes undrawn, and sunlight poured in over the neatly folded shirts. Deliberately he turned away from them. He'd be damned if he'd unpack until he could do so in the privacy of his own room.

A man had a right to his own closet.

Jacqueline MacNamara had been correct about one thing. He felt better after a full night's sleep. His mind was clearer. Though it wasn't something he cared to dwell on, he went over everything that had happened from the time he'd unlocked his door until he'd fallen, facefirst, into the guest bed.

He realized he'd been a fool not to toss her out on her pert little ear the night before, but that could be rectified. And the sooner the better.

He showered, taking his shaving gear into the bathroom with him, but meticulously replacing everything in the kit when he was finished. Nothing was coming out until it could be placed in his own cabinets and drawers. After he'd dressed, in light cotton pants and shirt, he felt in charge again. If he couldn't deal with a dippy little number like the brunette snuggled in his bed, he was definitely slipping. Still, it wouldn't hurt to have a cup of coffee first.

He was halfway down the stairs when he smelled it. Coffee. Strong, fresh coffee. The aroma was so welcome he nearly smiled, but then he remembered who must have brewed it. Strengthening his resolve, he continued. Another scent wafted toward him. Bacon? Surely that was bacon. Obviously she was making herself right at home. He heard the music, as well—rock, something cheerful and bouncy and loud enough to be heard a room away.

No, the nightmare wasn't over, but it was going to end, and end quickly.

Nathan strode into the kitchen prepared to shoot straight from the hip.

"Good morning." Jackie greeted him with a smile that competed with the sunshine. As a concession to him, she turned the radio down, but not off. "I wasn't sure how long you'd sleep, but I didn't think you were the type to stay in bed through the morning, so I started breakfast. I hope you like blueberry pancakes. I slipped out early and bought the berries. They're fresh." Before he could speak, she popped one into his mouth. "Have a seat. I'll get your coffee."

"Miss MacNamara—"

"Jackie, please. Cream?"

"Black. We left things a bit up in the air last night, but we've got to settle this business now."

"Absolutely. I hope you like your bacon crisp." She set a platter on the counter, where a place was already set with his good china and a damask napkin. She noticed that he'd shaved. With the shadow of beard gone, he didn't look quite as much like her Jake—except around the eyes. It wouldn't be wise, she decided, to underestimate him.

"I've given it a lot of thought, Nathan, and I think I've come up with the ideal solution." She poured batter onto the griddle and adjusted the flame. "Did you sleep well?"

"Fine." At least he'd felt fine when he'd awakened. Now he reached for the coffee almost defensively. She was like a sunbeam that had intruded when all he'd really wanted to do was draw the shades and take a nap.

"My mother's fond of saying you always sleep best at home, but it's never mattered to me. I can sleep anywhere. Would you like the paper?"

"No." He sipped the coffee, stared at it, then sipped again. Maybe it was his imagination, but it was the best cup of coffee he'd ever tasted.

"I buy the beans from a little shop in town," she said, answering his unspoken question as she flipped the pancakes with an expert hand. "I don't drink it often myself. That's why I think it's important to have a really good cup. Ready for these?" Before he could answer, she took his plate and stacked pancakes on it. "You've a wonderful view from right here." Jackie poured a second cup of coffee and sat beside him. "It makes eating an event."

Nathan found himself reaching for the syrup. It wouldn't hurt to eat first. He could still toss her out later. "How long have you been here?"

"Just a few days. Fred's always had an excellent sense of timing. How are your pancakes?"

It seemed only fair to give her her due. "They're wonderful. Aren't you eating?"

"I sort of sampled as I went along." But that didn't stop her from plucking another slice of bacon. She nibbled, approved, then smiled at him. "Do you cook?"

"Only if the package comes with instructions."

Jackie felt the first thrill of victory. "I'm really a very good cook."

"Studied at the Cordon Bleu, I imagine."

"Only for six months," she said, grinning at him. "But I did learn most of the basics. From there I decided to go my own way, experiment, you know? Cooking should be as much of an adventure as anything else."

To Nathan, cooking was drudgery that usually ended in failure. He only grunted.

"Your Mrs. Grange," Jackie began conversationally. "Is she supposed to come in every day, do the cleaning and the cooking?"

"Once a week." The pancakes were absolutely fabulous. He'd grown accustomed to hotel food, and as excellent as it had been, it couldn't compete with this. He began to relax as he studied the view. She was right, it was great, and he couldn't remember ever having enjoyed breakfast more. "She cleans, does the weekly

marketing, and usually fixes a casserole or something."
Nathan took another forkful, then stopped himself before he could again be seduced by the flavor. "Why?"

"It all has to do with our little dilemma."

"Your dilemma."

"Whatever. I wonder, are you a fair man, Nathan? Your buildings certainly show a sense of style and order, but I can't really tell if you have a sense of fair play." She lifted the coffeepot. "Let me top that off for you."

He was losing his appetite rapidly. "What are you getting at?"

"I'm out thirty-five hundred." Jackie munched on the bacon. "Now, I'm not going to try to make you think that the loss is going to have me on the street corner selling pencils, but it's not really the amount. It's the principle. You believe in principles, don't you?"

Cautious, he gave a noncommittal shrug.

"I paid, in good faith, for a place to live and to work for three months."

"I'm sure your family retains excellent lawyers. Why don't you sue your cousin?"

"The MacNamaras don't solve family problems that way. Oh, I'll settle up with him—when he least expects it."

There was a look in her eyes that made Nathan think she would do just that, and beautifully. He had to fight back a surge of admiration. "I'll wish you the best of luck here, but your family problems don't involve me."

"They do when it's your house in the middle of it. Do you want some more?"

"No. Thanks," he added belatedly. "Miss—Jackie—I'm going to be perfectly frank with you." He settled back, prepared to be both reasonable and firm. If he'd known her better, Nathan would have felt his first qualms when she turned her big brown eyes on him with a look of complete cooperation. "My work in Germany was difficult and tiring. I have a couple of months of free time coming, which I intend to spend here, alone, doing as little as possible."

"What were you building?"

"What?"

"In Germany. What were you building?"

"An entertainment complex, but that isn't really relevant. I'm sorry if it seems insensitive, but I don't feel responsible for your situation."

"It doesn't seem insensitive at all." Jackie patted his hand, then poured him more coffee. "Why should you, after all? An entertainment complex. It sounds fascinating, and I'd really love to hear all about it later, but the thing is, Nathan—" she paused as she topped off her own cup "—is that I kind of see us as two people in the same boat. We both expected to spend the next couple of months alone, pursuing our own projects, and Fred screwed up the works. Do you like Oriental food?"

He was losing ground. Nathan didn't know why, or when, the sand had started to shift beneath his feet, but there it was. Resting his elbows on the counter, he held his head in his hands. "What the hell does that have to do with anything?"

"It has to do with my idea, and I wanted to know what kind of food you liked, or particularly didn't like. Me, I'll eat anything, but most people have definite preferences." Jackie cupped her mug in both hands as she tucked her legs, lotus-style, under her on the stool. She was wearing shorts today, vivid blue ones with a flamingo emblem on one leg. Nathan studied the odd pink bird for a long time before he lifted his gaze to hers.

"Why don't you just tell me your idea while I still have a small part of my sanity?"

"The object is for both of us to have what we want — or as nearly as possible. It's a big house."

She lifted both brows as his eyes narrowed. That look, she thought again. That Jake look was hard to resist. Nathan's coming back when he did might have been the sort of odd bonus fate sometimes tossed out. Jackie was always ready to make the grab for it.

"I'm an excellent roommate. I could give you references from several people. I went to a variety of colleges, you see, so I lived with a variety of people. I can be neat if that's important, and I can be quiet and unobtrusive."

"I find that difficult to believe."

"No, really, especially when I'm immersed in my own project, like I am now. I write almost all day. This story's really the most important thing in my life right now. I'll have to tell you about it, but we'll save that."

"I'd appreciate it."

"You have a wonderfully subtle sense of humor, Nathan. Don't ever lose it. Anyhow, I'm a strong believer in atmosphere. You must be, too, being an architect."

"You're losing me again." He shoved the coffee aside. Too much stimulation, that must be it. Another cup and he might just start understanding her.

"The house," Jackie said patiently. Her eyes were the problem, Nathan decided. There was something about them that compelled you to look and listen when all you really wanted to do was hold your hands over your ears and run.

"What about the house?"

"There's something about it. The minute I set up here, everything just started flowing. With the story. If I moved, well, don't you think things might stop flowing just as quickly? I don't want to chance that. So I'm willing to make some compromises."

"You're willing to make some compromises," Nathan repeated slowly. "That's fascinating. You're living in my house, without my consent, but you're willing to make some compromises."

"It's only fair." There was that smile again, quick and brilliant. "You don't cook. I do." Jackie gestured with both hands as if to show the simplicity of it. "I'll prepare all of your meals, at my expense, for as long as I'm here."

It sounded reasonable. Why in the hell did it sound so reasonable when she said it? "That's very generous of you, but I don't want a cook, or a roommate."

"How do you know? You haven't had either yet."

"What I want," he began, careful to space his words and keep his tone even, "is privacy."

"Of course you do." She didn't touch him, but her tone was like a pat on the head. He nearly growled. "We'll make a pact right now. I'll respect your privacy and you'll respect mine, Nathan..." She leaned toward him, again covering his hand with hers in a move that was natural rather than calculated. "I know you've got absolutely no reason to do me any favors, but I'm really committed to this book. For reasons of my own, I've a great need to finish it, and I'm sure I can. Here."

"If you're trying to make me feel guilty because I'd be sabotaging the great American novel—"

"No, I'm not. I would have if I'd thought of it, but I

didn't. I'm just asking you to give me a chance. A couple of weeks. If I drive you crazy, I'll leave."

"Jacqueline, I've known you about twelve hours, and you've already driven me crazy."

She was winning. There was just the slightest hint of it in his tone, but she caught it and pounced. "You ate all your pancakes."

Almost guiltily, Nathan looked down at his empty plate. "I've had nothing but airplane food for twenty-four hours."

"Wait until you taste my crepes. And my Belgian waffles." She caught her lower lip between her teeth. "Nathan, think of it. You won't have to open a single can as long as I'm around."

Involuntarily he thought of all the haphazard meals he'd prepared, and about the barely edible ones he brought into the house in foam containers. "I'll eat out."

"A fat lot of privacy you'd have sitting in crowded restaurants and competing for a waiter's attention. With my solution, you won't have to do anything but relax."

He hated restaurants. And God knew he'd had enough of them over the past year. The arrangement made perfect sense, at least while he was comfortably full of her blueberry pancakes.

"I want my room back."

"That goes without saying."

"And I don't like small talk in the morning."

"Completely uncivilized. I do want pool privileges."

"If I stumble over you or any of your things even once, you're out."

"Agreed." She held out a hand, sensing he was a man who would stand by a handshake. She was even more certain of it when she saw him hesitate. Jackie brought out what she hoped would be the coup de grâce. "You really would hate yourself if you threw me out, you know."

Nathan scowled at her but found his palm resting against hers. A small hand, and a soft one, he thought, but the grip was firm. If he lived to regret this temporary arrangement, he'd have one more score to settle with Fred. "I'm going to take a spa."

"Good idea. Loosen up all those tense muscles. By the way, what would you like for lunch?"

He didn't look back. "Surprise me."

Jackie picked up his plate and did a quick dance around the kitchen.

Temporary insanity. Nathan debated the wisdom of pleading that cause to his associates, his family or the higher courts. He had a boarder. A nonpaying one at that. Nathan Powell, a conservative, upstanding member of society, a member of the Fortune 500, the thirty-two-year-old wunderkind of architecture, had a strange woman in his house.

He didn't necessarily mean strange as in unknown. Jackie MacNamara *was* strange. He'd come to that conclusion when he'd seen her meditating by the pool after lunch. He'd glanced out and spotted her, sitting cross-legged on the stone apron, head tilted back, eyes closed, hands resting lightly on her knees, palms up. He'd been mortally afraid she was reciting a mantra. Did people still do that sort of thing?

He must have been insane to agree to her arrangement because of blueberry pancakes and a smile. Jet lag, he decided as he poured another glass of iced tea Jackie had made to go with a truly exceptional spinach salad.

Even a competent, intelligent man could fall victim to the weakness of the body after a transatlantic flight.

Two weeks, he reminded himself. Technically, he'd only agreed to two weeks. After that time had passed, he could gently but firmly ease her on her way. In the meantime, he would do what he should have done hours ago—make certain he didn't have a maniac on his hands.

There was a neat leather-bound address book by the kitchen phone, as there was by every phone in the house. Nathan flipped through it to the *L*'s. Jackie was upstairs working on her book—if indeed there was a book at all. He would make the call, glean a few pertinent facts, then decide how to move from there.

"Lindstrom residence."

"Adele Lindstrom, please, Nathan Powell calling."

"One moment, Mr. Powell."

Nathan sipped tea as he waited. A man could become addicted to having it made fresh instead of digging crystallized chemicals out of a jar. Absently he drew a cigarette out of his pocket and tapped the filter on the counter.

"Nathan, dear, how are you?"

"Adele. I'm very well, and you?"

"Couldn't be better, though March insists on going out like a lion here. What can I do for you, dear? Are you in Chicago?"

"No, actually I've just arrived home. Your nephew Fred was, ah…house-sitting for me."

"Of course, I remember." There was a long, and to Nathan pregnant, pause. "Fred hasn't done something naughty, has he?"

Naughty? Nathan passed a hand over his face. After

a moment, he decided not to blast Adele with the sad facts of the situation, but to tone it down. "We do have a bit of a mix-up. Your niece is here."

"Niece? Well, I have several of those. Jacqueline? Of course it's Jacqueline. I remember now that Honoria— that's Fred's mother—told me that little Jack was going south. Poor Nathan, you've a houseful of MacNamaras."

"Actually, Fred's in San Diego."

"San Diego? What are you all doing in San Diego?"

Nathan tried to remember if Adele Lindstrom had been quite this scattered in Chicago. "Fred's in San Diego—at least I think he is. I'm in Florida, with your niece."

"Oh… Oh!" The second *oh* had enough delight in it to put Nathan on guard. "Well, isn't that lovely? I've always said that all our Jacqueline needed was a nice, stable man. She's a bit of a butterfly, of course, but very bright and wonderfully good-hearted."

"I'm sure she is." Nathan found it necessary to put the record straight, and to put it straight quickly. "She's only here because of a misunderstanding. It seems Fred…didn't understand that I was coming back, and he…offered the house to Jackie."

"I see." And she did, perfectly. Fortunately for Nathan, he couldn't see her eyes light with amusement. "How awkward for you. I hope you and Jacqueline have worked things out."

"More or less. You're her mother's sister?"

"That's right. Jackie favors Patricia physically. Such a piquant look. I was always jealous as a child. Otherwise, none of us have ever been quite sure who little Jackie takes after."

Nathan blew out a stream of smoke. "That doesn't surprise me."

"What is it now…painting? No, it's writing. Jackie's a novelist these days."

"So she says."

"I'm sure she'll tell a delightful story. She's always been full of them."

"I'll just bet."

"Well, dear, I know the two of you will get along fine. Our little Jack manages to get along with just about anyone. A talent of hers. Not to say that Patricia and I hadn't hoped she'd be settled down and married by now—put some of that energy into raising a nice family. She's a sweet girl—a bit flighty, but sweet. You're still single, aren't you, Nathan?"

With his eyes cast up to the ceiling, he shook his head. "Yes, I am. It's been nice talking to you, Adele. I'll suggest to your niece that she get in touch when she relocates."

"That would be nice. It's always a pleasure to hear from Jack. And you, too, Nathan. Be sure to let me know if you get to Chicago again."

"I will. Take care of yourself, Adele."

He hung up, still frowning at the phone. There was little doubt that his unwanted tenant was exactly who she said she was. But that didn't really accomplish anything. He could talk to her again, but when he'd tried to do that over lunch, he'd gotten a small, and very nagging, headache. It might be the coward's way, but for the rest of the day he was going to pretend that Jacqueline MacNamara, with her long legs and her brilliant smile, didn't exist.

Upstairs, in front of her typewriter, Jackie wasn't

giving Nathan a thought. Or if she was she'd twined him so completely with the hard-bitten and heroic Jake that she wasn't able to see the difference.

It was working. Sometimes, when her fingers slowed just a bit and her mind whipped back to the present, she was struck by the wonderful and delightful thought that she was really writing. Not playing at it, as she had played at so many other things.

She knew her family tut-tutted about her. All those brains and all that breeding, and Jackie could never seem to make up her mind what to do with them. She was happy to announce that this time she had found something, and that it had found her.

Sitting back, her tongue caught between her teeth, she read the last scene over. It was good, she was sure of that. She knew that back in Newport there were those who would shake their heads and smile indulgently. So what if the scene was good, or even if several chapters were good? Dear little Jack never finished anything.

In her stint at remodeling, she'd bought a huge rattrap of a house and scraped, planed, painted and papered. She'd learned about plumbing and rewiring, haunted lumberyards and hardware stores. The first floor— she'd always believed in starting from the bottom up— had been fabulous. She was creative and competent. The problem had been, as it always had been, that once the first rush of excitement was over something else had caught her interest. The house had lost its charm for her. True, she'd sold it at a nice profit, but she'd never touched the two upper stories.

This was different.

Jackie cradled her chin in her hand. How many times had she said that before? The photography studio, the dance classes, the potter's wheel. But this *was* different. She'd been fascinated by each field she'd tampered in, and in each had shown a nice ability to apply what she'd learned, but she was beginning to see, or hope, that all those experiments, all those false starts, had been leading up to this.

She had to be right about the story. This time she had to carry it through from start to finish. Nothing else she'd tried had been so important or seemed so right. It didn't matter that her family and friends saw her as eccentric and fickle. She *was* eccentric and fickle. But there had to be something, something strong and meaningful, in her life. She couldn't go on playing at being an adult forever.

The great American novel. That made her smile. No, it wouldn't be that. In fact, Jackie couldn't think of many things more tedious than attempting to write the great American novel. But it could be a good book, a book people might care about and enjoy, one they might curl up with on a quiet evening. That would be enough. She hadn't realized that before, but once she'd really begun to care about it herself she'd known that would be more than enough.

It was coming so fast, almost faster than she could handle. The room was stacked with reference books and manuals, writers' how-tos and guides. She'd pored over them all. Researching her subject was the one discipline Jackie had always followed strictly. She'd been grateful for the road maps, the explanations of pitfalls and the suggestions. Oddly, now that she was hip deep in the story, none of that seemed to matter. She was writing on instinct and by the seat of her pants. As far as she could remember—and her memory was keen—she'd never had more fun in her life.

She closed her eyes to think about Jake. Instantly her mind took a leap to Nathan. Wasn't it strange how much he looked like her own conception of the hero of her story? It really did make it all seem fated. Jackie had a healthy respect for fate, particularly after her study of astrology.

Not that Nathan was a reckless gunslinger. No, he was rather sweetly conservative. A man, she was sure, who thought of himself as organized and practical. She doubted seriously that he considered himself an artist, though he was undoubtedly a talented one. He'd also be a list-maker and a plan-follower. She respected that, though she'd never been able to stick with a list in her life. What she admired even more was that he was a man who knew what he wanted and had accomplished it.

He was also a pleasure to look at— particularly when he smiled. The smile was usually reluctant, which made it all the sweeter. Already she'd decided it was her duty to nudge that smile from him as often as possible.

It shouldn't be difficult. Obviously he had a good heart; otherwise he would have given her the heave-ho the first night. That he hadn't, though he'd certainly wanted to, made Jackie think rather kindly of him. Because she did, she was determined to make their cohabitation as painless for him as possible.

She didn't doubt that they could deal very nicely with each other for a few months. In truth, she preferred company, even his reluctant sort, to solitude.

She liked his subtlety, and his well-bred sarcasm. Even someone much less sensitive than she would have recognized the fact that nothing would have made him happier than to dispose of her. It was a pity she couldn't oblige him, but she really was determined to finish her book, and to finish it where she had started it.

While she was at it, she'd stay out of his way as much as was humanly possible, and fix him some of the best meals of his life.

That thought made her glance at her watch. She swore a little, but turned off her machine. It really was a pain to have to think about dinner when Jake was tethered by a leather thong to the wrist of an Apache brave. The knife fight was just heating up; but a bargain was a bargain.

Humming to herself, she started down to the kitchen.

Once again it was the scents that lured him. Nathan had been perfectly happy catching up on his back issues of *Architectural Digest*. He burrowed in his office, content simply to be there with the warm paneled walls and the faded Persian carpet. Terrace doors opened onto the patio and out to the garden. It was his refuge, with the faint scent of leather from books and the sharp light of sun through etched glass. If a man couldn't be alone in his office, he couldn't be alone anywhere.

Late in the afternoon he'd nearly been able to erase Jackie MacNamara and her conniving cousin from his mind. He'd heard her humming, and had ignored it. That had pleased him. A servant. He would think of her as a servant and nothing more.

Then the aromas had started teasing him. Hot, spicy aromas. She was playing the radio again. Loud. He really was going to have to speak to her about that. Nathan shifted in his office chair and tried to concentrate.

Was that chicken? he wondered, and lost his place

in an article on earth homes. He thought about closing the door, flipped a page and found the Top 40 number Jackie was playing at top volume juggling around in his head. Telling himself she needed a lecture on music appreciation, he set the magazine aside—after marking his place—then headed toward the kitchen.

He had to speak to her twice before she heard him. Jackie kept a hand on the handle of the frying pan, shaking it gently as she pitched her voice to a shout.

"It'll be ready in a few minutes. Would you like some wine?"

"No. What I'd like is for you to turn that thing off."

"To what?"

"To turn that thing—" Almost growling in disgust, Nathan walked over to the kitchen speaker and hit the switch. "Haven't you ever heard about inner-ear damage?"

Jackie gave the pan another shake before turning off the flame. "I always play the music loud when I'm cooking. It inspires me."

"Invest in headphones," he suggested.

With a shrug, Jackie took the lid off the rice and gave it a quick swipe with a fork. "Sorry. I figured since you had speakers in every room you liked music. How was your day? Did you get plenty of rest?"

Something in her tone made him feel like a cranky grandfather. "I'm fine," he said between his teeth.

"Good. I hope you like Chinese. I have a friend who owns a really wonderful little Oriental restaurant in San Francisco. I persuaded his chef to share some recipes." Jackie poured Nathan a glass of wine. She was using his Waterford this time. In the smooth and economical way she had in the kitchen, she scooped the sweet-

and-sour chicken onto a bed of rice. "I didn't have time
for fortune cookies, but there's an upside-down cake
in the oven." She licked sauce from her thumb before
she began to serve herself. "You don't want to let that
get cold."

Wary of her, he sat. A man had to eat, after all. As
he forked a cube of chicken, he watched her. Nothing
seemed to break her rhythm, or her breezy sense of self-
confidence. He'd see about that, Nathan thought, and
waited until she'd joined him at the bar.

"I spoke with your aunt today."

"Really? Aunt Adele?" Jackie hooked one bare foot
around the leg of the stool. "Did she give me a good
reference?"

"More or less."

"You brought it on yourself," she said, then began to
eat with the steady enthusiasm of one who liked food
for food's sake.

"I beg your pardon?"

Jackie sampled a bamboo shoot. "Word's going to
spread like wildfire, through the Lindstrom branch and
over to the MacNamaras. I imagine it'll detour through
the O'Brians too. That's my father's sister's married
name." She took a forkful of saffron rice. "I can't take
the responsibility."

Now it was he who'd lost his rhythm. Again. "I don't
know what you're talking about."

"The wedding."

"What wedding?"

"Ours." She picked up her glass and sipped, smiling
at him over the rim. "What do you think of the wine?"

"Back up. What do you mean, our wedding?"

"Well, I don't mean it, and you don't mean it. But

Aunt Adele will mean it. Twenty minutes after you spoke with her she'd have been chirping happily about our romance to anyone who'd listen. People do listen to Aunt Adele. I've never understood why. You're letting that chicken get cold, Nathan."

He set his fork down, keeping his voice even and his eyes steady. "I never gave her any reason to think we were involved."

"Of course you didn't." Obviously on his side, Jackie squeezed his arm. "All you did was tell Aunt Adele I was living here." The timer buzzed, so Jackie scooted up to pull the cake out of the oven. Wanting a moment to think, Nathan waited until she'd set it out to cool and joined him again.

"I explained there'd been a misunderstanding."

"She has a very selective memory." Jackie took another generous bite. "Don't worry, I won't hold you to it. Do you think there's enough ginger in this?"

"There's nothing to hold me to."

"Not between us." She sent him a sympathetic glance. "Don't let it ruin your appetite. I can handle the family. Can I ask you a personal question?"

Nathan picked up his fork again. Somehow he'd opened the door to his own house and fallen down the rabbit hole. "Why not?"

"Are you involved with anyone? It doesn't have to be particularly serious."

She liked the way his eyes narrowed. There was something about gray eyes, really gray eyes, that could cut right through you.

He debated half a dozen answers before settling on the truth. "No."

"That's too bad." Her forehead wrinkled briefly before smoothing out again. "It would have helped if you were, but I'll just make something up. Would you mind very much if I threw you over, maybe for a marine biologist?"

He was laughing. He didn't know why, but when he reached for his wine, his lips were still curved. "Not at all."

She hadn't counted on that—that his laugh would be so appealing. The little flutter came. Jackie acknowledged it, savored it briefly, then banked it down. It wouldn't do. No, it wouldn't do at all. "You're a good sport, Nathan. Not everyone would think so, but they don't know you like I do. Let me get you some more chicken."

"No, I'll get it."

It was a small mistake, the kind people make every day when they step into a doorway at the same time or bump elbows in a crowded elevator. The kind of small mistake that is rarely recognized and soon forgotten.

They rose simultaneously, both reaching for his plate. Their hands closed over it, and each other's. Their bodies bumped. He took her arm to steady her. The usual quick smile and the automatic apology didn't come from either of them.

Jackie felt her breath snag and her heart stumble. The feeling didn't surprise her. She was too much in tune with her emotions, too comfortable with them, to be surprised. It was the depth of them that caught at her. The contact was casual, more funny than romantic, but she felt as though she'd been waiting all her life for it.

She'd remember the feel of his hand, and the china, and the heat of his body as it barely brushed hers. She'd remember the look of surprised suspicion in his eyes, and the scent of spices and wine. She'd remember the quiet, the absolute and sudden quiet. As if the world had held its breath for a moment. For just a moment.

What the hell was this? That was his first and only coherent thought. He was gripping her harder than he should have, as if he were holding on—but that was absurd. However absurd it was, he couldn't quite make himself let go. Her eyes were so big, so soft. Was it foolish to believe he saw absolute honesty in them? That scent, her scent, was there, the one he'd first come across in his own bedroom. The one, Nathan thought now, that still lingered, ridiculously, after she'd moved into a guest room. He heard her breath suck in, then shudder out. Or maybe it was his own.

And he wanted her, as clearly and as logically as he'd ever wanted anything. It lasted only a moment, but the desire was strong.

They moved away together, with the quick, almost jerky motion one uses when one steps back from an unexpected flame. Jackie cleared her throat. Nathan let out a long, quiet breath.

"It's no trouble," she said.

"Thanks."

She moved to the stove before she thought she could breathe easily. As she scooped up chicken and vegetables, she wondered if this was one adventure she should have passed on.

# *Chapter Three*

When he looked at her something happened, something frantic, something she'd never experienced before. Her heart beat just a little too fast, and dampness sprang out on the palms of her hands. A look was all that was necessary. His eyes were so dark, so penetrating. When he looked at her it was as if he could see everything she was, or could be, or wanted to be.

It was absurd. He was a man who lived by the gun, who took what he wanted without regret or compassion. All of her life she'd been taught that the line between right and wrong was clear and wide, and couldn't be crossed.

To kill was the greatest sin, the most unforgivable. Yet he had killed, and would surely kill again. Knowing it, she couldn't care for him. But care she did. And want she did. And need.

Sitting back, Jackie reviewed Sarah's confused and contrasting feelings for Jake. How would a sheltered young woman, barely eighteen, respond to a man who had lived all his life by rules she couldn't possibly understand or approve of? And how would a man who had seen and done all that Jake Redman had seen and done react to an innocent, convent-bred woman?

There was no way their dealings with each other could run smoothly. Their coming together and its resolution couldn't be impossible, it just had to be difficult. Two different worlds, she thought. Two sets of values, two opposing ambitions. Those would be difficult conflicts to overcome. Then you added gunfights, betrayal, kidnapping and revenge. Just to keep things interesting. Still, for all the action and adventure, Jackie had come to think that the love story was really the heart of her book. How these two people were going to change and complement each other, how they would compromise, adjust and stand firm.

She didn't think Sarah or Jake would understand about emotional commitment or mutually supportive relationships. Those were twentieth-century terms. Her psychology course on modern marriage had given Jackie a basketful of catchphrases. The words might change, but love was love. As far as she was concerned, Sarah and Jake had a good chance. That was more than a great many people could say.

It occurred to her that that was all she wanted for herself. A good chance. Someone to love who would love her back, someone to make adjustments for, to make long-range plans with. Wasn't it strange that in making a relationship on paper she had begun to fantasize about making one for herself?

She wouldn't ask for perfection, not only because it would be boring but because she would never be able to achieve perfection herself. It wouldn't be necessary, or even appealing, to settle down with a man who agreed with you on every point.

Would she like dashing? Probably. It might be fun to have someone flash in and out of your life, dropping off dew-kissed roses and magnums of champagne. It would be a nice interlude, but she was dead certain she couldn't live with dashing. Dashing would never take out the trash or unclog a drain.

Sensitive. Jackie rolled the word around in her mind, coming up with a picture of a sweet, caring man who wrote bad poetry. Horn-rimmed glasses and a voice like cream. Sensitive would always understand a woman's needs and a woman's moods. She could be very fond of sensitive. Until sensitive began to drive her crazy.

Passionate would be nice, as well. Someone who would toss her over his shoulder and make mad love in sun-drenched fields. But it might get a bit tough to do that sort of thing once they hit eighty.

Funny, intelligent, reckless and dependable.

That was the trouble, she supposed. She could think of a dozen different qualities she would enjoy in a man, but not of a combination that would pull her in for the long haul. With a sigh, she cupped her chin in her hand and stared over the typewriter through the window. Maybe she just wasn't ready to think about wedding rings and picket fences. Maybe she'd never be ready.

It wasn't easy to accept, but if it was true she could see herself living in some quaint little house near the water and writing about other people's love affairs. She could spend her days dreaming up characters and places, puttering around in a garden and playing aunt to all the little MacNamaras. It wouldn't be so bad.

She wouldn't be a hermit, of course. And it wasn't as though she didn't appreciate men. Any man she'd ever been close to had possessed at least one of the qualities she admired. She'd cared for and about them, even loved them a little. But then, love was easy for her, falling in and falling out of it without bruises or scars. That wasn't real romance, she thought as she looked at the words she'd written. Real romance scraped off a little skin. It had to if love was going to bloom out of it and heal.

Lord, she was getting philosophical since she'd started putting words on paper. Maybe that explained her reaction to Nathan.

The problem was, though she was clever with words and always had been, she couldn't quite come up with the right ones to describe that one brief moment of contact.

Intense, confusing, illuminating, scary. It had been all of those, yet she wasn't sure what the sum of the parts equaled.

Attraction, certainly. But then, she'd found him attractive even when she'd thought she was hallucinating. Most women found dark, brooding types with aloof qualities attractive. God knew why. Yet that one moment, that quick link, had been more than simple attraction. The fact was, it hadn't been simple anything. She'd wanted him in the strong, vital way that usually came only with understanding and time.

I know you, something had seemed to say inside her. And I've been waiting.

He'd felt something too. She was certain of that. Maybe it had been that same kind of instant knowledge and instant desire. Whatever he'd felt hadn't pleased him, because he'd been very careful to avoid her for the better part of two days. Not an easy trick, since they were living in the same house, but he'd managed.

She still thought it had been rather rude of him to go out on his boat for an entire day and not ask her along.

Maybe he had to think things through. Jackie gauged him as the type of man who would have to compute and analyze and reason out every area of his life, including the emotional. That was too bad, but she'd have been the first to say that everyone was entitled to their own quirks.

He didn't have to worry about her, she decided as she dipped into a bowl of cheese curls. She wasn't interested in flirting with a relationship, and certainly not one with a man as buttoned-down as Nathan Powell. If she were, then he'd have reason to worry. Jackie chuckled to herself as she nibbled. She could be very tenacious and very persuasive when her mind was set. Fortunately for him, and perhaps for both of them, she was much too involved with writing to give him more than a passing thought.

Still, she checked her watch and noticed that it was nearly dinnertime and he wasn't back. His problem, she thought as she took another handful of cheese curls. She'd agreed to cook, but not to cater. When he came home he could make himself a sandwich. It certainly didn't matter to her.

She peered out her window at the sound of a boat, then settled back with the smallest of sighs when it passed by.

She wasn't really thinking of him, she told herself. She was just…passing the time. She didn't really wish he'd asked her to join him today so that they could have spent some time alone together, getting to know each other better. She wasn't really wondering what kind of man he was—except in the most intellectual terms.

What did it matter that she liked the way he laughed when he briefly let his guard down? It certainly wasn't important that his eyes were dark and dangerous one minute and quietly sensitive another. He was just a man, bound up in his work and his self-image in the same way she was bound up in her work and her future. It wasn't any of her business that he seemed more tense than he should be, and more solitary. It wasn't her goal in life to draw him out and urge him to relax and enjoy.

Her goal in life, Jackie reminded herself, was to finish the story, sell it and reap the benefits of being a published novelist. Whatever they might be. Straightening in her seat, she pushed Nathan Powell aside and went back to work.

This was what he'd come home for, Nathan told himself as he cruised down one of the narrow, deserted channels. Peace and quiet. There were no deadlines, no contract dates to worry about, no supply shortages to work around or inspectors to answer to. Sun and water. He didn't want to think beyond them.

He was beginning to feel almost like himself again. It was odd that he hadn't thought of this before—taking the boat out and disappearing for the day. He might have agreed to have a boarder for a couple of weeks, but that didn't mean he had to chain himself to the house. Or to her.

He couldn't say that it was entirely unpleasant having her there. She was keeping her end of the bargain.

Most days passed without him seeing her at all except in the kitchen. Somehow he'd even gotten used to hearing her pounding away at the keys of her typewriter for hours on end. She might have been writing nursery rhymes for all he knew, but he couldn't say she wasn't keeping at it.

Actually, there were a lot of things he couldn't say about her. The problem started with the things he could say.

She talked too fast. It might have seemed an odd complaint, but not for a man who preferred quiet and structured conversations. If they talked about the weather she'd mention her brief career as a meteorologist and end by saying she liked rain because it smelled nice. Who could keep up with that sort of thought pattern?

She anticipated him. He might just begin to think he could use a cold drink and he'd find her in the kitchen making iced tea or pouring him a beer. Though she hadn't yet indicated that she'd trained as a psychic, he found it disconcerting.

She always looked at ease. It was a difficult thing to fault her for, but he found himself growing tenser the more casual she became. Invariably she was dressed in shorts and some breezy top with no makeup and her hair curling as it chose. She stopped just short of being sloppy, and he shouldn't have found it alluring. He preferred well-groomed, polished women—women with a little gloss and style. So why couldn't he keep his mind off one coltish, unpainted throwback who didn't do anything more to attract him than scrub her face and grin?

Because she was different? Nathan could easily reject that notion. He was a man who preferred the comfortable, and the comfortable usually meant the familiar. There was certainly nothing remotely familiar about Jackie. Some might accuse him of being in a rut, but he thought himself entitled. When your career took you to different cities and different countries and involved different people and problems on a regular basis, you deserved a nice comfortable rut in your personal life.

Solitude, quiet, a good book, an occasional congenial companion over drinks or dinner. It didn't seem like too much to ask. Jacqueline MacNamara had thrown a wrench in the works.

He didn't like to admit it, but he was getting used to her. After only a few days, he was used to her company. That in itself, for a loner, was a shattering discovery.

Nathan opened the throttle to let his boat race. He might have been more comfortable if she'd been dull or drab. For social purposes he preferred refined and composed, but for a housemate—boarder, he reminded himself firmly—for a boarder he'd have been happy with dull.

The trouble was, no matter how quiet or unobtrusive she was for most of the day, she was impossible to ignore with her rapid-fire conversations, her dazzling smiles and her bright clothes. Especially since she never seemed to dress in anything that covered more than ten percent of her.

Maybe he could admit it now, alone, with the wind breezing through his hair and over his face, that as annoying and inconvenient as it was to have his sanctuary invaded, she was, well…fun.

He hadn't allowed himself a great deal of fun in the past few years. Work had been and still was his first priority. Building, the creative process and the actual nuts and bolts, absorbed his time. He'd never resented the responsibility. If anyone had asked him if he enjoyed his work, he would have given them a peculiar look and answered, "Of course." Why else would he do it?

He would have accepted the term *dedicated* but would have knit his brows at the word *obsessed,* though obsessed was exactly what he was. He could picture a building in his mind, complete, down to the smallest detail, but he didn't consider himself an artist when he drew up the blueprints. He was a professional, educated and trained, nothing more or less.

He loved his work and considered himself lucky to have found a profession for which he had both skill and affection. There were moments of sweaty, gritty work, head-throbbing concentration and absolute pride. Nothing, absolutely nothing, had ever given him the same thrill of accomplishment as seeing one of his buildings completed.

If he absorbed himself in his work, it wasn't that his life was lacking in other areas. It was simply that no other area had the same appeal or excitement for him. He enjoyed the company of women, but had never met one who could keep him awake at night the way an engineering problem with a building could.

Unless, of course, he counted Jackie. He didn't care to.

He squinted into the sun, then steered away from it until it spread its warmth across his back. Still his frown remained.

Her conversations were like puzzles he had to sort out. No one had made him think that intricately in years. Her constant cheerfulness was contagious. It would be

foolish to deny he hadn't eaten better since his childhood—and probably not even then.

She did have an affecting smile, he thought as he
wound his way down an alley of the waterway. And
her eyes were so big and dark. Dark, yes, but they had
this trick, this illusion of lighting up when she smiled.
And her mouth was so wide and so generous, always
ready to curve.

Nathan pulled himself up short. Her physical attri-
butes weren't of any consequence. Shouldn't be.

That one moment of connection had been a fluke.
And he was undoubtedly exaggerating the depth of it.
There might have been a passing attraction. That was
natural enough. But there certainly hadn't been the af-
finity he'd imagined. He didn't believe in such things.
Love at first sight was a convenience used by novelists—usually bad ones. And instant desire was only
lust given a prettier name.

Whatever he had felt, if he'd felt anything at all, had
been a vague and temporary tug, purely physical and
easily subdued.

Nathan could almost hear her laughing at him,
though he was alone on the water and the banks of
the waterway were almost deserted. Grimly he headed
home.

It was dusk when she heard his boat. Jackie was certain it was Nathan. For the past two hours her ears had
been fine-tuned for his return. The wave of relief came
first. He hadn't met with any of the hideous boating ac-
cidents her mind had conjured up for him. Nor had he
been kidnapped and held for ransom. He was back, safe
and sound. She wanted to punch him right in the mouth.

Twelve hours, she thought as she dived cleanly into

the pool. He'd been gone for nearly twelve hours. The man obviously had no sense of consideration.

Naturally, she hadn't been worried. She'd been much too busy with her own projects to give him more than a passing thought—every five minutes for the last two hours.

Jackie began to do laps in a steady freestyle to release her pent-up energy. She wasn't angry. Why, she wasn't even mildly annoyed. His life was most certainly his own, to do with exactly as he chose. She wouldn't say a word about it. Not a word.

She did twenty laps, then tossed her wet hair back before resting her elbows on the edge of the pool.

"Training for the Olympics?" Nathan asked her. He stood only a few feet away, a glass of clear, fizzing liquid in his hand. Jackie blinked water out of her eyes and frowned at him.

He was wearing shorts, pleated and pressed, and a short-sleeved polo shirt that was so neat and tidy it might have come straight from the box. Nathan Powell's casual wear, she thought nastily.

"I didn't realize you were back." She glanced at his feet as she lied. Despite all her accomplishments, Jackie had never been able to manage an eyeball-to-eyeball lie.

"I haven't been for long." She was annoyed, Nathan realized. He found it enormously satisfying. Abandoning his rule against small talk, he smiled down at her. "So, how was your day?"

"Busy." Jackie pushed away from the side and began lazily treading water. In the east, the sky was nearly dark, but the last light from the sun touched the pool and garden. She didn't trust the way he was smiling right now, but she found she liked it. There was probably nothing more tedious than a man a woman could trust unconditionally. "And yours?"

"Relaxing." He had an urge, odd and unexpected, to slide into the pool with her. The water would be cool and soft; so would her skin. Maybe he was punchy, Nathan thought, after a hot day on the water.

As she continued to float, Jackie studied him. He did look relaxed—for him. She'd already discovered he was one of those people who carried around tension like a responsibility. She smiled, forgiving him as abruptly as she'd become angry.

"Want an omelet?"

"What?" Distracted, he pulled himself back. She was wearing two thin strips as an excuse for a bathing suit. The water, and perhaps a trick of the light, made them glimmer against her skin. A great deal of skin.

"Are you hungry? I could fix you an omelet."

"No. No, thanks." He took a sip of his drink to ease a suddenly dry throat, then sat the glass down to stuff his hands in his pockets. "It's cooling off." If that was the best he could do, he thought with a scowl, he'd best put the lid on small talk again.

"You're telling me." After sleeking her hair back, Jackie pulled herself out of the pool. She was skinny, Nathan told himself. There was no reason such a skinny, even lanky woman should move so athletically. In the fading sunlight, drops of water scattered over her skin like some primitive decoration.

"I forgot a towel." She shrugged, then shook herself. Nathan swallowed and looked elsewhere. It wasn't wise to look when he'd begun to imagine how easy it would be to slip those two tiny swatches of material off her and slide back into the water with her.

"I should go in," he managed after a moment. "I've got reading to catch up on."

"Me too. I'm reading tons of Westerns. Ever try Zane Grey or Louis L'Amour?" She was walking toward him as she spoke, and he found himself fascinated by the way the water clung to and darkened her hair and lashes. "Great stuff. I'll take this in for you."

"That's all right."

For the second time they reached at the same instant. For the second time their fingers touched and tangled. Nathan felt hers tense on the glass. So she felt it, too. That jolt...that connection, as he'd come to think of it. It wasn't his imagination. Wanting to avoid it, Nathan loosened his grip and stepped back. For the same reason, Jackie mirrored his move. The glass tipped, teetering on the edge of the table. They made the grab simultaneously, caught it, then stood holding the glass between them.

It should have been funny, she thought, but she managed only a quick, nervous laugh. In his eyes she saw exactly what she felt. Desire, hot and dangerous and edgy.

"Looks like we need a choreographer."

"I've got it." His voice was stiff as they waged a brief tug-of-war.

After relinquishing the glass to him, Jackie let out a slow, careful breath. She made the decision quickly, as she believed all the best decisions were made. "It might be better if we just got it over with."

"Got what over with?"

"The kiss. It's simple, really. I wonder what it would be like, you wonder what it would be like." Though her voice was casual, she moistened her lips. "Don't you think we'd be more comfortable if we stopped wondering?"

He set the glass down again as he studied her. It wasn't a romantic proposal, it was a logical one. That appealed to him. "That's a very pragmatic way of looking at it."

"I can be, occasionally." She shivered a little in the cooling air. "Look, odds are it won't be nearly as important after. Imagination magnifies things. At least mine does." The smile came again, quick and stunning, with the flash of a dimple at the corner of her mouth. "You're not my type. No offense. And I doubt I'm yours."

"No, you're not," he answered, stung a bit.

She took this statement with an agreeable nod. "So, we get the kiss out of the way and get back to normal. Deal?"

He didn't know if she'd done it on purpose—in fact, he was all but certain she hadn't—but she'd managed a direct hit to his male pride. She was so casual, so damn friendly about it. So sure that kissing him would leave her unaffected. Kissing him would be like brushing a pesky fly aside. Get it over with and get back to normal. He'd see about that.

She should have been warned by the look in his eyes—what she still thought of as his Jake look. Perhaps she had been, but it was knowledge gained too late.

With one hand he cupped her neck so that his fingers tangled in her dripping hair. The touch itself was a surprise—quietly intimate. There was a quick and sudden instinct to back away, but she ignored it. Jackie was used to approaching things head-on. So she stepped forward, tilting her head up. She expected something pleasant, warm, even ordinary. It wasn't the first time in her life she'd gotten more than she'd bargained for.

Rockets. They were her first image as his lips closed over hers. Rockets, with that flash of color and that fast, deadly boom. It had always been the boom she'd liked the best. Her little murmur wasn't of protest but of surprise and of pleasure. Accepting the pleasure, she leaned into him and absorbed it.

She could smell the water on him, not the clear, chlorinated water of the pool, but the darker, more exciting water that ran out to sea. The air was cooling rapidly as night fell, but the chill was gone. Her skin warmed as she moved against him and felt the soft brush of his shirt, and then of his hands.

And she *had* been waiting. The knowledge clicked quietly into place. She had been waiting years and years for this. Just this.

Unlike Jackie, Nathan had stopped thinking almost instantly—or thought he had. She tasted...exotic. There had been no warning of that in her pretty, piquant looks and wiry body, no indication of milk and honey heated with spice. She tasted of the desert, of something a dying man might drink greedily in the oasis of his mind.

He hadn't meant to hold her, not closely. He hadn't meant to let his hands roam over her, not freely. Somehow he'd lost control over them. With each touch and stroke over her damp skin, he lost a bit more.

Her back was long and lean and slick. He trailed his fingers over it and felt her tremble. The need jolted again until his mouth was hard on hers, more demanding than he'd ever intended. He pillaged. She accepted. When her sigh whispered against his tongue, his heartbeat doubled.

She pressed against him, her mouth open and willing, her body soft but not submissive. Her generosity was all-consuming. As was his temptation.

She'd never forget this, Jackie thought, not one detail. The heavy, heated scent of flowers, the soft hum of insects, the lapping of water close by. She'd never forget this first kiss, begun at dusk and carried into the night.

Her hands were in his hair, a smile just forming on her lips, as they drew apart. Unashamed of her reaction to him, she let out a long, contented sigh.

"I love surprises," she murmured.

He didn't. Nathan reminded himself of that and pulled back before he could stroke a hand through her hair. It amazed him and infuriated him to see that it wasn't steady. He wanted, unbearably, what he had no intention of taking.

"Now that we've satisfied our curiosity, we shouldn't have any more problems."

He expected anger. Indeed, that came first, a flash in her eyes. They were exceptionally expressive, he thought, and felt a pang when he read hurt in them. Then that, like the anger, disappeared, to be replaced by amusement.

"Don't bet the farm on it, Nathan." She patted his cheek—though she would have preferred to use her fist—and strolled into the house.

She was going to give him problems, all right, she thought as the screen door shut behind her. And it would be her pleasure.

## Chapter Four

She would poison his poached eggs. Jackie could see the justice in that. He would come down for breakfast, cool-eyed and smug. She could even imagine what he'd be wearing—beige cotton slacks and a navy-blue shirt. Without a wrinkle in either.

She, giving him no reason to suspect, would serve him a lovely plate of Canadian bacon, lightly grilled, and poached eggs on toast. With a touch of cyanide.

He would sip his coffee. Nathan always went for the coffee first. Then he'd slice the meat. Jackie would fix herself a plate so everything would seem perfectly normal. They'd discuss the weather. A bit humid today, isn't it? Perhaps we're in for some rain.

As he took the first forkful of eggs, the sweat would break out cold on her brow as she waited…and waited.

In moments he would be writhing on the floor, gasping for air, clutching his throat. His eyes would be wide and shocked, then all too aware, as she stood over him, triumphant and smiling. With his last breath, he would beg for forgiveness.

But that wasn't subtle enough.

She was a great believer in revenge. People who forgave and forgot with a pious smile deserved to be stepped on. Not that she couldn't forgive small slights or unconscious hurts, but the big ones, the deliberate ones, required—no, demanded—payback.

She was going to give Nathan Powell the payback he deserved.

She told herself he was a cold fish, an unfeeling slug, a cardboard cutout. But she didn't believe it. Unfortunately for her, she'd seen the kindness and sense of fair play in him. Perhaps he was rigid, but he wasn't cold.

Maybe, just maybe, she had read too much into the kiss. Perhaps her emotions were closer to the surface than most people's, and there was a possibility that he hadn't heard the boom. But he'd felt something. A man didn't hold a woman as if he were falling off a cliff if he'd only slipped off a curb.

He'd felt something, all right, and she was going to see to it that he felt that and more. And suffered miserably.

She could take rejection, Jackie told herself as she ground fresh beans for coffee. Smashing something into dust gave her enormous satisfaction. Rejection was that part of life that toughened you enough to make you try harder. True, she hadn't had to deal with it very often, but she thought of herself as gracious enough to accept it when it was warranted.

Frowning, she watched the kettle begin to steam. It

wasn't as though she expected men to fall at her feet—though she had enough ego to want one to trip a little now and again. She certainly didn't expect pledges of undying love and fidelity after one embrace, no matter how torrid.

But damn it, there had been something special between them, something rare and close to wonderful. He'd had no business turning it off with a shrug.

And he'd pay, she thought viciously as she poured boiling water over the ground coffee. He'd pay for the shrug, for the pretending disinterest, and more, he'd pay for the night she'd spent tossing in bed remembering every second she'd been in his arms.

It was a pity she wasn't stunning, Jackie mused as she heated a skillet. Really stunning, with razor-edged cheekbones and a statuesque build—or petite and fragile-looking, with melting blue eyes and porcelain skin. Frowning a bit, she tried to get a good look at her reflection in the stainless-steel range hood. What she saw was distorted and vague. Experimenting, she sucked in her cheeks, then let them out again with a puff of air.

Since her appearance was something she couldn't change, she would make the very best of what she had. Nathan Powell, man of stone and steel, would be eating out of her hand in no time.

She heard him come in but took her time before turning. The skimpy halter made the most of her tanned back. For the first time in days she'd raided her supply of makeup. Nothing jarring, she'd told herself. Just a bit of blush and gloss, with most of the accent on the eyes.

Jackie tossed one of her best smiles over her shoulders and had to stifle a shout of laughter. He looked dreadful. Wasn't that a shame?

He felt worse. While Jackie had been fuming and tossing in her bed, Nathan had been cursing and turning in his own. Her cheerful smile made him want to bare his teeth and snarl.

One kiss and they'd get back to normal? He'd have liked to strangle her. Things hadn't been normal since she'd forced herself into his life. As far as he could recall, his body hadn't ached like this since he'd been a teenager, when, fortunately, his imagination had outdistanced his experience. Now he knew exactly what it could be like and had spent most of the night thinking about it.

"Morning, Nate. Coffee?"

Nate? *Nate?* Because he was sure it would hurt too much to argue, he merely nodded.

"Hot and fresh, just the way you like it." If her voice had been any sweeter, she'd have grown wings. "We have Canadian bacon and eggs on the menu this morning. Ready in five minutes."

He downed the first cup. He set it back on the counter, and she filled it again. She'd used a freer hand with her scent. Her fragrance still wasn't rich or overpowering, but this morning it seemed just a bit more pungent than usual. Remember? it seemed to say. Cautious, he glanced up at her.

Did she look prettier, or was it just his imagination? How did she manage to make her skin always look so glowing, so soft? It wasn't right, it wasn't even fair, that her hair could be constantly disheveled and appealing whether she was tossing a salad or napping on his couch.

He'd have sworn he'd never seen anyone look so alive, so vivid, in the morning. It was infuriating that she should be so fresh when he felt as though he'd spent the night being pummeled by rubber-tipped sledgehammers.

Despite his best intentions, his gaze was drawn to her mouth. She'd put something on it, something that left it looking as moist and as warm as he remembered it tasted. Dirty pool, he thought, and scowled at her.

"Mrs. Grange is coming in today."

"Oh?" Jackie smiled at him again as she turned the sizzling bacon. "Isn't that nice? Things really are getting back to normal, aren't they?" Jackie broke an egg, one-handed, and dropped it in the poacher. "Do you plan to be here for lunch?"

The yolk didn't break, and the shell was neatly dispatched. A nice trick, Nathan thought. He was sure she had a million of them. "I'll be in all day. I've got a lot of calls to make."

"Good. I'll be sure to fix something special." She turned to him again to give him a long, interested study. "You know, Nathan, you look a little haggard this morning. Trouble sleeping?"

No matter how much it cost him, he wouldn't snarl. "I had some paperwork I wanted to clear up."

Jackie clucked her tongue sympathetically as she arranged his breakfast on a plate. "You work too hard. It makes you tense. You should try yoga. There's nothing like a little meditation and proper exercise to relax the body and mind."

"Work relaxes me."

"A common misconception." Jackie set the plate neatly in front of him, then scooted around the counter. "The fact is that work occupies your mind and can take your mind off other problems, but it doesn't cleanse. Take a good massage."

Jackie began to knead his neck and shoulders while she spoke, pleased that at the first touch he jerked like a spring. "A really good massage," she continued as her fingers pressed and stroked, "relieves both mind and body of tension. A little oil, some soothing music, and you'll sleep like a baby. Oh, you've got yourself a real knot here at the base of your neck."

"I'm fine," he managed. In another minute the fork he was holding was going to snap in two. She had magic in her hands. Black magic. "I'm never tense."

Jackie frowned a moment, losing track of the purpose of the exercise. Did he believe that? she wondered. Probably. When a man was always tense, he obviously thought of it as normal. When her heart started to warm toward him, she lectured herself.

"Let's just say there's relaxed and there's relaxed." She concentrated on the teres minor. "After a really good rub, my muscles are like butter. I slide right off the table. I've got some wonderful oil. Hans swears by it."

"Hans?" Why was he asking? Nathan thought as, despite himself, he stretched under her hands.

"My masseur. He's from Norway and has the hands of an artist. He taught me his technique."

"I'll just bet," Nathan muttered, and had Jackie grinning behind his back.

God, who would have suspected he had muscles like this? The man drew up blueprints and argued with engineers. Jackie hadn't suspected that his conservative shirts hid all those wonderful ridges. Last night, when he'd held her, she'd been too dazed to notice how well he was built. She ran her hands over his shoulders.

"You've got a terrific build," she told him. "I've got lousy deltoids myself. When I was into bodybuilding, I never managed to do much more than sweat."

Enough was enough, Nathan thought. One more squeeze of those long, limber fingers and he'd do something embarrassing. Like whimpering. Instead, he spun around on the stool and caught her hands in his.

"What the hell are you trying to do?"

She didn't mind her heart skipping a beat. In fact, it was a delightful feeling. Still, she remembered that revenge was her first order of business.

"Just trying to loosen you up, Nate. Tension's bad for the digestion."

"I'm not tense. And don't call me Nate."

"Sorry. It suits you when you get that look in your eyes. That look," she explained, and she would have gestured if her hands hadn't been clamped in his. "The one that says shoot first and ask questions later."

He would be patient. Nathan told himself to count to ten, but only made it to four. "Careful, Jack. You're here on probation. You'd be wise to back off from whatever game you're playing."

"Game?" She smiled, but her eyes held the first hint of frost he'd ever seen in them. For some reason, even that attracted him. "I don't know what you're talking about."

"What about that stuff you put on your mouth?"

"This?" Deliberately she ran her tongue over her upper, then her lower lip. "A woman's entitled to a little lipstick now and then. Don't you like it?"

He wouldn't dignify the question with an answer. "You put stuff on your eyes, too."

"Are cosmetics against the law in this state? Really,

Nate—sorry, Nathan—you're being silly. Surely you don't think I'm trying to…seduce you?" She smiled again, daring him to comment. "I'd think a big strong man like you could take care of himself." She liked the way his eyes could darken from slate to smoke. "But if it stirs you up, I'll be certain to keep my mouth absolutely naked from now on. Will that be better?"

His voice was so soft, so very controlled, that she was fooled into thinking she was still at the wheel. "People who fight dirty end up in the mud themselves."

"So I've heard." She tossed back her head and looked at him from beneath her lashes. "But you see, I can take care of myself, too."

She saw then that she had misjudged him. Perhaps by no more than a few degrees, but such miscalculations could often be fatal. The look that came into his eyes was so utterly reckless, so coolly dangerous, that her heart thudded to a halt.

Jake was back, and his guns were smoking.

It would be more than a kiss now, whether she wanted it or not. It would be exactly as he chose, when he chose and how he chose. No amount of glib chatter or charming smiles was going to help.

When the doorbell rang, neither of them moved. With a hard, painful thump, Jackie's heart started again. Saved by the bell. She would have giggled if she hadn't been ready to collapse.

"That must be Mrs. Grange," she said brightly, just a shade too brightly. "If you'd let go of my hands now, Nathan, I'd be glad to answer the door while you finish your breakfast."

He did release her, but only after making her suffer through the longest five seconds of her life, during

which she believed he would ignore the door and finish what his eyes had told her he intended to do. Saying
nothing, Nathan let her go, then swiveled back around to
the counter. The pity of it was that he no longer wanted
coffee, but a nice stiff drink.

Jackie slipped out of the kitchen. She hoped his eggs
were stone-cold.

She loved Mrs. Grange. When Jackie opened the
door, she wasn't sure what to make of the large woman
in the flowered housedress and high-top sneakers. Mrs.
Grange gave Jackie a long, narrowed look with watery
blue eyes, pursed her lips and said, "Well, well."

Understanding the implications of that, Jackie smiled
and offered a hand. "Good morning. You must be Mrs.
Grange. I'm Jack MacNamara, and Nathan's stuck with
me for a few weeks because he can't bring himself to
toss me out. Have you had breakfast?"

"An hour ago." After she stepped inside, Mrs. Grange
set a huge canvas bag on the floor. "MacNamara. You
must be related to that no-account."

Jackie didn't need a name. "Guilty. We're cousins.
He's gone."

"And good riddance." With a sniff, Mrs. Grange cast
a look around the living area. Though she approved of
the fresh flowers, she was determined to withhold final
judgment. "I'll tell you like I told him. I don't clean up
after pigs."

"And who could blame you?" Jackie's grin was fast
and brilliant. If dear cousin Fred had tried to charm
Mrs. Grange, he'd fallen flat on his baby face. "I'm
using the guest room, the blue-and-white one? I'm
working in there, too, so if you'll just let me know where

that room fits into your schedule I'll make sure I'm out of your way. I'm planning on fixing lunch about twelve-thirty," she continued, mentally adjusting her menu with the idea of carving a few pounds from Mrs. Grange's prodigious bulk.

Mrs. Grange's lips pursed again. It was a rare thing for an employer to offer her a meal. For the most part she was treated with polite, and bland, disregard. "I brought some sandwiches."

"Of course, if you'd rather, but I was hoping you'd join us. I'll be upstairs if you need anything. Nathan's in the kitchen and the coffee's fresh." She smiled again, then left Mrs. Grange to begin while she went upstairs.

Throughout the morning, Jackie heard the sounds of vacuuming and the heavy thud of Mrs. Grange's sneakers moving up and down the hallway. It pleased her that the noise and activity didn't intrude on her concentration. A real writer, in her opinion, should have imagination enough to overcome any outside interference. By noon, she was well on her way to sending Jake and Sarah on another adventure.

Jackie decided on a cracked-wheat-and-parsley salad for the lunch break. With the radio on, she set about dicing and cubing and humming to herself while she tried to imagine what it would be like to outrun desperadoes. When Nathan came in, she turned the music down, then set a huge bowl on the counter.

"Iced coffee all right?"

"Fine." His answer was casual, but he was watching her. One wrong move, he thought, and he was going to pounce. He wasn't certain what would constitute a wrong move, or what he'd do once he'd pounced, but he was ready for her.

"I'd like to use the phone later, if you don't mind. Anything long-distance I'll charge to my credit card."

"All right."

"Thanks. I think it's about time to start planting the seeds of Fred's downfall."

With his fork halfway to his mouth, Nathan stopped. "What kind of seeds?"

"You're better off not knowing. Oh, hello, Mrs. Grange."

Annoyed with the interruption, Nathan turned to look at his housekeeper. "Mrs. Grange?"

"Sit down right here," Jackie said before Nathan could continue. "I hope you like this. It's called *tabouleh*. Very popular in Syria."

Mrs. Grange settled her bulk on a stool and eyed the bowl doubtfully. "It doesn't have any of that funny stuff in it, does it?"

"Absolutely not." Jackie set a glass of iced coffee next to the bowl. "If you like it, I'll give you the recipe for your family. Do you have a family, Mrs. Grange?"

"Boys are grown." Cautiously Mrs. Grange took the first forkful. Her hands, Jackie noticed, were work-reddened and ringless.

"You have sons?"

With a nod, Mrs. Grange dipped into the salad again. "Had four of them. Two of them are married now. Got three grandkids."

"Three grandchildren. That's marvelous, isn't it, Nathan? Do you have pictures?"

Mrs. Grange took another forkful. She'd never tasted anything quite like this. It wasn't cold meat loaf on rye, but it was nice. Real nice. "Got some in my bag."

"I'd love to see them." Jackie took a seat that set Mrs.

Grange squarely between her and Nathan. He was eating in silence, like a man who found himself placed next to strangers at a diner. "Four sons. You must be very proud."

"They're good boys." Her wide, stern face relaxed a bit. "The youngest is in college. Going to be a teacher. He's smart, that one, never gave me a minute's trouble. The others…" She paused, then shook her head. "Well, that's what having kids is all about. This is a real nice salad, Miss MacNamara. Real pretty."

"Jack. And I'm glad you like it. Would you like some more coffee?"

"No, I'd best get back to work. You want me to take those shirts to the cleaners, Mr. Powell?"

"I'd appreciate it."

"If you don't need to use it now, I'll do your office."

"That's fine."

She turned to Jackie, and her eyes were friendly. "Don't worry about keeping out of the way upstairs. I can work around you."

"Thanks. Don't bother, I'll get these." She started to gather up bowls as Mrs. Grange plodded out. Nathan frowned at her over the rim of his iced coffee.

"What was all that about?"

"Hmm?" Jackie glanced at him as she transferred the leftover salad into a smaller dish.

"That business with Mrs. Grange. What were you doing?"

"Eating lunch. Would you mind if I gave her the rest of this to take home?"

"No, go ahead." He drew out a cigarette. "Do you usually have lunch with the help?"

She looked at him again, one brow lifting. "Why not?"

Every answer he thought of seemed stilted and snobbish, so he merely shrugged and lit his cigarette. Because she could see he was embarrassed, Jackie let it pass.

"Is Mrs. Grange divorced or widowed?"

"What?" Nathan blew out a stream of smoke and shook his head. "How would I know? How do you know she's either?"

"Because she talked about her sons and her grandchildren, but she didn't mention her husband. Therefore it's elementary, my dear Nathan, that she hasn't got one." As an afterthought, she popped one last crouton into her mouth. "I opt for divorce because widows usually continue to wear a wedding ring. Hasn't it ever come up?"

"No." He brooded, staring into his coffee. For some reason he didn't want to confess that Mrs. Grange had worked for him for five—no, it was nearly six years now—and he hadn't known she had four sons and three grandchildren until five minutes ago. "It wasn't part of her job description, and I didn't want to pry."

"That's nonsense. Everyone likes to talk about their families. I wonder how long she's been single." She moved around the kitchen rinsing bowls, tidying counters. The rings on her fingers flashed with wealth, while her hands spoke of confidence. "I can't think of anything tougher than raising kids on your own. Do you ever think about that?"

"Think about what?"

"About having a family." She poured herself another glass with the idea of taking the coffee upstairs. "Thinking about kids always makes me feel very traditional. White picket fence, two-car garage, wood-paneled station wagon and all of that. I'm surprised you're not married, Nathan. Being a traditional man."

Her tone had him scowling. "I know when I've been insulted."

"Of course you do." She touched his cheek lightly with her fingertips. "Being traditional's nothing to be ashamed of. I admire you, Nathan, really I do. There's something endearing about a man who always knows where his socks are. When the right woman comes along, she's going to get a real prize."

His hand clamped over her wrist before she could draw away. "Have you ever had your nose broken?"

Absolutely delighted, she grinned at him. "Not so far. Want to fight?"

"Let's try this."

Jackie found herself sprawled over him as he sat on the stool. He'd caught her off balance, and she had to grab his shoulders to keep from falling on her face. She hadn't expected him to move that quickly, or precisely in that way. Before she could decide how to counter it—or whether she should counter it—his mouth was on hers. And it was searing.

He didn't know why he'd done it. What he'd really wanted to do, ached to do, was slug her. Of course, a man didn't slug a woman, so he'd really been left with no choice.

Why he'd thought a kiss would be revenge was beyond him now that it was begun. She didn't struggle, though he knew from the way her breath caught and her fingers tightened that he had at least surprised her.

But she couldn't have been more surprised than he.

Damn it, he wasn't the kind of man who yanked women around. Yet it seemed right when it was Jackie.

It seemed...fated. He could rationalize for hours, he could reason and deliberate until everything was crystal-clear. Then he could touch her and blow logic to smithereens.

He didn't want her. He was eaten up with wanting her. He didn't even like her. He was fascinated by her. He thought she was crazy. And he was beginning to be sure he was. Always he'd known there was a pattern to everything, a structure. Until Jackie.

He nipped his teeth into her bottom lip and heard her low, quiet moan. Apparently life wasn't always geometrical.

She'd asked for it, Jackie thought to herself. And, thank God, she'd gotten it. Thoughts of revenge, of making him suffer and sweat, flew out of her mind as she dived into the kiss. It was wonderful, sweet, sharp, hot, trembling, the way she'd imagined and hoped a kiss might be.

Her heart went into it, completely, trustingly. This was a man who could love her, accept her. She wasn't a fool, and she wasn't naive. She felt it from him as clearly as if he'd spoken the words. This was special, unique, the kind of loving poems were written about and wars were fought for. Some people waited a lifetime for only this. And not everyone found it. She knew it, and she wrapped her arms around him, ready to give him everything she was. No questions, no doubts.

Something was happening. Over the desire, over the passion, he could sense it. There was a change inside him, an opening, a recklessness. When her mouth was on his, her body melting in his arms, he couldn't think beyond the moment. That was crazy. He never thought of today without taking tomorrow into account. But now, just now, he could think only of holding her like this. Of tasting more of her, bit by slow bit. Of exploring her, discovering her. He couldn't think of anything but her.

It was insanity. He knew it, feared it, even as he pressed her closer. Sinking. He was sinking into her. It was an odd and erotic sensation to feel himself lose his grip. He had to stop this, and stop it cold, before whatever was growing inside him grew too big to be controlled.

He drew her away, struggling to be firm, planning to be cruel. If she smiled at him instead of striking back, he knew, he'd be on his knees. He knew he should tell her all bets were off, to pack her things and leave. But he couldn't. No matter how much he told himself he wanted her out of his life, he couldn't ask her to go.

"Nathan." Aroused, pliant, already in love, she cupped her hand over his cheek. "Let's give Mrs. Grange the rest of the day off. I want to be with you."

Words caught in his throat, trapped in a fresh surge of desire. He'd never known a woman who was more open with her feelings, more honest with her needs. She scared him to death. He gave himself an extra moment. He couldn't afford to have his voice sound unsteady or to have her see how flexible his resolve was.

"You're getting ahead of yourself." As if the kiss had been only a kiss, he set her back on the floor. He hadn't realized how much warmth she'd brought to him until he'd no longer been touching her. "I don't think having an affair is in your best interests, or mine, considering our current arrangement. But thanks."

She went pale, and he knew that he'd gone too far in his rush for self-protection.

"Jackie, I didn't mean that the way it sounded."

"Didn't you? Well, whatever." She was amazed, absolutely amazed, at how much it hurt. She'd always dreamed of falling in love, deeply, blindly, beautifully in love. So this was how it felt, she thought as she pressed a hand to her stomach. The poets could keep it.

"Jack, listen—"

"No, I'd really rather not." When she smiled at him now, he realized just how special her genuine smile was. "No explanations required, Nathan. It was only a suggestion. I should apologize for coming on too strong."

"Damn it, I don't want an apology."

"No? Well, that's good, because I think I'd choke on it. I really should get back to work, but before I go there's just one thing." Deadly calm, Jackie picked up her glass of iced coffee and emptied it in his lap. "See you at dinner."

She worked like a maniac, barely noticing when Mrs. Grange came in to change the bed linen and dust the furniture. She was both amazed and infuriated at how close, how dangerously close, she'd been to tears. It wasn't that she minded shedding tears. There were times when she enjoyed nothing more than a wailing crying jag. But she knew that if she gave in to this one she wouldn't enjoy it a bit.

How could he have been so insensitive, so unfeeling, as to think she'd been offering him nothing more than sex, a quick afternoon romp? And how could she have been so stupid as to think she'd fallen in love?

Love took two people. She knew that. Wasn't she even now pouring her heart out in a story that involved two people's feelings and needs? And those feelings hadn't sprung out of a kiss but out of time and struggle.

Same old Jack, she accused herself. Still believing that everything in life came as easily as slipping off a log. She'd deserved a swift kick and gotten one. But deserving or not, it didn't make it any less humiliating that Nathan had been the one to plant it.

Mrs. Grange cleared her throat for the third time as she fluffed Jackie's pillows. The minute the typewriter stilled, she stepped in.

"You sure do type fast," she began. "You do secretarial work?"

There was no reason to take out her foul mood on the housekeeper, Jackie reminded herself as she forced a smile. "No, actually I'm writing a book."

"Is that so?" Interested, Mrs. Grange walked to the foot of the bed to tug on the spread. "I like a good story myself."

Mrs. Grange was the first person Jackie had told about her writing who hadn't raised a brow or rolled her eyes. Encouraged, she swiveled around in her chair. The devil with Nathan, she thought. Jacqueline R. MacNamara had come to write a book, and that was just what she was going to do.

"Do you get much of a chance to read?"

"Nothing I like better after a day on my feet than to sit down with a nice story for an hour or two." Mrs. Grange edged a little closer, passing a dustrag over the lamp. "What kind of book are you writing?"

"A romance, a historical romance."

"No fooling? I'm partial to love stories. You been writing long?"

"Actually, this is my first try. I spent about a month

doing research and compiling information and dates and things, then I just dived in."

Mrs. Grange shifted her gaze to the typewriter, then looked back at the lamp. "I guess it's like painting. You don't want anybody looking till it's all done."

"Are you kidding?" Laughing, Jackie tucked her feet under her. "I've been dying for somebody to want to read some of it." But not her family, Jackie thought, nibbling on her lower lip. They had already seen too much of what she'd begun, then left undone. "Want to see the first page?" Jackie was already whipping it from the pile and offering it.

"Well, now." Mrs. Grange took the typed sheet and held it out at arm's length until she focused on it. She read with her lips pursed and her eyes narrowed. After a moment she let out three wheezes that Jackie recognized as a laugh. Nothing, absolutely nothing, could have pleased her more.

"You sure did start out with a bang, didn't you?" There was both admiration and approval in Mrs. Grange's eyes as she looked over the end of the sheet. "Nothing like a gunfight to pique the interest."

"That's what I was hoping. Of course, it's just a first draft, but it's going fast." She accepted the page back and studied it. "I'm hoping to have enough to send off in a couple of weeks."

"I'll be mighty pleased to read the whole thing when you've finished."

"Me too." Jackie laughed again as she placed the first page on top of the pile. "Every day when I see how many pages I've done I can't believe it." A bit hesitantly, she laid her hand on top of the manuscript pages.

"I haven't figured out what I'm going to do when it's all finished."

"Well, I guess you'll just have to write another one, won't you?" Bending, Mrs. Grange hefted her box of cleaning tools and clumped out.

Why, she was right, Jackie thought. Win or lose, life didn't begin or end on the first try. There couldn't be anyone who knew that better than herself. If something worked, you kept at it. And if something didn't work, and you wanted it, you kept right at that, too.

Turning around, she smiled at the half-typed page in her machine. She could apply that philosophy nicely to her writing. And while she was at it she might just apply it to Nathan.

# Chapter Five

He was furious with himself. Still, it was easier, and a lot more comfortable, to turn his fury on her. He hadn't wanted to kiss her. She'd goaded him into it. He certainly hadn't wanted to hurt her. She'd forced him to do so. In a matter of days she'd turned him into a short-tempered villain with an overactive libido.

He was really a very nice man. Nathan was certain of it. Sure, he could be tough-minded, and he was often an impatient perfectionist on the job. He could hire and fire with impersonal speed. But that was business. In his personal life he'd never given anyone reason to dislike him.

When he saw a woman socially, he was always careful to see that the rules were posted up front. If the relationship deepened, both would be fully aware of its possibilities and its limitations. No one would ever have called him a womanizer.

Not that he didn't have a certain number of female...
friends. It would be impossible for a grown man, a
healthy man, to go through life without some companionship and affection. But, damn it, he made the moves,
the overtures—and there was a certain flow to how
these things worked. When a man and a woman decided to go beyond being friends, they did so respon-
sibly, with as much caution as affection. By the time
they did, if they did, they'd developed a certain rapport
and understanding.

Groping in the kitchen after a parsley salad wasn't
his idea of a sensible adult relationship.

If that was old-fashioned, then he was old-fashioned.

The problem was, that kiss over the kitchen counter
had meant more, had shaken him more, than any of the
carefully programmed, considerate and mature relationships he'd ever experienced. And it wasn't the way he
wanted his life to run.

He hadn't learned much from his father, other than
how to knot a tie correctly, but he had learned that a
woman was to be treated with respect, admiration and
care. He was—always had been—a gentleman. Roses
for the proper occasion, a light touch and a certain
amount of courtship.

He knew how to treat a woman, how to steer a relationship along the right course and how to end one without scenes and recriminations. If he was overly careful
not to allow anyone to get too close, he had good reason.
Another thing he'd learned from his father, in reverse,
was never to make promises he wouldn't keep or establish bonds he would certainly break. It had always
been a matter of pride to him that whenever it had be-

come necessary to end a relationship he and the woman involved had parted as friends.

How could he and Jackie part as friends when they hadn't yet become friends? In any case, Nathan considered himself sharp enough to know that if a relationship was begun, then ended, with a woman like Jackie, it wouldn't end without scenes or recriminations. The end, he was sure, would be just as explosive and illogical as the beginning.

He didn't like mercurial personalities or flash-fire tempers. They interfered with his concentration.

What he needed to do was to get back in gear—start the preliminaries on his next project, resume his social life. He'd spent too much time on the troubles and triumphs with the complex in Germany. Now that he'd gotten home, he hadn't had a peaceful moment.

His own fault. Nathan was willing to accept responsibility. His uninvited guest had another week—after all, she had his word on that. Then she was out. Out and forgotten. Well, out, in any case.

He started upstairs with the intention of changing and drowning himself in the pool. Then he heard her laugh. It was just his bad luck, he supposed, that she had such an appealing laugh. He heard her speak in that quicksilver way she had, and he stopped. Her bedroom door was open, and her voice raced out, It wasn't eavesdropping, he told himself. It was, after all, his house.

"Aunt Honoria, what in the world gave you that idea?" Kicked back in a chair, Jackie held the phone between her shoulder and chin as she painted her toenails. "Of course I'm not annoyed with Fred. Why should I be? He did me a wonderful favor." Jackie dipped her brush in the bottle of Sizzling Cerise polish and played her cards close to her chest. "The house is absolutely perfect, exactly what I'd been looking for, and Nathan—Nathan's the owner, darling—yes, he's just adorable."

She held her foot out to admire her handiwork. Between writing and cooking, she hadn't had time for a pedicure in weeks. No matter how busy, her mother would have said, a woman should always look her best from head to toe.

"No, dear, we've worked things out beautifully. He's a bit of a hermit, so we keep to ourselves. I'm fixing his meals for him. The darling's developing a bit of a paunch."

Outside the door, Nathan automatically reached a hand to his stomach.

"No, he couldn't be sweeter. We're rubbing along just fine. He might be one of my uncles. As a matter of fact, his hairline's receding just like Uncle Bob's."

This time both of Nathan's hands went to his hair.

"I'm just glad I could put your mind at ease. No, be sure to let Fred know everything couldn't be better. I'd have gotten in touch with him myself, but I wasn't sure just where he'd popped off to."

There was a pause. For some reason, Nathan felt it was a particularly cold one.

"Of course, dear, I know exactly how our Fred is."

In the hallway, Nathan heard little murmurs of agreement and a few light laughs. He was just about to continue when Jackie spoke again.

"Oh, Aunt Honoria, I nearly forgot. What was the name of that wonderful Realtor you used on the Hawkins property?"

Jackie switched feet and moved in for the kill.

"Well, dear, it's rather confidential still, but I know I

can trust you. It seems there's this block of land, about twenty-five acres, South of here, a place called Shutter's Creek. Yes, it is rather precious, isn't it? In any case… you will keep this to yourself, won't you?"

Jackie smiled and continued to paint as she received her aunt's assurances. Aunt Honoria's promises were as easily smeared as wet nail polish. "Yes, I knew you would. Anyway, it's being sold at rock bottom, and naturally I wouldn't have been interested. Who would? It's hardly more than a swamp at this point. But the beauty is, dear, that Allegheny Enterprises—you know, the contractors who put up all those marvelous resorts? Yes, that's the one. They're scouting out the location. They're thinking about pumping it and filling it in and putting up one of those chichi places like they did in Arizona. Yes, it was marvelous what they did with a few acres of desert, wasn't it?"

She listened a few more moments, knowing how to play a line until the bait was well taken.

"Just a little tip from a friend of mine. I want to snap it up quickly, then resell it to Allegheny. Word from my friend is that they'll pay triple the asking price. Yes, I know, sounds too good to be true. Do keep this under your hat, Auntie. I want to see if I can have the Realtor push this through settlement before the lid's off."

Jackie listened for a moment as she debated putting on a third coat.

"Yes, it could be exciting, and very hush-hush. That's why I don't want to tip my hand to the Realtor here in Florida. No, I haven't said a thing to Mother and Daddy yet. You know how I love surprises. Oh, darling, there's the door. Must run. Do give my best to everyone. I'll be in touch. *Ciao*."

Delighted with herself, Jackie stretched in the chair and sent it spinning in a circle.

"Well, hello, Nathan."

"I don't know where you get your information," he began, "but unless you want to lose even more money, I'd look for someplace other than Shutter's Creek. It's twenty-five acres of sludge and mosquitoes."

"Yes, I know." With the ease of the limber, Jackie brought her leg around so that she could blow on her painted toenails. Nathan wouldn't have been surprised if she'd tucked her heel behind her ear and grinned at him. "And unless I miss my guess, dear old Fred will own all those lovely mosquitoes within forty-eight hours." Smiling at Nathan, she pillowed her head on her folded arms. "I always figure when you pay back you should pay back where it'll hurt the most. For Fred, that's his wallet."

Impressed, Nathan stepped farther into the room. "You planted the seeds of his downfall?"

"Exactly, and like Jack's beanstalk, it should sprout overnight."

Nathan mulled it over. It was a nasty trick, a very nasty trick. He only wished he'd thought of it. "How do you know he'll go for it?"

Jackie merely continued to smile. "Want to make a wager on it?"

"No," he said after a moment. "No, I don't think I do. How much are they asking an acre?"

"Oh, only two thousand. Fred should be able to beg, borrow or steal fifty without too much trouble." Deciding against a third coat, she capped the bottle. "I always pay my debts, Nathan. Without exception."

He was aware he'd been warned and decided he deserved it. "If it's any consolation, I doubt I'll be able to drink iced coffee again."

She crossed her legs lazily. "I suppose that's something."

"And I'm not losing my hair."

She flicked her gaze over it. It was thick and full and dark. She could remember with absolute clarity how it had felt between her fingers. "Probably not."

"Nor do I have a paunch."

With her tongue caught between her teeth, she let her glance slide down to his taut and very flat stomach. "Well, not yet."

"And I am not adorable."

"Well…" Her eyes were laughing when they came back to his. "Cute, then—in a staid and very masculine sort of way."

He opened his mouth to argue, then decided it was safer to give up. "I'm sorry," he said instead before he knew he'd meant to tell her.

Jackie's eyes softened along with her smile. Revenge always took a back seat to an apology. "Yes, I think you are. Do you like fresh starts, Nathan?"

So it was that easy. He should have known it would be that easy with her. "Yes, actually, I do."

"All right, then." She unwound herself from the chair. If he found himself looking at her legs again, he was only human. When she stood, she offered a hand. "Friends?"

He knew he could have given her a list of reasons they couldn't be, certainly a lengthy one of reasons why they shouldn't be. But he put his hand in hers. "Friends. Do you want to take a swim?"

"Yeah." She could have kissed him. God, she wanted

to. Lecturing herself, Jackie smiled instead. "Give me five minutes to change."

She took less than that. When she arrived, Nathan was just surfacing. Before he had the chance to shake the water out of his eyes and spot her, she dived in beside him. She came up cleanly, head tilted back so that her hair was slick against her head.

"Hi."

"You move fast."

"Mostly." She moved into a smooth sidestroke and did a length and a half. "I love your pool. That helped sell me on the place, you know. I grew up with a pool, so I'd have hated to spend three months without one."

"Glad I could oblige," he told her, but it didn't come out nearly as sarcastic as he'd expected. She smiled and switched to a breaststroke that barely rippled the water. "I take it you do a lot of swimming."

"Not as much as I used to." With what looked like no effort at all, she rolled onto her back to float. "I was on a swim team for a couple of years in my teens. Gave some serious thought to the Olympics."

"I'm not surprised."

"Then I fell in love with my swim coach. His name was Hank." She sighed and closed her eyes on the memory. "I couldn't seem to concentrate on my form after that. I was fifteen and Hank was twenty-five. I imagined us married and raising a relay team. He was only interested in my backstroke. I've always been able to go backward well."

"You don't say."

"No, really. I was all-state with my backstroke. Anyway, Hank was about five-eight, with shoulders like I beams. I've always been a sucker for shoulders." She opened her eyes briefly to study him. Without a shirt, his body seemed tougher and more disciplined than she had expected. "Yours are very nice."

"Thanks." He discovered it was both relaxing and invigorating to float beside her.

"Also, Hank had the greatest blue eyes. Like lanterns. I wove some wonderful fantasies around those eyes."

Irrationally he began to detest Hank. "But he was only interested in your backstroke."

"Exactly. To get him to notice me, I pretended I was drowning. I imagined him pulling me out and doing mouth-to-mouth until he realized he was madly in love and couldn't live without me. How was I supposed to know that my father had picked that day to come in and watch practice?"

"No one could have."

"I knew you'd understand. So there's my father jumping into the pool in his three-piece wool suit and Swiss watch. Neither were ever quite the same again, by the way. By the time he dragged me to the side he was hysterical. Some of my teammates thought it was a reaction from shock, but my father knew me too well. Before I could blink, I was off the swim team and on the tennis courts. With a female pro."

"Your father sounds like a very wise man."

"Oh, he's as sharp as they come, J. D. MacNamara. No one's ever been able to put anything over on him for long. God knows I've tried." She sighed and let the water lap around her. "He'll get a tremendous charge out of it when I tell him about the sting I pulled on Fred."

"You're close to your family?"

Jackie thought, but couldn't be sure, that his voice sounded wistful. "Very. Sometimes almost too much,

which may be why I'm always pulling myself off somewhere to try something new. If Daddy had his way, I'd
be safely housed in Newport with the man of his choice,
raising his grandchildren and keeping out of trouble.
Do you have any family here in Florida?"

"No."

She didn't have any doubts about it this time. The
subject was definitely on posted ground. Not wanting
to irritate him again so soon, Jackie let it pass. "Want
to race?"

"Where?" He nearly yawned as he said it. He couldn't
remember the last time he'd been so completely relaxed.

"To one end and back to the other. I'll give you a
three-stroke lead."

He opened his eyes at that. Jackie was treading water
now, her face only inches from his. As he looked at her,
Nathan realized he could yank her to him and have his
mouth on hers in a heartbeat. Racing, he decided, was
a much better idea.

"Fine." He took three easy strokes, then saw the bul-
let pass him. Amused, and challenged, he kicked in.

It might have been a few years since she'd been on a
swim team, but after five yards Nathan saw that she'd
retained her competitive spirit. With some women, with
most women, he'd have been inclined to lose, knowing that the woman involved would know he'd done
so purposely.

He didn't feel inclined to lose to Jackie.

When they touched the wall and rolled into a turn,
they were head-to-head. He couldn't, as he'd expected,
sprint ahead of her. Her long legs propelled her forward, and her slim arms cut through the water in quick,
smooth strokes. Gradually he inched ahead, one stroke,

then two, with the advantage of his longer reach. When they came to the side he touched only half a body length ahead.

"I must be slipping." A little breathless, Jackie leaned her forearms on the edge, pillowed her cheek on them and studied him. His skin was shiny with water now, drops running off of and clinging to muscular forearms and shoulders. The kind of arms and shoulders, Jackie thought, that a woman could depend on. "You're in good shape, Nathan."

"You too." He was out of breath himself.

"No handicap next time."

He grinned. "I'll still beat you."

"Maybe." Jackie dragged a hand through her hair so that it curled, wet and charming, around her face. "How's your tennis?"

"Not bad."

"Well, that's a possibility." She pulled herself up and out, then sat on the edge, legs dangling. "How about Latin?"

"What about Latin?"

"We could have a Latin tournament."

With a shake of his head, he pulled himself up to sit beside her. "I don't know any Latin."

"Everyone knows some Latin. Corpus delicti or magna cum laude." She leaned back on her elbows. "I can never understand why they call it a dead language when it's used every day."

"That's certainly something to think about."

She laughed. She couldn't help it. He had such a droll way of telling her he thought she was crazy. When his eyes were light and friendly and the smile was beginning to play around his mouth, he seemed like someone she'd known all her life. Or wished she had.

"I like you, Nathan. I really do."

"I like you, too. I think." It wasn't possible not to smile back at her, just as it wasn't possible not to look at her if she was anywhere nearby. She drew you in. Being with her was like plunging into a cold lake on a sultry day. It was a shock to the system, but a welcome one.

Before he realized what he was doing, Nathan reached over to tuck a dripping curl behind her ear. It wasn't like him; he didn't touch casually. The moment his fingers brushed her cheek he knew it was just one more mistake. How could you want more when you weren't even certain what it was you were taking?

As he started to draw away, she leaned up just a little and took his hand in hers. She brought his fingers to her lips in a gesture that stunned him with the naturalness of it.

"Nathan, is there some woman I should be concerned about?"

He didn't pull away, though he knew he should. Somehow his fingers had curled with hers and were holding on. "What do you mean?"

"I mean, you said you weren't involved, but I wondered if there was someone. I don't mind competing, I just like to know."

There was no one. Even if there had been, her memory would have vanished like a puff of smoke. That was what worried him. "Jack, you're taking two steps to my one."

"Am I?" She shifted. It only took a small movement to have her lips whisper against his. She didn't press, content for now with only a taste. "How long do you think it'll take you to catch up?"

He didn't remember moving, but somehow his hands were framing her face. He could feel the water turning to steam on his skin. It should have been easy, uncomplicated. She was willing, he was desirous. They were adults who understood the rules and the risks. There were no promises between them, and no demands for any.

But even as her lips parted beneath his, even as he took what she offered and ached for more, he knew there would be nothing simple about it.

"I don't think I'm ready for you," he murmured, but lowered her onto the concrete apron of the pool.

"Then don't think." Her arms went around him. She'd been waiting. There was no way she could explain to him that she'd been waiting for him, just for him, all her life. It was so easy, so natural, to want him and to give in to that wanting.

Somehow, even as a girl, she'd known there would only be one man for her. She hadn't known how or when she'd find him, or even if she would. Without him, she would have been content to live on her own, satisfying herself with the love of family and friends. Jackie had never believed in settling for second best.

But now he was here, his mouth on her mouth, his body warming hers. She didn't have to think about tomorrow or the day after that when she was holding a lifelong dream in her arms.

What she wanted was here and now. Turning into him, Jackie murmured his name and cherished the sensation of being wanted in turn.

She wasn't like other women. But why? He'd wanted

before, been charmed and baffled and achy before. But not like this. He couldn't think when he was close to her. He could only feel. Tenderness, passion, frustration, desire. It was as if when he held her intellect clicked off and emotion, pure emotion, took over.

Was it that she was every man's fantasy? A generous, willing woman with needs and demands to match a man's—a woman without inhibitions or pretenses. He wished he could believe it was that. He wanted to believe it was only that. But he knew it was more. Somehow it was much more.

And he was losing himself, degree by degree, layer by layer. All his life he'd known where he was going and why. It wasn't possible, it wasn't right, to allow this—to allow her—to change it.

He had to stop it now, while he still had a choice, or at least while he could still pretend he had one.

Slowly, and with much more difficulty than he'd imagined, he pulled away from her. The sun was hanging in the west, still bright, vivid enough to bring out the highlights in her hair. It wasn't just brown as he'd thought, it had dozens and dozens of variations of the shade. Soft, warm, rich. Like her eyes. Like her skin.

He forced himself not to lift a hand to her cheek to touch just once more.

"We'd better go in."

She'd melted inside. Completely. He could have asked anything of her in that moment and she'd have given it without a second thought. Such was the power of loving. She blinked, struggling against coming back to earth. If the choice had been hers, and hers alone, she would have stayed where she was, in his arms, forever.

But she wasn't a fool. He wasn't talking about going

in to continue what they'd begun, but to end it. She closed her eyes, accepting the hurt.

"Go ahead. I think I'll get a little more sun."

"Jack."

She opened her eyes. He was surprised to see such patience in them. He shifted away, knowing that if he remained too close he'd touch her again and start the merry-go-round spinning. "I don't like to start anything until I know how it's going to finish."

She let out a long sigh because she understood. "That's too bad. You miss an awful lot that way, Nathan."

"And make less mistakes. I don't like to make mistakes."

"Is that what I am?" There was just enough amusement in her voice for him to be relieved.

"Yes. You've been a mistake right from the beginning." He turned to her again, noting that she was looking at him the way he sometimes saw her look when she was putting together a complicated dish. "You know it would be better if you didn't stay here."

She lifted a brow. It was the only change in the quietly intense look. "Are you kicking me out?"

"No." He said it too quickly and cursed himself for it. "I should, but I don't seem to be able to."

She laid a hand on his shoulder lightly. He was tense again. "You want me, Nathan. Is that so terrible?"

"I don't take everything I want."

She frowned a moment, thinking. "No, you wouldn't. You're too sensible. It's one of the things I like best about you. But you will take me eventually, Nathan. Because there's something right about us. And we both know it."

"I don't sleep with every woman who attracts me."

"I'm glad to hear it." Jackie sat up completely, tucked up her knees and wrapped her arms around them. "Indulging like that is dangerous in more ways than one." Turning her head, she studied him. "Do you think I sleep with every man who raises my blood pressure?"

Restless and not entirely comfortable, he moved his shoulders. "I don't know you or your lifestyle."

"Well, that's fair." She preferred things to be fair. "Let's get the sex out of the way, then. It dims the romance a bit, but it's sensible. I'm twenty-five, and I've fallen in and out of love countless times. I like falling in better, but I've never been able to stick. Nathan, this might be difficult for you to accept, but I'm not a virgin."

When he shook his head and dropped his chin on his chest, she patted his shoulder.

"I know, shocking, isn't it? I confess, I've been with a man. Actually, I've been with two. The first time was on my twenty-first birthday."

"Jack—"

"I know," she interrupted with a wave of her hand. "That's a little late in this day and age, but I hate to follow trends. I was crazy about him. He could quote Yeats."

"That explains it," Nathan muttered.

"I knew you'd understand. Then a couple of years ago I was into photography. Moody black-and-whites. Very esoteric. I met this man. Black leather jacket. Very sullen good looks." There was more amusement in her eyes now than sentiment.

"He moved in with me and sat around being attractive and despondent. It only took me a couple of weeks to discover I wasn't meant to be depressed. But I got some wonderful pictures. Since then, there hasn't been anyone who's made my toes curl. Until you."

He sat still, wondering why he should be glad there had only been two important men in her life. And why he was now jealous of both of them. After a moment he looked at her again. The light had changed subtly. It warmed her skin now.

"I can't decide whether you have no guile whatso-ever or if you have more than anyone I've ever met."

"Isn't it nice to have something to wonder about? I guess that's why I want to write. You can 'I wonder' yourself from beginning to end." She was silent only a moment. Jackie's debates with herself never lasted long. "Nathan, there's another thing you might want to wonder about. I'm in love with you."

She rose after she told him, feeling it would be best for both of them.

"I don't want you to worry about it," she said as he sat in stunned silence. "It's just that I hate it when people try to pretend things away. Good things, I mean. I think I'll go in after all and change before I start dinner."

She left him alone. He wondered if anyone else could drop a bombshell so casually, then wander off without checking the damage. Jackie could.

He frowned, watching the way the sun danced in di-amonds on the water. There was a boat running north. He could just hear the purr of the motor. The air smelled richly of spring, flowers sun-warmed and burgeoning, grass freshly cut. The days were lengthening, and the heat remained well into evening.

That was life. It went on. It had a pattern.

She was in love with him.

That was absurd…so why wasn't he surprised? It all had to do with who she was, he decided. While he wasn't one to use words like *love* casually, she would be much freer with words, and with feelings.

He didn't even know what love meant to her. An attraction, an affection, a spark. That would be more than enough for many people. She was impetuous. Hadn't she just told him she'd fallen in and out of love countless times? This was just one more adventure for her.

Wasn't that what he wanted to believe? If it was, why did the thought leave him cold and angry?

Because he didn't want to be another adventure. Not for her. He didn't want her to be in love with him…but if she was, he wanted it to be real.

Rising, Nathan walked over to where his land gave way to the wall and the wall to the water. Once his life had moved that smoothly—like a calm channel flowing effortlessly out to sea. That was what he wanted, and that was what he had. He didn't have time to deal with impulsive women who talked about love and romance.

Sometime in the future there would be time for such things—with the proper woman. Someone sensible and polished, Nathan thought. Then he wondered why that suddenly sounded like a nice piece of furniture instead of a wife.

She was doing this to him, he realized, and he resented it. She had no business telling him she was in love with him, making him think that maybe, just maybe, what he was feeling was—

No. He brought himself up short as he turned to scowl back at his house. It was beyond ridiculous to imagine, even for an instant, that he could be in love with her. He barely knew the woman, and for the most part she was an annoyance. If he was attracted it was simply because she was attractive. And he'd kept himself so tied up with work in Germany that he hadn't had time for the softer things a man needed.

And, damn it, that was a lie. Disgusted, he turned back to the water again. He did feel something for her. He wasn't sure what or why, but he felt it. He wanted more than to tumble into bed with her and satisfy an itch. He wanted to be with her, hold her, let that low, fascinating voice drain away his tensions.

But that wasn't love, he assured himself. It might have been a little like caring. That was almost acceptable. A man could come to care for a woman without sinking in over his head.

But not a woman like Jackie.

Dragging a hand through his hair, he started back to the house. They weren't going to talk about this, not now, and not later. Whatever it took, he was going to get back to normal.

He told himself it was expedient, not cowardly, to go in through the side door and avoid her.

# Chapter Six

Jackie wasn't ashamed of having told Nathan what she felt. Nor did she wish the words back. One of her firmest beliefs was that it was useless to second-guess a decision once it had been made.

In any case, taking the words back or regretting them wouldn't change the fact that they were true. She hadn't meant to fall in love with him, which made it all the sweeter and more important. At other times in her life she had seen a man, thought that he might be the one and set about falling in love.

With Nathan, love had come unexpectedly, without plan or consideration. It had simply happened, as she had always secretly hoped it would. In her heart she'd known that love couldn't be planned, so she'd begun to believe that it would never be there for her.

He was not the perfect match for her, at least not in the way she'd once imagined. Even now she couldn't be sure he had all the qualities she had sometimes listed as desirable in a man.

None of that mattered, because she loved him.

She was willing to give him time—a few days, even a week—to respond in whatever way suited him. As far as she was concerned, there were no doubts as to how things would resolve themselves. She loved him. Fate had taken a hand, in the person of cousin Fred, and tossed them together. Perhaps Nathan didn't know it yet. As she whipped eggs for a soufflé, Jackie smiled. In fact, she was sure Nathan didn't know it yet, but she was exactly what he needed.

When a man was logical, conservative and—well, yes, even just a tad stuffy—he needed the love and understanding of a woman who wasn't any of those things. And that same woman—herself, in this case—would love the man, Nathan, because he was all the things he was. She would find his traits endearing and at the same time not allow him to become so starched he cracked down the middle.

She could see exactly the way it would be for them over the years. They would grow closer with an understanding so keen that each would be able to know what the other was thinking. Agreement wouldn't always be possible, but understanding would. He would work at his drawing board and attend his meetings, while she wrote and took occasional trips to New York to lunch with her publisher.

When his work took him away, she'd go with him, supporting his career just as he would support hers. While he supervised the construction of one of his buildings, she would fill reams of notebooks with research.

Until the children came. Then, for a few years, they would both stay closer to home while they raised their family. Jackie didn't want to imagine boys or girls or hair color, because something that precious should be a surprise. But she was sure that Nathan would be a marshmallow when it came to his children.

And she would be there for him, always, to knead the tension from his shoulders, to laugh him out of his sullen moods, to watch his genius grow and expand. With her, he would smile more. With him, she would become more stable. She would be proud of him, and he of her. When she won the Pulitzer they would drink a magnum of champagne and make love through the night.

It was really very simple. Now all she had to do was wait for him to realize how simple.

Then the phone rang.

With her mixing bowl held in the crook of her elbow, Jackie picked up the receiver from the wall unit. "Hello."

After a brief hesitation came a beautifully modulated voice. "Yes, is this the Powell residence?"

"Yes, it is. May I help you?"

"I'd like to speak to Nathan, please. This is Justine Chesterfield calling."

The name rang a bell. In fact, it rang several. Justine Chesterfield, the recently divorced darling of the society pages. The name opened doors in Bridgeport, Monte Carlo and St. Moritz. All in the proper season, naturally. Jackie believed in premonitions, and she didn't care for the one she was having at the moment.

She was tempted to hang up, but she didn't think that would solve anything.

"Of course." Her mother would have been delighted

with the richly rounded tones. "I'll see if he's available, Mrs. Chesterfield."

It was ridiculous to be jealous of a voice over the phone. Besides, she didn't have a jealous bone in her body. Regardless, Jackie gained enormous satisfaction from sticking her tongue out at the receiver before she went to find Nathan.

Since he was just coming down the stairs, she didn't have to look far. "You have a phone call. Justine Chesterfield."

"Oh." He had a flash of guilt that baffled him. Why should receiving a call from an old friend make him feel guilty? "Thanks. I'll take it in my office."

She didn't linger in the hall. Not on purpose, anyway. Could she help it if she had a sudden and unavoidable itch on the back of her knee? So she stood, scratching, while Nathan stepped into his office and picked up the phone.

"Justine, hello. A few days ago. A new housekeeper? No, that was…" How did he, or anyone, explain Jackie? "Actually, I've been meaning to call you. Yes, about Fred MacNamara."

When she decided that if she scratched much longer she'd draw blood, Jackie wandered back into the kitchen. Once there, she stared at the phone. It would be easy to pick up the receiver, very slowly, very quietly—just to see if he was still on the line, of course. She began to, and very nearly did. Then, with a muttered oath, she set it back on the hook. Audibly.

She wasn't interested in anything he had to say to *that woman*. Already Justine had taken on an italicized quality in her mind. Let him explain to *her* why he had a woman living with him. Because the idea amused her,

Jackie turned up the radio a little louder and began to sing along with it.

With the care of a woman who loved to cook, she continued to mix the soufflé. She wouldn't slam pots and pans around the kitchen. Jackie knew how to control herself. She didn't make a habit of it, but she knew how. It was only a phone call, after all. As far as Jackie knew, *that woman* had phoned Nathan to make a plug for her favorite charity. Or maybe she wanted to remodel her den. There were a dozen very innocent and perfectly logical reasons for Justine Chesterfield to call Nathan.

Because she wants to get her hooks into him, Jackie thought, and made herself pour the soufflé mixture into the pan without spilling a drop.

"Jackie?"

She turned, as careful with her smile as she'd been with the batter. "All done? Did you have a nice chat with Justine?"

"I wanted to let you know I'll be going out so you wouldn't worry about dinner."

"Mmm-hmm." Without missing a beat, Jackie set a cucumber on the chopping block and began to slice it. "I wonder, did Justine's second—or is it third--divorce ever come through?"

"As far as I know." He paused a moment, leaning against the doorjamb as he watched Jackie bring the knife down with deadly accuracy. Jealousy, he thought, recognizing it when it slammed into his face. He had a jealous woman on his hands, through no fault of his own. Nathan opened his mouth, then shut it again. He'd be damned if he'd explain himself. Perhaps it was absurd, but if she thought he and Justine were romantically involved it might be the best thing for everyone. "I'll see you later."

"Have a good time," she said, and brought the knife down with a satisfying *thwack*.

Jackie didn't turn, nor did she stop her steady slicing until she heard the front door shut. Blowing the hair out of her eyes, she poured the soufflé mixture down the drain. She'd eat a hot dog.

It helped to get back to work, to hear the comforting hum of her typewriter. What helped even more was the development of a new character. Justine—make that Carlotta—was the frowsy, scheming, overendowed madam of the local brothel. Her heart was brass, like her hair. She was a woman who used men like poker chips.

Jake, being only a man, was taken in by her. But Sarah, with the clear eyes of a woman, saw Justine— Carlotta—for exactly what she was.

Afraid of his growing feelings for Sarah, Jake turned to Carlotta. The cad. Eventually Carlotta would betray him, and her betrayal would nearly cost Sarah her life, but for now Sarah had to deal with the fact that the man she'd come to love would turn to another woman to release his passion.

Jackie would have preferred to make Carlotta frumpy and faded. She'd even toyed with a wart, Just a small one. But a hard-faced woman wouldn't do justice to Jake or her book. Dutifully tearing up the first page, Jackie got down to business.

Carlotta was stunning. In a cold, calculated sort of way. Jackie had seen Justine's picture often enough to describe her. Pale and willowy, with eyes the clear blue of a mountain lake and a thin, almost childish mouth.

A slender neck and wheat-blond hair. There were ice-edged cheekbones and balletic limbs. Taking literary license, Jackie allowed herself to toughen the looks, add a few dissipated lines and a drinking problem.

As she wrote, she began to see the character more clearly, even began to understand Carlotta's drive to use and discard men, to make a living off their baser drives and weaknesses. She discovered that Carlotta had had a miserable childhood and an abusive first marriage. Unfortunately, this softened her mood toward Justine even as she had Carlotta plotting dreadful problems for Jake and Sarah.

When Jackie ran out of steam, it was still shy of midnight. Telling herself it had nothing to do with waiting up for Nathan, she dawdled, applying a facial she remembered once or twice a month at best, filing her nails and leafing through magazines.

At one she deliberately turned the bedside light off, then lay staring at the ceiling.

Maybe everyone was right after all. Maybe she *was* crazy. A woman who fell in love with a man who had virtually no interest in her had to be asking for trouble. And heartache. This was her first experience with real heartache, and she couldn't say she cared for it.

But she did love him, with all the energy and devotion she was capable of. It wasn't anything like the way it had been with the Yeats buff or the leather jacket. They had brought on a sense of excitement—the way a runner might feel, she thought, when she was about to race the fifty-yard dash full-out. It was different, very different, from preparing for a marathon. The excitement was still there, but with it was a steady determination that came from the knowledge of being ready to start and finish, of being prepared for the long haul.

Like her writing, Jackie thought, and sat up in bed. The parallel was so clear. With all her other projects there had been that quick, almost frantic flash of energy and power. It had been as if she'd known going in that there would be a short, perhaps memorable thrill, then disenchantment.

With the writing, there had been the certainty that this was it for her. It hadn't been her last chance so much as her only one. What she was beginning now was the one thing she'd been looking for through all the years of experimenting.

Falling for Nathan was precisely the same. Other men she'd cared for had been like stepping-stones or springboards that had boosted her up for that one and only man she would want for the rest of her life.

If someone had gotten in the way of her and her writing, would she have tolerated it? Not for a minute. Mentally pushing up her sleeves, she settled back. No one was going to step in the way of her and her man, either. Justine Chesterfield was going to have a fight on her hands.

He'd been home for nearly an hour, but Nathan sat in his parked car and let the smoke from his cigarette trail out the window. It was an odd thing for a man to be wary about going into his own house, but there it was, She was in there. In the bedroom. Her bedroom now, It would never be just a guest room again.

He'd seen her light burning, and he'd seen her light shut off. She might be sleeping. He wasn't sure he'd ever get a decent night's sleep again.

My God, he wanted to go in, walk up the stairs into her room and lose himself in the promise of her. Or the threat.

There was nothing in his feelings for her that made sense, nothing he could put his finger on and analyze. Over and over again his mind played back the way she'd looked at him as they'd sat by the pool, the way her skin had felt with water drying on it, the way her voice had sounded.

*I'm in love with you.*

Could it be, could it possibly be that easy for her? Yes, he thought it was. Now that he was beginning to know and understand her, he was sure that falling in love and declaring that love would be as natural for Jackie as breathing. But this time she was in love with him.

He could take advantage of it. She wouldn't even blame him for it. He could, without conscience or guilt, do exactly what he was dreaming of doing— walk into her room and finish what had been started that evening.

But he couldn't. He'd never be able to forget the way her eyes had looked. Trusting, honest and incredibly vulnerable. She thought she was tough, resilient. And he believed that she was, to a point. If she really loved him and he hurt her by casually taking what love urged her to give, she wouldn't bounce back.

So how did he handle her?

He'd thought he'd known earlier that evening. Going to see Justine had been a calculated move to distance himself from Jackie and to show both her and himself how ridiculously implausible any relationship between them would be.

Then he'd found himself in Justine's elegant condo with its gold-and-white rooms and its tasteful French antiques and he'd been unable to think of anything but Jackie. There'd been an excellent poached salmon, prepared to a turn by Justine's housekeeper. Nathan had found himself with a yen for the spicy chicken Jackie had prepared that first night.

He'd smiled as Justine, dressed in sleek white lounging pajamas, her wheat-colored hair twisted back in a sleek knot, had served him brandy. And he'd thought of the way Jackie looked in shorts.

With Justine he'd discussed mutual friends and compared viewpoints on Frankfurt and Paris. Her voice was low and soothing, her observations were concise and mildly amusing. He'd remembered the fits and starts and wild paths Jackie's conversations could take.

Justine was an old friend, a valued one. She was a woman he had always been completely at ease with. He knew her family, and she knew his. Their opinions might not always agree precisely, but they were invariably compatible. Over the ten years they'd known each other, they'd never become lovers. Justine's marriages and Nathan's travels had prevented that, though there had always been a light and companionable attraction between them.

That could change now, and they were both aware of it. She was single, and he was home. There would very likely never be a woman he knew better, a woman better suited to his tastes, than Justine Chesterfield.

He'd wanted, as he'd sat comfortably, to be back in his kitchen watching Jackie concoct a meal, even if the damn radio was playing.

He thought it entirely possible that he was losing his mind.

The evening had ended with a chaste, almost brotherly kiss. He hadn't wanted to make love with Justine, though God knew he was stirred up enough to need a woman. It infuriated him to realize that if he'd slept with Justine he would have thought of Jackie and felt like an adulterer.

There was no doubt about it. He was going crazy.

Giving up on trying to reason, even with himself, Nathan got out of the car. As he let himself in to the house he thought a long soak in the whirlpool might tire him out enough to let him sleep.

Jackie heard the movement downstairs and sat up in bed again. Nathan? She hadn't heard a car drive up and stop. She'd been listening for his return for over a half hour, and even in a half doze she would have heard. Crawling down to the foot of the bed, she strained to hear.

Silence.

If it was Nathan, why wasn't he coming upstairs? Annoyed because her heart was beginning to race, she crept to the door and peeked out.

If it was Nathan, why was he walking around in the dark?

Because it wasn't Nathan, she decided. It was a burglar who'd probably been watching the house for weeks, learning the routine and waiting for his chance. He'd know that she was alone in the house and asleep, so he'd broken in to rob Nathan blind.

With a hand to her heart, she glanced back toward her bed. She could call the police, then crawl under the covers. It sounded like a wonderful idea. Even as she took the first tiptoeing step back, she stopped.

But what if she hadn't really heard anything other than the house settling? If Nathan wasn't already fed up, he certainly would be if he got home from *that woman*'s and found the house full of police because she'd jumped the gun.

Taking a deep breath, Jackie decided to creep down and make sure there was a good reason to panic.

She descended the stairs slowly, keeping her back to the wall. Still no sound. The house was absolutely dark and absolutely silent. A burglar had to make some noise when he stole the family silver.

Probably just your imagination, she told herself as she reached the lower landing. In the dark she strained her ears but still heard nothing. As her heartbeat slowed to normal she decided to take one quick check around the house, knowing her imagination would play havoc if she went back to bed without satisfying her curiosity.

She began to whistle, just under her breath, as she moved from room to room. There was no one there, of course, but if there was, Jackie preferred to have them know she was on her way. Jackie's imagination, according to her mother, had always been bizarre.

By the time she'd wound through the living room, passed by Nathan's office and the powder room and gone into the dining area, she'd imagined not just your everyday intruder but a gang of psychotic thugs who'd recently escaped from a maximum-security prison in Kentucky. Determined to beat her own wayward fantasies, she stepped into the kitchen. Every light in the house blazed behind her. Now, as she reached for the switch in the kitchen, she heard a shuffle of footsteps.

Her fingers froze, but her mind didn't. They were in the sunroom—at least six of them by now. One of them had a scar running from his temple to his jawline and had been serving time for bludgeoning senior citizens in their sleep. She took a step back, thinking of the phone in her room behind a locked door when the footsteps came closer.

Too late, her mind flashed. Going with impulse and desperation, she grabbed the closest weapon—the soufflé pan. Swinging it above her head, she prepared to defend herself.

When Nathan stepped into the room, dressed only in his briefs, it was a toss-up as to who was the more surprised. He jerked back, finding himself ridiculously embarrassed as Jackie let out a scream and dropped the pan. It landed with a resounding clatter just before she doubled over with hysterical giggles.

"What the hell are you doing, sneaking around the house?" If it wouldn't have made him feel that much more foolish, Nathan would have grabbed a dishcloth for cover.

Jackie slammed both hands over her mouth as she gasped and choked. "I thought you were six men with homicidal intentions. One of you had a scar, and the little one had a face like a weasel."

"So naturally you came down to beat us all off with a soufflé pan."

"Not exactly." Still giggling, she propped herself against the counter. "I'm sorry, I always laugh when I'm terrified."

"Who doesn't?"

"It was just that I thought there was a burglar, then I convinced myself there wasn't, and then..." She began to hiccup. "Then I thought you were this gang from Kentucky led by a man named Bubba. I need some water." Grabbing a glass, Jackie filled it to the rim while Nathan tried to follow.

"You've obviously picked the right field at last, Jack. With an imagination like that, you'll make a million."

"Thanks." Picking up the glass, she drank while running her finger in circles over the bottom.

"What the hell are you doing now?"

"Getting rid of the hiccups. Surefire." She set the glass down and waited. "See? All clear. Now it's your turn. What were you doing sneaking around the house in the dark in your underwear?"

"It's my house."

"Right you are. And it's very nice underwear, too. Sorry I scared you."

"You didn't scare me." Finding his temper once more on a short fuse, he bent down and scooped up the pan. "I was about to take a spa and decided I wanted a drink."

"Oh. Well, that explains that." Jackie pressed her lips together. It wouldn't do to start giggling again. "Did you have a nice time?"

"What? Yes, fine." This was a hell of a time, Nathan decided, to notice that she was wearing nothing but an oversize T-shirt with a faded picture of Mozart on the front. With care and effort, he kept his eyes on her face, but it didn't help very much. "I don't want to keep you up."

"Oh, that's okay. I'll fix you a drink."

"I can do it." He had his hand on her wrist before she could open the cupboard.

"No need to be cranky. I said I was sorry."

"I'm not cranky. Go to bed, Jack."

"I'm bothering you, aren't I?" she murmured as she turned to face him. With her free hand, she reached up to touch his cheek. "That's nice."

"Yes, you're bothering me, and it's not particularly

nice." Her face was scrubbed free of cosmetics, but her scent still lingered. "Now go to bed."

"Want to come with me?"

His eyes narrowed at the smile in hers. "You're going to push too far."

"It was only a suggestion." She felt a wave of tenderness as she thought of how he would view his position and what was happening between them. An honorable man who thought his intentions were dishonorable. "Nathan, is it so hard for you to understand that I love you and want to make love with you?"

He didn't want it to make sense, couldn't allow it to make sense. "What's hard for me to understand and impossible for me to believe is that anyone could consider themselves in love after a matter of days. Things don't work that easily, Jack."

"Sometimes they do. Look at Romeo and Juliet. No, that's a bad example when you think of how things worked out." Fascinated by his mouth, warmed by the memory of how it felt on hers, she traced it with her fingertip. "Sorry, I guess I can't think of a good example right now because I'm thinking about you."

His stomach wound itself into a tight knot. "If you're trying to make this difficult, you're succeeding."

"Impossible was the idea, but I'll settle for difficult." She shifted closer. Their thighs brushed. Her eyelids lowered. "Kiss me, Nathan. Even my imagination falls short of what it's like when you do."

He swore at her, or tried to, but his mouth was already against hers. Each time it was a little sweeter, a little sharper, a little more difficult to forget. He was losing, and he knew it. Once he gave in to his own needs, he wasn't sure he'd be able to pull back. Nor did he know precisely what he would find himself trapped in.

She was a drug to a man who had always been obsessively clear-minded, a slide down a cliff to one who had always been firmly surefooted.

And she was naked beneath that loose shirt. Soft and naked and already warm for him. He found himself reaching, testing, taking, even as warning bells rang inside his head.

DANGER. PROCEED AT YOUR OWN RISK.

His own risk. He'd always carefully calculated the risk, the odds, the degrees and angles, before he took the first step. Her body seemed to have been molded for his hands, for his pleasure, for his needs. There was no way to calculate this, or her, or what happened every time they touched each other.

It was so easy, so mindlessly easy, to take the next step. Blindly, recklessly. She was murmuring his name as her hands glided up his back, then down to his hips. He could feel every curve and angle of her body as his hands moved over and under the thin cotton. How could it be so familiar yet so fresh, so comforting yet so unnerving?

He wanted to scoop her up, to wallow in her, to lose himself. It would have been so easy. Her body was poised against his, ready, waiting, eager. And the heat, the heat he'd begun to recognize and expect, was weighing down on his brain. There was nothing and no one he'd ever wanted more.

Somewhere in the back of his mind he heard a door slam and a key turn in a lock. In a last attempt at self-defense, he pulled her away.

"Hold it."

Sighing, half dreaming, she opened her eyes. "Hmm?"

If she kept looking at him like that he was going to

fall apart. Or rip that excuse for nightgear off her back. "Look, I don't know why this is happening, but it has to stop. I'm not hypocrite enough to say I don't want you, but I'm not crazy enough to start something that's going to make us both miserable."

"Why should making love make either of us miserable?"

"Because it could never go beyond that." Because she swayed toward him, he put his hands on her shoulders. Damn it, she was trembling. Or he was. "I don't have room for you, for anyone, in my life, Jack. I don't want to make room. I don't think you understand that."

"No, I don't." She leaned forward to brush her lips over his chin. "If I believed it, I'd think it was very sad."

"Believe it." But he was no longer certain he did. "My work comes first. It takes all my time, my energy and my concentration. That's the way I want it. A blistering affair with you has its appeal, but…for some reason I care about you, and I don't think that's all you want or need."

"It doesn't have to be all."

"But it does, and that's something for you to think about." He had to stay calm now, calm enough to make her listen. "In six weeks I go to Denver. When I've finished there, it's Sydney. After that I don't know where I'll be or for how long. I travel light, and that doesn't include a lover, or the worry about someone waiting for me back home."

She shook her head as she took a small step back. "I wonder what happened to make you so unwilling to share yourself, so determined to keep to some straight-and-narrow path. No curves, no detours, Nathan?" She tilted her head to study him. There was no anger in her eyes, just a sympathy he didn't want. "It's more than sad, it's sinful, really, to turn away someone who loves you because you don't want to spoil your routine."

He opened his mouth so that the words nearly tumbled out. Reasons, explanations, an anger he barely remembered or thought he'd forgotten. Years of control snapped into place.

"Maybe it is, but that's the way I live. The way I've chosen to live." He'd hurt her again, badly this time. The shiver of pain sliced back at him, and he knew he was hurting himself, as well. "I can tell you that if you were another woman it would be a lot easier to turn away. I don't want to feel what I'm feeling for you. Do you understand?"

"Yes. I wish I didn't." She looked down at the floor. When her eyes lifted again, the hurt was still there, but it had been joined by a flash of something stronger. "What you don't understand is that I don't give up. Blame it on the Irish. A stubborn breed. I want you, Nathan, and no matter how far you run or how fast, I'll catch up. When I do, all your neat little plans are going to tumble like a stack of dominoes." Taking his face in her hands, she kissed him hard. "And you'll thank me for it, because no one's ever going to love you the way I do."

She kissed him again, more gently this time, then turned away. "I made some fresh lemonade, if you still want a drink. Night."

He watched her go with the sinking feeling that he could already hear the clatter of dominoes.

# Chapter Seven

She should have hated him. Sarah wanted to, wished the strong, destructive emotions would come, filling all the cracks in her feelings, blocking out everything else. With hate, a coolheaded, sharply honed hate, she would have felt in control again. She needed badly to feel in control again. But she didn't hate him. Couldn't.

Even knowing Jake had spent the night with another woman, kissing another woman's lips, touching another woman's skin, she couldn't hate him. But she could grieve for the loss, for the death of a beauty that had never had the chance to bloom fully.

She had come to understand what they might have had together. She had nearly come to accept that they belonged together, whatever their differences, whatever the risks. He would always live by his gun and by his own set of rules, but with her, briefly, perhaps reluctantly, he had shown such kindness, such tenderness.

There was a place for her in his heart. Sarah knew it. Beneath the rough-hewn exterior was a man who believed in justice, who was capable of small, endearing kindnesses. He'd allowed her to see that part of him, a part she knew he'd shared with few others.

Then why, the moment she had begun to soften toward him, to accept him for what and who he was, had he turned to another woman, a woman of easy virtue?

*A woman of easy virtue?* Jackie said to herself, and rolled her eyes. If that was the best she could come up with, she'd better hang it up right now.

It hadn't been one of her better days. Nathan had been up and gone before she'd started breakfast. He'd left her a note—she couldn't even say a scribbled note, because his handwriting was as disciplined as the rest of him—telling her he'd be out most of the day.

She'd munched on a candy bar and the last of the ginger ale as she'd mulled over the current situation. As far as she could see, it stank.

She was in love with a man who was determined to hold her, and his own feelings, at arm's length. A man who insisted on rationalizing those feelings away— not because he was committed to another woman, not because he was suffering from a fatal disease, not because he was hiding a criminal past, but because they were inconvenient.

He was too honorable to take advantage of the situation, and too stubborn to admit that he and she belonged together.

No room in his life for her? Jackie thought as she pushed away from the typewriter and began to pace. Did he really believe she would take a ridiculous statement like that and back off? Of course she wouldn't, but what bothered her more was that he would make a statement like that in the first place.

What made him so determined not to accept love when it was given, so determined not to acknowledge his own emotions? Her own family could sometimes be annoyingly proper, but there had always been a wealth of love generously given. She'd grown up unafraid of feelings. If you didn't feel, you weren't alive, so what was the purpose? She knew Nathan felt, and felt deeply, but whenever his emotions took control he stepped back and put up those walls.

He did love her, Jackie thought as she flopped down on the bed. She couldn't be mistaken about that. But he was going to fight her every inch of the way. So she'd handle it. It wasn't that she objected to a good fight, it was just that this one hurt. Every time he drew back, every time he denied what they had together, it hurt a little more.

She'd been honest with him, and that hadn't worked. She'd been deliberately provocative, and that hadn't done so well, either. She'd been annoying, and she'd been cooperative. She wasn't sure what step to take next.

Rolling onto her stomach, she debated the idea of taking a nap. It was midafternoon, she'd worked nonstop since breakfast, and she couldn't drum up any enthusiasm for the pool. Perhaps if she went to sleep with Nathan on her mind she would wake up with a solution. Deciding to trust the Fates—after all, they'd gotten her this far—she closed her eyes. She'd nearly dozed off when the doorbell rang.

Someone selling encyclopedias, she thought groggily, with the idea of ignoring them. Or it was three men in white suits passing out pamphlets for a tent revival—which actually might be fairly interesting. With a yawn, she snuggled into the pillow. She'd nearly shut off her mind when a last thought intruded. It was a telegram from home, and someone had been in a horrible accident.

Springing up, she sprinted downstairs.

"Yes, I'm coming!" As she pushed the hair out of her eyes, she yanked the door open.

It wasn't a telegram or a door-to-door salesman. It was Justine Chesterfield. Jackie decided it really wasn't one of her better days. She leaned on the door and offered a chilly smile.

"Hello."

"Hello. I wonder if Nathan might be around."

"Sorry, he's out." Her fingers on the knob itched to close the door quietly and completely. That would be rude. Jackie could almost hear her mother upbraiding her. She took a long breath before moderating her tone. "He didn't say where he was going or when he'd be back, but you're welcome to wait if you'd like."

"Thanks." They exchanged appraising glances before Justine stepped over the threshold.

The woman's dressed as if she's just stepped off a yacht, Jackie thought nastily. In Hyannis Port. At the beginning of the season. Justine's tall, softly curved body was set off nicely by white slacks and a boat necked silk T-shirt in crimson. She'd added a quietly elegant necklace of twisted gold links and discreetly stylish matching earrings. Her hair had been left down to wave gently on her shoulders, scooped back at the temples by two mother-of-pearl combs.

She was perfect. Perfectly lovely, perfectly groomed, perfectly mannerly. Jackie was glad she could hate her.

"I hope I'm not disturbing you...." Justine began.

"Not at all." Jackie gestured toward the living room. "Make yourself at home."

"Thanks." Justine wandered in, then set her envelope bag on a small table. The bag matched her open-toed white snakeskin pumps. "You must be Jacqueline, Fred's cousin."

"I must be."

"I'm Justine Chesterfield. An old friend of Nathan's."

"I recognized your voice." Ingrained manners had Jackie offering a hand. As their fingers touched briefly, a smile hovered around Justine's mouth. Unfortunately for Jackie, the smile was friendly and entirely too appealing.

"And I yours. According to Nathan, Fred's as devious as he is charming."

"More so, believe me." So this was the kind of woman Nathan preferred. Quietly polished, quietly stylish, quietly stunning. Trying not to sigh, Jackie played hostess. "Can I get you something? A cold drink, some coffee?"

"I'd love something cold, if you wouldn't mind."

"All right, have a seat. I'll just be a minute."

Jackie muttered to herself the entire time she fixed lemonade and arranged shortbread cookies on Nathan's Depression glass platter. It rarely occurred to her to think how she looked when she planned on staying in. But she would have picked today to wear her most comfortable and most ragged pair of cutoffs, with a baggy athletic-style T-shirt in garish green-and-yellow stripes. There was a small fortune in gold and gems on her fingers, and her feet were bare. The Sizzling Cerise on her toes had begun to chip.

The hell with that, she thought, and made one vague and futile attempt to finger-comb her hair. She'd let Ms. Sleek-and-Stylish have her say.

She was sure that Sarah would have been just as gracious to Carlotta, but she had a feeling that Sarah was a much nicer person than Jacqueline R. MacNamara. Determined to give Nathan nothing to snarl about, she lifted the tray and started back to her guest. Nathan's guest.

The sunlight and the strong masculine colors of the room were certainly flattering to Justine. It didn't help to admit it, but Jackie was nothing if not honest.

"This is awfully nice of you," Justine began as she took a seat. "Actually, I was hoping we'd have a chance to talk. Are you very busy? Nathan told me you were working on a book."

"He did?" It was surprise more than a desire to chat that had Jackie sitting. She hadn't thought Nathan even remembered she was writing, much less that he would tell someone else about it. And Justine was the second person, after Mrs. Grange, who hadn't smirked when she'd spoken of her writing.

"Yes, he said you were writing a novel and that you were very dedicated and disciplined about your work. Nathan's a big believer in discipline."

"So I've noticed." Jackie discovered she didn't mind sipping a glass of lemonade after all. Justine had just handed her the perfect route to make her excuses and disappear back upstairs. After a second sip, Jackie decided to detour around it. "As it turns out, I was just taking a break when you rang the bell."

"That's lucky." Justine chose a cookie and nibbled. Her scent was very sophisticated, not opulent but rich and feminine. Jackie noticed that her nails were long, rounded and painted a pale rose. She wore only one ring, a stunning opal surrounded by diamonds. "I suppose I should apologize first."

Jackie left off her study long enough to lift a brow. "Apologize?"

"For the mix-up here between you and Nathan." Justine noticed with a little stab of envy that Jackie's skin was free of cosmetics and as clear as springwater. "It was I who talked Nathan into letting Fred move in while he was away in Europe. It seemed like such a perfect solution at the time, as Nathan was concerned about leaving his house empty for that length of time and Fred seemed to be at loose ends."

"Fred's always at loose ends," Jackie said over the rim of her glass. She looked at Justine with a trace of sympathy. Fred's charm might not have swayed Mrs. Grange, but the housekeeper was the exception to the rule. "He also has a way of making you believe he can spin straw into gold. As long as you're paying for the straw."

"So I understand." Appreciation for the analogy showed in Justine's eyes. "I feel, well…a little guilty that Fred absconded with your money under false pretenses."

"No need." Jackie took a healthy bite out of a cookie. "I've known Fred all my life. If anyone should have seen through him, I should have. In any case," she added with what she thought was a wonderfully cool smile, "Nathan and I have come to a satisfactory arrangement."

"So he said." Justine took another sip of lemonade,

watching Jackie over the rim. "Apparently you're a first-class cook."

"Yes." She didn't believe in denying the truth, but she wondered what else Nathan had felt obligated to tell Justine. If they were going to fight, she thought restlessly, why didn't they just get on with it?

"I've never been able to put two ingredients together and have either one come out recognizable. Did you really study in Paris?"

"Which time?" Despite herself, Jackie smiled. She hadn't wanted to like Justine. True, the woman was very cool and very polished, but there was something kind in her eyes. Kindness, no matter what the package, always drew her in.

Justine smiled in return, and the restraint between them lowered by another few degrees. "Miss MacNamara—Jacqueline—may I be frank?"

"Things usually get done faster that way."

"You're not at all what I expected."

Jackie sat back, tucking up her legs Indian-style. "What did you expect?"

"I always thought when Nathan became besotted about someone she'd be very sleek and self-contained. Possibly boring."

The lemonade that was halfway down Jackie's throat had to be swallowed in a hard gulp. "Back up. Did you say Nathan was besotted?"

"A wreck. Didn't you know?"

"He hides it well," Jackie murmured.

"Well, it was perfectly obvious to me last night." The heat in Jackie's eyes came instantly and automatically. "We've never been anything but friends, by the way."

Justine gave a small shrug. "If I were in your position, I'd appreciate someone making that clear to me."

The heat simmered a moment longer, then snuffed itself out. She didn't often feel like a fool, but she was willing to accept it when she did. "I do appreciate it—your telling me, and the fact that you've never been anything but friends. Would you mind if I asked you why?"

"I've wondered myself." With the ease of a woman who never gained an ounce, Justine took another cookie. "The timing's never been quite right. I'm not independent." This was said with another shrug. "I enjoy being married, being part of a couple, so I end up doing it quite a bit. I was married when I met Nathan. Then, after my first divorce, we were in different parts of the country. It's continued to work out about the same way for close to a decade. In any case, it's enough to say that I was always involved with someone else and Nathan was always involved with his work. For his own reasons, he prefers things that way."

Jackie wanted to ask why, suspected that Justine might have some of the answers. But she couldn't go that far. If what she had with Nathan was going to work, the explanations would have to come from him. "I appreciate you telling me. I suppose I should tell you that you're not what I expected, either."

"And what did you expect?"

"A calculating adventuress with icicles on her heart and designs on my man. I spent most of last night detesting you." When Justine's lips curved at the description, Jackie was very glad she'd refrained from giving Carlotta that wart.

"Then I wasn't wrong in thinking you care about Nathan?"

"I'm in love with him."

Justine smiled again. There was a trace of wistfulness in it that told Jackie more than words could have. "He needs someone. He doesn't think so, but he does."

"I know. And it's going to be me."

"Then I'll wish you luck. I didn't intend to when I came."

"What changed your mind?"

"You invited me in and offered me a drink when you wished me to hell."

Jackie grinned. "And I thought I was so discreet."

"No, you weren't. Jack…that's what Nathan calls you, isn't it?"

"Most of the time."

"Jack, my track record with relationships isn't what you would call impressive—in fact, let's continue to be frank and admit it's lousy—but I'd like to offer you a little advice."

"I'll take anything I can get."

"Some men need more of a push than others. Use both hands with Nathan."

"I intend to." With her head tilted to one side, Jackie considered. "You know, Justine, I have this cousin. Second cousin on my father's side. Not Fred," she said quickly, "This one's a college professor at the University of Michigan. Do you like the intellectual type?"

With a laugh, Justine set down her glass. "Ask me again in six months. I'm on sabbatical."

When Nathan arrived home a few hours later, he knew nothing of Justine's visit or of the conclusions that had been reached in his living room. Perhaps that was for the best.

It was bad enough that he was glad to be home. It was a different sort of glad from the feeling he'd had when he'd arrived from Germany. Then he'd been looking forward to the familiar, to solitude, to the routine he had set for himself over the years. He didn't—wouldn't have—considered it stuffy, just convenient.

Now a part of him, a part he still wasn't ready to acknowledge, was glad to come home to Jackie. There was an anticipation, a surge of excitement at knowing she was there to talk with, to relax with, even to spar with. The unfamiliar, and the companionship, added a new dimension to an evening at home. The challenge of outmaneuvering her had become a habit he hadn't been aware of forming. Somewhere along the line he'd stopped resenting the fact that she'd invaded his privacy.

He heard the music the moment he opened the door. It wasn't the rock he'd grown accustomed to hearing from the kitchen but one of Strauss's lovely and sensual waltzes. Though he wasn't sure if her change in radio stations was something to worry about, he was cautious as he slipped into his office to put away his briefcase and the reinforced tubes that held the blueprints from his project in Denver.

Loosening his tie, he started into the kitchen. As usual, something smelled wonderful.

She wasn't wearing her habitual shorts. Instead, she wore a jumpsuit in some soft, silky material the color of melted butter. It didn't cling to her body so much as shift around it, offering hints. Her feet were bare, and she wore one long wooden earring. She was busy slicing a round loaf of crusty bread. He had a sudden feeling, strong and lucid, that he should turn and run, as fast and as far as he could. Because it annoyed him, Nathan stepped through the archway.

"Hello, Jack."

She'd known he was there, but she managed to look mildly and credibly surprised when she turned. "Hi." He looked so attractive in a suit, with the knot of his tie pulled loose. Because her heart turned to mush, she walked over and kissed his cheek. "How was your day?"

He didn't know what to make of her. So what else was new? But he did know that her casual greeting kiss was exactly what he'd needed, and it worried him. "Busy," he told her.

"Well, you'll have to tell me all about it, but you should have some wine first." She was already pouring two glasses. The sun hit the liquid as it rushed into the crystal and shot it through with gold. "I hope you're hungry. It'll be ready in just a couple minutes."

He accepted the wine and didn't ask why her timing always seemed so perfect. It made him wonder if she'd managed to slip a homing device on him. "Did you get much done today?"

"Quite a bit." Jackie began to arrange the bread she'd sliced in a basket. "I had a little lull this afternoon, but things really picked up afterward." Her lips curved as she lifted her wine, and once again he had the feeling that there was something he should know, but he didn't want to ask. "I've decided to concentrate on the first hundred pages for the next week or so, until it's ready to send off to an agent I know in New York."

"That's good," he managed, wondering why the idea sent him into a panic. He wanted her to progress, didn't he? The more she did, the less guilty he'd feel about telling her that her time was up. No amount of logic could erase the niggling fear that she would tell him she no longer needed the house to work in and was moving on. "It must be going well."

"Better than I expected, and I always expect quite a lot." The timer buzzed, and she turned to the oven. Fortunately, the move hid her smile. "I thought we'd eat on the patio. It's such a nice evening."

The warning bells sounded again, but they were dimmer and less urgent. "It's going to rain."

"Not for a couple of hours yet." With her hands buried in oven mitts, she drew out a casserole. "I hope you like this. It's called *schinkenfleckerln*." Jackie whipped out the foreign name like a native.

There was something very homey and nonthreatening about the pot of browned noodles and ham in bubbling sauce. "It looks terrific."

"A very simple Austrian recipe," she told him. That explained the Viennese waltz, he thought. "Grab the bread, will you? I've already set up outside."

Again, she timed it perfectly. The sun was dropping in the sky. The clouds that were gathering to bring rain during the night were tipped with pink and orange. The air was cool, with a catchy breeze from the east that brought just a hint of the sea.

The round patio table was set for two. Informally. Nathan would have to have stretched a point to call it deliberately romantic. Colorful mats she must have bought herself were under his white everyday dishes. She'd added flowers, but they were only a few sprigs of daisies in a colored bottle. The bottle wasn't his, either, so he could only suppose that she'd been foraging in some of the local shops.

He settled back as Jackie began the business of serving. "I haven't thanked you for all the meals."

She only smiled as she sat across from him. "That was the deal."

"I know, but you've gone to more trouble than you had to. I appreciate it."

"That's nice. I really like to cook when there's someone to share it with. Nothing more depressing than cooking for one."

He hadn't thought so. Once. "Jack..." She looked up at him, her eyes big and round and soft, and he lost track of what he'd planned to say. Groping, he picked up his wine. "I, ah...I feel like we got off on the wrong foot. Since we're both victims, so to speak, I'd like to call a truce."

"I thought we had."

"An official one."

"All right." She lifted her glass and tapped it against his. "Live long and prosper."

"I beg your pardon?"

Jackie chuckled into her wine. "I should have known you wouldn't be a fan of *Star Trek*. That's the Vulcan greeting, Nathan, but to keep it simple, I'll just wish you the best."

"Thanks." Unconsciously he loosened his tie a little more. "Why don't you tell me about your book?"

It was a first, Nathan decided, to see Jackie speechless. Her lips parted, not to smile or to toss a quip, but in utter surprise. "Really?" she managed after a moment.

"Yes, I'd like to hear what it's about." He picked up a hunk of bread and began to butter it. "Don't you want to talk about it?"

"Well, yes, it's just that I didn't think you were interested. You never asked, or even commented, and I know that I usually beat people over the head with whatever I'm doing at the time because I get too involved and lose perspective. So I thought it would be better if I just kept the book to myself since I was already driving you crazy. I figured under the circumstances, counting Fred and six months in Frankfurt, you'd probably hate it anyway."

Nathan scooped up some of the casserole, chewed and considered. "I understand that," he said. "I can't tell you how much that terrifies me, but I understand. Now, why don't you tell me about your book?"

"Okay." She moistened her lips. "I've set it in what is now Arizona, in the 1870s—a decade or so after the Mexican War, when it was ceded to the U.S. as part of New Mexico. I'd toyed around with doing a generational thing and starting in the eighteenth century, when it was still a European settlement, but I found that I wanted to get into the meat right away."

"No meat in the eighteenth century?"

"Oh, pounds of it." She took a piece of bread herself and shredded it before she realized she was nervous. "But Jake and Sarah weren't alive then. My protagonists," Jackie explained. "It's really their story, and I was too impatient to start the book a hundred years before they came along. He's a gunfighter and she's convent-bred. I liked the idea of putting them in Arizona because it really epitomizes America's Old West. The Earps, the Claytons, Tombstone, Tucson, Apaches." Nerves disappeared as she began to imagine. "It gives it that nice bloody frontier tradition."

"Shoot-outs, bounty hunters and Indian raids?"

"That's the idea. The setup has Sarah coming West

after her father dies. He, Sarah's father, had led her to believe that he's a prosperous miner. She's grown up in the East, learning all the things that well-bred young ladies of good families are supposed to learn. Then, after his sudden death, she comes out to the Arizona Territory and discovers that for all the years she was living in moderate luxury back East, her father had barely been scraping by on this dilapidated gold mine, spending every penny he could spare on her education."

"Now she's penniless, orphaned and out of her element."

"Exactly." Pleased with him, Jackie poured more wine. "I figure that makes her instantly vulnerable and sympathetic, as well as plunging her into immediate jeopardy. Anyway, it doesn't take her long to discover that her father didn't die in an accidental cave-in, but was murdered. By this time, she's already had a few run-ins with Jake Redman, the hard-bitten gun-for-hire renegade who stands for everything she's been taught to detest. He saved her life during an Apache raid."

"So he's not all bad."

"A diamond in the rough," Jackie explained over a bite of bread. "See, there were a lot of miners and adventurers in the territory during this period, but the War between the States and troop withdrawal were delaying settlement, so the Apaches were still dominant. That made it a very wild and dangerous place for a gently bred young woman to be."

"But she stays."

"If she'd turned to run, she'd have been pitiful rather than sympathetic. Big difference. She's compelled to discover who killed her father and why. Then there's the fact that she's desperately, though unwillingly, attracted to Jake Redman."

"And he to her?"

"You've got it." She smiled at him as she toyed with her wine. "You see, Jake, like a lot of men—and women, for that matter—doesn't believe he needs anyone, certainly not someone who would interfere with his lifestyle and convince him to settle down. He's a loner, has always been a loner, and intends to keep it that way."

His brow lifted as he sipped. "Very clever," he said mildly.

Pleased that he saw the correlation, she smiled. "Yes, I thought so. But Sarah's quite determined. Once she discovers that she loves him, that her life would never be complete without him, she wears him down. Of course, Carlotta does her best to botch things up."

"Carlotta?"

"The town's leading woman of ill repute. It's not so much that she wants Jake, though of course she does. They all do. But she hates Sarah and everything Sarah stands for. Then there's the fact that she knows Sarah's father had been murdered because, after five years, he'd finally hit the mother lode. The mine Sarah now holds the claim for is worth a fortune. That's as far as I've gotten."

"But how does it end?"

"I don't know."

"What do you mean, you don't know? You're writing it, you have to know."

"No, I don't. In fact, I'm almost certain if I knew, exactly, it wouldn't be half as much fun to sit down every day." She offered him more of the casserole, but he shook his head. "It's a story for me, too, and I am getting closer, but it's not like a blueprint, Nathan."

Because she could see he didn't understand, she leaned closer, elbows propped on the table. "I'll tell you why I think I'd never have made a good architect, though I found the whole process fascinating and the idea of taking an empty lot and bringing it alive with a building incredible."

He glanced over again at that. What she'd said, and how she'd phrased it, encompassed his own feelings so perfectly that he could almost believe she'd stepped into his mind.

"You have to know every detail, beginning to end. You have to be certain before you take out the first shovel of dirt how it's going to end up. When you build, you're not just responsible for creating an attractive, functional piece of work. You're also responsible for the lives of the people who will work or live in or pass through the building, climb the stairs, ride the elevators. Nothing can be left to chance, and imagination has to conform to safety and practicality."

"I think you're wrong," he said after a moment. "I think you'd have made an excellent architect."

She smiled at him. "No, just because I understand doesn't mean I can do. Believe me, I've been there." She touched his hand easily, friend to friend. "You're an excellent architect because not only do you understand, but you're able to combine art with practicality, creativity with reality."

He studied her, both moved and pleased by her insight. "Is that what you're doing with your writing?"

"I hope so." She sat back to watch the clouds roll in. It would rain soon after nightfall. "All my life I've been scrambling around, looking for one creative outlet after another. Music, painting, dancing. I composed my first sonata when I was ten." Her lips tilted in a self-deprecating grin. "I was precocious."

"No, really?"

She chuckled as she slipped her hand under the bowl of her glass. "It wasn't a particularly good sonata, but I always knew there was something I had to do. My parents have been very patient, even indulgent, and I didn't always deserve it. This time…I guess this sounds silly at my age, but this time I want them to be proud of me."

"It doesn't sound silly," he murmured. "We never grow out of wanting our parents' approval."

"Do you have yours, Nathan?"

"Yes." The word was clipped. Because he heard it himself, he added a smile. "They're both very pleased with the route my career's taken."

She decided to press just a little farther. "Your father isn't an architect, is he?"

"No. Finance."

"Ah. That's funny, when you think of it. I imagine our parents have had cocktails together more than once. J.D.'s biggest interests are in finance."

"You call your father J.D.?"

"Only when I'm thinking of him as a businessman. He'd always get such a kick out of it when I'd march into his office, plop on his desk and say, 'All right, J.D., is it buy or sell?'"

"You're very fond of him."

"I'm crazy about him. Mother, too, even when she nags. She's always wanting me to fly to Paris and be redone." With only the faintest of frowns, she touched the tips of her hair. "She's certain the French could find a way to make me elegant and demure."

"I like you the way you are."

Again he saw that quick look of astonishment on her face. "That's the nicest thing you've ever said to me."

He thought, as he stared into her eyes, that he heard the first rumble of thunder. "We'd better get this stuff inside. Rain's coming."

"All right." She rose easily enough and helped clear the table. It was foolish to be moved by such a simple statement. He hadn't told her she was beautiful or brilliant. He hadn't said he loved her madly. He'd simply told her that he liked her the way she was. Nothing he could have said would have meant more to a woman like Jackie.

Inside the kitchen, they worked together for a few moments in companionable silence.

"I suppose," she began, "since you're dressed like that, you didn't spend the day at the beach."

"No, I had meetings. My clients from Denver."

Jackie looked at what was left in the wine bottle, decided it wasn't enough to cork and poured the remainder into their glasses. "You never mentioned what you were going to build."

"S and S Industries is putting a branch in Denver. They need an office building."

"You designed another one of them in Dallas a few years ago."

Surprised, he glanced over. "Yes, I did."

"Is this one going to be along the same lines?"

"No. I went for slick and futuristic in Dallas. Lots of glass and steel, with an uncluttered look. I want something more classic for this. Softer, more distinguished lines."

"Can I see the drawings?"

"I suppose, if you'd like."

"I really would." She dried her hands on a cloth, then handed him his half-filled glass. "Can I see them now?"

"All right." He didn't question the fact that he wanted her to see them, that her opinion mattered to him. Both were new concepts for him, and something to think about later. They walked through the house as the light grew dim from the gathering clouds.

His desk was clear. Nathan would never have gone to a meeting without dealing with any leftover paperwork or correspondence. Drawing the blueprints from the tube, he spread them out. Genuinely interested, Jackie leaned over his shoulder with her lips pursed.

"The exterior is brown brick," he began, trying to ignore the brush of her hair against his cheek as she leaned closer. "I'm using curves rather than straight lines."

"It has a deco look."

"Exactly." Why hadn't he noticed her scent earlier? Was he just growing accustomed to it, or was it because she was standing so close, close enough to touch or to taste with the slightest effort? "I've arched the windows, and…"

When he let his words trail off, she glanced up and smiled. Understanding and patience shouldn't make a man uncomfortable, but he looked back deliberately at the papers on his desk.

"And every individual office will have at least one. I've always felt that it's more conducive to productivity if you don't feel caged in."

"Yes." She was still smiling, and neither of them were looking at the blueprints. "It's a beautiful building, very strong without being oppressive. Classic without being staid. The trim and accents are in rose, I imagine."

"To blend with the bricks." Her mouth was rose, a very soft, very subtle rose. He found himself turning his head just enough to taste it.

This time he knew he heard thunder, and it was much closer.

He drew away, shaken. Without speaking, he began to roll up the blueprints.

"I'd like to see the sketches of the interior."

"Jack—"

"It's not really fair to leave things half done."

Nodding, Nathan unrolled the next set. She was right. He supposed he'd known that all along. A thing begun required a finish.

# Chapter Eight

Jackie drew a long, steadying breath. She felt like a diver who'd just taken the last bounce on the board. There could be no turning back now.

She hadn't known when she'd started the evening that he would allow her to get this close. The defenses he had were lowering, and the distance he insisted on was narrowing. It was difficult, very difficult, to accept that the reason for that might only be his own desire. But if that was all he could feel for her now, that was all she would ask for. Desire, at least, was honest.

She couldn't love him any more than she already did. That was what she had thought, but now she knew it wasn't true. With every step closer, with every hour spent with him, her heart expanded.

Patient, even sympathetic to his dilemma, she listened while he explained the floor plans.

It was an excellent piece of work. Her eye and her knowledge were sharp enough to recognize that. But so was he. An excellent piece of work. His hands were wide palmed and long fingered, tanned from the hours he spent outdoors watching over his projects, artistic in their own competent, no-nonsense way. His voice was strong, masculine without being gruff, cultured without being affected. There was a trace of lime scent on his skin from his soap.

She murmured in agreement and put a hand on his arm as he pointed out a facet of the building. There were muscles beneath the creaseless material of his tailored, conservative suit. She heard his voice hesitate at her touch. And she, too, heard the thunder.

"There'll be an atrium here, in the executive offices. We're going to use tile rather than carpet for a cooler, cleaner look. And here…" His mouth was drying up on the words, his muscles tightening at her casual touch. He found it necessary to sit.

"The boardroom?" Jackie prompted, and sat on the arm of his chair.

"What? Yes." His tie was strangling him. Nathan tugged at it and struggled to concentrate. "We'll continue with the arches, but on a larger scale. The paneling will—" He wondered why in the hell the paneling had ever mattered. Her hand was on his shoulder now, kneading away the tension he hadn't even been aware had lodged there.

"What about the paneling?"

What about it? he thought as she leaned forward to trail one of her slender, ringed fingers over the prints. "We're going with mahogany. Honduras."

"It'll be beautiful. Now, and a hundred years from now. Indirect lighting?"

"Yes." He looked at her again. She was smiling, her head tilted just inches above his, her body curved just slightly toward him. The ink on the blueprint of his life seemed to fade. "Jack, this can't go on."

"I agree completely." In one lithe move, she was in his lap.

"What are you doing?" It shouldn't have amused him. His stomach had just contracted into a fist, one with claws, but he found himself smiling at her.

"You're right, this can't go on. I'm sure you're going as crazy as I am, and we can't have that, can we?" A trio of rings glittered on her hand as she tucked her hair back.

"I suppose not."

"No. So I'm going to put a stop to it."

"To what?" He put a hand on her wrist as she slipped off his tie.

"To the uncertainty, to the what-ifs." Ignoring his hand, she began to unbutton his shirt. "This is very nice material," she commented. "I'm taking full responsibility, Nathan. You really have no say in the matter."

"What are you talking about, Jack?" He took her by the shoulders when she started to peel off his jacket. "What the hell do you think you're doing?"

"I'm having my way with you, Nathan." She pressed her mouth to his, and the laugh he'd thought he was ready to form became a moan. "It's no use trying to fight it, you know," she murmured against his lips as she pulled off his jacket. "I'm a very determined woman."

"So I see." He felt her tug at his shirt from the waistband of his slacks and tried again. "Jack—damn it, Jackie, we'd better talk about this."

"No more talk." She nipped lightly at his collarbone, then slid her tongue to his ear. "I'm going to have you, Nathan, willing or not." She closed her teeth over his earlobe. "Don't make me hurt you."

This time he did laugh, though not steadily. "Jack, I outweigh you by seventy pounds."

"The bigger they are…" she told him, and unhooked his slacks. In an automatic defensive gesture, his hands covered hers.

"You're serious."

She drew back far enough to look at him just as the first slice of lightning lit the sky. The flash leaped into her eyes as if it had always been there, waiting. "Deadly." With her eyes on his, she caught the zipper of her jumpsuit between her thumb and fingers and drew it down. "You're not getting out of this room until I'm finished with you, Nathan. Cooperate, and I'll be gentle. Otherwise…" She shrugged, and the jumpsuit slithered tantalizingly down her shoulders.

It was too late, much too late, to pretend he didn't want to be with her, didn't have to be with her. The game she was playing was taking the responsibility and the repercussions away from him and onto her. Though it touched him, he couldn't allow it.

"I want you." He brushed her cheeks with his hands and combed his fingers through her hair as he said it. "Come upstairs."

She turned her face so that her lips pressed into his palm. It was a gesture of great tenderness, a gesture that bordered on submission. But when she looked back at him, she shook her head. "Right here. Right now." Jackie pressed her open mouth to his, leaving him no choice.

She tantalized, tormented, teased. Her body curled itself around his, and her lips were quick and urgent. They lingered on his, drawing in, drawing out, then sped away to trace the planes and angles of his face. His blood was hammering. He could feel it, in his head, in his loins, in his fingertips. Her hands were unmerciful…wonderful…as they roamed over him.

No hesitation. She didn't know the meaning of the word. Like the storm that whipped at the windows, she was all flash and fire. A man could get burned by her, he thought, and always bear the scars. Yet his arms banded around her, holding her hard and close as he fought to maintain some control. She was driving him beyond the limits he'd always set for himself, away from reason, away from the civilized.

That was his own breath he heard, fast and uneven. That was his skin springing moist and hot from a need that had grown titanic in mere moments. He was pulling the material from her shoulders with a gnawing demand to feel her flesh against his. And it was with an insatiable greed that he took it.

"Jack." His mouth was against her throat as he tasted, devoured. More…he could only think of having more. He'd have absorbed her into him if he'd known how. "Jack," he repeated. "Give me a minute, will you?"

But her mouth was just as greedy when it came to his. She only laughed.

He swore, but even the oath caught in his throat. He was tearing the jumpsuit from her as they slid to the floor.

She couldn't make her fingers work fast enough.

Jackie pulled and yanked to strip the last barriers of his clothing away. She wanted to feel him, all of him. As they rolled over on the carpet, her skin was on fire from the friction of flesh against flesh.

She'd thought she would guide him, coerce, cajole, seduce. She'd been wrong. Like a pebble in a slingshot, she'd been flung high and fast, no longer in control. But with some trace of reason, she knew he was as lost as she.

Desire held control, steered by a love only one of them could admit. But in the lamplight, with the storm reaching its peak, desire was enough.

Wrapped together, they rolled mindlessly, each searching and finding more. The capacity for intense concentration was inherent in them both, but neither had used it so fully in the act of love until tonight. The clothes they'd discarded tangled with their naked legs and were kicked heedlessly away. Rain, tossed by a restless wind, hit the windows like bullets but was ignored. Something teetered on a table as it was jolted, then thudded to the carpet. Neither of them heard.

There were no murmured promises, no whispered endearments. Only sighs and shudders. Neither were there tender caresses or gentle kisses. Only demands and hunger.

Breath heaving, Nathan moved above her. Lightning still flashed sporadically, highlighting her face and hair. Her head was thrown back, her eyes clear and open, when he took her.

Perfect. Naked, damp and dazed, Jackie curled into him while that one word ran around in her head. Nothing had ever been so perfect. His heart was still pounding against hers, his breath still warming her cheek. The rain had slowed, and the thunder was only a murmur in the distance. Storms passed. Some storms.

She hadn't needed the physical act of love to confirm her feelings for Nathan. Lovemaking was only an extension of being in love. But even with her vivid and often far-reaching imagination, she'd never known anything could be like this.

He'd emptied her, and he'd filled her.

No matter how many times they came together, no matter how many years they shared, there would never be another first time. Her eyes closed, her arms wrapped around him, she savored it.

He didn't know what to say to her, or if he was capable of speech at all. He'd thought he knew himself, the man he was and the man he'd chosen to be. The Nathan Powell he'd lived with most of his life wasn't the same man who had plunged so recklessly into passion, giving and taking with greedy disregard.

He'd lost all sense of time, of place, even of self, as he'd driven himself restlessly, even abandonedly, into her. The way he had never done before. The way, he already understood, he would never do again. Unless it was with Jackie.

He should have taken her with more care, and certainly with more consideration. But once begun he had lost whatever foothold he'd still had on reason and had cartwheeled off the cliff with her.

It had been what she'd wanted—what he'd wanted—but did that make it right? There had been no words, no questions. He hadn't even given a thought to his responsibility or her protection. That had made him wince a bit even as he stroked a hand through her hair.

They'd have to talk about that, and soon, because he was going to have to admit that what had happened between them was going to happen again. That didn't make it permanent, he assured himself as his hand fitted possessively over the curve of her shoulder.

"Jack?"

When she tilted her head to look up at him, he was struck by such an unexpected wave of tenderness that he couldn't speak at all. Lips curved, she leaned closer and pressed them to his. It took no more than that to have the embers of desire glowing again. The fingers that had been stroking her hair tightened and dragged her closer. Limber and sleek, she shifted onto him.

"I love you, Nathan. No, don't say anything." Her lips nibbled and rubbed against his as she sought to soothe more than to arouse. "You don't have to say anything. I just need to tell you. And I want to make love with you again and again."

Her hands had already told him as much, and now her mouth was moving lower, nipping and gliding along his neck. His response was so immediate it stunned him.

"Jack, wait a minute."

"No more complaints," she murmured. "I ravished you once, and I can do it again."

"Thank God for that, but wait." Firmly now, thinking only of her, he drew her away by the shoulders. "We have to talk a minute."

"We can talk when we're old—though I did want to mention that I'm crazy about your carpet."

"I've grown fond of it myself. Now, hold on," he said again when she tried to squirm away from his restraining hands. "Jack, I'm serious."

She let out a huge and exaggerated sigh. "Do you have to be?"

"Yes."

"All right, then." She composed her features and settled herself comfortably. "Shoot."

"I'm already doing it backward," he began, furious with himself. "But I don't intend to make the same mistake again. Things happened so quickly before that I never asked, never even thought to ask, if it was all right."

"Of course it was all right," she began with a laugh. "Oh." Her brows rose as realization struck. "You really are a very good man, aren't you?" Despite his grip on her shoulders, she managed to kiss him. "Yes, it's all right. I realize I look like a scatterbrain, but I'm not. Well, at least I'm a responsible one."

The tenderness crept back unexpectedly, and he cupped her face in his hands. "You don't look like a scatterbrain. You may act like one, but you look beautiful."

"Now I know I'm getting to you." She tried to say it lightly, but her eyes glistened. "I'd like you to think I'm beautiful. I always wanted to be."

Her hair fell over her brow, tempting him to brush at it, to tangle his fingers in it. "The first time I saw you, when I was tired and annoyed and you were sitting in my whirlpool, I thought you were beautiful."

"And I thought you were Jake."

"What?"

"I'd been sitting there, thinking about my story, and about Jake—the way he looked, you know." Her fingers roamed over his face as she remembered. "Build, coloring, features. I opened my eyes and saw you and thought...there he is." She rested her cheek on his chest. "My hero."

Troubled, he curled an arm around her. "I'm no hero, Jack."

"You are to me." She shimmied up his body a bit, then rested her forehead against his. "Nathan, I forgot the strudel."

"Did you? What strudel?"

"The apple strudel I made for dessert. Why don't I dish some out and we can eat it in bed?"

Later, he thought, later he'd think about Jackie's idea of love and heroes. "Sounds very sensible."

"Okay." She kissed the tip of his nose, then smiled. "Your bed or mine?"

"Mine," he murmured, as though the word had been waiting to be said. "I want you in mine."

Laziness was its own reward. Jackie embraced the idea as she stretched in bed. Nothing seemed more glorious at the moment than to sleep in after so many days of rising early and going straight to the typewriter.

She snuggled, half dozing, pretending she was twelve and it was Saturday. There had been nothing she'd liked better at twelve than Saturdays. But as she shifted her leg brushed against Nathan's. It took no more than that for her to be very, very glad she was no longer twelve.

"Are you awake?" she asked without opening her eyes.

"No." His arm came around her possessively and remained.

Still drowsy, a smile just forming on her lips, she nibbled on him. "Would you like to be?"

"Depends." He shifted closer to her, enjoying the

quiet, cozy feel of warm body against warm body. "Did we get all the strudel out of the bed?"

"Can't say for sure. Shall I look?" With that, Jackie tossed the sheets over their heads and attacked him.

She had more energy than she was entitled to, Nathan thought later as she lay sprawled over him. The sheets were now balled and twisted somewhere below their feet. Still trying to catch his breath, he kept his eyes half-shut as he looked at her.

She was long and lean and curved very subtly. Her skin was gold in the late-morning light, except for a remarkably thin line over her hips where it remained white, unexposed to the sun. Tousled from the pillow and from his hands, her hair sprang in a distracted halo.

He'd always thought he preferred long hair on a woman, but with Jackie's short, free-swinging style he could stroke the curve at the back of her neck. He did so now, and she began to purr like a satisfied cat.

What was he going to do with her?

The idea of nudging her gently along was no longer even a remote possibility. He wanted her with him. Needed her. *Need.* That was a word he'd always been careful to avoid. Now that it had slammed into him, he hadn't any idea how to handle it.

He tried to think of what he would do tomorrow, a week, even a month from now, without her. His mind remained stubbornly blank. This wasn't like him. He hadn't been like himself since she'd spun her way into his life.

What did she want from him? Nathan detested himself because he knew he wouldn't ask her. He already knew what she wanted, as if it had been discussed and debated and deliberated. She loved him, at least for today. And he...he cared for her. *Love* was one four-letter word he wouldn't allow himself. Love meant promises. He never made promises unless he was sure he could keep them. A promise given casually and broken was worse than a lie.

With the morning sun shining through the windows and the birds singing the praises of spring, he wished it could be as simple as Jackie would like it. Love, marriage, family. He knew all too well that love didn't guarantee the success of a marriage and that marriage didn't equal family.

His parents had a marriage in which love no longer was an issue. No one would ever have accused the three of them of being a family.

He wasn't his father, Nathan thought as he held Jackie and studied the ceiling. He'd made certain that he would never be his father. But he understood the pride in success and the drive for accomplishment that had been his father's. That were still his father's. And were his.

He shook his head. He hadn't thought of his father or his lack of family life as much in a decade as he had since he'd met Jackie. She did that to him, as well. She made him consider possibilities that he'd rejected long ago with perfect logic and sense. She made him wish and regret what he'd never had reason to wish or regret before.

He couldn't let himself love her, because then he would make promises. And when the promises were broken he'd hate himself. She deserved better than what he could give her or, more accurately, what he couldn't give her.

"Nathan?"

"Hmm."

"What are you thinking about?"

"You."

When she lifted her head, her eyes were unexpectedly solemn. "I hope not."

Puzzled, he combed his fingers through the tangle of her hair. "Why?"

"Because you're tensing up again." Something came and went in her face—the first shadow of sorrow he'd ever seen in it. "Don't regret. I don't think I could bear it."

"No." He drew her up to cradle her in his arms. "No, I don't. How could I?"

She turned her face into his throat. He didn't know she was forcing back tears, and she couldn't have explained them to him. "I love you, Nathan, and I don't want you to regret that, either, or worry about it. I want you to just let things happen as they're meant to happen."

He tilted her head back with a finger under her chin. Her eyes were dry now. His were intense. "And that's enough for you?"

"Enough for today." The smile was back. Even he couldn't detect the effort it cost her. "I never know what's going to be enough for tomorrow. How do you feel about brunch? You haven't had my crepes yet. I make really wonderful crepes, but I don't remember if there's any whipping cream. There's always omelets, of course—if the mushrooms haven't dried up. Or we could make do with leftover strudel. Maybe we should have a swim first, and then—"

"Jack?"

"Uh-huh?"

"Shut up."

"Right now?" she asked as his hand slid down to her hip.

"Yes."

"Okay."

She started to laugh, but his lips met hers with such quiet, such fragile tenderness that the laughter became a helpless moan. Her eyes, once alight with amusement, shuttered closed at the sound. She was a strong woman, often valiant in her way, but she had no defense against tenderness.

It had been just as unexpected for him. There had been no flash of fire, no rumble of thunder. Just warmth, a drugging, languorous warmth that crept under his skin, into his brain, into his heart. With one kiss, one easy merging of lips, she filled him.

He hadn't thought of her as delicate. But she was delicate now, as her bones seemed to dissolve under his hands, leaving her smaller somehow, softer. Woman at her most vulnerable. As the kiss spun out, he lifted a hand to her cheek, as if to hold her there, captive.

Patience. She'd known there was a steady, rock-solid patience in him. But until now he'd never shown it to her. Compassion. That, too, she'd sensed in him. But to feel it now, to have him give her the gift of it, was more precious than diamonds. She was lost in him again, not in the frantic race she'd become used to, but in a slow, lengthy search she already knew would lead her where she had always wanted to go.

He caressed where he'd once taken greedily. Her skin was like satin and shivered under his touch. There was a fluidity to her now rather than a frenzy, a quiescence that had taken the place of energy.

His fingertips skimmed over her, and he delighted in making discoveries in territory already conquered. The same woman, yet a different one; her generosity was still there, but merged now with a vulnerability that humbled him. He found her flavor somehow sweeter. When he pressed his lips to her breast, he felt her heartbeat. It hammered fast, not with the heady, energetic rhythm of their past loving, but quick and light.

Experimentally he ran a finger over the inside of her wrist, feeling her pulse beating there, as well. For him. Curling his fingers through hers, he brought them to his lips to kiss and caress them one by one.

The bottom seemed to drop out of her world. With each touch she had fallen deeper, still deeper, into his. Into him. Now, as he did nothing more than brush his mouth over her fingertips, she tumbled headfirst into the dark, trusting him implicitly to catch her.

He could have asked her anything, demanded anything. In that moment her love was so overwhelming that she would have granted any wish without a thought to self or survival. It wasn't possible for her to gather him close and take their loving to another plane. He had a prisoner. Though he might not know it, she would stay enslaved as long as he'd have her.

He only knew that something had changed yet again. He was protector now as well as lover, giver as well as taker. The excitement that knowledge brought was tinged with a trace of fear he struggled to ignore. He couldn't think about tomorrow and tomorrow's consequences when he wanted her, possibly more, impossibly more, than he had only moments ago. She wouldn't object if he took her quickly, if he dragged them both to the top without preamble or delicacy. Perhaps it was because of that, because he understood that she would accept him on any terms, that he found himself needing to give her everything he could.

Slow loving. Almost tortuous. Tender stroking. Lazy tastes. There were quiet sighs that rippled the air until even the sunlight seemed to dim. If it had been possible, he would have had flowers for her, a bouquet of them. Soft petals, shimmering fragrances; he would have poured them over her skin. But he only had himself.

It was enough. He was more than enough for her. She showed him that in the way her lips parted, in the way her arms encircled him. No dream she'd ever indulged in, no wish she'd ever given herself, could compare with the reality of him cherishing her.

His hands were so cool, so calm, on her skin. With each touch she felt herself glow. The heat came from within her now, so that it was possible to bank it, to prevent it from becoming overpowering. Just flickers of flame, burning softly.

As gentle as he, she reached for him, offering the pleasure and temptation of unconditional love. When she trembled, he murmured. In reassurance. And she, who had never believed she would need a man to watch over her, understood that she would wither to dust without him.

Generosity, given without restrictions. That she offered, openhanded, was no longer a surprise to him. But to discover that he could give equally, to find that he was compelled to match her, was something new.

He slipped into her, and the tenderness remained.

Slow, harmonious movements. A breath caught, then sighed away like the wind. With his mouth on hers, they continued. Like a Viennese waltz, their dance was light and elegant. When the tempo increased, they surged with the music, spinning, whirling, their eyes open and locked together.

The dance ended as gently as it had begun.

The sun was higher now. Contentedly, her body curved into his, Jackie watched the curtains move with the faint breeze. If she concentrated hard enough she could catch the light fragrance of flowers from the garden below. Nothing identifiable, but a mixture of scents that spoke of spring and new life.

Every moment of the hours they'd had together was lodged firmly in her mind. She knew she would take them out often and enjoy them over and over.

"You know what I'd like?" she asked him.

"Hmm?" If he hadn't been so dazed, it would have amazed him that he could be dozing in bed this close to noon.

"To stay here, right here in this bed, all day."

"We've got a pretty good start."

Her grin wicked, she turned to face him. Nose to nose, she leered. "Why don't we—" She swore when the phone rang. "It's the wrong number," she told him, climbing over his shoulder as he reached for it. "It's just a woman with a squeaky voice who's going to tell you your name's been selected in a sweepstakes and you've won ten free magazine subscriptions as long as you pay $7.75 a month for handling."

He hesitated a moment because when she said it it was too easy to believe. "What if it isn't?"

"Ah, but what if it is? Do you have enough willpower to resist ten free magazines a month? Be sure, Nathan. Be very sure."

He put a hand over her face and shoved her back against the pillows. "Hello."

"You were warned," Jackie said in a voice that spoke of doom. This time he put the pillow over her face.

"Carla?"

"Carla?" Her voice was muffled by the pillows. Jackie tossed it aside and sank her teeth into his shoulder.

"Ouch! Damn it! No, Carla, I— What is it?" To protect himself, Nathan rolled and trapped Jackie under him. "Yes, I was expecting that." Ignoring the flailing arms and muttered curses beneath him, Nathan listened. "All right, we'll push up the schedule if necessary. No, I've already taken care of that from here. Set this up for tomorrow. Nine. Ten, then," he said. "Contact Cody. I'll want him there. Fine, Carla." Jackie wriggled beneath him and made loud gasping noises. He ignored that, as well. "Yes, I've enjoyed having a few days of relaxation. See you tomorrow."

When he leaned over to hang up the receiver, Jackie managed to squirm out from under him. Face flushed, pulling in exaggerated gulps of air, she thudded a pillow over his head.

"So," she began. "You decided to smother me so that you could run off with the Italian countess and make mad, illicit passion in the Holiday Inn. Don't try to deny it," she warned. "The signs are all too clear."

"Okay. Which Italian countess was that?"

"Carla." She slammed the pillow at him again, aiming lower, then had to bite back a laugh when he grabbed her around the waist. "No, don't try to make up, Nathan. It's too late. I've already decided to murder both you and the countess. I'll electrocute you while you're sharing your bubble bath. No jury would convict me."

"Not if they did a psychiatric profile first."

She made another grab, this time for a very vulnerable area. He avoided her by throwing her onto her back and once again using his body to shield and protect himself. Arms locked, they rolled. Nathan was just beginning to enjoy it when her momentum sent them tumbling to the floor.

Out of breath and rubbing his shoulder, he narrowed his eyes. "You are crazy."

Jackie straddled him and planted her arms on either side of his head. "Okay, Powell, if you value your life, come clean. Who's Carla?"

He considered her. Her eyes were bright, her cheeks flushed with amusement. Her wide, incredible mouth was curved. Casually he cupped her hips in his hands. "You want the truth?"

"And nothing but."

"The Countess Carla Mandolini and I have been having a blazing adulterous affair for years. She fools her husband, the elderly and impotent count, by doubling as my secretary. The fool actually believes that the twins are his."

He really was adorable, Jackie decided as she leaned closer. "A likely story," she told him just before her mouth covered his.

# Chapter Nine

"All right, Nathan, consider yourself kidnapped. You might as well go peacefully."

As he wrapped a towel around his waist, Nathan glanced up. Without bothering to knock, Jackie pushed open the door to the bathroom and strode in. He should be used to it by now, he thought as he secured the towel. She could pop up anytime and anywhere.

"Mind if I put my shoes on?"

"You've got ten minutes."

Before she could turn to go, he had her by the arm. "Where have you been?"

He was becoming too attached to her, Nathan told himself even as the words came out. When he'd woken up alone that morning it had taken all of his control not to dash around the house looking for her. They'd been lovers three days, and already he felt bereft if she wasn't beside him when he opened his eyes in the morning.

"Some of us have work to do, even on Saturdays." She let her gaze roam down, then up. He was damp, tanned and mostly naked. She thought it a pity she'd made plans. "Downstairs in ten minutes, or I'll make you suffer."

"What's going on, Jack?"

"You're not in a position to ask questions." With a last smile, she left him. He heard her run lightly downstairs.

What did she have in store for him now? Nathan wondered as he reached for his razor. With Jackie there were never any guarantees, and there was rarely any rhyme or reason. It should have annoyed him, he thought as he lathered his face. It was supposed to annoy him. He'd already planned his day.

A few hours in his office dealing with the preliminaries on the Sydney project and snipping any loose ends from Denver would take care of the morning. After that he'd thought it might be nice to treat Jackie, and himself, to lunch and tennis at the country club. Being kidnapped hadn't been in his plans.

But he wasn't annoyed. Nathan brought the razor over lather and beard in short, smooth strokes. Because he'd left the window open, the mirror was only lightly steamed at the edges. He could see himself clearly. What had changed?

He was still Nathan Powell, a man with certain responsibilities and priorities. It wasn't a stranger looking back at him in the mirror, but a man he knew very well. The eyes were the same, as was the shape of the face, the hairline. If he looked the same, why didn't he feel the same? More, why couldn't he, a man who knew himself so well, put his finger on exactly what his feelings were?

Shaking the thought aside, he rinsed off the traces of lather. It was absurd. He was exactly who he had always been. The only change in his life was Jackie.

And what the hell was he going to do about her?

It wasn't a question he could avoid much longer. The more involved he became with her, the more certain he was that he was going to hurt her. That was something he would regret the rest of his life. In a matter of weeks he would have to leave her to go to Denver. He couldn't leave her with promises and vows, nor could he expect her to stay when he couldn't tell her what she needed to hear.

He wanted to believe she was nothing more than a few colorful pages in the very straightforward book of his life. But he knew, he already knew, that as his life went on he would keep turning back to look over those few pages again and again.

They should talk. He slapped on aftershave that left his skin cool and stinging. It was up to him to see that they did, quietly, seriously and as soon as possible. The world, as much as he might now wish it could be, was not composed of two people. And neither of them had begun to live the moment they'd met.

"You're running out of time, Nathan."

Jackie's voice came rushing up the stairs and caught him daydreaming. Daydreams were also something new in his life. Swearing at himself, Nathan whipped off the towel and began to dress.

He found her in the kitchen, securing the lid on a cooler, while on the radio some group from the fifties harmonized about love and devotion.

"You're lucky I decided to be generous and give you another five minutes." She turned to study him. He wore black shorts with a white shirt, and his hair was still slightly damp. "I guess it was worth it."

He was almost but not quite used to her frank and unabashed appraisals. "What's going on, Jack?"

"I told you. You're kidnapped." She stepped forward to slip her arms around his waist. "If you try to escape, it'll go hard on you." Pressing her face in his throat, she began to sniff. "I love your aftershave."

"What's in the cooler?"

"Surprises. Sit down, you can have some cereal."

"Cereal?"

"Man doesn't live by hotcakes alone, Nathan." She kissed him quick. "And some bananas." She moved away to get one, changed her mind and took two. As she peeled her own, she began to explain. "You might as well consider yourself my hostage for the day and make this simple."

"Make what simple?"

"We've both been working hard the last few days—well, except for one very memorable day." She smiled as she took the first bite. "And that was exhausting in its own way. So…" She slapped a palm on the cooler. "I'm taking you for a ride."

"I see." Nathan sliced the banana over a bowl of cornflakes. "Anywhere in particular?"

"No. Anywhere at all. You eat, I'll put this in the boat."

"Boat?" He paused, the banana peel in his hand. "My boat?"

"Of course." Hefting the cooler, she turned back with an easy smile. "As much as I love you, Nathan, I know even you can't walk on water. Coffee's hot, by the way, but make it quick, will you?"

He did, because he was more interested in what she had up her sleeve than in a bowl of cold cereal. She'd left the radio on, he supposed for his benefit. After he'd rinsed his bowl, Nathan switched it off. As a matter of course he went to check the front door. Jackie had left it open. He shut it, locked it, then went to join her.

Outside, he found her competently storing supplies in the hatch. She wore a visor in a blazing orange that matched her shorts and the frames of a pair of mirrored wraparound sunglasses.

"All set?" she asked him. "Cast off, will you?"

"You're driving?"

"Sure. I was practically born on a boat." She slipped behind the wheel and tossed a look over her shoulder as Nathan hesitated, his hands on the line. "Trust me. I looked at a map."

"Well, then." Wondering if he was taking his life in his hands, he cast off and came aboard.

"Sun block," she said, handing him a tube. With that she pulled smoothly away from the dock. "How do you feel about St. Thomas?"

"Jack…"

"Only kidding. I've thought what a kick it would be to travel the whole Intracoastal. Take a whole summer and just cruise."

He'd thought of it, too, as something he might find time for—someday. After retirement, perhaps. When Jackie said it, it seemed possible it could happen tomorrow. And it made him wish it would happen tomorrow. He only murmured as he watched her handle the boat.

He should have known she'd be fine. Maybe she

couldn't remember to close doors behind her, but it seemed to him that whatever she did she did with careless skill. Her hand was light on the wheel as she negotiated the channel. Even when she picked up speed, he relaxed.

"You picked a good day for a kidnapping."

"I thought so." She threw him a grin, then settled more comfortably in her seat.

The boat handled like a dream. Of course, she'd known that Nathan would keep it in tip-top shape. That was one of the things she admired about him. He didn't take his possessions for granted. If it belonged to him, it deserved his attention. Too many people she knew, herself included, could develop a casual disregard for what was theirs. She'd learned something from him about pride of possession and the responsibility that went along with it.

She belonged to him now. Jackie hoped he'd begin to care for her with the same kind of devotion.

You're moving too fast, as usual, she cautioned herself. Caution was something else she'd learned from Nathan. It had to be enough, for now, that he no longer looked alarmed whenever she told him she loved him. The fact that he was beginning to accept that she did was a giant step. And soon—eventually, she thought, correcting herself—eventually he would accept the fact that he loved her back.

She knew he did. It wasn't a matter of wish fulfillment or hopeful dreams. She saw it when he looked at her, felt it when he touched her. Because she did, it made it that much more difficult to wait.

She'd always looked for instant gratification. Even as a child she'd been able to learn quickly and apply what she'd learned so that the rewards came quickly. Writing had shown her more than a love for storytelling. It had also shown her that some rewards were best waited for. Having Nathan, really having him, would be worth waiting a lifetime.

She turned down an alley of water where the bush was thick and green. It was hardly wide enough for two boats to pass. Near the verges, limbs of deadwood poked through the surface like twisted arms. Behind them the wake churned white, while ahead the water was darker, more mysterious. Above, the sun was a white flash, hinting, perhaps threatening, of the sultry summer still weeks away. Spray flew, glinting in the light. The motor purred, sending a flurry of birds rocketing above the trees.

"Ever been on the Amazon?"

"No." Nathan turned to her. "Have you?"

"Not yet," she told him, as if it were only a small oversight. "It might be something like this. Brown water, thick vegetation hiding all sorts of dangerous jungle life. Is it crocodiles or alligators down there?"

"I couldn't say."

"I'll have to look it up." A dragonfly dashed blue and gleaming across the bow, catching her attention. It skimmed over the water without making a ripple, then flashed into the bush. "It's wonderful here." Abruptly she cut the engine.

"What are you doing?"

"Listening."

Within moments the birds began to call, rustling through the leaves and growing bold in the silence. Insects sent up a soprano chorus. There was a watery plop, then two, as a frog swallowed an insect for an early lunch. Even the water itself had sound, a low, murmurous voice that invited laziness. From far off, too far off to be important, came the hum of another boat.

"I used to love to go camping," Jackie remembered. "I'd drag one of my brothers, and—"

"I didn't know you had any brothers."

"Two. Fortunately for me, they've both taken an avid interest in my father's many empires, leaving me free to do as I please." He couldn't see her eyes as she spoke, but from the tone of her voice he knew they were smiling.

"Never any interest in being a corporate climber?"

"Oh, God, no. Well, actually, I did think of being chairman of the board when I was six. Then I decided I'd rather be a brain surgeon. So I was more than happy when Ryan and Brandon took me off the hook." Lazily she slipped out of her deck shoes to stretch her toes. "I've always thought it would be difficult to be a son of a demanding father and not want to follow in his footsteps."

She'd said it casually, but Nathan was so completely silent that she realized she'd hit part of the mark. She opened her mouth to question, then shut it again. In his own time, she reminded herself. "Anyway, even though it often took blackmail to get one of my brothers to go with me, I really loved sitting by the fire and listening. You could be anywhere you wanted to be."

"Where did you go?"

"Oh, here and there. Arizona was the best. There's something indescribable about the desert when you're sitting beside a tent." She grinned again. "Of course, there's also something special about the presidential suite and room service. Depends on the mood. You want to drive?"

"No, you're doing fine."

With a laugh, Jackie kicked the motor on. "I hate to say it, but you ain't seen nothin' yet."

She spun the boat through the waterway, taking any out-of-the-way canal or inlet that caught her fancy. She was delighted to chug along behind the *Jungle Queen*, Lauderdale's triple-decker party boat, and wave to the tourists. For a time she was content to follow its wake and direction as it toured the Intracoastal's estates.

The houses pleased her, with their sweeping grounds and sturdy pillars. She enjoyed the flood of the spring flowers and the wink and shimmer of the pools. When another boat passed, she'd make up stories about the occupants that had Nathan laughing or just rolling his eyes.

It pleased her just as much to turn off the more traveled routes and pretend she was lost in the quiet, serpentine waters where the brush grew heavy and close at the edges. Shutting down again under the shade of bending palms and cypress, she took out Jackie's idea of a picnic.

There was Pouilly-Fuissé in paper cups, and cracked crab to be dug out with plastic forks, and tiny Swiss meringues, white and glossy. After she'd badgered Nathan into taking off his shirt, she rubbed sunblock over him, rambling all the while about the idea of setting a book in the Everglades.

But what she noticed most as she stroked the cream over his skin was that he was relaxed. There was no band of tension over his shoulders, no knot of nerves at the base of his neck. When he reciprocated by applying the cream to wherever her skinny blue tank top exposed her skin, there was none in her, either.

When the cooler was packed away again, she jumped back behind the wheel. The morning laziness was over, she told him. Turning the boat around, she headed out.

She burst into Port Everglades to join the pleasure and cruise ships, the freighters and sailboats. Here the water was wide and open, the spray cool and the air full of sound.

"Do you ever come here?" she shouted.

"No." Nathan clamped a hand on the orange visor she'd transferred from her head to his. "Not often."

"I love it! Think of all the places these ships have been before they come here. And where they're going when they leave. Hundreds of people, thousands, come here on their way to—I don't know…Mexico, Cuba."

"The Amazon?"

"Yes." Laughing, she turned the boat in a circle that had spray spurting up the sides. "There are so many places to go and see. You don't live long enough, you just can't live long enough to do everything you should." Her hair danced madly away from her face as she rode into the wind. "That's why I'm coming back."

"To Florida?"

"No. To life."

He watched her laugh again and raise her arm to another boat. If anyone could, Nathan thought, it would be Jackie.

He let her have her head. Indeed, he didn't know if he could have stopped her if he'd been inclined to. Besides, he'd long since acknowledged that he enjoyed the race.

At midafternoon, she pulled up to a dock and advised

Nathan to secure the lines. While he obliged, she dug her purse out of the hatch.

"Where are we going now?"

"Shopping."

He held out a hand to help her onto the pier. "For what?"

"For anything. Maybe nothing." With her hand in his, she began to walk. "You know, spring break's nearly here. In a couple of weeks the college crowd will flock to this, the mecca of the East."

"Don't remind me."

"Oh, don't be a stick-in-the-mud, Nathan. Kids have to blow off steam, too. But I was thinking the shops would be a madhouse then, and as much as I might appreciate that, you wouldn't, so we should do this now."

"Do what now?"

"Shop," she explained patiently. "Play tourist, buy tacky souvenirs and T-shirts with vulgar sayings, haggle over a shell ashtray."

"I can't tell you how much I appreciate you thinking of me."

"My pleasure, darling." She planted a quick kiss on his cheek. "Listen, unless I miss my guess, this is something you never do."

He was surprised when she paused, waiting for his answer. "No, it's not."

"It's time you did." She adjusted the visor to a cockier angle. "You very sensibly moved south and chose Fort Lauderdale because of its growth, but you don't take too many walks on the beach."

"I thought we were going shopping."

"It's the same thing." She slipped her arm around his waist. "You know, Nathan, as far as I can see, you don't have one T-shirt with a beer slogan, a rock concert or an obscene saying."

"I've been deprived."

"I know. That's why I'd like to help you out."

"Jack." He stopped, turning around to gently take her shoulders. "Please don't."

"You'll thank me later."

"We'll compromise. I'll buy a tie."

"Only if it has a naked mermaid on it."

Jackie found exactly what she wanted bordering Las Olas Boulevard. There was a labyrinth of small cross streets bulging with shops selling everything from snorkels to sapphires. Telling him it was for his own good, Jackie dragged him into a small, crowded store with a doorway flanked by two garish red flamingos.

"They're becoming entirely too trendy," she said to Nathan with a flick of her hand toward the slim-legged birds. "It's a shame I'm so fond of them. Oh, look, just what I've always wanted. A music box with shells stuck all over it. What do you suppose it plays?"

Jackie wound up what Nathan considered one of the most hideous-looking things he'd ever seen. It played "Moon River."

"No." Jackie shook her head over the melody. "I can do without that."

"Thank God."

Chuckling, she replaced it and began to poke through rows of equally moronic whatnots. "I understand, Nathan, that you have an eye for the aesthetic and harmonious, but there really is something to be said for the ugly and useless."

"Yes, but I can't say it here. There are children present."

"Now take this."

"No," he said as she held up a pelican made entirely of clamshells. "Please, I can't thank you enough for the thought, but I couldn't."

"Only for demonstration purposes. This has a certain charm." She laughed as his brow rose. "No, really. Think of this. Say a couple comes here on their honeymoon and they want something silly and very personal to remember the day by. They need something they can look at in ten years and bring back that very heady, very intimate time before insurance payments and wet diapers." She flourished the bird. *"Voilà."*

*"Voilà?* One doesn't *voilà* a pelican, especially a shell one."

"More imagination," she said with a sigh. "All you need is a little more imagination." With what seemed like genuine regret, she set the pelican down. Just when he thought it was safe, Jackie dragged him over to a maze of T-shirts. She seemed very taken with one in teal with an alligator lounging in a hammock drinking a wine cooler. Passing it by, she dragged out one of a grinning shark in dark glasses.

"This," she told him grandly, "is you."

"It is?"

"Absolutely. Not to say you're a predator, but sharks are notorious for being loners, and the sunglasses are a symbol of a need for privacy."

He studied it, frowning and intrigued. "You know, I've never known anyone to be philosophical about T-shirts."

"Clothes make the man, Nathan." Draping it over her arm, she continued to browse. When she loitered by a rack of ties screen-printed with fish, he put his foot down.

"No, Jack, not even for you."

Sighing at his lack of vision, she settled for the shirt.

She hauled him through a dozen shops until pictures of neon palms, plastic mugs and garish straw hats blurred in his head. She bought with a blatant disregard for style or use. Then, suddenly inspired, she shipped off a huge papier-mâché parrot to her father.

"My mother will make him take it off to one of his offices, but he'll love it. Daddy has a wonderful sense of the ridiculous."

"Is that where you get it?"

"I suppose." Hands on her hips, she turned in a circle to be certain she hadn't missed anything. "Well, since I've done that, I'd better run by that little jewelry store and see if there's anything appropriate for my mother." She pocketed the receipt, then relieved Nathan of two packages. "How are you holding up?"

"I'm game if you are."

"You're sweet." She leaned over, between packages, to kiss him. "Why don't I buy you an ice-cream cone?"

"Why don't you?"

She grinned at that, thinking he was certainly coming along. "Right after I find something tasteful for my mother," she promised, and she proved as good as her word.

Some fifteen minutes later, she chose an ebony pin crusted with pearls. It was a very mature, very elegant piece in faultless taste.

The purchase showed Nathan two things. First that she glanced only casually at the price, so casually that he was certain she would have bought it no matter what the amount. An impulse buyer she certainly was, but he sensed that once she'd decided an item was right, the dollar amount was unimportant. And second that the pin was both conventional and elegant, making it a far cry from the parrot she'd chosen for her father.

It made him wonder, as she loitered over some of the more colorful pieces in the shop, if her parents were as different as her vision of them.

He'd always believed, perhaps too strongly, that children inherited traits, good and bad. Yet here was Jackie, nothing like a woman who would wear a classically tasteful pin, and also nothing like a man who had spent his adult life wheeling and dealing in the business world.

Moments later, he had other things to worry about. They were out on the street again, and Jackie was making arrangements to rent a bicycle built for two.

"Jack, I don't think this is—"

"Why don't you put those packages in the basket, Nathan?" She patted his hand before paying for the rental.

"Listen, I haven't been on a bike since I was a teenager."

"It'll come back to you." The transaction complete, she turned to him and smiled. "I'll take the front if you're worried."

Perhaps she hadn't meant to bait him, but he didn't believe it. Nathan swung his leg over and settled on the front seat. "Get on," he told her. "And remember, you asked for it."

"I love a masterful man," she cooed. Nathan found his lips twitching at the phony southern accent as he set off.

She'd been right. It did come back to him. They pedaled smoothly, even sedately, across the street to ride along the seawall.

Jackie was glad he'd taken the lead. It gave her the opportunity to daydream and sightsee. Which, she thought with a smile, she would have done even if she'd been steering. This way, she didn't have to worry about running into a parked car or barreling down on pedestrians. Nathan could be trusted to steer true. It was only one more reason she loved him.

Matching her rhythm to his, she watched his shoulders. Strong and dependable. She found those both such lovely words. Strange…she'd never known she would find dependability so fiercely attractive until she'd found it. Found him.

Now he was relaxed, enjoying the sun and the day in it. She could give that to him. Not every day of the week, Jackie mused. He wouldn't always fall in with whatever last-minute plans she cooked up. But often enough, she thought, and wished there wasn't so much space between them so that she could wrap her arms around him and just hug.

He'd never pictured himself biking along the oceanfront—much less enjoying it. The fact was, Nathan rarely even came to this section of town. It was for tourists and teenagers. Being with Jackie made him feel like both. She was showing him new things not only about the city where he'd lived for nearly a decade but about the life he'd had more than thirty years to experience.

Everything about her was unexpected. How could he have known that the unexpected could also be the fresh? For a few hours he hadn't given a thought to Denver or penalty clauses or the responsibilities of tomorrow. He hadn't thought of tomorrow at all.

This was today, and the sun was bright, and the water was a rich blue against the golden sand. There were children squealing as they played in the surf, and there was the smell of oils and lotions. Someone was walking a dog along the beach, and a vendor was hawking nachos.

Across the street, beach towels waved colorfully over rails, making a tawdry little hotel seem exotic. He could smell hot dogs, he realized, and some kind of colored ice was being sold to children so that it would drip sticky down their arms as they slurped it. Oddly enough, he had a sudden yen for it himself.

When he looked up, he spotted the black-and-yellow colors of a kite shaped like a wasp. It had caught the wind and was climbing. A light plane flew over, trailing a flowing message about the special at a local restaurant.

He took it all in, wondering why he'd thought the beach held no magic for him. Perhaps it hadn't when he'd been alone.

On impulse, he signaled Jackie, then stopped.

"You owe me some ice cream."

"So I do." She slipped lithely off the bike, kissed him, then backtracked a few steps to a vendor. She considered, debated and studied her choices, taking a longer and more serious deliberation over ice cream on a stick than she had over a five-hundred-dollar brooch. After weighing the pros and cons, she settled on chocolate and nuts wrapped around a slab of vanilla.

Stuffing her change in her pocket, she turned and saw Nathan. He was holding a big orange balloon. "Goes with your outfit," he told her, then gently looped the string around her wrist.

She was going to cry. Jackie felt the tears well up. It was only a ball of colorful rubber held by a string, she knew. But as symbols went, it was the best. She knew that when the air had finally escaped she would press the remains between the pages of a book as sentimentally as she would a rose.

"Thanks," she managed, then dutifully handed him the ice cream before she threw her arms around him.

He held her close, trying not to show the awkwardness he was suddenly feeling. How did a man deal with a woman who cried over a balloon? He'd expected her to laugh. Kissing her temple, he reminded himself that she rarely did the expected.

"You're welcome."

"I love you, Nathan."

"I think maybe you do," he murmured. The idea left him both exhilarated and shaken. What was he going to do about her? he wondered as his arms tightened around her. What the hell was he going to do about her, and them?

Looking up, Jackie saw the concern and the doubt in his eyes. She bit back a sigh, touching his face instead. There was time, she told herself. There was still plenty of time.

"Ice cream's melting." She was smiling as she brushed his lips with hers. "Why don't we sit on the wall while we eat it? Then you can change into your new shirt."

He cupped her chin in his hand, lingering over another kiss. He didn't know Justine had used the word *besotted* in describing his feelings for Jackie, but that was precisely what he was.

"I'm not changing shirts on the street."

She smiled again and took his hand.

When their hour was up, they pedaled back. Nathan was wearing his shark.

# *Chapter Ten*

From the doorway, Jackie watched Nathan drive off. She lifted her hand as his car headed down the street. For a moment there was only the sound of his fading engine breaking the morning quiet. Then, standing there, she heard the neighborhood noises of children being loaded into cars for school, doors slamming, goodbyes and last-minute instructions being given.

Nice sounds, Jackie thought as she leaned against the doorjamb. Regular everyday sounds that would be repeated morning after morning. There was a solidity to them, and a comfort.

She wondered if wives felt this way, seeing off their husbands after sharing that last cup of coffee and before the workday really began. It was an odd mixture of emotions, the pleasure of watching her man tidily on his way and the regret of knowing it would be hours before he came back.

But she wasn't a wife, Jackie reminded herself as she wandered away from the door without remembering to shut it. It didn't do any good to imagine herself as one. It did less good to regret knowing that Nathan was still far from ready for commitments and wedding rings.

It shouldn't be so important.

Chewing on her bottom lip, she started back upstairs. Mrs. Grange was already scrubbing and mopping the kitchen, and she herself had enough work to do to keep her occupied throughout the day. When Nathan came home, he would be glad to see her, and they'd share the casual talk of couples.

It couldn't be so important.

She was happy, after all, happier with Nathan than she'd ever been before or than she could imagine herself being without him. Since there had never been any major tragedies in her life, that was saying quite a lot. He cared for her, and if there were still restrictions on how much he would allow himself to care, what they had now was more than many people ever had.

He laughed more. It was very gratifying to know she'd given him that. Now, when she put her arms around him, it was a rare thing for her to find him tense. She wondered if he knew he reached for her in his sleep and held her close. She didn't think so. His subconscious had already accepted that they belonged together. That they were together. It would take a bit longer for him to accept that consciously.

So she'd be patient. Until Nathan, Jackie hadn't realized she had such an enormous capacity for patience. It pleased her to be able to find a virtue in herself that, because it had so seldom been tapped, seemed to run free.

He'd changed her. Jackie took her seat in front of

her typewriter, thinking Nathan probably didn't realize that, either. She hadn't fully realized it herself until it had already happened. She thought of the future more, without the need for rose-colored glasses. She'd come to appreciate the ability to make plans—not that she wouldn't always enjoy an interesting detour, but she'd come to understand that happiness and good times didn't always hinge on impulse.

She'd begun to look at life a little differently. It had come home to her that a sense of responsibility wasn't necessarily a burden. It could also bring a sense of satisfaction and accomplishment. Seeing something through, even when the pace began to drag and the enthusiasm began to wane, was part of living. Nathan had shown her that.

She wasn't certain she could explain it to him so that he would understand or even believe her. After all, she'd never given anyone reason to believe she could be sensible, dependable and tenacious. Things were different now.

Surprised at her own nerves, she looked down at the padded envelope sitting beside the neatly typed pile of manuscript pages. For the first time in her life, she was ready to put herself on the line. To prove herself, Jackie thought, taking a deep breath. To prove herself to herself first, then to Nathan, then to her family.

There was no guarantee that the agent would accept the proposal, nor, though he'd been gracious and marginally encouraging, that he would find anything appealing in her work. Risks didn't frighten her, Jackie told herself. But still she hesitated, not quite able to take the next step and slip the pages into the envelope. This risk frightened her. It hurt to admit it, but she was scared to death. It was no longer just a matter of telling an entertaining story from start to finish. It was her future on the line now, the future she had once blithely believed could take care of itself. If she failed now, she had no one to blame but herself.

She couldn't, as she had with so many of her other projects, claim that she'd discovered something that interested her more. Writing was it, win or lose, and somehow, though she knew it was foolish, the success or failure of her work was inevitably tied up with her success or failure with Nathan.

She crossed her fingers tight, eyes closed, and recited the first prayer that came into her head, though "Now I lay me down to sleep" wasn't quite appropriate. This done, Jackie shoved the proposal into the bag. Clutching it to her chest, she ran downstairs.

"Mrs. Grange, I've got to go out for a few minutes. I won't be long."

The housekeeper barely glanced up from her polishing. "Take your time."

It was done within fifteen minutes. Jackie stood in front of the post office, certain she'd just made the biggest mistake of her life. She should have gone over the first chapter again. A dozen glaring errors leaped into her mind, errors that seemed so obvious now that the manuscript was sealed and stamped and handed over to some post office clerk she didn't even know.

It occurred to her that there had been a wonderful angle she hadn't bothered to explore and that her characterization of the sheriff was much too weak. He should have chewed tobacco. That was the answer, the perfect answer. All she had to do was go in and stick a wad of tobacco in his mouth and the book would be a best-seller.

She took a step toward the door, stopped and took a step back. She was being ridiculous. Worse, if she didn't get hold of herself, she was going to be sick. Weak-kneed, she sat on the curb and dropped her head into her hands. Sink or swim, the proposal was going to New York, and it was going today. It amazed her to remember that she'd once thought of celebrating with champagne when she had enough to ship off. She didn't feel like celebrating. She felt like crawling home and burying herself under the covers.

What if she was wrong? Why hadn't she ever considered the fact that she could be totally and completely wrong—about the book, about Nathan, about herself? Only a fool, only a stupid fool, left herself without any route to survival.

She'd poured her heart into that story, then sent it off to a relative stranger who would then have the authority to give a thumbs-up or a thumbs-down without any regard for her as a person. It was business.

She'd given her heart to Nathan. She'd held it out to him in both hands and all but forced him to take it. If he tried to give it back to her, no matter how gently he handled it, it would be cracked and bruised.

There were tears on her cheeks. Feeling them, Jackie let out a little huff of disgust and dragged the heels of her hands over them. What a pitiful sight. A grown woman sitting on a curb crying because things might not work out the way she wanted them to. She sniffled, then rose to her feet. Maybe they wouldn't work out and she'd have to deal with it. But in the meantime she was going to do her damnedest to win.

* * *

By noon, Jackie was sitting at the counter, elbows up, looking at Mrs. Grange's latest pictures of her grandchildren while they shared a pasta salad.

"These are great. This one here…Lawrence, right?"

"That's Lawrence. He's three. A pistol."

Jackie studied the little towhead with the smear of what might have been peanut butter on his chin. "Looks like a heartbreaker to me. Do you get to spend much time with them?"

"Oh, now and again. Don't seem enough, though, with grandkids. They grow up faster than your own. This one, Anne Marie, she favors me." A big knuckled finger tapped a snapshot of a little girl in a frilly blue dress. "Hard to believe now—" Mrs. Grange patted an ample hip "—but I was a good-looking woman a few years and a few pounds back."

"You're still a good-looking woman, Mrs. Grange." Jackie poured out more of the fruit drink she'd concocted. "And you have a beautiful family."

Because the compliment had been given easily, Mrs. Grange accepted it. "Families, they make up for a lot. I was eighteen when I ran off to marry Clint. Oh, he was something to look at, let me tell you. Lean as a snake and twice as mean." She chuckled, the way a woman could over an old and almost faded mistake. "I was what you might call swept away."

She took a bite of pasta as she looked back. It didn't occur to her that she was talking about private things to someone she hardly knew. Jackie made it easy to talk. "Girls got no sense at that age, and I wasn't any different. Marry in haste, they say, but who listens?"

"People who say that probably haven't been lucky enough to have been swept away."

Admiring Jackie's logic, Mrs. Grange smiled. "That's true enough, and I can't say I regret it, even though at twenty-four I found myself in a crowded little apartment without a husband, without a penny, and with four little boys wanting their supper. Clinton had walked out on the lot of us, smooth as you please."

"I'm sorry. It must have been awful for you."

"I've had better moments." She turned then, seeing Jackie looking at her not with polite interest but with eyes filled with sympathy and understanding. "Sometimes we get what we ask for, Miss Jack, and I'd asked for Clint Grange, worthless snake that he was."

"What did you do after he'd left?"

"I cried. Spent the night and the better part of a day at it. It felt mighty good, that self-pity, but my boys needed a mother, not some wet-eyed female pining after her man. So I took a look around, figured I'd made enough of a mess of things for a while and decided to fix what I could. That's when I started cleaning houses. Twenty-eight years later, I'm still cleaning them." She looked around the tidy kitchen with a sense of simple satisfaction. "My kids are grown up, and two of them have families of their own. I guess you might say Clint did me a favor, but I don't think I'd thank him if we happened to run into each other in the checkout line at the supermarket."

Jackie understood the last of the sentiment, but not the beginning. If a man had left her high and dry with three children, hanging was too good for him. "How do you figure he did you a favor?"

"If he'd stayed with me, I'd never have been the same

kind of mother, the same kind of person. I guess you could say that some people change your life by coming into it, and others change it by going out." Mrs. Grange smiled as she finished off her salad. "Course, I don't suppose I'd shed any tears if I heard old Clinton was lying in a gutter somewheres begging for loose change."

Jackie laughed and toasted her. "I like you, Mrs. Grange."

"I like you, too, Miss Jack. And I hope you find what you're looking for with Mr. Powell." She rose then, but hesitated. She'd always been a good mother, but she'd never been lavish with praise. "You're one of those people who change lives by coming in. You've done something nice for Mr. Powell."

"I hope so. I love him a lot." With a sigh, she stacked Mrs. Grange's snapshots. "That's not always enough, is it?"

"It's better than a stick in the eye." In her gruff way, she patted Jackie's shoulder, then went about her business.

Jackie thought that over, nodded, then walked upstairs, where she went to work with a vengeance.

Long after Mrs. Grange had gone home and afternoon had turned to evening, Nathan found her there. She was hunched over the machine, posture forgotten, her hair falling into her face and her bare feet hooked around the legs of the chair.

He watched her, more than a little intrigued. He'd never really seen her work before. Whenever he'd come up, she'd somehow sensed his approach and swung around in her chair the moment he'd entered.

Now her fingers would drum on the keys, then stop,

drum again, then pause while she stared out of the window as if she'd gone into a trance. She'd begin to type again, frowning at the paper in front of her, then smiling, then muttering to herself.

He glanced over at the pile of pages to her right, unaware that the bulk of them were copies of what she'd mailed that morning. He had an uncomfortable feeling that she was more done than undone by this time. Then he cursed himself for being so selfish. What she was doing was important. He'd understood that since the night she'd spun part of the tale for him. It was wrong of him to wish it wouldn't move so quickly or so well, but he'd come to equate the end of her book with the end of their relationship. Yet he knew, even as he stood in the doorway and watched her, that it was he who would end it, and soon.

It had been a month. Only a month, he thought, dragging a hand through his hair. How had she managed to turn his life upside down in a matter of weeks? Despite all his resolutions, all his plans to the contrary, he'd fallen in love with her. That only made it worse. Loving, he wanted to give her all those pretty, unrealistic promises. Marriage, family, a lifetime. Years of shared days and nights. But all he could give her was disappointment.

It was best, really for the best, that Denver was only two weeks away. Even now the wheels were turning that would keep him at the office and in meetings more and at home less. In twelve days he would get on a plane and head west, away from her. Nathan had come to understand that if he didn't love her, if it were only need now, he might be tempted to make those promises to keep her there.

She deserved better. Despite both of them, he was going to make sure she didn't settle for less.

But there were twelve days left.

Quietly he moved toward her. When her fingers stilled again, he laid his hands on her shoulders. Jackie came off the chair with a yelp.

"I'm sorry," he said, but he had to laugh. "I didn't mean to startle you."

"You didn't. You scared me out of my skin." She sank back into the chair with a hand to her heart. "What are you doing home so early?"

"I'm not. It's after six."

"Oh. No wonder my back feels like it belongs to an eighty-year-old weight lifter."

He began to massage her shoulders. That, too, was something he'd learned from her. "How long have you been at it?"

"I don't know. Lost track. Right there... Mmm." Sighing her approval, she shifted under his hands. "I was going to set an alarm or something after Mrs. Grange left, but Burt Donley rode into town, and I forgot."

"Burt Donley?"

"The cold-blooded hired hand of Samuel Carlson."

"Oh, of course, Burt."

Chuckling, she looked over her shoulder. "Burt murdered Sarah's father, at Carlson's bidding. He and Jake have unfinished business from Laramie. That's when Burt gunned down Jake's best friend—in the back, of course."

"Of course."

"And how was your day?"

"Not as exciting. No major shootouts or encounters with loose women."

"Lucky for you I happen to be feeling very loose." She rose, sliding her body up his until her arms were linked around his neck. "Why don't I go see what I can mix together for dinner? Then we'll talk about it."

"Jack, you don't have to cook for me every night."

"We made a deal."

He stilled her mouth with a kiss, a longer and more intense one than he'd realized he needed. When he drew away, her eyes had that soft, unfocused look he'd come to love. "I'd say all those bets were off. Wouldn't you?"

"I don't mind cooking for you, Nathan."

"I know." She could have no idea how such a simple statement humbled him. "But I'd guess of the two of us you've had the tougher day." He drew her closer, wanting to smell her hair, brush his lips over her temple. He was hardly aware that his hands had slipped under her shirt just to stroke the long line of her back. "I'd offer to go down and throw something together, but I doubt you'd be able to eat it. Over the past few weeks I've learned my cooking's not just bad, it's embarrassing."

"We could send out for pizza."

"An excellent idea." He drew her toward the bed. "In an hour."

"An even better idea," she murmured, and melted into him.

Later, much later, after the sun had set and the cicadas had started their serenade, they sat on the patio, an empty carton between them and wine growing warm in glasses. The silence between them had stretched out, long and comfortable. Lovemaking and food had left them content. There was an ease between that usually came only from years of friendship or from complete understanding.

The moon was round and white and generous with its light. With her legs stretched out and her eyes half closed, Jackie decided she could happily stay where she was for hours. It could be like this, just like this, she thought, for the rest of her life.

"You know, Nathan, I've been thinking."

"Hmm?" He stirred himself enough to look at her. Moonlight did something special to her skin, to her eyes. Though he knew he would remember her best in the sunlight, with energy vibrating through her, there would be times when he would need a memory like this—of Jackie, almost bonelessly relaxed, in the light of a full moon.

"Are you listening?"

"No, I'm looking. There are times you are incredibly lovely."

She smiled, almost shyly, then reached out to take his hands. "Keep that up and I won't be able to think at all."

"Is that all it takes?"

"Do you want to hear my idea or not?"

"I'm never sure if I want to hear your ideas."

"This is a good one. I think we should have a party."

"A party?"

"Yes, you know what a party is, Nathan. A social gathering, often including music, food, drink and a group of people brought together for entertainment purposes."

"I've heard of them."

"Then we've passed the first hurdle." She kissed his hand, but he could tell that her mind was already leaping forward. "You've been back from Europe for weeks now and you haven't seen any of your friends. You do have friends, don't you?"

"One or two."

"There we go, over the second hurdle." Lazily she stretched out her legs, rubbing the arch of her foot over his calf. "As a businessman and a pillar of the community—I'm sure you're a pillar of the community—it's practically your obligation to entertain."

He lifted a brow. "I've never been much of a pillar, Jack."

"That's where you're wrong. Anyone who wears a suit the way you do is an absolute pillar." She grinned at him, knowing she'd ruffled his feathers. "A man of distinction, that's you, darling. A tower of strength and conservatism. A dyed-in-the-wool Republican."

"How do you know I'm a Republican?"

Her smile became sympathetic. "Please, Nathan, let's not debate the obvious. Have you ever owned a foreign car?"

"I don't see what that has to do with it."

"Never mind, your politics are entirely your affair." She patted his hand. "Myself, I'm a political agnostic. I'm not entirely convinced they exist. But we're getting off the subject."

"What else is new?"

"Let's talk party, Nathan." As she spoke, she leaned closer, enthusiasm already bubbling. "You've got those fat little address books at every phone in the house. I'm sure out of them you could find enough convivial bodies to make up a party."

"Convivial bodies?"

"A party's nothing without them. It doesn't have to be

elaborate—just a couple dozen people, some nice little canapés and an air of good cheer. It could be a combination welcome-home and bon-voyage party for you."

He glanced over sharply at that. Her eyes were steady and a great deal more serious than her words. So, she was thinking about Denver, too. It was like her not to have mentioned it directly or to have asked questions. His fingers tightened on hers. "When did you have in mind?"

She could smile again. Now that his leaving had been brought up and acknowledged, she could push it firmly to the back of her mind. "How about next week?"

"All right. I have an agency we can call."

"No, a party's personal."

"And a lot of work."

She shook her head. She wasn't able to explain that she needed something to keep her mind occupied. "Don't worry, Nathan. If there's one thing I know how to do, it's throw a party. You take care of contacting your friends. I'll do the rest."

"If that's what you want."

"Very much. Now that that's settled, how about a swim?"

He glanced over at the pool. It was inviting and tempting, but so was sitting doing nothing. "Go ahead. The idea of changing into a suit seems too complicated."

"Who needs a suit?" To prove a point, she rose and shimmied out of her shorts.

"Jack..."

"Nathan," she said, mimicking his tone, "one of the ten great pleasures of life is skinny-dipping in the moonlight." The thin bikinis she wore joined her shorts. Her baggy T-shirt skimmed her thighs. "You have a very private pool here," she continued. "Your neighbors would need a stepladder and binoculars to sneak a peak." Carelessly she pulled the T-shirt over her head and stood, slim and naked. "If they want to that badly, we may as well oblige them."

His mouth went dry. He should have been beyond that by now. Over the past few weeks he'd seen, touched, tasted every inch of her. Yet watching Jackie poised at the edge of the pool, her body gold and gleaming in the moonlight, made his heart thud like a teenager's on a first date.

She rose on her toes, arched and dived cleanly into the water. And surfaced, laughing. "God, I've missed this." Her body glimmered beneath the surface, darker and somehow more lush with the illusion of moonlight and water. "I used to sneak out at one in the morning to swim like this. My mother would have been horrified, even though there was a six-foot wall around the estate and the pool was hidden by trees. There was something wonderfully decadent about swimming nude at one in the morning. Aren't you coming in?"

He was already having trouble breathing, and he only shook his head. If he went in, he wouldn't do much swimming.

"And you said you weren't a pillar of the community." She laughed at him and trailed her fingers through the water. "All right, then, I guess I've got to get tough. It's for your own good." With a sigh, she lifted a hand out of the water. Like a child playing cowboy, she pointed it at him, finger out, thumb up. "Okay, Nathan, get up slow. Don't make any sudden moves."

"Give me a break, Jack."

"This is a hair trigger," she warned him. "Get up, and keep your hands where I can see them."

He couldn't have said why he did it. Maybe it was the full moon. He rose to a more interesting view.

"Okay, strip." She touched her tongue to her top lip. "Slow."

"You really are out of your mind."

"Don't beg, Nathan, it's pitiful." She cocked her thumb back over an invisible hammer. "Do you have any idea what a .38 slug can do to the human body? Take my word for it, it's not a pretty sight."

With a shrug, he pulled off his shirt. It wouldn't hurt to go in wearing his shorts. "You haven't got the guts to use that thing."

"Don't bet on it." But her lips twitched as she struggled with a grin. "Come a step closer with your pants on and I'll blow off a kneecap. Something like that gives a whole new meaning to the word *pain*."

She was crazy, he had no doubt about that. But apparently some of it had rubbed off. Nathan unsnapped his shorts and stepped out of them. She was going to get a surprise when he joined her in the water.

"That's good, very good." Deliberately she took her time evaluating him. "Now the rest."

With his eyes on hers, he stripped off his briefs. "You have no shame."

"Not a bit. Aren't you lucky?" Laughing, she gestured with her imaginary gun. "Into the pool, Nathan. Face the music."

He dived in, no more than an arm's length from her. When he surfaced, Jackie was treading water and smiling. "You dropped your gun."

She glanced down, as if surprised, at her open hand. "So I did."

"Let's see how tough you are unarmed."

He lunged for her, but she was quick. Anticipating him, Jackie dived deep, kicked out and glided under him. When she surfaced, she was six feet away with a smug smile. "Missed," she said lightly, and waited for his next move.

Slowly they circled, eyes locked. Jackie bit her lip, knowing that if she gave in to the laughter she would be sunk in more ways than one. Nathan was as strong a swimmer as she, but she was counting on speed and agility to see her through. Until she was ready to lose.

He advanced, she evaded. He feinted, she adjusted. He maneuvered, she outmaneuvered. For the next few minutes there were only the sounds of insects and lapping water, giving them both a sense of solitude. Suddenly inspired, he brought a hand out of the water, cupping his fingers in his palm, pointing the index and cocking the thumb.

"Look what I found."

That was all it took to have her laughter breaking through. In two long strokes, he had her.

"Cheat. You cheated. Nathan, there's hope for you yet." Giggling, she reached to hug him. Then his hand was hard and fast around her hair. The roughness was so uncharacteristic that her eyes flew to his. What she saw had her breath catching. This time it was her mouth that went dry. "Nathan," she managed before her lips were imprisoned by his.

The need was fiercer, edgier, more frenzied than it had ever been before. He felt as though his body were full of springs that had all been wound too tightly.

Against his own, her heart was beating desperately as he dived into her mouth, taking, tasting, devouring all. His teeth scraped her lips, his tongue invaded, tantalized by her breathless moan. Her body, at first taut as wire, went limp against him. They slipped beneath the surface without a thought for air.

The water enveloped them, making their movements slow and sluggish but no less urgent. The sensuous kiss of the cool, night-darkened water flowed around them, then ran off in torrents as they rose above it, still wrapped close.

Her first submission had passed. Now she was as desperate and anxious as he. She clung to him, head thrown back as he brought her up so that he could suckle her damp, water-cooled breasts. With each greedy pull, her stomach contracted and her pulse thudded out the new rhythm. The fingers on his shoulders dug in, leaving thin crescents. Then her mouth was on his again, thirsty.

She took her hands under, then over him, while her mind spun faster than her movements. Their bodies were captured in a slow-motion dream world, but their thoughts, their needs, raced.

Reaching down, he found her, cool and inviting. At his touch, his name burst from her. The sound of it across the quiet moonlight had his madness growing. She clung to him, her hands slipping over his slick body, then grasping for purchase. Her lips were wet and open when he took them again.

Jackie found her back braced against the side of the pool. Trembling with anticipation, she opened for him, then groaned when he filled her. Her hands fell lifelessly in the water, and he was there, holding her, moving in her.

The moonlight was on her face, making it both exotic and beautiful, but he could only press his own into her shoulder and ride the wave.

# *Chapter Eleven*

Some people were born knowing how to entertain, and Jackie was one of them. The fact that she was using a party as a way of blocking out the knowledge that she had only a few more days until Nathan left didn't mean she was any less determined to make it a success.

She wrote for eight, sometimes ten, hours a day, losing herself in another romance, in another catastrophe. When she wasn't chained to her machine, she was shopping, planning menus, checking off lists and supplies.

She insisted on doing all the cooking herself but had decided to enlist Mrs. Grange to help serve and her son, the future teacher, to tend bar.

She was delighted when Nathan joined her in the kitchen the afternoon of the party, his sleeves rolled up and his mind set on helping her make hors d'oeuvres. Determined he was, and clumsy. Jackie found both traits endearing. Tactfully she buried his attempts on the bottom tray.

Jackie, optimistic about the weather, had planned to set up tables outside so that the guests could wander out among the colored lights she'd hung. Her faith was rewarded when the day remained clear and promised a star-filled, breezy night.

She rarely worried about the success or failure of a party, but this was different. She wanted it to be perfect, to prove to herself and to Nathan that she belonged in his world as much as she belonged in his arms.

She had only a matter of days left before he would fly thousands of miles away from her. It was difficult not to dwell on that, and on the fact that he had never told her what he wanted of her. What he wanted for them. She refused to believe that he still considered permanence impossible.

He'd never told her he loved her. That was a thought that hit her painfully at the oddest times. But he'd shown her in so many ways. Often he'd call her in the middle of the day just to hear her voice. He'd bring her flowers, from his garden or from a roadside stand, just when the ones she'd put in a vase had begun to fade. He'd draw her close, just to hold her after lovemaking, after passion had ebbed and contentment remained.

A woman didn't need words when she had everything else.

The hell she didn't.

Pushing back her gnawing doubts, Jackie told herself that for once she would have to be content with what she had instead of what she wanted.

An hour before the party she began to pamper herself. This was one of her mother's traditions that Jackie

approved of. She was using her old room after telling
Nathan he'd only be in her way. There was some truth
in that, but more, Jackie had discovered she wanted to
add a touch of mystery to the evening. She wanted him
to see not the step-by-step preparation but the completed woman.

A long, leisurely bubble bath was first on her list.
She soaked, the radio playing quietly while she looked
out through the skylight over the tub. The only clouds
in the sky were as harmless as white spun sugar.

She took time and care with her makeup, shooting
for the exotic. When she studied her face from every
angle in the mirror, she was satisfied with the results.
She indulged in the feminine pleasure of slathering on
perfumed cream before she took the dress she'd bought
only the day before out of the closet.

Nathan was already downstairs when she started
out. She could hear him talking to Mrs. Grange, and
she could hear the woman's gruff replies. Always one
to enjoy a bit of drama, Jackie put her hand on the rail
and started slowly down.

She wasn't disappointed. Nathan glanced up, saw her
and stopped in midsentence. Intent on him, she didn't
notice the tall sandy-haired man beside Mrs. Grange.
Nor did she see his mouth fall open.

Her eyes dominated her face, smudged on the lids
with blending tones of bronze. Her hair, a combination
of nature and womanly art, was windswept and cun-
ningly tousled. Oversize silver stars glinted at her ears.

When Nathan could drag his gaze away from her
face to take in the rest of her, it was another shock to
the system.

The dress she'd chosen was stunning, eye-burning

white that fell in a narrow column from her breasts to her ankles, leaving her shoulders bare and her arms unadorned but for the dozen silver bracelets that encircled her arm from her wrist almost to her elbow. Smiling, she reached the bottom, then turned in a circle, revealing the slit in the back of the dress that reached to midthigh.

"What do you think?"

"You're stunning."

Finishing the circle, she studied him in turn. No one wore a black suit with quite as much style as Nathan, Jackie thought. It must have been that broad-shouldered, muscled body that gave conservatism a dangerous look. She took a step closer to kiss him. Then, with her hand in his, she turned to Mrs. Grange.

"I really appreciate you helping us out tonight. And this is your son? You must be Charlie."

"Yes, ma'am." He swallowed audibly, then accepted the hand she offered. His palm was sweaty. His mother hadn't told him that Miss Jack was a goddess.

"It's nice to meet you, Charlie. Your mom's told us a lot about you. Shall I show you where we've set up the bar?"

Mrs. Grange gave him an elbow in the ribs. The boy looked as if he had rocks in his head when he stared that way. "I'll show him what he needs to know. Come on, Charlie, get the lead out."

Charlie went with his mother—because she had a death grip on his arm—but sent one last moonstruck look over his shoulder.

"The kid's jaw dropped on his shoes when he saw you."

With a laugh, Jackie tucked her arm through Nathan's. "That's kind of sweet."

"Mine hit the floor."

She looked at him, nearly level with him in her heeled sandals. "That's even sweeter."

"You always manage to surprise me, Jack."

"I hope so."

With his free hand he touched her shoulder, then ran his fingertips down her arm. "This is the first time I remember wishing a party was over before it began." It wasn't her usual scent tonight, but something stunningly sexy and taunting. "What did you do to yourself up there?"

"Tricks of the trade." She had to shift only slightly for her lips to meet his. "It's still me, Nathan."

"I know." His arm curled around her waist to keep her there. "That's why I wish the party was over."

"Tell you what." She slid her hands over his shoulders. "When it is, we'll have one all our own."

"I'm counting on it." He lowered his lips to hers as the doorbell rang.

"Round one," she said. Keeping his hand in hers, she went to answer the door.

Within an hour, the house was milling with people. Most of them were every bit as interested in finding out about the woman in Nathan's life as they were in an evening of socializing. She didn't mind. She was just as curious about them.

She discovered Nathan knew a wide variety of people, from the staunch and stuffy to the easygoing. It took only a smile and a greeting for her to click with Cody Johnson, an architect who had joined Nathan's firm two years before. He favored scuffed boots and faded jeans but had made a concession to formality by tossing on a suit jacket. Since her brother favored the same style and brand, Jackie recognized it as murderously expensive. He clamped a hand over hers, looked her up and down with eyes as brown as her own, then winked.

"I've been wanting to get a look at you."

"Check out the boss's outside interests?"

"Something like that." He still held her hand, but there was nothing flirtatious in the gesture. Jackie had the feeling that Cody got his impressions as much by touch as by sight. "One thing you can never fault Nathan for is his taste. I always figured whenever he looked more than twice at a woman she'd have to be special."

"That seemed like both a compliment and approval."

"You could say that." He didn't often give both so easily. "I'm glad, because Nathan's a good friend. The best. You planning on sticking around?"

Her brow lifted. Though she preferred direct questions, Jackie didn't feel obligated to respond with a direct answer. "You cut right through, don't you?"

"Hate to waste time."

Yes, she decided, she liked Cody Johnson just fine. With her hand still in his, she looked over and spotted Nathan. "I plan on sticking around."

His lips curved. He had one of those quick, arrogant grins that women found devastating. Because, Jackie thought, a woman could never be sure what he was thinking. "Then why don't I buy you a drink?"

Tucking her arm through his, she headed for the bar. "Have you met Justine Chesterfield?"

His laugh was full and rich. Jackie liked that as much as she did the sun-bronzed hair that fell over his forehead. "Anyone ever tell you you're clear as glass?"

"Hate to waste time."

"I appreciate that." He stopped at the bar and was

amused by the way the college boy gaped at his hostess. "She's a nice lady, but a little rich for my blood."

"Is there anyone special?"

"Depends. You got a sister?"

With a laugh, Jackie turned and ordered champagne. Neither of them noticed Nathan watching them with a small, preoccupied frown.

He wasn't a jealous man. Nathan had always considered that one of the most foolish and unproductive emotions. Not only was jealousy the green-eyed monster, it invariably made the affected party look, and act, like an idiot.

He was neither an idiot nor jealous, but watching Jackie with Cody made him feel suspiciously like both. It was not, Nathan discovered, a sensation that could be enjoyed or ignored.

Cody was certainly more her type. Nathan managed to smile at the squeaky-voiced engineer who thought he had his attention. Cody could easily have passed for a gunfighter. Jackie's diamond-in-the-rough Jake Redman. That was Cody, with his loose limbed, rangy build and his sun-bleached hair that always looked as though it were one week past time for the barber. And there was the drawl. Nathan had always considered Cody's slight drawl soothing, but it began to occur to him that a woman might find it exciting. Some women

Added to that was a deceptively laid-back attitude, a total lack of interest in convention and a restless, unerring eye for quality. Fast cars, late nights and bright lights. That was Cody.

When Nathan saw Jackie glance up and laugh into Cody's wide grin, he considered the potential satisfaction of strangling them both.

Ridiculous. Nathan sipped his drink, then reached for a cigarette. He wasn't fully aware that he rarely wanted—needed—a cigarette these days. Cody was a friend, probably the best friend Nathan had now, or had ever had. And Jackie... What was Jackie?

Lover, friend, companion. A delight and, oddly enough, a rock. It was strange to think of someone who looked and acted like a butterfly as something so solid and secure. She could be loyal when loyalty was deserved and strong when strength was needed. But rock or not, he'd given her no reason to pledge her fidelity. For her own good. He didn't want to cage her in or narrow her horizons.

The hell he didn't.

Cutting off the engineer in midsentence, Nathan made a vague excuse and moved toward Jackie.

She was laughing again, her face glowing with it, her eyes brilliant as they slanted upward over the rim of her champagne flute. "Nathan, you didn't tell me your associate was the kind of man mothers warn their daughters about." But as she spoke, her hand linked casually with Nathan's. It was the kind of ease that spoke of certain intimacy.

"I'm happy to take that as a compliment." Cody was drinking vodka straight up, and he toasted her with the squat glass. "Nice party, boss. I've already complimented you on your taste."

"Thanks. You know there are tables loaded with food outside. Knowing your appetite, I'm surprised you haven't found them."

"I'm on my way." He sent Jackie a final wink, then sauntered off.

"Well, that was certainly a subtle heave-ho," she commented.

"It seemed he was taking up a great deal of your time."

Her head swiveled around, her brows lifted, and then her face glowed again with a fresh smile. "That's nice. That's very, very nice." She brushed her lips lightly over his. "Some women don't care for possessive men. Myself, I like them a lot. To a point."

"I simply meant—"

"Don't spoil it." She kissed him again before she tucked her arm through his. "Well, shall we stroll around looking convivial, or shall we dive into that food before I starve to death?"

He raised her hand to his lips. The quick bout of jealousy, if that was what it was, hadn't caused him to look or act like an idiot. That was one more thing he'd have to rearrange his thinking about.

"We'll dive," he decided. "It's hard to be convivial on an empty stomach."

The evening was a complete success. Cards and calls came in over the next few days complimenting and commenting. Invitations were extended. It should have been a delightful time for Jackie. She had met Nathan's friends and associates and had won them over. But it wasn't Nathan's friends and associates who mattered. The bottom line was Nathan himself, and he was going to Denver.

It was no longer something she could think about later, not when his plane ticket was tucked in his briefcase. She'd been to Denver herself once, to sit on the fifty-yard line at Mile High Stadium and cheer. She'd enjoyed it well enough. Now she hated it, as a city and as a symbol.

He was leaving in a matter of hours, and they'd settled nothing. Once or twice he'd tried to talk to her, but she'd put him off. It was cowardly, but if he was going to brush her out of his life, she wanted every moment she could grab before it happened.

Now she was out of time, but she'd made herself a firm promise. He would at least tell her why. If he didn't want her any longer—wouldn't let himself want her— she would have the reasons.

She braced herself outside the bedroom door, squared her shoulders, then walked in. "I brought you some coffee."

Nathan glanced up from his packing. "Thanks." He'd thought he'd been miserable a few times before in his life. He'd been wrong.

"Need any help with this?" She lifted her own cup and sipped. Somehow it was easier to have serious, life-altering discussions when you were doing something as casual as drinking coffee.

"No, I'm almost finished."

Nodding, she sat on the edge of the bed. If she paced, as she wanted to, it would be easy to slam the cup against the wall and watch it shatter. As she wanted to. "You haven't said how long you'll be out of town."

"That's because I can't be sure." He'd never hated packing before. It had always been just one more small, slightly annoying chore. He hated it now. "It could be three weeks, more likely four, on this first trip. If we don't run into any major complications, I should be able to spot-check it as we go."

She sipped again, but the coffee was bitter. "Should I be here when you get back?"

It was like her to put it that way, not a demand or even a request, but a question. He wanted to say yes, please, yes, but "It's up to you" was what he told her.

"No, it's not. We both know how I feel, what I want. I haven't made a secret out of it." She paused a moment, wondering if she should feel a loss of pride. But none came. "Now it comes down to what you feel and what you want."

Her eyes were so solemn. There was no hint of a smile on her lips. He missed that, already missed that bright, vivid look she wore the way other women wore jewelry. "You mean a lot to me, Jackie." The word *love* was there, in his mind, in his heart, but he couldn't say it. "More than anyone else."

It amazed her that she was almost desperate enough, almost hungry enough, to accept those crumbs and be content. But she lifted a brow and continued watching him. "And?"

He packed another freshly laundered shirt. He wanted to choose the right words, say the right thing. Over and over during the last twenty-four hours he'd imagined what he would say to her, what he would do. In one wildly satisfying fantasy he'd dragged her to the airport with him and they'd flown away together. On a shell pelican.

But this was real. If he couldn't give her anything else, he could give her fairness.

"I can't ask you to stay, to wait, then live your life day by day. That's not what I want for you, Jack."

The hurting came from his honesty. He wouldn't lie or give her what she thought might be the comfort of pretense. "I'd like you to take a step back and tell me what you want for yourself. Is it what you had before, Nathan? Peace and quiet and no complications?"

Wasn't it? But somehow, when she said it, that life no longer sounded settled and comfortable, it sounded stagnant and boring. Yet it was the only one he was sure of. "I can't give you what you want," he said, struggling for calm. "I can't give you marriage and family and a lifetime commitment, because I don't believe in those things, Jack. I'd rather hurt you now than hurt you consistently over the rest of our lives."

She said nothing for a moment, afraid she would say too much. Her heart had gone out to him. There had been more misery in those last few words than she'd known he felt, or could feel. Though she hurt with him, she wasn't sorry she'd dredged it up.

"Was it that bad?" she said quietly. "Were you that unhappy growing up?"

He could have sworn at her for putting her slim, sensitive finger on the core of it. "That's not relevant."

"Oh, it is, and we both know it." She rose. She had to move, just a little, or the tension inside of her was going to explode and shatter her into a million pieces. "Nathan, I won't say you owe me an explanation. People are always saying, 'He owes me,' or 'I owe him.' I've always felt that when you do something for someone, or give something away, that you should do it freely or not at all. So there's no debt." She sat again, calmer, then looked at him again. "But I have to say that I think it's right for you to tell me why."

He fished out a cigarette and lit it as he sat on the opposite end of the bed. "Yes, you're right. You're entitled to reasons." He was silent for a long time, trying to sort out the words, but it wasn't possible to plan them. So he simply began.

"My mother came from a wealthy and established family. She was expected to make a good marriage. A proper marriage. She'd been raised and educated with that in mind."

Jackie frowned a little, but tried to be fair. "That wasn't so unusual a generation ago."

"No, and it was the rule of thumb in her family. My father had more ambition than security, but had earned a reputation as an up-and-comer. He was, I've been told, dynamic and charismatic. When my mother fell in love with him, her family wasn't overjoyed, but they didn't object. Marriage to her gave my father exactly what he wanted. Family name, family backing, a well-bred wife who could entertain properly and give him an heir."

Jackie looked down at her empty cup. "I see," she murmured, and she was beginning to.

"He didn't love her. The marriage was a business decision."

He paused again, studying the column of smoke rising toward the ceiling. Was that the core of it? he wondered. Was that what had damaged his parents, and him, the most? Restless, he moved his shoulders. It was history, ancient history.

"I don't doubt that he had a certain amount of affection for her. He wasn't able, he'd never been able, to give too much of himself. His business took him away from home quite a bit. He was obsessed with making a fortune, with personal and professional success. When I was born, he gave my mother an emerald necklace as a reward for producing a son."

She started to speak, struck by the bitterness in his

tone, then closed her mouth. Sometimes it was best only to listen.

"My mother adored him, was almost fanatic about it. As a child I had a nurse, a nanny and a bodyguard. She was terrified of what he might do if anything happened to me. It wasn't so much that she worried about me as a son, but as *his* son. His symbol."

"Oh, Nathan..." she began, but he shook his head.

"She told me in almost those words when I was five, six years old. She told me that and a great deal more once her feelings for him had changed. I rarely saw either of them when I was growing up. She was so determined to be the perfect society wife, and he was always flying off somewhere or another to close a deal. His idea of being a father consisted of periodic checks on my progress in school, lectures on responsibility and family honor. The trouble was, he had no honor himself."

With slow, deliberate motions he crushed out his cigarette. "There were other women. My mother knew and ignored it. He told me once there was nothing serious in those relationships. A man away from home so often required certain comforts."

"He told you?" Jackie demanded, stupidly shocked.

"When I was sixteen. I believe he considered it a heart-to-heart. My mother's feelings for him were dead by that time, and we were living like three polite strangers in the same house."

"Couldn't you have gone to your grandparents?"

"My grandmother was dead. She might have understood. I can't be sure. My grandfather considered the marriage a success. My mother certainly never complained, and my father had lived up to his potential. He would have been horrified if I'd arrived on his doorstep saying I couldn't live in the same house with my own parents. Besides, I had the place to myself a great deal of the time."

Privacy, she thought. She certainly understood his need for privacy. But what would it have done to a young boy to have his privacy in such an unhealthy place? "It must have been terrible for you."

She thought of her own family, wealthy, prestigious, respected. But their house had never been quiet, not the way she imagined Nathan's childhood home. It had never been cold. Hers had been filled with screams of laughter and accusations. With fists raised, the emotion in the threat heatedly real at the moment, then laughed about later.

"Nathan," she began slowly, "did you ever tell them how they made you feel?"

"Once. They were simply appalled with me for my lack of gratitude. And my lack of graciousness in bringing up the subject. You learn not to beat your head against a wall that isn't going to move and find other ways."

"What other ways?"

"Study, personal ambitions. I can't say they ceased to exist for me as parents, but I shifted priorities. My father was away when I graduated from high school. I went to Europe that summer, so I didn't see him again until I was in college. He'd discovered I was studying architecture and came, he thought, to pull the rug out from under my feet.

"He wanted, as you put it once, for me to follow in his footsteps. He expected it. He demanded it. I'd lived under his thumb for eighteen years, totally cowed by my, and my mother's, perception of him. But something had happened. When I'd decided I wanted to build, the idea, the dream of that, became bigger than he."

"You'd grown up," she murmured.

"Enough, apparently, to stand up to him. He threatened to stop my tuition. I had a responsibility to him and the family business. That's all the family was, you see. A business. My mother was in full agreement. The fact was, once she'd stopped loving him, she couldn't have cared less. For her, I was my father's son."

"Surely that's too harsh, Nathan. Your mother—"

"Told me she hadn't wanted me." He reached for another cigarette, then broke it in half. "She said she believed if I hadn't been born her marriage could have been saved. Without the responsibility of a child she could have traveled with my father."

Her face had gone very white. She didn't want to believe him. She didn't want to think that anyone could be so cruel to her own child. "They didn't deserve you." Swallowing a lump of tears, she rose to go to him.

"That's not the point." He put his hands out, knowing if she put her arms around him now he would fall apart. He had never spoken of this with anyone before, hadn't wanted to think it through stage by stage. "I made a decision that day I faced my father. I had no family, had never had one and didn't need one. My grandmother had left me enough to get me through college. So I used that, and took nothing from him. What I did from that point, I did on my own, for myself. That hasn't changed."

She let her arms rest at her sides. He wouldn't allow her to comfort him, and as much as her heart ached to, her mind told her that perhaps it wasn't comfort he needed.

"You're still letting them run your life." Her voice wasn't soft now, but angry, angry with him, angry for him. "Their marriage was ugly, so marriage itself is ugly? That's stupid."

"Not marriage itself, marriage for me." Fury hit him suddenly. He'd opened up an old and tender wound for her, yet she still wanted more. "Do you think people only inherit brown eyes or a cleft chin from their parents? Don't you be stupid, Jack. They give us a great deal more than that. My father was a selfish man. I'm a selfish man, but at least I have the common sense to know I can't put myself, you or the children we'd have through that kind of misery."

"Common sense?" The MacNamara temper, famed for generations, leaped out. "You can stand there spouting off that kind of drivel and call it common sense? You haven't got enough sense to fill a teaspoon. For God's sake, Nathan, if your father had been an ax murderer, does that mean you'd be lunging around looking for people to chop up? My father loves raw oysters, and I can't stand to look at them. Does that mean I'm adopted?"

"You're being absurd."

"I'm being absurd? *I'm* being absurd?" With a sound of disgust, she reached for the closest thing at hand— a nineteenth-century Venetian bowl—and smashed it to the floor. "You obviously wouldn't recognize absurd if it shot you between the eyes. I'll tell you what's absurd. Absurd is loving someone and having them love you right back, then refusing to do anything solid about it because maybe, just maybe, it wouldn't work out perfectly."

"I'm not talking about perfect. Damn it, Jack, not that vase."

But it was already a pile of French porcelain shards on the floor. "Of course you're talking about perfect. Perfect's your middle name. Nathan Perfect Powell, projecting his life years into the future, making certain there aren't any loose ends or uneven edges."

"Fine." He swung her around before she could grab something else. "That should be enough right there to show you I'm right about this, about us. I like things done a certain way, I do plan ahead and insist on completing things as carefully as they're begun. You, by your own admission, never finish anything."

Her chin came up. Her eyes were dry. The tears would come later, she knew, torrents of them. "I wondered how long it would take you to throw that in my face. You're right about one thing, Nathan. The world's made up of two kinds of people, the careful and the careless. I'm a careless person and content to be so. But I don't think less of you for being a careful one."

He let out a quiet breath. He wasn't used to fighting, not unless it was over the quality of materials or working conditions for his men. "I didn't mean that as an insult."

"No? Well, maybe not, but the point's taken. We're not alike, and though I think we're both capable of a certain amount of growth and compromise, we'll never be alike. That doesn't change the fact that I love you and want to spend my life with you." This time she grabbed him, by the shirtfront. "You're not your father, Nathan, and I'm sure as hell not your mother. Don't let them do this to you, to us."

He covered her hands with his. "Maybe if you weren't

so important it would be easier to risk it. I could say all right, we want each other, so let's take the chance. But I care for you too much to go into this with two strikes against me."

"You care too much." The tears were going to come, and soon, so she backed away. "Damn you for that, Nathan. For not having the guts to say you love me, even now."

She whirled around and ran out. He heard the front door slam.

# *Chapter Twelve*

"The masons lost two days with the rain. I'm putting on double shifts."

Nathan stood at the building site, squinting into the sun, which had finally made an appearance. It was cold in Denver. Spring hadn't floated in gently. The few hopeful wildflowers that had poked up had been carelessly trampled over. By next spring, the grounds would be green and trimmed. Looking at the raw steel and, through the skeleton of the building, he already saw it.

"Considering the filthy weather you've been having, there's been a lot of progress in just under three weeks." Cody, a Stetson shading his eyes, his booted feet planted wide apart, looked at the beams and girders. Unlike Nathan, he didn't see the finished product. He preferred this stage, when there were still possibilities. "It looks good," he decided. "You, on the other hand, look like hell."

"It's always nice to have you around, Cody." Studying his clipboard, Nathan began a steady and detailed analysis of work completed and work projected. Schedules had to be adjusted, and deadlines met.

"You seem to have everything under control, as usual."

"Yeah." Nathan pulled out a cigarette, cupping his hands over his lighter.

As the flame leaped on, Cody noticed the shadows under Nathan's eyes, the lines of strain that had dug in around his mouth. To Cody's mind, there was only one thing that could make a strong man look battered. That was a woman.

Nathan dropped his lighter back in his pocket. "The building inspector should make his pass through today."

"Bless his heart." Cody helped himself to a cigarette from Nathan's pack. "I thought you were quitting these?"

"Eventually." One of the laborers had a portable radio turned up full. Nathan thought of Jackie blaring music through the kitchen speakers. "Any problems back home?"

"Businesswise? No. But I was about to ask you the same thing."

"I haven't been there, remember? Got an update on the Sydney project?"

"Ready to break ground in about six weeks." He took another drag, then broke the filter off the cigarette. Cody figured if you were going to kill yourself you might as well do it straight out. "You and Jack have a disagreement?"

"Why?"

"Because from the looks of you you haven't had a

decent night's sleep since you got out here." He found a bent pack of matches in his pocket, remembered the club that was printed on the front with some fondness, then struck a match. "Want to talk about it?"

"There's nothing to talk about."

Cody merely lifted a brow and drew in more smoke. "Whatever you say, boss."

Nathan swore and pinched at the tension between his eyes. "Sorry."

"Okay." He stood quiet for a time, smoking and watching the men at work. "I could do with some coffee and a plateful of eggs." He pitched the stub of the cigarette into the construction rubble. "Since I'm on an expense account, I'll buy."

"You're a sport, Cody." But Nathan walked back to the pickup truck.

Within ten minutes they were sitting in a greasy little diner where the menu was written on a chalkboard and the waitresses wore holsters and short shocking-pink uniforms. There was a bald man dozing over his coffee at the counter and booths with ashtrays in the shape of saddles. The smell of onions hung stubbornly in the air.

"You always could pick a class joint," Nathan muttered as they slid into a booth, but all he could think of was how Jackie would have enjoyed it.

"It ain't the package, son." Cody settled back and grinned as one of the waitresses shrieked out an order to a stocky, grim-faced man at the grill.

A pot of coffee was plopped down without being asked for. Cody poured it himself and watched the steam rise. "You can keep your fancy French restaurants. Nobody makes coffee like a diner."

Jackie did, Nathan thought, and found he'd lost his taste for it.

Cody grinned up at the frowsy blonde who stopped, pad in hand, by their booth. "That blue plate special. I want two of them."

"Two blue plates," she muttered, writing.

"On one plate, darling," he added.

She looked over her pad and let her gaze roam over him. "I guess you do have a lot to fill up."

"That's the idea. Bring my friend the same."

She turned to study Nathan and decided it was her lucky day. Two hunks at her station, though the dark one looked as if he'd put in a rough night. Or a week of rough nights. She smiled at Nathan, showing crooked incisors. "How do you want your eggs, sweetie?"

"Over light," Cody told her, drawing her attention back to him. "And don't wring all the grease out of the home fries."

She chuckled and started off, her voice pitched high. "Double up on a couple of blue plates. Flip the eggs but make it easy."

For the first time in weeks, Nathan had the urge to smile. "What is the blue plate?"

"Two eggs, a rasher of bacon, home fries, biscuits and coffee by the barrel." As he took out one of his own cigarettes, Cody stretched his legs to rest his feet on the seat beside Nathan. "So, have you called her?"

It wasn't any use pretending he didn't want to talk about it. If that had been the case, he could have made some excuse and remained on the building site. He'd come because Cody could be counted on to be honest, whether the truth was pretty or not.

"No, I haven't called her."

"So you did have a fight?"

"I don't think you could call it a fight." Frowning, he remembered the china shattering on the floor. "No, you could call it that."

"People in love fight all the time."

Nathan smiled again. "That sounds like something she'd say."

"Sensible woman." He poured a second cup of coffee and noted that Nathan had left his untouched. "From the looks of you, I'd say whatever you two fought about, she won."

"No. Neither of us did."

Cody was silent for a moment, tapping his spoon on the table with the tinny country song playing on the jukebox. "My old man was big on sending flowers whenever he and my mother went at each other. Worked every time."

"This isn't as simple as that."

Cody waited until two heaping plates were set in front of them. He sent the waitress a cheeky wink, then dug in. "Nathan, I know you're the kind of man who likes to keep things to himself. I respect that. Working with you the last couple of years has been an education for me, in organization and control, in professionalism. But I figure by this time we're more than associates. A man has trouble with a woman, it usually helps if he dumps it out on another man. Not that another man understands women any better. They can just be confused about it together."

A semi pulled up in front of the diner's dusty window, gears groaning. "Jack wanted a commitment. I couldn't give her one."

"Couldn't?" Cody took his time pouring honey on a biscuit. "Isn't the word *wouldn't?*"

"Not in this case. For reasons I don't want to get into, I couldn't give her the marriage and family she wanted. Needed. Jack needed promises. I don't make promises."

"Well, that's for you to decide." Cody scooped up more eggs. "But it seems to me you're not too happy about it. If you don't love her—"

"I didn't say I didn't love her."

"Didn't you? Guess I misunderstood."

"Look, Cody, marriage is impossible enough when people think alike, when they have the same attitudes and habits. When they're as different as Jack and I, it's worse than impossible. She wants a home, kids and all the confusion that goes with it. I'm on the road for weeks at a time, and when I come home I want..." He let his words trail off because he no longer knew. He used to know.

"Yeah, that's a problem, all right," Cody continued as if Nathan weren't staring out of the window. "I guess dragging a woman along, having her to share those nameless hotel rooms and solitary meals, would be inconvenient. And having one who loved you waiting for you when you got home would be a pain."

Nathan turned back from the window and gave Cody a level look. "It would be unfair to her."

"Probably right. It's better to move on and be unhappy without her than risk being happy with her. Your eggs are getting cold, boss."

"Marriages break up as often as they work out."

"Yeah, the statistics are lousy. Makes you wonder why people keep jumping in."

"You haven't."

"Nope. Haven't found a woman mean enough." He grinned as he shoveled in the last of his eggs. "Maybe I'll look Jack up next week." The sudden deadly fury on Nathan's face had Cody stretching an arm over the back of the booth. "Figure this, Nathan, when a woman puts light into a man's life and he pulls the shade, he's asking for somebody else to enjoy it. Is that what you want?"

"Don't push it, Cody."

"No, I think you've already pushed yourself." He leaned forward again, his face quietly serious. "Let me tell you something, Nathan. You're a good man and a hell of an architect. You don't lie or look for the easy way. You fight for your men and for your principles, but you're not so hardheaded you won't compromise when it's time. You'll still be all of those things without her, but you could be a hell of a lot more with her. She did something for you."

"I know that." He shoved his all-but-untouched meal aside. "I'm worried about what I might do to her. If it were up to me…"

"If it were up to you, what?"

"It comes down to the fact that I'm not better off without her." That was a tough one to bring out in the open, to say plainly and live with. "But she may be better off without me."

"I guess she's the only one who can answer that." He drew out his wallet and riffled through bills. "I figure I know as much about this project here as you."

"What? Yes, so?"

"So I got an airline ticket in my room. Booked to leave day after tomorrow. I'll trade you for your hotel room."

Nathan started to make excuses, to give all the reasons why he was responsible for the project. Excuses, he realized, were all they would be. "Keep it," he said abruptly. "I'm leaving today."

"Smart move." Cody added a generous tip to the bill.

Nathan arrived home at 2:00 a.m. after a frenzied stop-and-go day of traveling. He'd had to route through St. Louis, bump into Chicago, then pace restlessly through O'Hare for two and a half hours waiting for his connection to Baltimore. From there he took his only option, a puddle jumper that touched down hourly.

He was sure she'd be there. He'd kept himself going with that alone. True, she hadn't answered when he'd called, but she could have been out shopping, in the pool, taking a walk. He didn't believe she'd left.

Somewhere in his heart he'd been sure all along that no matter what he'd said or how they'd left things she would be there when he returned. She was too stubborn and too self-confident to give up on him because he'd been an idiot.

She loved him, and when a woman like Jackie loved, she continued to love, for better or for worse. He'd given her worse. Now, if she'd let him, he was going to try for better.

But she wasn't there. He knew it almost from the minute he opened his front door. The house had that same quiet, almost respectful feel it had had before she'd come into it. A lonely feel. Swearing, he took the steps two at a time, calling her.

The bed was empty, made up with Mrs. Grange's no-nonsense tucks. There were no colorful shirts or grubby shoes tossed anywhere. The room was neat as a pin. He detested it on sight. Still unable to accept it, he pulled open the closet. Only his own ordered clothes were there.

Furious with her, as well as himself, he strode into the guest room. And had to accept. She wasn't there, curled under tangled sheets. The clutter of books and papers was gone. So was her typewriter.

He stared for a long time, wondering how he could ever had thought it preferable to come home to order and peace. Tired, he sat on the edge of the bed. Her scent was still there, but it was fading. That was the worst of it, to have a trace of her without the rest.

He lay back on the bed, unwilling to sleep in the one he'd shared with her night after night. She wasn't going to get away with it, he thought, and instantly fell asleep.

"It's worse than pitiful for a grown man to cheat at Scrabble."

"I don't have to cheat." J. D. MacNamara narrowed his eyes and focused them on his daughter. "*Zuckly* is an adjective, meaning graceful. As in 'the ballerina executed a zuckly pirouette.'"

"That's a load of you-know what," Jackie said, and scowled at him. "I let you get away with *quoho*, Daddy, but this is too much."

"Just because you're a writer now doesn't mean you know every word in the dictionary. Go ahead, look it up, but you lose fifty points if you find it."

Jackie's fingers hovered over the dictionary. She knew her father could lie beautifully, but she also knew he had an uncanny way of coming out on top. With a sigh of disgust, she dropped her hand. "I'll concede. I know how to be a zuckly player."

"That's my girl." Pleased with himself, he began to

add points to his score. Jackie lifted her glass of wine and considered him.

J. D. MacNamara was quite a man. But then, she'd always known that. She supposed it was Nathan's description of his own father, his family life, that had made her stand back and appreciate fully what she'd been given. She knew her father had a tough-as-nails reputation in the business world. He derived great pleasure from wheeling and dealing and outwitting competitors. Yet she'd seen the same self-satisfied look on his face after pulling off a multimillion-dollar business coup as she saw on it now as he outscored his daughter in a game of Scrabble.

He just loved life, with all its twists and turns. Perhaps Nathan was right about children inheriting more than eye color, and if she'd inherited that joie de vivre from her father, she was grateful.

"I love you, Daddy, even if you are a rotten cheat."

"I love you, too, Jackie." He beamed at the totals. "But I'm not going to let that interfere with destroying you. Your turn, you know."

Folding up her legs, she propped her elbows and stared owlishly at her letters. The room was gracefully lit, the drapes yet to be drawn as sunset exploded in the eastern sky. The second parlor, as her mother insisted on calling it, was for family or informal gatherings, but it was a study in elegance and taste.

The rose-and-gray pattern of the Aubusson was picked up prettily in soft floor-length drapes and the upholstery of a curvy sofa. Her mother's prize collection of crystal had been moved out some years before when Jackie and Brandon had broken a candy dish while wrestling over some forgotten disagreement. Patricia had stubbornly left a few dainty pieces of porcelain.

There was a wide window seat in the east wall, where Jackie had hidden playing hide-and-seek as a child and dreamed of her latest crush as a teenager. She'd spent thousands of hours in that room, happy ones, furious ones, tearful ones. It was home. She hadn't fully understood or appreciated that until now.

"What's the matter with you, girl? Writers are supposed to have a way with words."

Her lips twitched a bit. J.D. had already fallen into the habit of calling her a writer several times a day. "Off my case, J.D."

"Hell of a way to talk to your father. Why, I ought to take a strap to you."

She grinned. "You and who else?"

He grinned back. He had a full, generous face with that oh-so-Irish ruddy skin. His eyes were a bright blue even through the glasses he had perched on his nose. He wore a suit because dressing for dinner was expected, but the vest was unbuttoned and the tie pulled crooked. A cigar was clamped between his big teeth, a cigar that Patricia tolerated in dignified silence.

Jackie pushed her letters around. "You know, Daddy, I've just began to think about it, but you and Mother, you're so different."

"Hmm?" He glanced up, distracted from the creative demands of inventing a new word.

"I mean, Mother is so elegant, so well-groomed."

"What am I, a slob?"

"Not exactly." When he frowned, she spread out her letters on the board. "There, *hyfoxal*."

"What the hell is this?" J.D. waved a blunt finger at the word. "No such thing."

"It's from the Latin for sly or cleverly adept. As in 'My father is well-known for his hyfoxal business dealings.'"

In answer, J.D. used a brief four-letter word that would have had his wife clucking her tongue. "Look it up," Jackie invited. "If you want to lose fifty points. Daddy," she said to distract him again, "how do you and Mother stay so happy?"

"I let her do what she does best, she lets me do what I do best. Besides, I'm crazy about the old prude."

"I know." Jackie felt her eyes fill with the tears that never seemed far away these days. "I've been thinking a lot lately about what you've both done for me and the boys. And loving each other might be the most important part of all."

"Jack, why don't you tell me what's on your mind?"

She shook her head but leaned over to stroke his cheek. "I just grew up this spring. Thought you'd like to know."

"And does growing up have anything to do with the man you're in love with?"

"Just about everything. Oh, you'd like him, Daddy. He's strong, sometimes too strong. He's kind and funny in the oddest sorts of ways. He likes me the way I am." The tears threatened again, and she put a hand to her eyes, pressing hard for a moment. "He makes lists for everything and always makes sure that *B* follows *A*. He, uh…" Letting out a long breath, she dropped her hands. "He's the kind of man who opens the door for you, not because he thinks it's the gentlemanly or proper thing to do, but because he is a gentleman. A very gentle man." She smiled again, her tears under control. "Mother would like him, too."

"Then what's the problem, Jackie?"

"He's just not ready for me or for the way we feel about each other. And I'm not sure how long I can wait for him to get ready."

J.D. frowned a moment. "Want me to give him a kick in the pants?"

That made her laugh. She was up and in his lap, her arms tight around him. "I'll let you know."

Patricia glided into the room, slim and pretty in a silk sheath the same pale blue as her eyes. "John, if the chef continues to throw these disgraceful temper tantrums, you're going to have to speak to him yourself. I'm at my wit's end." She went to the bar, poured a small glass of dry sherry, then settled in a chair. She crossed her legs, which her husband still considered the best on the East Coast, and sipped. "Jackie, I came across a new hairdresser last week. I'm convinced he could do wonders for you."

Jackie grinned and blew her hair out of her eyes. "I love you, Mother."

Instantly, and in the way Jackie had always adored, Patricia's eyes softened. "I love you too, darling. I meant to tell you that your tan is wonderfully flattering, particularly with your coloring, but after all I've been reading lately I'm worried about the long-term effects." Then she smiled in a way that made her look remarkably like her daughter. "It's good to have you home for a little while. The house is always too quiet without you and the boys."

"Won't be seeing too much of her now." J.D. gave

her a fatherly pinch on the rump. "Now that she's a big-time author."

"It's only one book," she reminded him, then grinned. "So far."

"It did give me a great deal of satisfaction to mention, very casually, of course, to Honoria that you'd sold your manuscript to Harlequin Historicals." Patricia took a delicate sip as she settled back on the cushions.

"Casual?" J.D. gave a shout of laughter. "She couldn't wait to pick up the phone and brag. Hey, there, what do you think you're doing?"

Jackie turned back from her study of his letters. "Nothing." She gave him a loud kiss on the cheek. "You're doomed, you know. You're never going to be able to use that ridiculous collection."

"We'll see about that." J.D. dumped her off of his lap, then rubbed his palms together. "Sit down and shut up."

"John, really," Patricia said, in a tone that had Jackie running over to hug her. When the doorbell rang, Jackie straightened, but her mother waved her back. "Philip will get the door, Jacqueline. Do fix your hair."

Dutifully Jackie dragged her fingers through it as their graying butler came to the parlor entrance. "I beg your pardon, Mrs. MacNamara, but there's a Nathan Powell here to see Miss Jacqueline."

With a quick squeal, Jackie leaped forward. Her mother's firm command stopped her. "Jacqueline, sit down and pretend you're a lady. Philip will show the man in."

"But—"

"Sit down," J.D. told her. "And shut up."

"Quite," Patricia murmured, then nodded to Philip. She sat with a thud.

"And I'd take that sulky look off your pointy face," her father suggested. "Unless you want him to turn right around and leave again."

Jackie gritted her teeth, glared arrows at him, then settled down. Maybe they were right, she thought. Just this once, she'd look before she leaped. But when she saw him she would have been out of her chair in an instant if her father's foot hadn't stamped down on hers.

"Jack." There was something strained and husky about his voice, as though he hadn't spoken for days.

"Hello, Nathan." Pulling herself in, she rose easily and offered a hand. "I didn't expect you."

"No, I…" He felt suddenly and completely foolish standing there in a travel-stained suit with a brightly ribboned box under his arm. "I should have called."

"Of course not." As if there had never been any strain between them, or any passion, she tucked her arm through his. "I'd like you to meet my parents. J. D. and Patricia MacNamara, Nathan Powell."

J.D. shoved himself to his feet. He'd already made his assessment, and if he'd ever seen a more lovesick, frustrated man before, he couldn't bring it to mind. It was with both sympathy and interest that he offered a hand.

"Pleased to meet you. Admire your work." He shook his hand with a hefty pumping stroke. "Jack's told us all about you. I'll get you a drink."

Nathan managed to nod through these rapid-fire statements before turning to greet Jackie's mother. This was what she would look like in twenty or twenty-five years, Nathan realized with a jolt. Still lovely, with her skin clear as a bell and the grace that only years could add.

"Mrs. MacNamara, I apologize for dropping in on you like this."

"No need for that." But it pleased her that he had the manners to do so. She took stock in much the same way her husband had and saw a breeding and a kindness that she approved of. "Won't you sit down, Mr. Powell?"

"Well, I—"

"Here you are, nothing like a nice shot of whiskey to put hair on your chest." J.D. slapped him on the back as he offered the glass. "So you design buildings? Do any remodeling?"

"Yes, when there's—"

"Good, good. I'd like to talk to you about this building I'd had my eye on. Place is a mess, but it has potential. Now if I—"

"Excuse me." Forgetting his manners, Nathan shoved the glass back in J.D.'s hand and grabbed Jackie's arm. Without another word, he dragged her through the terrace doors he'd spotted.

"Well." Patricia raised both brows as if scandalized and hid her smile in her drink. J.D. merely hooted and downed the whiskey himself.

"Up to planning a wedding, Patty, old girl?"

The air was balmy and full of flowers. The stars were close enough to touch, vying with the moon for brilliance. Nathan noticed none of it as he stopped, dropped his package on a gleaming white table and hauled Jackie into his arms.

She fit perfectly.

"I'm sorry," he managed after a moment. "I was rude to your parents."

"That's all right. We often are." She lifted both hands to his face and studied him. "You look tired."

"No, I'm fine." He was anything but. Searching for lost control, he stepped back. "I wasn't sure you'd be here, either."

"Either?"

"You were gone when I got home, and then I tracked down your apartment, but you weren't there, either, so I came looking here."

Hoping she could take it slowly, she leaned back against the table. "You've been looking for me?"

"For a couple of days."

"I'm sorry. I didn't expect you back from Denver until next week. Your office certainly didn't."

"I came back sooner than— You called my office?"

"Yes. You came back sooner than what, Nathan?"

"Sooner than expected," he said with a snap. "I left Cody in charge, dumped the project in his lap and flew home. You'd gone. You'd left me."

She nearly flew at him, laughing, but decided to play it out. "Did you expect me to stay on?"

"Yes. No. Yes, damn it." He dragged both hands through his hair. "I know I hadn't any right to expect it, but I did. Then, when I got home, the house was empty. I hated it there without you. I can't think without you. That's your fault. You've done something to my brain." He'd begun to pace, which made her lift a brow. The Nathan she'd come to know rarely made unnecessary moves. "Every time I see something I wonder what you'd think about it, what you'd say. I couldn't even eat a blue plate special without thinking about you."

"That's really dreadful." She drew a breath. It needed to be asked. "Do you want me back, Nathan?"

There was fury in his eyes when he turned, a kind

of vivid, blazing fury that made her want to launch herself into his arms again. "Do you want me to crawl?"

"Let me think about it." She touched the bow on the package, wondering what was inside. Wondering was almost as good as knowing. "You deserve to crawl a bit, but I don't have the heart for it." She smiled at him, her hands folded neatly. "I hadn't gone anywhere, Nathan."

"You'd cleared out. The place was tidy as a tomb."

"Didn't you look in the closet?"

Impatience shimmered, then stilled. "What do you mean?"

"I mean, I hadn't left. My clothes are still in the guest room. I couldn't sleep in your bed without you, so I moved, but I didn't leave." She touched his face again, gently. "I had no intention of letting you ruin your life."

He grabbed her hand as if it were a lifeline. "Then why are you here and not there?"

"I wanted to see my parents. Partly because of the things you'd told me. It made me realize I needed to see them, to thank them somehow for being as wonderful as they are. And partly because I wanted to tell them I'd finally done something from beginning to end." Her fingers curved nervously over his. "I sold my book."

"Sold it? I didn't know you'd sent it in."

"I didn't want to tell you. I didn't want you to be disappointed in me if it didn't work."

"I wouldn't have been." He drew her close. Her scent, so needed, was all around him. It was only then that he understood that you could come home even without the familiar walls. "I'm happy for you. I'm proud of you. I wish…I wish I'd been here."

"This is something I had to do, this first time, by

myself." She shifted back, not out of his arms, but circled by them. "I'd like you to be around the next time."

His fingers tensed on the back of her waist, and his eyes went dark. Jake's look, she thought yet again, giddy with love for him. "It's that easy? All I had to do was walk in and ask?"

"That's all you've ever had to do."

"I don't deserve you."

She smiled. "I know."

With a laugh, he swung her in a circle, then brought her down to crush his lips to hers in a long, breathless kiss. "I came prepared to make all kinds of offers and promises. You aren't going to ask for any."

"That's not to say I wouldn't like to hear them." She laid her head on his shoulder. "Why don't you tell me what you've got in mind?"

"I want you, but I want it to be right. No long separations, no broken promises. I'm doing something I should have done a year ago and making Cody a partner."

When she drew her head back, he noticed that her eyes could be as shrewd as her father's. "That's an excellent decision."

"A personal one, as well as a business one. I'm learning, Jack."

"I can see that."

"Between the two of us, the pressure will lighten enough to make it possible to start a family, a real family. I don't know what kind of husband I'll make, or father, but—"

She touched her fingers to his lips. "We'll find out together."

"Yes." Reaching up, he took her hands again. "I'll

still have to travel some, but I hope you'll agree to come with me whenever you can."

"Just try to stop me."

"And you'll be there to make certain I don't forget that marriage and family come first."

She turned her face into his throat. "You can count on it."

"I'm doing this backward. I do that a lot since I met you." He ran his hands down her arms, then drew her away. "I wanted to tell you that since I found you everything changed for me. Losing you would be worse than losing my eyes or my arms, because without you I can't see or touch anything. I need you in my life, I want you to share it all with me. We can learn from each other, make mistakes together, and I love you more than I know how to say."

"I think you said it very nicely." She sniffled, then shook her head. "I don't want to cry. I look really awful when I cry, and I want to be beautiful tonight. Let me have my present, will you, before I start babbling?"

"I like it when you babble." He pressed a kiss to her brow, to her temple, to the dimple at the corner of her mouth. "Oh, God, I do owe cousin Fred."

Jackie gave a watery laugh. "He's trying to find a buyer for twenty-five acres of swampland."

"Sold." He caught her face in his hands again, just to look, just to touch what was more real to him than his own heart. "I do love you, Jack."

"I know, but you can repeat yourself all you want."

"I intend to, but first I think you should have this." He picked up the package and offered it to her. "I wanted you to have something that would show you, if

I couldn't make myself clear, how I felt about you. How you'd given me hope for a future I never believed in."

She dragged the heels of her hands under her eyes. "Well, let's see. Diamonds are forever, but I've always had a fondness for colored stones." She ripped at the paper ruthlessly, then pulled out her gift.

For a moment she was speechless, standing in the moonlight, her cheeks still gleaming with tears. In her hands was a shell-covered pelican. When she looked at him again, her eyes were drenched. "Nobody understands me the way you do."

"Don't change," he murmured, holding her close again with the tacky bird between them. "Let's go home, Jack."

\* \* \* \* \*